TEXAS PRIDE

VIVIENNE SAVAGE

Edited by
HOT TREE EDITING

PAYNE & TAYLOR

TEXAS PRIDE

WILD OPERATIVES #5

By Vivienne Savage

***

http://www.viviennesavage.com

1

SASHA

*B*ass boomed from the powerful speakers, filling the air with the pounding noise of a recent hip-hop single. While awaiting a drink from the bartender, I observed the dozens of scantily clothed bodies writhing beneath a kaleidoscope of colorful club lights.

Within minutes of entering and finding my seat, the smell of sweat, perfume, and hairspray had overwhelmed my nose. Dancers packed as close as sardines on the floor and mingled their unique scents as they became one living, breathing presence rolling to the beat of the music.

Maybe I was a glutton for punishment for subjecting myself to yet another night at Club Hysteria, the hottest nightclub in Houston, because nothing called to me more than the bed I'd left behind at home. Despite an hour of waxing, primping, and preening for the evening, I couldn't summon the energy to throw myself onto the dance floor.

Another bust. Another wasted night. I'd told the girls

there were better ways to meet our goals, but of course, no one listened to me until they were bitten in the ass and needed my advice. To dull the bitter taste of disappointment, I ordered a White Russian at the bar and returned to my seat. At least Hysteria used real cream— not the good stuff Nandi used when she mixed our drinks, but it was better than thin, cheap milk. I raised the glass to my lips and let the delicious mixture slide over my tongue.

"Excuse me, baby. You here with somebody?"

A young man gripped the back of the chair on the opposite end of the table and leaned forward. His blue eyes glittered with interest beneath a shaggy mess of ash brown curls, and when he smiled, one of his cheeks dimpled. The short sleeves of his fitted T-shirt revealed a tight, muscular body and a tribal tattoo sleeve on his left arm. He looked like a frat boy, the kind of kid who chugged booze and mainlined Everclear for kicks.

Way too young for me, the sensible aspect of my conscious whispered.

Probably energetic and frisky though, my inner lioness purred.

Most likely half my age and still in college, Miss Prissy disagreed.

Thankfully, I didn't look my age. No shifter ever did. As a lioness shifter from South Africa, the fountain of youth had been imprinted in my genes, a natural part of me I could never shake.

Maybe the hunt was back on after all. "Mm, no unfortunately."

"That's a damn shame, pretty lady like you here all alone."

At least he hadn't used a totally cheesy pick-up line. That was one point in his favor, I supposed. I smiled and pushed aside my empty glass. "Not so alone anymore, am I? I've got you here to keep me company. So what do I call you?"

"I'm David."

"Sasha."

"Wanna dance?"

"Sure."

With David guiding me by the hand, we navigated a floor swarmed with glossy, perspiring bodies until we reached a pocket in the crowd. The music filled me, and I moved to the beat, letting the pulsing rhythm guide the sway of my hips. A twist put my back to his chest, and we ground close.

By the end of the song, every male eye within the vicinity had darted toward us.

Maybe the night wouldn't be wasted after all. Maybe I'd have a conquest to drag back to Nandi and Isisa the way wild lionesses took home their kills. The girls—*my* girls—loved it when I brought home a tasty dish for them to sample. And we hadn't had a delicious man in months. Sometimes Isisa only watched, because that was her thing, but what mattered most was that we were all fulfilled in some way.

When David escorted me back to the table with his arm around my waist, the subtle aroma of sweat and tobacco wafted from his skin. He smoked, and in my excitement, I hadn't picked it up before we hit the dance floor.

Shit. There'd already been enough to knock him out of the running as a potential mate, and smoking was the final straw that broke the camel's back. Us girls had sketched out the perfect list of desired traits, requirements for a future husband chiseled in stone.

And if it wasn't the odor of cigarettes clinging to David's skin, it would have been his age, his immaturity, the fact that he was still probably in college. Why couldn't this be like the romance novels I read where women met their ideal match while standing at the bar?

Between the three of us, no man would ever be enough. I could have looked the other way and ignored a few cigs, but Isisa would never bend on what she'd deemed an unforgivably gross habit. She took her health seriously, and if one of us made her miss the morning five-mile run, she sulked the rest of the day.

"What's a sexy lady like you doing here all alone?"

"My roommates work tomorrow, so they hit the hay early," I explained.

At that moment, Nandi and Isisa lay cuddled together in bed, since I'd drawn the short straw for the night's hunt. Sometimes we took turns, sometimes we pulled straws, but one of us always went on the prowl for a man up for the task of satisfying three women at once.

"Where you from? You can't be American with an accent like that." David flashed an eager grin and feigned interest in learning more about me.

"South Africa." Searching for men was like fishing, and if the girls weren't so thirsty, I would have thrown him back and tried to reel in a bigger, better catch. "I was born in Africa, but I came to the states as a child to live with my mother."

"Oh man. Africa. Like elephants and lions Africa. I bet you saw them all the time, right?"

"Mm-hmm. If you know where to look, it can be like seeing a squirrel or a hare in your backyard here." Sightings were exceptionally frequent when those same lions were family.

"So, you want a drink?"

"I'd be glad for another White Russian."

"My pleasure. Be right back."

My quarry disappeared into the throng at the bar. Better him than me. So many sweaty bodies pressed together, everyone wrangling to catch the barkeeper's attention in the most obnoxious way possible, always triggered my annoyance. Give me wide-open spaces over claustrophobic crowds.

David must have had a trick or two up his sleeve. He returned sooner than I expected with two drinks and passed one to me. "A White Russian for the lady."

"Thank you."

My would-be lay for the night watched me closely from across the table, holding his shot in one hand but not sipping. A strange odor offended my nose as I raised my glass for a sip. Discreetly, I swished the drink and inhaled again.

Flunitrazepam. Also known as Rohypnol by its trade name. While it was tasteless and odorless to humans when mixed in a drink, the drug was known for loss of inhibitions and amnesia. I'd performed a rape kit on a girl named Kerry only a month ago at the hospital, and the toxicology report had pinned Rohypnol as the culprit.

And now someone had laced my drink with it, albeit clumsily, as tiny little particles of white clung to the inside rim of the glass just above the creamy line of liquid. When my gaze rose from the glass to the man opposite me, his eager smile raised the fine hairs on my nape. Every sense, both related to my shifter half and female intuition, told me to splash the drink in his face and flee. Better yet, call the police and hold the cup for evidence.

Then I wondered how many times he'd done this shit before. How many Kerrys had he served a treacherous glass of sedative and booze? Because for every girl who came forward at the police station, there had to be a dozen more who wept at home in their showers and wondered how the hell their night on the town went so wrong.

Maybe I wasn't the first, but I'd for damn sure be his last.

Aware of his eyes on me, I raised the glass to my lips and slammed it back. Then I was out of the seat and taking him by the hand, relying on preternatural stamina as my shield. A few sedatives wouldn't do shit to me. As part of Ian's special operatives team, we'd all drugged ourselves numerous times before to test our endurance against a variety of concoctions.

This would be child's play.

"Let's go again," I coaxed him.

We danced for fifteen minutes longer until I feigned a stumble and swayed against him. It didn't take much longer afterward for David to guide me from the floor and into the parking lot where the fresh, balmy Texas air tossed my blonde hair. The kiss of the breeze against my perspiring brow alleviated the chemical fog enough to continue the act.

Clutching David by both hands, words escaped my lips in a breathy whisper against his cheek. "I don't feel so good. Can you take me home? I think I drank too much."

"Sure thing, babe. Sure."

The headache and blurry vision were only a temporary setback. Those would fade, even if the world was currently spinning around me and turning topsy-turvy like I'd taken a crack to the skull. Heavy eyelids threatened to close, and exhaustion crept into noncooperative limbs until the moment we reached a battered green pickup truck.

What if it had been some other girl? What if it was someone who couldn't defend herself? The what-ifs became fuel, motivating me into the passenger seat where I collapsed in a heap, no longer completely feigning the disorientation.

David drove for twenty minutes, never asking where I lived.

"Here we are, baby, safe and sound."

"Am I home?"

He chuckled and leaned across the center console. He slid a hand over my lap and wriggled his hand beneath my skirt. I clamped my thighs and denied him the feel he wanted. "Damn, I bet you're going to be tight. We're back home now. Want me to carry you up to bed?"

All I managed was a moan while suppressing the need to vomit.

He helped me from the car, keeping one arm tight around my waist. Through my blurred vision, I made out a dusty-looking apartment building with brown brick and grimy windows. Inside wasn't any better. The lights in the hallway flickered, and the stairwell smelled like stale cigarettes. The stench worsened the migraine initiated by the drugs.

The apartment was a bachelor's haven infused with

the odor of old gym socks and sour sweat. Old pizza boxes piled on a greasy, food-smeared kitchen counter, and two other guys sat on the beat-up sofa in front of the flat screen.

"Oh shit, you got one!" the nearest exclaimed. He was heavyset, sporting a real stocky build, glasses, and dark hair.

"Hell yeah, man," David said. "And you're happy to be here, aren't you, Sasha?" He lolled my head forward and back a few times while I gazed around through half-lidded eyes.

"You found a blonde named Sasha? I thought that was a stereotype." The second guy on the couch resembled Arnold Schwarzenegger at the top of his bodybuilding career. A big jock of a guy, probably a football player. He whistled and stepped close. "And she's hot as fuck, too. Check out those tits."

"Didn't they ask for a white chick though?" the chunky one asked.

David snickered. "I thought she was."

"Nah, look at those lips. She's probably a mutt." Then he grinned. "Bet her nips are brown."

Mutt? Barely contained rage trembled through my body.

"Help me get her to the bedroom, Pete. She's heavier than she looks," David said. "Get the condoms, Al."

"Yeah, sure. I got her."

Possession of me exchanged hands from David to the musclebound guy named Pete. He carried me into the back room and unceremoniously dumped me on an unmade bed covered by a scratchy, gray woolen blanket. A nearby tripod aimed a video camera toward the bed.

"Let's get this dress off of her," David said.

"It's skintight. May have to rip it."

"Rip it then. That'll get us a shitload of upvotes when we get it online."

Distracted by the promise of seeing more skin, Pete leaned over my body and grasped the hemline of the black dress I'd worn. Before fabric ripped in his hands, my hips bucked up from the bed and both thighs surrounded his neck. A hard twist yanked him down to the mattress, and then the assailant became the helpless victim, thrashing against the smelly bedcovers.

Faster than he could shout in surprise, I flipped him beneath me and straddled his shoulders before launching a fist into his nose. One. Two. I pounded him a third time, punches faster than cobra strikes.

"What the fuck's going on?" David cried.

Their other friend stood at the foot of the bed with his pants down and cock out. After twisting from my perch on Mr. Biceps, I dove like a wild cat to knock Al to the floor. Satisfied with the crack of his head bouncing off the ground, I sprang to my feet to confront David.

He charged and ran into my open palm. Hell if I knew what he thought he'd accomplish by rushing me, but all he earned for his effort was a broken nose, a gut punch that doubled him over, and an uppercut that knocked him back up. He and Pete could sport matching shiners.

"Holy shit! You said you gave her the shit!" Al cried from the floor.

Muscular arms surrounded my waist from behind. Pete's hot, alcohol-laden breath washed over my neck as he lifted my feet from the floor. Smashing the back of my head into his face made him set me back down, but he kept his arms locked around my chest. With strength that was a combination of natural athleticism, hard work, and shifter genes, I pushed him backward until his spine hit the wall. His breath heaved from his chest on a choking wheeze and his arms dropped.

By then, Al had recuperated enough to fetch a knife, though it did him no good; his attempt too slow and inadequate to use the weapon correctly. Between my reflexes and military training, I twisted the blade from his grip.

After slipping my hand around the back of his neck, I thrust him into the wall and crashed his face into it.

"Fuck this! I'm out of here!" Pete yelled before he burst out the door.

I glared at his retreating form. "Coward."

"Dude, we're sorry. We're sorry. Don't hurt us anymore," David pleaded from the ground. "We didn't actually do anything to you yet. Just let us go. I mean, you can walk out the door and we can forget this happened."

How many of their victims had asked for mercy too, begging to be let go, pleading with him not to do it?

"You want to rape women, yes? Rape someone now."

I crushed David's balls beneath my heel. He shrieked like I was killing him. Too bad I couldn't.

Battered and bruised as they were, fear of another ass kicking kept Al in line for me to hogtie him. As for the other predator, I slammed his face against the floor again for good measure before restraining him too. Rummaging through their belongings and hunting around the bathroom revealed a stash of narcotics and sedatives. Not to mention the spindle of DVDs labeled by physical traits and dates. Blonde Gangbang 5/17. Black Threesome

4/21. Underage Asian Girl 9/13. That was only three days ago.

The nausea struck like an emotional fist to the gut, and everything in my belly came up in the grimy toilet. I flushed with the bottom of my foot, avoided touching anything else in the apartment, and stumbled outside with my heels in one hand.

I stood barefoot on a sidewalk encrusted with petrified gum. Gross. It took less than a minute to schedule a lift from a ride sharing app on my phone. With that accomplished, I swiped through my contacts list and dialed the only friend I could trust with my current situation.

"MacArthur." His drowsy voice grumbled a hello into the phone.

"I'm sorry for waking you, Ian, but I need a favor."

The sleepy man sighed. "Sasha, it's..." He paused, presumably to check the time. "It's past midnight. You couldn't wait until morning?"

"Someone tried to rape me."

Bedsprings creaked. *"What?* Where are you? I'll be there as soon as—"

"I don't need you to come here, silly. I need your connections. They're a group of college kids with a whole stash of illegal drugs and... and tapes. I beat the shit out of them before they could do anything."

"If you beat the shit out of them, what do you want me to do?"

"I need you to use your pull with the Houston PD. Get them arrested on something that doesn't require me to testify and become involved. All the evidence they need is right here I think."

"Fine. Forward me your location, and I'll get some guys out there who know what to do," Ian said.

"Thanks. Love you."

"Love you too, kitty. Are you sure you don't need me? I can be there in under an hour."

"I'll be fine. Call me tomorrow with an update."

We ended the call as the Lyft driver pulled up to the side of the street. By then, the enhanced metabolism granted by my shifter abilities had cleansed most of the Rohypnol from my system.

It could have been worse. It could have been so much worse. I could have been human, and the story would have ended another way without the three assholes nursing their bruises and two of them in lockup for a host of sex-related crimes.

I could have been one of the girls on the tape.

～

*R*ambling thoughts followed me from the car into the elevator, unshakable worries refusing to let loose even when I entered the tranquil atmosphere of a penthouse shared by my pridemates.

For the first time since the entire ordeal began, the battle rhythm of my racing pulse eased. Centering myself, I closed my eyes and dragged in deep inhalations, letting the comfort of home and our chic digs welcome me within a fragrant embrace. Nothing worked better than erasing the stank memory of an illegal sex den than Nandi's sugar cookie Scentsy melts. She had a fragrance for every season. The season of the pumpkin would arrive soon.

Home. I'm safe now.

After tossing my heels into the corner beside our front door, I maneuvered into the kitchen and set my phone on the counter. I'd carried it and my ID in the lace band of my thigh-highs, the satin soft nylons secured by an overpriced garter belt from my favorite lingerie company.

Nandy and Isisa had to be asleep by now, probably wrapped in each other's arms. After a bath, or maybe even a long soak amidst peach-scented bubble bath, I'd crawl into bed and join them. The image brought a smile to my face until I saw the pale glow of a light from the upstairs office.

She's at it again. Writing at two in the morning? Really?

Nandi was the homebody. We dragged her out into the sun every so often, but it was usually a lost cause. She'd rather sit behind her computer building her reading audience, joining book parties, and typing up the erotica that paid her share of the bills.

Isisa and I wouldn't mind it so much if she left home sometimes to breathe in the fresh air and hunt.

"Well? Where is he?" Isisa whispered from the shadows.

Jerking toward the sound of her voice and twisting my upper body to face danger brought my hip into the edge of the dishwasher. I swore before shooting her a dirty look. "What the hell are you doing up?"

Isisa had one hand out toward me, though she blinked and withdrew it. "Sorry. I was on my way from the kitchen when the door opened. I hid to catch a peek at your find…"

I kneaded my aching hipbone. "There's no one tonight."

"No one?" Nandi had popped out of the office. She peered down over the second-floor railing and pushed her glasses up on her nose. She had a mild astigmatism in her human form, not uncommon among some types of shifters, and the screen hurt her eyes after a while.

"Why did you come back empty-handed?" Isisa asked.

While I fretted in the mirror over blemishes and acne, Nandi and Isisa enjoyed flawless complexions smooth as black satin. Their silhouettes were reminiscent of obsidian statues given life by a wizard searching for the perfect women despite their differing frames and shapes.

"Because the only idiot I met tried to rape me."

Nandi's gold eyes grew saucer large. She leapt over the rail and dropped down beside me with effortless grace. "Are you hurt? Did he hurt you?" Her gentle hands cupped my face while Isisa searched my body for injuries.

"It's okay. Relax. The police are going to take care of it. I made a call to Ian, and he's put some guys on the case." If I told them more, if I shared anything else about what I saw and what could have happened, Nandi wouldn't sleep for the rest of the night.

I'd tell Isisa. She had the stomach for tolerating things our sensitive Nandi struggled to handle.

"Maybe this is a bad idea. Maybe we should give up on it and accept that we're alone but together," Nandi said. "Since we have each other."

"No," Isisa said, shaking her head.

Nandi crossed her arms beneath her generous breasts. "I don't like this anymore. We've tried everything from clubs to Tinder and Match.com, but you're the two risking your safety to meet guys we never like. I'm happy with both of you. Aren't you happy with what we have?"

"I'm happy," Isisa said. She hesitated and bit her lower lip. "But it isn't the same."

"What isn't the same?" Disgust dripped from Nandi's voice, and she rolled her eyes. "Some asshole almost hurt Sasha, and if getting some dick means we have to put either of you in danger out there, I'm fine with our battery-operated boyfriends."

I sighed. "I'm happy, too, but we deserve more."

"More? Like what?" Nandi demanded.

"Don't pretend you don't feel the same hole, because I know you do. There's something missing, and no amount of writing porn on your computer is going to fix it," I said.

Nandi flinched. "It's not *porn*." And then the moisture glistened in her eyes, shimmered against her impossibly long lashes, and I felt like the world's biggest asshole.

Usually Isisa said the stupid and impulsive things. Sighing, I moved close to my pridemate and drew her into a hug. "I love you, Nandi. And I love your books. I just wish we had that kind of romance for ourselves. Don't we deserve to have a man of our own?"

"Yes, but… I don't want you to be in danger."

"I wasn't in danger. Not once." In a gentler, softer voice I murmured, "Don't you still want a baby?"

Silence fell over the kitchen. A baby had been the one thing we all wanted, but the dream eluded us at every turn. Once upon a time, I should have been a mother.

Then fate had dashed those dreams to ribbons and turned my hopes into nightmares. I blinked a few times to alleviate the burning behind my eyelids, but it didn't help, and my vision blurred.

"I do," Nandi whispered. "I still want a baby. We can do a donor though, can't we?"

Isisa shook her head. "Neither you nor I had an ideal father, and Sasha's died too soon. While I don't doubt we could raise a child, or several alone without a man, it isn't something I want for our little one if possible. I would like to reserve that option for when all else fails."

"But I do think we need to change up our plans. We're never going to find a good, quality type of man by trolling bars. Some good lays, maybe, but not the kind of guy we want to keep around for us. Definitely not the kind of guy we want around to raise a family with us."

Isisa nodded in agreement. "You're right. I began to think along the same lines after you left."

"So did I," Nandi admitted. "The Internet is full of trolls and guys only wanting booty."

"It would have been nice to touch some muscles tonight though," Isisa lamented. "I'm sorry you had a rough night, but I'm even more sorry some creep almost hurt you. Want me to run you a bath?"

"Please."

"Want us to join you?" Nandi asked.

As if she needed my answer. "Double please."

Isisa ran the bath while Nandi fawned over me, and all discussion related to finding the ideal mate to complete our pride ended. By the end of the night, I slept cradled between them, safe, secure, and loved.

2

SASHA

*T*he sound and smell of sizzling bacon woke me from slumber. Beside me, Isisa mumbled in her sleep and curled closer in against my side. Morning cuddles made for the best cuddles, so I nuzzled my face into the crook of her neck.

"Nandi is making breakfast. Time to wake up."

"Don't wanna," Isisa grumbled.

"C'mon, sleepyhead." My fingers tickled up her rib cage until she squealed with laughter. It wasn't often that she was in the snuggly kind of mood.

"All right, I'm up, I'm up!"

Before I could crawl from bed, Isisa laced her fingers in my hair and drew me down to the disheveled sheets. The sweet surrender of her kisses, her exploring fingers, and her loving mouth were all I needed to overcome the traumatic memories of the previous night.

The mattress dipped and bedsprings creaked beneath Nandi's weight as she joined us. Despite the scent of bacon and spiced maple syrup, breakfast became the furthest thing from my mind.

By the time we rolled out of bed and shambled into the kitchen, our bacon had gone cool. Isisa warmed the bacon in the skillet while I settled on a stool in the breakfast nook and admired her long legs. She had pulled on a T-shirt and panties but nothing else. As far as I was concerned, there weren't a sexier pair of legs in the world.

My gaze drifted from Isisa to Nandi. Out of the three of us, she had the best tits, hands down, and her snug tank top showed them off. She glanced over and grinned, as if sensing my thoughts, so I blew a kiss and winked at her. She blew one back in return then fetched three coffee mugs from the cabinet.

"So, new game plan," Isisa declared. "No more bars."

I nodded. "No more bars. If we want a man who deserves us, we need to search for him in better places."

"Libraries?" Nandi suggested. She set out creamer and sugar on the counter beside the mugs.

"That'll work for a book nerd like you, but I want someone who won't study his phone the entire time we're at the Museum of Fine Arts," Isisa muttered.

Nandi scrunched her nose. "I like art."

"You had your face in your phone the *whole* time, like you were glued to it."

"I was taking photos for Instagram!"

While they argued over the museum and our last date, I dreamed up the ideal man and a host of perfect traits from a love for his family to a fondness for fishing, swimming, and hiking. "I don't care about art or books, though I suppose it would be nice to have a man with a taste for camping and hiking. A hunter maybe. Someone who wouldn't freak about having a lioness take down a deer in front of him," I said.

Isisa pursed her lips. "An athletic hunter would be nice." She slid a plate in front of me then served Nandi before taking her own seat. "So, we want a nerdy outdoorsman with class *and* balls." She snorted. "Yeah. That's really going to happen."

"It could happen," I pointed out. "I mean, technically we just described Ian, but he's taken."

Nandi snuck a bacon slice from Isisa's plate. "Then we still need to figure out where to meet such a man. Maybe…"

"Maybe what?" I asked, speaking around a mouthful of eggs.

Nandi dropped her gaze to her lap. "Maybe we should take a trip to Africa. Find another lion."

Before I could reject the idea, Isisa dropped her fork and slammed her palm against the counter surface. "No."

Nandi flinched back from the sharp slap of skin against marble and stared at her.

Isisa's reaction didn't come as a surprise, her experience with lion shifters different from mine. My father had been a good man, and he'd been slaughtered protecting my mother and me from hunters seeking skins and trophies. Isisa's father had been a monster who terrorized them and ruled his pride with an iron fist.

For a while, we ate in silence, neither talking nor looking at one another. When she finished eating, Nandi shoved her plate into the dishwasher and went to the office to write.

"You shouldn't have yelled at her," I said.

"I didn't even raise my voice."

"You have this thing where you yell without yelling. Plus, you know, the whole smacking thing."

An uneasy, fleeting smile came to Isisa's face. "I suppose I owe her an apology. But you have to admit it would be nice if she'd let this shifter thing go."

"Why? Isisa, my love, all lions are not the same. Your father was a bastard, but there are some out there who care for their prides."

"We don't need a man to come rule over us like some king of the urban jungle," Isisa spit out bitterly. "I don't want a lion shifter. I don't want *any* shifter."

"I respect your feelings, and I love you so much, but I think we're making a mist—" Providing the interruption we needed, Disney music spilled from the cell phone I'd abandoned on the kitchen counter. Taylor had noticed my phone unattended a few months ago and changed my ringtone to The Lion King's opening theme. I swept it up and peered at the caller ID. Ian.

Isisa's eyes raised to my face. "Go ahead. I need more coffee if we're going to talk about this and come to any kind of compromise."

"All right. I'll be right back then. It's probably Ian checking in on me." I kissed her cheek. Eager for fresh air and the privacy to discuss the previous night's events if Ian needed me to rehash what happened, I crossed the floor and hurried onto the lower-level balcony. We had four in all: an enormous deck located off the living room, another off the downstairs bedroom, one off Nandi's office, and a fourth located from the master bedroom. Once the door shut behind me, I squinted against the sun and raised the phone to my ear. The tang of chlorine and water reached my nose, wafting off the surface of our private pool. "Morning, Ian."

"Morning, sweetheart. I figured you'd be awake by now. How are you? Do you need anything? Is there *anything* Leigh or I can do for you?"

Not only had Ian been the commander of our interbranch military operative team, but in the years since we'd all left the active service, he'd been a good friend to all of us. More than a friend. A father figure, a brother, whatever the situation called for whenever we needed him.

If I hadn't handled last night's situation, Ian would have peeled out of his driveway and blown down the highways. "As good as anyone can be after escaping an attack. I'm good. Really. The only thing they injured were my knuckles when I beat them."

A low chuckle spilled through the phone. "Good. Is this a good time to discuss the details?"

I stole a look at Isisa through the blinds. She'd poured another cup of coffee and was reading the nutrition information on the back of some zucchini banana chocolate chip muffins. "As good as any. No one's listening, so I can be candid."

"All right. Do you want the good news or bad news first?"

"Good," I said, lowering to a deck chair.

"My associates with HPD took in those two guys you left in the apartment, and of course, those two rolled over and squealed on their pal. He's in lockup along with them." A quiet lull passed between us before Ian spoke again. "Plenty of evidence found on scene."

"Yeah, I saw."

"Christ, Sasha, how'd you end up there anyway?"

Unashamed, but certainly not proud of the personal risks we'd all taken during our most desperate moments, I told Ian about my visit to the club. He listened without interruption or condescension, even after I told him we'd done it many times before without peril.

"You know what?" Ian finally said after a long, awkward silence.

"What?" Great. Now he'd probably tell me how irresponsibly I behaved, or worse, that I'd disappointed him.

"You should have tossed the damn drink in his face."

My held breath escaped with a laugh. "If I did, we might have lost our evidence."

"True. God knows those three needed the ass kicking you gave them. Anyway, my acquaintance recovered the video and filed it into evidence, but if you ask for it, I'll make it disappear. The choice is yours."

With the phone cradled between my ear and shoulder, I settled on one of the deck chairs and considered his offer. Involvement in a sexual assault case was the last thing I'd wanted. It could have gone differently, but it hadn't, because the gifts I'd inherited from my parents had provided all the protection a gun couldn't have provided.

"Think about it and get back with me. No rush."

"Thanks, Ian. So, what happens now?"

"The police try to identify any of the young women in the videos and compare the information with recent sexual crimes. They'll test genetic data from the perps against a few dozen unsolved rape kits."

The thought made me shudder, but I hoped the

investigation would bring a modicum of closure to other women out there in the world. Girls like Kerry.

"Anyway, if you need to talk to anyone, Leigh and I are here for you. Don't forget that, okay?"

"I'm okay. Honest. As difficult as it was to leave them alive with their throats intact, I made the choice to drink a spiked cocktail. I'm glad they're off the streets. Now what's the bad news?"

"That this is bigger than those three idiots, but they had no useful information to offer. They received cash and mailed digital copies of their videos, stored on flash drives. When we tried to pull up the owner of the PO Box, we got squat. The box was registered to an elderly man who died two years ago."

"I'm sorry to hear that."

"Yeah, well, we'll keep looking at it on our end, and I'll let you know if I find out anything."

Ian and I chatted for a short while longer before he made me promise to visit him, Leigh, and their daughter Sophia soon. When I ended the call, Isisa stepped outside and joined me on the low seat.

"Good news?"

"All three of them are in custody. Ian wants to know if I'll come forward."

"Will you?"

"I haven't decided yet. Did you apologize to Nandi?"

"Not yet. I will in a moment."

Despite the enormity of the unfinished conversation lingering between us, we sat in silence for a while, both of us gazing down at the world below the edge of the balcony railing. We lived in an enormous high-rise located at the edge of the Discovery Green, walking distance from Minute Maid Park and St. Raphael's Hospital where I worked. Prime real estate, enormous mortgage payments each month, and absolute beauty that made the sacrifices we'd made to get there worth it.

"We didn't want to argue with you. All we tried to say is that it would be prudent to give the idea due consideration."

Isisa's jaw clenched, but she dipped her chin. Her spine curved, and the eye contact between us ended. "Fine. If that's what you two need."

"I want what's best for all of us. We're not going to let some guy come between us. Ever. I'm not saying we have to go find a lion, only that we don't rule them out from the start."

Wrapping my arms around her didn't ease the tension in her body. It remained long enough for each beat of my heart to echo like a sledgehammer strike between my ears. Slowly, muscle by muscle, she relaxed in my arms until she hugged me close with her head on my shoulder.

"Times are different now. If he's some asshole who tries to put his hands on any of us, we'll kick his ass. All right?"

Isisa tucked her face beneath my throat. "All right."

My mother had smuggled my twin brother Sebastian and me from South Africa days after Dad was killed by trophy hunters coveting our pride's white pelts. He'd been a good man, a just and fair leader who ruled with love, but the moment another alpha moved in on his territory, life had become absolute chaos.

Sometimes lion alphas gave in to their bestial natures, and they'd claim the widowed females of slain pride leaders as if they were markers on a poker table. Some mothers fled with her babies, but the cruel reality was that they often had no resources available to them.

The worst of those terrible practices ended with Mum's generation. Eventually, lionesses who lost a mate banded together to defend their little ones in teams. They escaped to human cities, found jobs wherever they could as maids, cooks, and even nannies. They worked their fingers to the bone in factories and raised their offspring in cramped flats away from the wild plains we loved.

Some of them, like my mum, relocated to different countries altogether. I owed everything to her, a wonderful childhood and a successful adulthood, because she'd been the first role model in my life to teach me there was always a way forward if I was willing to work to find it.

"He won't be like your father. I promise. It won't ever come to that. You may think Nandi is the one we have to protect, but if someone tried to hurt you, her claws would come out. We'd never choose a man over you. Ever." Punctuating words with kisses eased the remaining tension in her shoulders.

Isisa had lived a different childhood. I met her in the summer after my thirteenth birthday. Five years had passed since my mother had fled with me and my twin brother to America, and in that time, she'd worked toward gaining citizenship.

Our mothers met through a mutual friend, a leader of a secret support group for widowed shifters. Isisa's mother had entered the country illegally, unlike us, and needed shelter after escaping an abusive husband planning to sell their eleven-year-old daughter to another pride leader. Isisa had been the intended child bride. We housed them for five years until her mother was on her feet again, growing closer the entire time.

I didn't realize I'd fallen in love with my best friend until the day I left for boot camp.

As for my mother, now that she'd aged out of her breeding years, she'd accepted a man outside of our species—the sexiest Siberian tiger shifter I ever laid eyes on. Every so often, Mom and my silver fox stepdad booked a room at the nearby Ritz Carlton and showed up to visit over the weekend. They took us out to dinner, and I showed them the local nightlife. Nikolai loved the House of Blues, and we had one within walking distance.

"Fine. I won't rule them out," she relented. "But don't expect me to dance for joy, either."

"But you shake your ass so nicely," I teased.

"Smart-ass." She grinned and leaned in for a kiss.

"We good?"

"We're good," she agreed. "Now I'll go ensure the same with Nandi."

"Better take a peace offering."

Isisa hesitated. "Brownies bad or ice cream bad?"

Considering Nandi had abandoned her recent diet attempts and fallen off the sweets wagon, there probably wasn't any such thing as overkill. "I'd suggest brownies a la mode, just to be safe."

3

ESTEBAN

I tossed my hard hat into the truck's rear cab and fell into the waiting driver's seat. The day had been nonstop action, our construction crew on the go every minute since my arrival to the development site. Due to circumstances beyond our control, we'd fallen behind schedule two weeks ago. Anything wrong that could happen had happened, the series of unfortunate events ranging from family illnesses to injuries off site.

Damn. I wondered if we were cursed or something. What deity did we piss off? Why did God have to choose now to piss in my Cheerios like I'd done something? Maybe my mother was right and I'd skipped out on too many of the religious services she always begged me to join.

Whether it was divine intervention or just plain bad luck, we were cutting it close to not meeting the next project milestone, and I had no choice but to hire additional hands, pay outrageous overtime rates, and work on the crew alongside my guys instead of handling the administrative details.

Not that I minded leaving the office behind and returning to the field. I enjoyed the warm sun and the cool breeze whistling beneath my hard hat.

We'd recently expanded our business into Houston and taken on an enormous contract from a wealthy entrepreneur with some eccentric ideas about making "affordable" luxury housing in the suburbs. Julien Edward Dupont the Third, Esquire—as he introduced himself— had bought up a bunch of land and looked for a reliable, family-owned business to hire.

Through sheer luck and good fortune, Mr. Dupont had noticed my status as a USMC veteran and selected us, choosing Castillo Construction over a big-time company spreading its hooks across Texas. We'd lost jobs to the Medrano family in the past. They always outbid us on contracts, preyed on immigrants desperate to earn two dollars an hour, and bribed officials who should have busted them for shady practices.

The amount of money on the line for our current deal was more than we'd ever taken in before, and made up for a light year of business. We'd been contracted to build thirty-six brand new houses and a community recreation center with a massive pool and athletics center.

While I enjoyed working on developments like this, my true love belonged to jobs that placed me on beams a hundred feet or more above ground with only a safety harness between me and certain death. I hadn't had a job like that in forever, but that was how I'd gotten my start with the Marines.

Dragging in a few breaths and shaking off the stress of

the day, I kneaded the tension knot rippling from my nape to the small of my back. Little sparks of agony flared down my spine like the kiss of a knife blade between each vertebra.

I never minded working alongside my crew, because a true leader did more than issue orders. What did bother me was that the company's sterling reputation would take a hit if we surpassed the strict schedule set by the developer.

Two of the guys walked side by side toward a battered Honda parked on the street. Sergio, my little brother, would drive that damned thing until it fell to pieces. He paused at my driver's door and glanced through the window.

"See you at dinner, *hermano?*"

"Like I'd risk Mamá's fury."

"She'd come and find you if you did. Probably drag you to the table."

I grinned. "I might be a little late completing some errands, but I'll be there. Let her know?"

"Sure."

Errands covered everything from refilling my tank for the morning commute to fetching an order from the hardware store for a long-term personal project at home. I'd decided to build a deck and fence in the property, exhausted with a neighbor's dog harassing my fosters. If not for Samuel helping out for a few dollars in his pocket or Sergio spending the occasional afternoon alongside me to drop posts, I would have given up and hired a fence builder.

Pride wouldn't let me do that though. Now that I'd started the job, I'd finish this shit. I just hoped someone shot me the next time I had a bright idea to fence in twenty-two acres of forest. In the meantime, I'd completed a much smaller boundary securing just the immediate backyard. It was enough room for them to roam a couple hours and handle their business, but no true space for running.

With the window cracked and the autumn air whistling through my sweat-dampened hair, I sang along to the classic rock station filling my cab with the energetic tunes of Aerosmith.

Before I could butcher "Dream On" any further with my rendition of Steven Tyler's wail, the phone I'd tossed into the beverage compartment lit up with an incoming call from an old friend. I tapped a button on the steering wheel to accept Nadir's call, filtering his voice through a Bluetooth connection and out the car speakers.

"Sup, man?" he asked.

"Na'much. Driving home from work. What's up?"

"Just calling to see if you're still coming over tomorrow?"

"To be your manual labor after a week of hard work? Since you promised beer and your mom's cooking, yeah, I'll be there."

"Thanks, I really appreciate it. I've got a whole side of rib eye to cut up into steaks, too."

"Sounds good."

I'd agreed over a week ago to help Nadir move into his new home, but that had been before the shit hit the fan at work.

Damn, sleeping in on a Saturday would have been euphoric.

"See you tomorrow."

We ended the call as I entered the little community five minutes east of The Woodlands. My parents had lived on the peaceful lane for as long as I could remember, the house built while I was a toddler and my parents newly married. Today, most of my extended family lived within a few miles of each other.

As a wedding gift to my younger brother ten years ago, Pops had built Sergio a house of his own down the road. A few months ago, we did the same for Mariana and her new husband.

Other families gave newlyweds microwave ovens and can openers. Our family gave the entire deal from top to bottom to show our love. Maybe that was the advantage of having our own construction company.

Or maybe it was Mamá's way of keeping all her children together. Since we all lived within two square miles of each other, we held family dinner on the first Friday of every month. Rain or shine, she expected all her children to be present and had been holding the tradition since I'd moved out on my own. God help whoever decided to skip Mamá's dinner, because weathering that storm of guilt was more trouble than it was worth.

That included illnesses. I'd learned about ten years ago to bring my sniffles to the table, because if my ass wasn't sitting in that chair to drink Abuelita's manzanilla tea, Mamá would come and get me.

By the time I arrived home, took out the pups I was fostering, showered, and trimmed my beard—before my mother could comment on the length—I was already running behind by a half hour. Instead of walking as usual, I drove the half mile down the road and parked in the drive. My mother met me on the porch with her hands on her hips and a deep crease between her brows.

A few tenacious pink blossoms still clung to the immense double rose of Sharon bushes flanking the porch steps, and the late-blooming summer honeysuckle beneath the windows released a sweet fragrance into the air. I don't know how she did it, but Mamá knew how to make them flower all year long. Her ability to coax flowers out of dry soil was damned near supernatural. So was her glower.

"Sorry. Work ran late, and I hit traffic." One kiss to her cheek smoothed away the disapproving lines.

"You work too hard. Sergio managed to come home on time."

"Sergio isn't in charge."

"You're losing weight. Look at you, Esteban. You're skinnier and skinnier each time I see you."

"I'm not skinnier than I was last week."

She fussed over me in Spanish and guided me ahead of her into the dining room. Pops had already taken his seat at the head of the long table he and I had built together when I was a teen. Our original nine had grown into fifteen, not counting the abundance of cousins who lived in the area. We'd since built another table for the youngest members of the family and visiting relatives, but with Mariana and her new husband on their honeymoon and Eduardo out of town for the weekend on business, only a few of us were around and only the main table was in use.

My youngest brother glowered at me. "About time you showed up. Can we eat now?" He looked at our parents with a hopeful expression. At seventeen, a senior in high school, Samuel was the last of us waiting to leave the nest.

"After we say grace," Mamá admoi

Once I took my seat, she led us

raised the cover from the dish and the

arroz con pollo wafted into the air, rel

onion, garlic, tomato, sweet peppers,

seasoned with fresh herbs grown in the

My stomach cramped with hunger until I had the first heavenly bite.

Damn. If I could survive Mamá digging into my personal life, I'd show up for dinner more often.

"When are you going to bring home a nice woman to introduce to us?"

And she'd now set a brand-new record. Less than two minutes into the meal. I withheld a groan and cut into my chicken. "Ma, we discussed this."

"We discussed nothing. When are you going to take time away from the job to have a social life and to do things other young men do?"

"I'm forty-three. Far from being a young man."

"You're young to me, and you'll always be my baby," she disagreed. "Tell him he's too young to spend all of his life behind a desk, Ernesto."

My father groaned. The matter of my personal life had been an issue of contention between them, with Pops taking a hands-off approach. "He's old enough to make his own decisions, although I wonder if I retired and left the business to him too early."

"Pops—"

"No. It's a big responsibility, son. You're doing an amazing job, but there's more to life than work."

While Castillo Construction Co. was a family business, only a few of us had taken any interest. I'd worked

Pops from the time I returned from the
s. Sergio had been with our dad the longest, but he
n't wanted a top leadership position. Hadn't wanted to
be the boss of all the bosses, and he'd deferred the role
to me.

Mariana handled the administrative office for us, but
with her away on a luxury cruise, I'd had the stupid idea
to absorb her duties into mine. Should have trained
Selene when we had the chance, but my youngest sister
would laugh at me now if I asked for her help. Besides,
she'd just begun her final year of college. It was too late to
burden her with my problems.

"What are you doing this weekend?" Mamá asked.
"Sylvia's daughter Rochelle will be in from San Antonio,
and I'm sure she would appreciate someone to show her
around The Woodlands. Perhaps even Houston."

"I'm busy helping a friend tomorrow."

Her expression deflated, lips pursed into a thin line
and eyes staring into my soul. "The entire day?"

"Old Marine pal, Mamá. He's got twenty years of stuff
to move across Houston. It'll be an all-day thing."

"Oh."

The calculating look in her eyes didn't fade, and I
knew from that moment that she wouldn't let the
discussion end there.

An hour later, Selene came to fetch me from the
kitchen at our mother's behest. I'd been loading plates,
cutlery, and silverware into the washer while Samuel
scrubbed the pots and platters in the sink.

"Dammit. Can't he help me first?"

Selene rolled her eyes. "If you're going to bitch about a
few dishes, I'll help you."

Leaving my younger siblings behind to wash up and clean after dinner, I sought out our mother in her knitting room. She had a room for her sewing projects, needlework, and anything else involving yarn or fabric. She'd made Mariana's wedding dress with her own hands, toiling in that room for days until my sister had a dress worth more than any designer gown.

When I entered the room, Mamá was sitting at the table cutting fabric and humming to herself.

"Is that the fabric Selene chose for her graduation dress?"

"It is. So proud of our girl."

My little sister would be graduating in the spring with a bachelor's degree in mathematics after sacrificing multiple summers of her free time and taking enormous course loads. She was a machine, preparing to undertake the path of becoming a teacher. After that, she planned to return for her master's in education.

"You needed me, Mamá?"

"Come in and sit. You and I, we haven't talked much lately."

"We talk all the time," I said, taking a seat nearby but out of her way.

"Not about important things. I worry about you, *mijo*. When are you going to date again? You haven't been the same since Gabriela left." When I didn't answer, she carried on. "You're still in love with her, aren't you?"

"What?" Startled by the absurd question, I barked out a laugh and shook my head while waving both hands in denial. "No. Far from it. I've been over Gabriela since we signed the papers and ended our marriage." And I'd been on a couple dates.

"Good. That lying pu—"

"*Mamá.*"

"Esteban, she lied to you. She lied and told you things that were not true."

"She never lied to me. She changed her mind, and that's okay. Everyone changes their minds sometimes, and I'm glad she was able to tell me she didn't want kids."

"Only after eleven years of stringing you along. It wasn't right. You don't lie to a man and tell him you want children then hold him in a marriage so many years. It just isn't right." Mamá shook her head. "It's okay to not want kids, I understand, but what she did to you was not right."

I sighed.

Gabriela had been my childhood crush, my high school sweetheart, my first wife, and the expected mother of my children. I'd proposed to her two weeks prior to enlisting in the Marines, and three years later once I had some stability, we married. But she was never happy. The life of a military wife didn't appeal to her, and while we'd discussed having children, she'd always promised once we settled somewhere permanently, she'd be ready.

When I discharged to help Pops with the business, Gabriela had more excuses. I'd understood. I'd listened. Whenever she placed new stipulations upon building our family, I busted my ass to make it work.

We separated one month before moving into the brand-new home I'd built because she'd claimed she needed a house large enough for kids. The divorce came not long after that. When I'd served the papers, she signed without any complaints or requests to make it work.

And that was the end of eleven years of marriage.

"You deserve someone much better than Gabriela, and you won't find that someone if you bury yourself beneath work. Why don't you let your father return to the business?"

"You wanted Pops to retire, remember?"

"I did, but now I see the strain it places on you. Besides, now he sits around spending money. He shops all day at Amazon, finding things to buy that we don't need."

I smiled. "I'll tell him to get a hobby."

She harrumphed. "At least let him work in the office."

"You know he won't stay in there. Besides, it's still his business. If he really wanted to come back to work, he would. Let him find something else to do to occupy his time at home."

"He *has* a hobby. He wants to raise a steer. A *steer*! He bought this four-thousand-dollar meat grinder and all of this equipment for processing our own meat."

"About time. I'm tired of paying the butcher to process these deer."

"That isn't the point! He is looking for things to buy now. Who needs five deep freezers? According to him, five still isn't enough."

Somehow, I managed to keep from laughing at her horrified outrage. "It'll pay for itself eventually. He can even set up a stall at the farmer's market to sell some of our excess meat. That'll get him out of your hair for a while too."

Mamá narrowed her eyes at me. "But that means more money. He would need a food handler's license."

Damn. I couldn't sneak anything past her. "It's inexpensive. He'd need a temporary food establishment permit, and I'll help him get it. You worry so much about money. Pops won't overspend."

"That's what you say, but you don't have to live with him and that damned device always making purchases. He speaks to it now more than he talks to me." She sulked. "Tells it what he wants to buy, and two days later the mailman brings it."

"I'll have a talk with him about the dangers of Internet shopping. All right?"

"Fine."

Mamá twisted around to resume her work. And I hurried the hell away before she remembered to delve into my love life again.

~

*N*adir's family lived in an upscale community on the suburban outskirts of Houston. I arrived at nine as promised and drove him to pick up a U-Haul. Then it was back to the house for the hard work.

How did one man acquire so much crap while in the Marines? Better yet, how did his family find the room to store it all? Was there a single item in the attic that *didn't* belong to my buddy? Sweat poured down my brow and stung my eyes, trickling down my back in rivulets. I used my shirt to dry my face.

"Esteban, would you like a glass of sweet tea?" Roksana called.

Fuck yes. "Yes, ma'am. Just a moment." With dust and cobwebs in my hair, I emerged from the hatch and accepted a cool glass of sweet tea from Nadir's mother.

She smiled. "Thank you for coming to help Nadir with this. Are you sure you boys don't want us to help?"

Guzzling the entire glass didn't quench my thirst. Their attic could have substituted as a medieval torture device. Or a sauna for someone on a budget. The contractors who built the house had cut corners with ventilation.

"Thanks, but we've got it. I think you did enough work getting it all up there to begin with."

She laughed and wiped my face with the dishtowel in her hands, cleaning a few cobwebs from my beard. "You're a good friend. Always have been. Nadir was on the phone a moment ago and says backup should arrive shortly. He asked a few others to help out."

"Sounds good. I think I'll step out for some fresh air and see how much room is left in the truck."

When we'd rented the midsize truck, I hadn't anticipated the sheer amount of bullshit this dude had collected. While the rest of us had spent our money on drinks during deployments, or hoarded our earnings away, Nadir used his income to amass an impressive collection of silk rugs, brass and copper knickknacks, unique furniture, and handmade suits.

Tall, narrow windows with panels of stained glass framed the front door, giving me a good look outside. As I reached for the knob, I stopped, struck dumb by the sight only a few yards away.

The most beautiful woman I'd ever seen exited the driver's side of a cherry red Corvette convertible parked in the circle drive. The satin finish of the paint job glistened beneath the sun and faded to gold around the hood and fenders. As much as I wanted to fawn over the car, I wanted the owner more. She moved with the easy, long-legged gait of a woman confident in her looks, her languid stride reminding me of a panther on a stroll.

And she was heading this way.

Holy hell.

I opened the door, eager to get a better look. Her sleeveless pink top revealed toned arms, thin fabric clinging around a slim waist, and high, full breasts. A matching set of leggings hugged the most perfect thighs I'd ever wanted wrapped around my waist.

Goddamn.

4

SASHA

*N*adir's mother and father lived in a quaint neighborhood in Kingwood filled with brick homes and horseshoe drives. My Corvette slid into the circle drive a few yards behind the open U-Haul. I didn't recognize the gray pickup truck in front of Nadir's SUV.

Thank God. He called in more help. Nadir had picked the worst time to move. Russ was stuck at home caring for their son while his wife recuperated from the flu, Ian was busy sponsoring some kind of superhero initiative in D.C., our friend Juni couldn't get away from a bossy client, and Taylor had swept his wife away on a Caribbean cruise.

That left me. Only me. Julia, our other mutual friend, had triplets newly entered into their terrible twos, and better things to do with her time than delving into an attic. If I'd been smart, I would have dragged Nandi out with me for the fresh air, or Isisa for the workout.

Forewarned about their attic, I'd donned black and pink compression leggings and a tank. I drew my hair into a ponytail while crossing the yard. The humidity was already turning the sleek waves into frizz and silky curls, the unfortunate drawback of being biracial.

The door opened before I reached the porch, framing a tall man with a sturdy build—laborer's muscles honed by work instead of sculpting in a gym. Broad shoulders and impressive arms corded with muscle strained the limits of a drab olive T-shirt. He aimed a welcoming smile at me from a tanned face accented with a dark mustache and short beard trimmed to follow his jawline.

Holy shit. My heart lurched in my chest, and I halted in my tracks, feet stuck to the ground. I couldn't move, and why would I want to? My lioness was still, like a predator honing in on her prey.

"Are you okay?"

I snapped out of it and forced a bright smile to my face. "I'm great. Hi." My mouth had gone dry at the sight of him, my heart pounding a jackhammer's rhythm in my chest. The last thing I needed was for Señor Hotty to think I was having a breakdown on Nadir's walkway.

His abs looked rock hard beneath his sweat-dampened T-shirt, and he had the most amazing brown eyes that crinkled at the corners when he smiled. Lost in those eyes, my stare resumed.

Nadir crossed over and hugged me, oblivious to my distress. He smelled of sweat and dust, of the stale air of the attic we'd be crawling through soon. He'd drawn his black hair back from his face and tied it into a tail, though a few strands clung tenaciously against his damp cheeks. "Glad you were able to make it. I really appreciate your help, Sasha."

I wiggled and pushed against his chest with both

hands. "Of course, anything for you. Besides, I always like catching up with your folks. Just stop rubbing your funk off on me."

"Ahem." The sexy stranger with the dark eyes cleared his throat.

"Oh. This is Esteban." Nadir stepped back and clapped his friend on the shoulder. "We served in the same unit together until this guy decided to abandon me."

"Hey. One reenlistment was enough. Not my fault you didn't escape while you could."

I chuckled at their good-natured, brotherly teasing. "I blame insanity and a love of money for my decision to remain the full twenty, otherwise I might have also abandoned ship."

"You a Marine too?" Esteban's eyes traveled over me, introducing a thrill of pleasure. My entire body flushed with warmth, and my chest tightened until I battled to take normal breaths. In all my life, I'd never met a man I instantly wanted to drag into bed. A man who made my entire body tingle with one smoldering look.

"N-no," I stuttered out.

"Oh yeah, right. I should have introduced her as *Doctor* Sasha Vogt. Sash was an officer in the Navy," Nadir explained to his friend. "She served as the medic in my spec-ops team."

My uncooperative brain stalled again, and with great effort, I managed to respond. "Hi." *Derp. Great. He must be fascinated by the ditzy blonde who can't string together a complete sentence.*

Esteban chuckled. "I think we covered that part already." He took my hand and initiated mere seconds of contact I didn't want to end when electricity jumped between us and skated up my arm.

His warm hand was tough and calloused, scarred across the back of his knuckles. He had the hands of a man who worked for a living, not a man who based his career out of an office or skyscraper calling the shots to his minions down below. Visions skimmed through my mind of Esteban removing my clothes, those same hands traveling my naked body and caressing my sensitive places with a textured touch.

I shot a self-conscious glance down to my boobs, fearing my tightening nipples were visible. My choice of a padded T-shirt bra saved me some embarrassment.

"Sorry. I think I had a brain fart. Lack of coffee before leaving home."

"Nice to meet you, too, Sasha. So a doctor, yeah? What's your field of medicine?"

"I'm a trauma doctor, and I am blessedly not on call today. So you guys have me all to yourselves." *You especially have me for as long as you want me,* I thought.

Nadir's mother intercepted us at the door and folded me into a tight hug. Before I could become of use to the guys, she stole me away into the kitchen. She loved me. His whole family did. Nadir's younger twin sisters barreled into the kitchen on my heels and attacked me in unison, each one hugging my waist.

Way younger sisters. Nadir had turned thirty-nine a couple months ago, but the twins were about to celebrate their fifth birthdays

"Sasha, will you play dolls with me?" Sabella asked, batting her thick lashes.

"No, she needs to come play in the sandbox with me," Sahar argued.

While nearly identical in looks, the girls were worlds apart in personality. Sahar was the tomboy of the dark-haired pair, while Sabella loved to dress up and dance around the house with her favorite toys.

"Girls, I have to help your big brother first. Then I promise to hang around to play with both of you for as long as you like." I'd cleared the entire day, and with exception to an emergency at the hospital, I didn't plan to go in.

"Okay," they chimed in unison. The girls scampered off as quickly as they'd ambushed me, and I settled with Roksana. We sipped coffee while I humored her with chat about the practice, promised to meet her for lunch soon at our favorite cafe near the medical center, and eventually headed outside.

The guys had a good start, and I lingered on the covered porch a moment to admire them both, though my gaze was always drawn back to Esteban. His shirt stretched taut over his muscular back, dampened with sweat from working in the sun. The last days of Texas's unforgiving summer were cruel, but he had a beautiful tan that turned him golden-brown like a Latin American god.

"Are you going to make yourself useful or what?" Nadir called over. "If so, my room is full of stuff ready to load."

"Whatever you say, boss!"

The next hour passed moving furniture and trading friendly jibes. Esteban picked on Nadir as much as I did, teasing him for his expensive tastes and compulsive need to only buy hardwood furnishings.

"I like things that will last," Nadir countered. "I'd rather buy one expensive thing that will survive for years than buy cheap and replace it three or four times."

"Geez, Nadir, how many rugs did you buy over in the Gulf?" I grunted beneath the weight of yet another rolled carpet. Six more had already been loaded in the truck, all different colors and patterns.

"I'm leaving two for my mom and one each for the girls. There are only two left after that one."

"Only two left," I mimicked under my breath, rolling my eyes. Nadir was a great guy, but he had a definite eye for all things luxurious. He was also somewhat of a neat freak. I remembered giggling at photos of his ultra-tidy space in the barracks. When Juni and I had dared him to feminize his space, he met our challenge by covering his tiny cot in Hello Kitty sheets and a pink blanket.

"So, Esteban, are you going to help him unload all this stuff at his new place tomorrow?"

Nadir had bought a condo in the same building as me, and I'd make sure to hop home for lunch if he was going to be there.

"Nah. I only took Saturday off this weekend. I got a full work day tomorrow overseeing several pool installations in these lots we're finishing up."

Damn. So much for that. "Oh, so you work in construction?" I queried, curious to learn whatever I could about him.

"Esteban owns his company," Nadir answered for the man. We all paused to rest with cold beers beneath a shady oak. "Ian volunteered to come help me move in.

Said he had some business to handle in town once he flies in tomorrow morning. Russ may come too, depending on how Daniela and the baby are feeling."

"Awww. Is she still colicky at night?" I thought back to the last time I'd seen Russell, about a week ago. He'd looked like a zombie.

"Oh yeah. Plus, Mateo has the flu."

"Poor guy," I mumbled, shaking my head. "So what'd you do in the Corps?" I aimed my attention back toward Esteban. Nadir raised a brow at me from behind his friend, but I ignored him.

His rich chuckle stirred butterflies in my stomach. "Nothing as exciting as you two. I went in as an engineer, reenlisted once, and I went back to the family business when I was done. It was a good experience but just not the right career for me."

"No shame in that," I replied. *God, you still have the body for it,* I thought. I let my eyes travel over biceps straining beneath his rolled-up T-shirt sleeves.

An hour later, we'd cleared most of Nadir's belongings from the attic. Since he lived in the barracks while deployed, he'd always shipped his major purchases and souvenirs back home. He had oodles, along with enough clothes to stock his own department store.

"Are you the menswear king or something? What's up with all the suits, man?" Esteban teased him.

Nadir grunted. "Some of those are hand tailored, made specifically for me."

I hung back a few steps to appreciate the view of Esteban from behind. He wore his jeans fitted, and the snug denim hugged his ass just right. "I guess you don't share his fondness for fine garments," I quipped, suppressing the urge to grab double handfuls and squeeze his butt like I was testing fruit at the grocer. It was a thing of absolute beauty.

"Nah. I mean, don't get me wrong, I have a couple suits for special occasions, but nothing like Nadir. He fussed at me the last time we enjoyed the Houston nightlife."

"You like clubbing?"

"With the right company, I do. It's not my preferred entertainment or anything."

An invitation hung on the tip of my tongue. Wary of intruding on some other woman's property, my gaze darted to his hand for signs of a ring. Nothing. Not even a tan line.

I needed to know more about him. "Nadir, can I talk to you a second?" Without waiting for his answer, I curled my fingers around his bicep and dragged him from the lawn and into the foyer.

"The hell was that about?"

"Is he married?" I whispered.

"Huh?"

"I said, is your friend married?"

"No, why?"

I wanted to shake him but couldn't tell if Nadir was intentionally obtuse to tease or genuinely confused.

"I want his number, but I don't want to hit on a married man," I hissed back at him.

"Oh! No, he's pretty single. I think he divorced like seven or eight years ago. Maybe ten."

"Divorced, huh?"

Nadir shrugged. "Yeah. If I recall, he married his childhood sweetheart or something, but they divorced a couple years after he got out."

I leaned forward. "And?"

"And what?"

"Why'd he get divorced?"

"How the hell should I know? We didn't talk about it in detail. Look, if you're interested… oh noooo."

I straightened my spine, alarmed. "Oh no what?"

"Not you, too."

Heat suffused to my cheeks. "I think so. I… can barely focus when he's in my line of sight." Whenever shifters met their intended mate, a magical connection occurred, drawing us to our fated other half and making them irresistible. Four of our friends had already experienced it.

"He's a good guy. If he was an asshole, I wouldn't have asked for his help moving my things. Go for it."

"But what if the girls don't feel the same way?"

"Then there's no better way to test it than to have them meet him, right? Take him out for a date, get him back to your place and let the twins lay eyes on him."

"They're not twins, Nadir."

"Yeah, I know, but they look close. I like to pretend you're all sisters so I don't imagine you three doing naked things all alone together."

I shoved him in the shoulder. "You're such a dick."

After a pep talk from Nadir, I stepped onto the porch and returned to maneuvering boxes to fit into the storage.

We finished loading the truck in time for dinner. Nadir's father, Hazim, returned from a grueling day at St. Luke's Hospital. Roksana was a doctor too with admission privileges at Texas Children's Hospital. She was a pediatrician, so the three of us bonded often over chats about our patients and retreats we planned to attend.

Sabella and Sahar kept Esteban busy, asking question after question at the dinner table. The girls were like my little spies, and they didn't even know it.

"Do you have kids?" Sabella asked.

"Do you *like* kids?" Sahar followed up before the poor man could answer the first question.

"No and yes," he replied, laughing.

Their father eyed them. "Eat your kebabs."

"Awww," both girls groaned in unison.

Dammit. Foiled.

After dinner, while Roksana shuffled the girls off to their baths, Nadir, Esteban, and I stepped outside. The sunset painted the sky in gold and dusky purple streaks. After so many years, it still didn't compare to an African sunset on the savannah, gleaming gold behind the baobab trees. But it was close enough, and the company improved the view. I could have drank Esteban in all evening.

"Thanks for the help, both of you." Nadir leaned against the porch rail. "At least you won't have to figure out how to cram this stuff in the elevator."

"Ian's a Tetris champ," I replied, laughing. "He'll have you doing military pack style maneuvers in no time."

"Sorry I'm going to miss meeting him." Esteban checked his watch. "Anyway, I should be heading out. I want to break ground tomorrow bright and early. It was nice meeting you, Sasha."

"Same."

As Esteban crossed the yard to his truck, Nadir raised one dark brow at me. "What are you waiting for. He's getting away."

Once I found my courage, I darted down the walking

path at a jog before Esteban could gun the engine. I tapped on the glass.

"Hey," he said.

"Hey back to you." I leaned against the truck's driver side door and aimed a bright smile at Esteban, inviting the sexy Latino to linger. His hand never raised to the ignition. "So I was wondering when you planned to take your next day off."

"Friday, why?" His brown eyes narrowed. Then he twisted in the seat and peered through the window at Nadir. "Did he send you to beg me for more help?"

"No, nothing like that," I laughed. "Wanna meet up for drinks?"

Esteban stared at me until the offer clicked. "Sure," he blurted out, his eager voice widening my smile even more.

"Great. Here, let me put my number in your phone."

It wasn't until after we'd exchanged numbers and I'd watched him drive away that the true significance of the situation stole my breath away. One after the other, I'd watched my closest friends discover their fated mates in the most unlikely ways, and at last, I may have finally found the missing piece to our pride.

≈

Two hours later, after a shower and change of clothing, I still couldn't believe my luck. Keeping Esteban's discovery to myself ate me up inside, but I waited until Isisa returned from a business dinner before I sprang the good news on both.

Nandi and I had eaten Chinese takeout and shared a bottle of wine. She was sprawled across her stomach on the couch, lazily tossing a ball across the floor for our goldendoodle to fetch.

With my laptop resting on my thighs, I searched Esteban's name over social media.

Found him. Five mutual friends with Esteban Castillo of Conroe, Texas. Contract Manager at Castillo Construction Co.

I buzzed with excitement and waited until Isisa stepped out of her pumps. "I found a man."

Nandi propped her weight onto an elbow and stared at me. "Are you searching OkCupid again?"

"No. I met a man today while moving furniture for Nadir. An amazing man. A *gorgeous* man."

Isisa pressed her lips together and stared at me. Then she sighed and dropped into the seat beside me. "Does this gorgeous man have a name or a photo we can see?"

"He has a Facebook," I replied, sliding the laptop to her.

She sucked in a breath. "Okay. He's definitely an eleven on the one-to-ten attraction scale."

"Glad to know you agree."

"So he's nice?" Nandi asked. "Smart?"

"He was an engineer in the Marines, and he runs his own construction company. I think that counts."

Nandi clicked the friend request button. I slapped her hand, reflexes too slow to stop her. "Why did you do that?"

She stuck her tongue out at me. "Because I want to see the things on his wall that are reserved for friends only."

"He probably doesn't even—"

A notification popped up to let me know my request had been accepted.

And that acceptance opened the door to a slew of hidden posts and photographs. Nandi sighed as she scrolled through them. "He looks like a book cover model."

"Awww, look. He has an enormous family."

Nandi clicked the next photo, revealing the image of Esteban with a small child. The caption indicated it was his youngest niece. "And seems to be good with children."

"So, I take it from your reactions that I did the right thing by getting his number and inviting him out for a date with me?"

Isisa snorted. "If you didn't make date plans with him, Nandi would be mourning your death right now because I might have smothered you with this pillow."

"Will you bring him to meet us?"

"If things go well, yes. If he turns out to be a jerk in disguise, I'll ditch him and there won't be anything lost." I'd get over the mate attraction eventually.

Now I only had to hope that my first impression of Esteban hadn't steered me wrong.

5

ESTEBAN

"Your friend is hot as hell, but why is she single?" I paused at the intersection, stopped by a red light on my way to pick up Sasha for our date.

"Uh, I'll let her answer that for you," Nadir said, voice filtered through the Bluetooth device curved around my ear. My older Lexus didn't have phone to stereo capability like the truck.

"Man, come on. Don't be that way. I need some serious intel before I go into this."

"You're not going into a combat zone."

"If you knew how long it's been since I dated, you wouldn't say that. Anyway, we've been chatting and texting for the past couple days, and I can't find one thing wrong with her. She's breathtaking, but she has more than looks and a sweet body. She isn't a gold digger, and she has a career of her own. What's the catch?"

"Honestly? She asked me the same thing about you."

"What'd you tell her?" I asked, watching for the green light.

"Nothing more than I'm going to tell you. She's newly single, you're newly single. Talk about it on your date."

"I've been divorced for eleven years. That isn't newly single."

"And living like a widower the entire time, man. Look, take it easy and enjoy yourself. Both of you have a lot in common."

I took him at his word and pulled in front of her building fifteen minutes later. She waited for me in front of the glass doors, dressed in a pencil skirt and an off-the-shoulder silver top. She wore her hair twisted into some kind of elegant, neck-baring updo, but a few wispy curls escaped the opal clips pinning it in place.

Everything about Sasha was sensual from the style of her clothes to the confidence in her stride. I lowered the window when she approached.

"Here," she said, passing me a plastic card. "Scan this for entry and go down to lot four on sublevel two. Isisa doesn't have a car, so we use her space for guests. There are a dozen places to eat here within walking distance. It'll save us time in traffic." Her pink-glossed lips pursed. "And we won't need a designated driver."

Smart woman.

I followed her directions and took the garage elevator to the building's lobby. She lived in a posh skyrise with rental fees larger than my monthly paycheck. A well-dressed doorman in a spiffy suit and black coat opened the door for me, and I rejoined her on the sidewalk.

"I like your car. It's yours, too? I was expecting the truck."

"Nah. The truck is for work mostly," I explained. "You decide on a place to eat yet?"

"Pappadeaux sounds good to me. Although we have one nearby, I've never been, so when you suggested it I looked the place up online and made a reservation for a table." A genuine smile curved her lips. Then she peeked at me from beneath her long lashes, pulling off this coy look that sent a pulse right to my cock.

"And?"

"I've never had oysters before. Are they any good?"

"The oysters are awesome, but if you ask me, the gator is the best."

"I'm willing to try it."

A five-minute stroll from her building brought us to the seafood kitchen on the Discovery Green's southwestern corner. An amicable hostess led us to a quiet table near the back, not too far from the enjoyable music of a live band playing rock near the standing bar.

Once the hostess left, I glanced up from my unfolded menu. "Are you one of those girls who picks at a salad the entire date because she's afraid of picking up a pound or messing up her lipstick?"

"Or looking like a pig?" she suggested, a widening grin on her face. "One, I make it a point to never touch a salad unless it is covered in an overwhelming amount of bacon. Two, my lipstick is smudgeproof. Nandi sells it. And three, I'm not ashamed to stuff my face in front of anyone, and will probably eat more than you. I missed lunch today."

"Outeat me? Doubt it."

"You haven't seen me in action before."

"Wanna share a seafood platter then?"

Amusement danced in her blue eyes. She leaned forward, "You caught me during a generous moment, so I suppose I can share with you."

When the waitress arrived to take our order, before I had a chance to utter a word, Sasha took command of the situation and ordered fried gator with baked oysters on the half shell topped with crab, spinach, and hollandaise sauce for our appetizers. She ordered the seafood platter with an upgrade for additional shrimp while slipping me a smug smile from across the table.

"Catfish or tilapia?" the waitress asked.

Sasha raised a brow at me. "One of each?"

"Fine with me."

"Oh, and please bring a dessert menu. I would also like a Purple Voodoo."

I passed the menu to the server. "And a Grand Hennessy for me."

"Will there be anything else?"

"That's all. We'll keep one menu just in case."

All right. Attractive, capable of taking charge, and unafraid of eating in public. All good qualities I'd been searching for since parting from Gabriela. All qualities she'd lacked aside from having a pretty face. At my age, pretty faces were just the cherry on the sundae, not the entire dessert.

Sasha sipped her water then leaned forward, blue eyes trained to my face. "What do you do for fun?"

"Sadly, nothing very exciting. I like to camp when the weather is nice. When it's not, I stay home with a good book or help out with the dogs at the shelter. I spend time with my family and occasionally babysit a niece or nephew."

"You volunteer at the animal shelter?" Her brows raised.

"I do. I foster pit bulls since it can be hard finding good homes for them, too. They're likely to be put down before any other dog, so the shelter calls me when they have too many animals. The two I'm looking after now were seized during a fighting ring bust. The breeder intended to raise them as fighting dogs, but they were rescued in time. I've had them for a month now."

"That's…" I expected her to say lame when her voice trailed, but a soft look came to her expression. "That's really sweet of you. My housemate has a little puppy that we drove to Kentucky to get. He was a puppy mill dog seized during a bust, and a friend of ours, well, she's heavily into all that kind of stuff. So, Annette drove with us to pick up all these puppies and Isisa kept one."

"What kinda dog?"

"A goldendoodle. Sweetest fuzzball you've ever seen. He has pretty much claimed Isisa's lap as his own. Loves her to death, but he'll come play with Nandi and me when he has no choice. She named him Simba."

"Good for her. Takes a lot of dedication to help out a puppy mill dog."

Her smile broadened. "Isisa is a good person. So… um, you said camping? Tents? Popup trailer? Cabin rental?"

"Tents, otherwise it's like cheating," I said. "My brothers and I go out to a friend's property a lot to camp, fish, and hunt. Sometimes one of my little sisters comes along."

"You hunt?"

Crap. Why'd I say that? The last time the subject of my hunting came up on a date, the girl expressed so much outrage the date was over before it had a chance to begin. She did everything but call me a filthy murderer.

"I'm not a trophy hunter or anything like that. I get a hog and a couple deer each season for meat, that's all. We have a pretty big family and—"

"I'm not judging," Sasha blurted.

"Oh."

"I hunt, too," she explained. "All three of us do, but Isisa and me mostly. Nandi's the introvert among us. If it's fish or small animals, she'll clean whatever we kill and bring back, but God forbid she leaves the computer for a while to come with us these days. She's always on the next story."

"The next story?"

"Oh, yeah, about that." Sasha chuckled and tucked an escaped curl of white-blonde hair behind her ear. My gaze followed the movement, attention lingering on her slim neck, defined shoulders, the hint of cleavage and plump bosom visible beneath the ruffled lace edge of her top.

"You don't have to tell me, if it's private."

"No, nothing like that. Not really. Nandi is a writer."

"Like for Random House or something like that?"

"Mm, no. Self-published. She hit the New York Times list for the first time about a year ago. Now they're making one into a movie."

"Really?" Everything about Sasha intrigued me, right down to her housemates. "Anything I'd be familiar with?"

Sasha cleared her throat and blushed. "Vampire romance. It's all very, uh… quite steamy, lots of mutual biting and sex."

Definitely not something I'd be familiar with. "I have a

younger sister into books like that. Our mother is always on her for reading on her phone at the table."

The waitress arrived with our appetizer and drinks, setting down my Hennessy cocktail then Sasha's enormous glass. I squinted at it. My sister always ordered that one, preferring the coconut vodka, hibiscus grenadine, and pineapple over the other mixed drinks.

"What?"

"That's a huge drink."

"Pfft, yours is almost the same size. Besides," she said, winking, "I'm not on call."

I grinned back at her. "Have three then. I've been here enough with the family to know everything on the menu is good."

We divided slivers of crispy potato stick and tender morsels of deep-fried, battered gator onto our plates then took a few of the baked mussels.

"Dibs on the crab cake when the platter gets here," Sasha said.

"Only if I can have the stuffed crab."

Her lips pursed. After a moment, she nodded. "Fine. But I get a bite."

"You drive a hard bargain, ma'am."

We demolished the appetizers before the server returned with our platter of steaming seafood overflowing with bits of deep-fried crawfish and butterfly shrimp.

As dinner progressed and conversation continued, we discussed everything from our time aboard our respective ships to adjusting to civilian life. Sasha offered me a bite of the coveted crab cake. From her fingers. It melted in my mouth, and then I wondered if she'd do the same.

The waitress arrived with another wave of drinks and our dessert, placing a honey-flavored martini in front of Sasha and a Cat-30 Hurricane in front of me. Her Queen Bee looked delicate beside my tall glass of rum, soda, cognac, and Fassionola syrup.

Without breaking eye contact with me, Sasha licked the rim of her martini glass, tongue tracing over the sugar and cinnamon-crusted edge like an unspoken promise. "I love this drink. It's amazing." Sasha's satisfied moan caressed my ears like sex, a sound of pure pleasure and culinary delight. My imagination placed her beneath me, making those same noises.

Whoa, man. First date, let's not get ahead of ourselves.

"You think that's good, try this pecan pie. I'm not usually a fan of sweet potato—"

"Heathen."

I grinned and took another bite. "But this is divine."

Sasha leaned forward across the table, revealing another delectable hint of cleavage. "Do you know what else would be divine?"

"Uh-huh." Desperate to claim her mouth, I leaned the short distance and kissed her. She tipped her face up to meet me, lips parted, the taste of lemon, honey, vanilla, and Hennessy on her tongue. I moaned at the taste of her and pulled back, aware of diners at adjacent tables.

"That wasn't pie," she whispered, her gaze fixed on my face. "But as far as dessert goes, I think that was my favorite."

Our waitress showed up at precisely the wrong moment to ask if we needed anything else. Or maybe it was the right moment, distracting me from a raging hard-on and a desire to peel Sasha from the chair and into the nearest restroom. Two pairs of feet, one stall, and a possible arrest on my record for drunken, disorderly conduct.

Head in the game, man. Focus.

Meanwhile, my cock reminded me of how long it had been since I'd been laid. A two-year dry spell convinced me any trouble would be worth the cost of bail.

"Sir?"

I cleared my throat. "Just the check, please."

We polished off our desserts while we waited. Once everything had been paid, which I insisted on doing, we strode out into the evening arm in arm, her plump bosom snugly pressed against my bicep.

The chaos of the city surrounded a green park lit by dozens of lanterns, setting romantic ambiance for the remainder of our date. "This is nice, living on the edge of the park."

"Yeah, we love it," Sasha said. "There's a dog park and a jogging trail, so it works out really well for us. Nandi sometimes goes down to the reading room for a change in scene when she's writing."

Our stroll brought us to the edge of Kinder Lake where Halloween decorations hung from the trees. Music carried on the breeze from an outdoor stage with a large crowd gathered around it. The area was beautiful—and properly spooky, in a fun way—but fuck if it held a candle to Sasha.

We paused beside an oak strung with amber and purple twinkle lights, facing each other on the path with the glow of the colorful bulbs on our skin. Her smile was brighter, more dazzling than our surroundings. "I've never come here at night before," Sasha said.

"It's never too late for new experiences."

Her touch skated down my forearm until she found my hand and laced our fingers. She linked our other hands and stepped in close enough for her breath to whisper against my cheek. "I'm glad we went out tonight. Thank you."

"I feel like I should be thanking you for the company. You're…" Wonderful. Like a gift from heaven. A golden angel just for me after years of unsuccessful attempts to get back into the dating game and losing interest within moments of sitting down alongside the wrong women.

"I'm what?" Her head tilted, blue eyes alive with mirth and laughter.

"Too good to be true."

Sasha kissed the corner of my mouth. Wanting another taste of her, I turned my head to capture her lips, savoring the last trace of sweet dessert.

"Want to come up for a cup of coffee?" she asked at the end, breathless from our kiss.

Was she inviting me in for coffee or more? I hesitated. *Head out of the gutter. She probably wants me to sober the fuck up before I hit the road.* "Yeah. Coffee sounds great."

The walk back to her building took us less than ten minutes. The same doorman welcomed us both with a smile and a tip of his hat. The lobby reminded me of a fancy hotel in a way, with marble floors, chandelier lighting, cozy seating, and a courtesy desk. Sasha bypassed the first set of elevators and led me to a second bay in the back. Swiping a card called one of them down to us.

Damn. Personal elevator?

"This one only goes to the top four levels," she said when she caught me staring.

"Queen of the tower, huh?"

"Well, there *are* three of us. Helps when you're sharing the cost."

"True enough. Where's Nadir at in here? I haven't had a chance to visit yet."

"Floor six. I've only popped in once. He asked me to help him move some furniture around. After moving the couch, like, five times I put my foot down."

"Ha! Sounds like Nadir."

The doors opened, and we stepped inside. Sasha hit the top floor.

"Fair warning. My housemates are inquisitive, so you'll have to forgive me if they're around."

"That's fine." I'd play a game of twenty questions with them if it meant five more minutes in Sasha's company.

She led the way inside and it took everything I had not to gape. They had a two-story penthouse from what I could see, and everything had a touch of opulence to it. Marble countertops, floors I was certain were real hardwood, and a vaulted ceiling in the main room. Through a set of glass french doors to my right, there was a large balcony with a set of patio chairs beneath an enormous umbrella. It was too dark to see anything beyond that.

"That you, Sasha?" a voice called from the kitchen.

"No, I'm a burglar come to take all of your valuables," Sasha called back. She giggled and squeezed my hand. "Yeah, it's me, and I have company."

Holy shit. She's hot, too, was my first thought when the woman came into view from around the corner. While

Sasha was blonde and fair-skinned, her athletic friend could have been a sculpted bronze work of art given life, her flawless complexion as dark as cocoa. Radiant, like she was glowing.

"You must be Esteban. I'm Isisa."

"Nice to meet you." Somehow I managed to find the words instead of panting like a dog.

"Where's Nandi?" Sasha asked.

"Picking up food from the desk downstairs. You must have missed her in the elevator. She should be back—" The door opened up behind us, and Isisa grinned. "Right now, actually."

"You're home!" a softer voice exclaimed. "Oh, and you brought your... date?"

"Yeah, this is Esteban, Nandi."

I smelled cookies before the third woman came into view. She came around with a large white box in her hands marked with some bakery's logo.

Wow. It's like walking into a dream or something. Or an amateur porn flick. They're all gorgeous, and this feels like a setup.

Isisa and Nandi could have been sisters with at least thirty or forty pounds between them. The slimmer woman wore her hair in thin braids, but Nandi—the curvier one—had wild, untamed curls floating around her shoulders, appearing rust red beneath the apartment lights.

My eyes didn't know where to focus—on Sasha's perfect ass, Isisa's long legs, or Nandi's generous cleavage. I wanted to bury my face between her breasts.

What the hell is wrong with me? I snapped out of it, dismissing fantasies of Isisa's toned calves around my waist. Sasha wouldn't be happy to know I'd just had a very detailed fantasy of banging both of her close friends moments after our introduction. I didn't plan to share it.

Something about her—about all of them—kicked up my libido and brought back memories of being a hormonal teenage boy.

"Nandi?" Sasha whispered. "Are you okay?"

Nandi flinched and jerked back, her round eyes still trained on my face. "I'm fine. I… It was very nice meeting you, Esteban." Without another word, she scurried away and ascended the stairs without a backward glance.

"I have some… things to put together for court. I, uh, enjoy the rest of the night. Both of you." Isisa took Nandi's lead and vanished up the stairs.

"Did I do something wrong?"

Sasha shook her head. "Nandi is shy, and Isisa is a workaholic. You didn't do anything. Come on."

After she dragged me by the hand into her kitchen, she made coffee for both of us and we settled in her living room on the couch. With her close against my side, we sipped our hot drinks.

"This is some place you have here," I said, both to convey admiration and to break the silence.

"You're not at all intimidated?" she asked.

"Should I be?"

She bit her lower lip and glanced away only to shyly dart her eyes back to my face again a moment later. "I've dated a guy or two before in the past who wasn't comfortable with the way we live."

"Why's that?"

"The three of us pull a lot of cash. Between my pay as a doctor, Nandi's royalties, and the money Isisa makes in her practice, we're quite comfortable. I'm not saying that to brag, just to be honest with you."

"If your career and their success is enough to chase a man away, then he's not much of a damned man at all. Besides, I'm interested in you, not your money, chica. Relax. Now when do I get to see you again?"

Sasha's expression brightened. "Whenever you want. Uh, within reason. I can text you a list of the days I'll be free from the hospital, and we can work something out…" She set her coffee aside then turned until we faced each other. Electric blue eyes studied me in quiet scrutiny.

"Good." Alone at last, I leaned in and claimed the kiss I'd wanted all along. Desire and growing hunger turned it into something more than I'd intended, rough and dominating, fingers threading through her updo. Receptive to my advance, her lips parted, her coffee-flavored tongue sweet against mine.

Everything I'd needed and wanted bubbled to the surface in one kiss. I squeezed one breast in my palm. She moaned into my mouth and pressed closer. Instead of a bra, I found the edge of a pasty denying the hard nipple I wanted to tease.

One yank would rip her top away and expose her to me. But not when her roomies could walk out at any moment.

Then again… A dirty little fantasy flit through my mind, involving Sasha naked in my lap and her two friends walking in on us. Then joining us.

I found my self-control and pulled back, leaving her lips swollen and pink from my assault. "Time for me to get going."

"I'll get my schedule to you tomorrow." There was a

breathiness to her voice, and her blue eyes were dilated and unfocused.

"I... I have a busy week ahead of me catching up on a project, and a weekend camping with my family, but..." *Damn.* I wouldn't have time to see her for nearly two weeks.

"That's okay. I'm not going anywhere." She kissed me again, an affectionate brush against my lips. "If you find time, I can try to find time too."

With a promise to consult each other the next day, she hugged me at the door and I made my way down her private elevator to the garage level. Somehow, I'd met the perfect woman. Sasha was smart, down-to-earth, a top-notch kisser, gorgeous, and kind—everything I'd ever dreamed of finding in a woman since my divorce.

So why couldn't I get her friends off my mind?

≈

SASHA

*A*fter shutting the door, I turned around to find Nandi and Isisa standing at the rail outside of the office. Two pairs of dazzled golden eyes stared down at me.

"Did you both feel it?" I asked, uncertain.

"How could I not?" Isisa asked. "That was intense. I thought I'd tear his clothes off in the living room." Nandi nodded in silent agreement, and they both came down to join me in the living room.

"It's confirmed then. He's the one. We didn't have to troll a bar for him. We didn't need an online Internet profile. You stumbled on him by chance and... he's wonderful. We listened to both of you talking the whole time," Isisa said.

Sweet relief released the tension from my shoulders. The last thing I ever wanted was for a man to come between us, and no amount of physical attraction between me and Esteban would have mattered if they didn't feel the tug, too.

"What do we do now?" Nandi asked. "He likes you, but that doesn't mean he'll want..." She dragged in a long breath, exhaling it with a sigh.

"We tell him the truth. Upfront. We're a package deal. If he's into me, then he must feel something for you as well, no? That's how fated mates work. Mom always said that when she and her pack sister met Dad, he couldn't resist either of them."

"Then why didn't he show it?" Nandi asked. Uncertainty glinted in her eyes.

"Because he's human, and that's rude," Isisa answered along with a playful shove. "Would he get another date with Sash if he drooled over us in her face?"

"Actually," I mused, "I'm pretty sure I saw him checking out your tits, Nandi. Not that I can blame him." I reached over and caressed the side of one full breast.

Nandi tucked her chin, perpetually shy and easy to fluster with compliments until we dragged the sex kitten out of her. When we made eye contact again, her golden eyes brightened. "So what's next?"

"Next, I go and see what sort of man he is. I'm going to watch him hunt with his family."

∾

*E*steban surprised me with Starbucks a few days later. I received a text from him asking how I liked my java, so we met in the hospital lobby and enjoyed a walk together in the cooling autumn breeze.

"God, it feels great," I muttered. "Thanks for the coffee."

"Perfect hunting weather. My brother and cousin already prepared our gear for the weekend."

"I don't know... As much as I enjoy hunting, what I'd really like right now is time on a boat with a fishing pole. Peaceful, still water." I wouldn't mind a swim through a cool river, then a lazy bask alongside it in the fading sun. I sighed and sipped my coffee. We traveled arm in arm, me in my scrubs alongside a fine man in his construction boots, jeans, and T-shirt.

"We'll have to go fishing one weekend. I don't know about the boat, but I do have access to a cozy cabin up at Lake Conroe."

"Really? I'd love that."

"Do you still want to go to the zoo?"

"Of course. I'm looking forward to it."

Maybe the Houston Zoo wasn't the ideal second date location for some women, but for me, I'd be happy anywhere with the open breeze through my hair, the sun on my skin, and my handsome man alongside me. I squeezed up to his side again and kissed his cheek.

"We don't have to go if you'd like something else."

"Oh no, I'm cool with it."

"You're sure?" he asked again. "There's about a hundred other points of interest around Houston if fuzzy animals aren't your thing."

"To be honest, I used to visit Club Hysteria hoping to meet a nice guy, and now that I've met you, I'm happy anywhere we can get to know each other."

"Damn," he muttered. "You're making me regret I have plans this weekend."

His pained expression made me laugh. "No, you go have fun. If you make a good haul and are feeling adventurous, I can cook dinner for you with some of the meat."

"I'll gladly take that challenge."

6

ESTEBAN

*M*r. Dupont never visited our site during business hours. If we weren't receiving an enormous sum of money for building his private community, I'd have told him to stick his demands for an early morning inspection where the sun didn't shine.

Instead of laying warm in bed for another two hours, I parked my truck beside the mobile office and chugged coffee. Glaring at the digital readout didn't change the time from 4:25 a.m. to a reasonable hour.

If he wasn't always a punctual bastard, I would have hidden from the cold inside the mobile administration office. In lieu of our office in downtown Conroe, I'd picked up a secondhand RV a couple years ago because a few blue outhouses weren't enough for our expanding crew. A local rock and roll band had given me a deal to take it off their hands while they upgraded to a luxury party bus.

We took it to our larger worksites, furnishing it with a couch, television, table, chairs, a couple fridges, microwave, and stove. I used the bedroom as an office, setting my laptop on an old desk.

And it had a heater for times like this when we were freezing our asses off. Thankfully, I didn't need to retreat inside. Dupont's sleek automobile slid through the open gates five minutes later, and my client emerged from his car to smile like we'd arranged this meeting at noon instead of early fucking o'clock.

At my height, I towered above most guys, but Dupont barely reached the shoulders of my six-foot-six frame. He wore his blond hair drawn back from his angular face, secured by a single black ribbon.

"Good morning, Mr. Castillo," Dupont said in this posh, sophisticated accent that was borderline French and British, the kind of voice my little sister called audible sex.

"Morning, Mr. Dupont."

"I see there's been immense progress since my last visit two weeks ago."

"You'd see quite a bit more if you visited during the day," I pointed out, finding willpower I hadn't exerted since my days in the Marines. "At this time of the morning, it's too dark to see anything more than the silhouettes of the buildings."

The smile didn't fade. "Yes, of course. You're right, and I owe you my apologies for dragging you out at this dreadful hour. Other pressing matters require my attention once we're finished here, however, and I truly can't leave them waiting."

I lied through my teeth. "Accommodating hectic schedules is no problem, sir."

The dude was a hotshot attorney to the stars known for handling divorces of Hollywood's rich and famous couples. I imagined him flying off on his private jet to visit a starlet preparing to take her philandering husband for millions.

Maybe I was in the wrong business.

"Right. Anyway, if you'll follow me, sir." I picked up a battery-powered lamp and led him into one of the houses. My work boots thudded over the hardwood floors, and moonlight threw shadows across the spacious room. "This house and the other eleven homes in the first wave are ready for final electrical installations."

"And wave two?"

"Ready for framing."

"Excellent. Have you applied the window film here?"

"Yeah. I put my man on that yesterday. He's only completed a couple of the houses, but he'll be done before the week ends."

"I would appreciate your personal attention to the matter of the solar film. It's very important that every window receives the treatment."

"Sure. I planned to inspect his work anyway on each house."

"Thank you."

"The subcontractor arrives tomorrow to install the countertops to your specifications."

"Excellent. I understand my shipment arrived to their warehouse three days ago."

"Yeah. They were quite, uh, impressed." My pal David had called me to babble about the selection of premium marble, dyed concretes, and other high-end materials he'd received to complete the project.

"Is this the house with the basement?"

"Yeah. Your storm shelter is here."

Dupont's "no price is too great" ideology meant that we'd had to subcontract the work to another company specializing in basements. They were a rarity in Texas, and he'd wanted four of them—one in each of the three largest homes, and a huge one beneath the recreation center.

I led him to one of the five bathrooms and swept the portable lamp over the interior to reveal an enormous shower built from natural stone. We hadn't installed the doors yet, and it stood open, my light glinting off the glossy fixtures. He stepped inside and inspected the porcelain tiles.

"Beautiful work. It's come a long way since my last visit. When will you install the interior doors?"

"That will be one of the last items, after all the painting is done. The doors you specifically requested for the basements are due to be shipped in a week."

"Right on time. Good, good. This is all looking excellent."

After he saw the kitchen, the opening to the basement, and the upstairs bedroom, my satisfied client meandered outside and down the lane of packed dirt. I expected him to complain about getting muck on his fancy loafers, but he only smiled.

"Fabulous."

"I'm glad you're satisfied."

"Well then, I leave the rest in your capable hands, Mr. Castillo. I'm happy to see I've placed my trust in the right company. The right man."

"Thank you."

"Do let me know if you require anything else. Until our next meeting."

A chauffeur in a stiff uniform emerged from Dupont's BMW. After a courteous nod to me, he opened the rear passenger side door and held it until my client settled inside.

≈

A late night on the phone with Sasha and an early morning with Dupont took its toll around two in the afternoon. Jesús must have pitied me, because he made an impromptu trip to Starbucks and returned to the site with a triple espresso shot venti-sized coffee that made my heart vibrate like a jackhammer in my chest. Coffee was as good as liquid gold on days like these.

"Bless you, you caffeine-bearing angel."

"Remember this when it's time for raises, boss."

I sipped the sweet, caramel-flavored drink and closed my eyes. A raise? Hell. I was planning Christmas bonuses for everyone, a secret kept between myself and Mariana until we narrowed down the amount. Dupont's generosity, as well as the additional money he'd paid when we all signed his NDA, had made this project a magical golden goose.

Jesús sat on the breakroom bench beside me. "Thank God it's Friday, huh? So how did it go with our rich snob? He satisfied with our work?"

"Decent. He walked around a little. Didn't hang around more than an hour as usual."

"I guess a guy like that wants to know where his money is going. Can't say I blame him. When you got a multi-million-dollar project like this, you don't leave it up to chance that everybody's doing what they should. If you had twenty-five million dollars to pour into a private community, you'd be up our asses too every couple weeks."

"If I had twenty-five million dollars to blow, I'd pay someone else to be up our asses. I get what you mean though."

"Glad it was you and not me or Sergio. There's something about him that unnerves me, man."

I snorted. "Dupont weighs as much as one of your thighs and would probably faint if you waved a hammer at him in a menacing way. What is there to be afraid of?"

"It's just something about his look, okay? Anyway, you need anything else from me before I take off? Got a doc appointment to get to."

"You do? Crap, I totally forgot. Nah, go ahead, man. We got everything handled here. You're still coming hunting with us though, right?"

"Yeah. Wouldn't miss it for nothin'."

7

SASHA

A huge group of humans stomped through the woods with their bows, but my sensitive hearing painted an unfair perception of them. Unseen by the gang, I prowled low and to their rear with a great distance between us, using the waist-high brush and unkempt grass to my advantage. With my white fur, I'd stand out like a sore thumb if I didn't play it safe.

I'd been shadowing them all day. Thanks to keen senses, I didn't need to be close to eavesdrop on their conversations, and since this was Ian's property, I knew the lay of the land like the back of my hand. Mostly it had been friendly banter and plotting for the hunt.

One of the younger men, Ignacio, paused to scan the surrounding foliage. I ducked down and pressed my belly to the grass. "Dude, your friend was cool to let us hunt on his property like this." He was heavyset, baby faced, and as tall as Esteban. College age at the most.

As I stalked the group, I'd learned most of their names already, identifying one of the men among them as his brother Sergio and a few as subordinates on his crew. Angelo and Lalo were also his younger brothers.

Esteban chuckled. "Not my friend, Nacho. Friend of a friend. I guess the guy owns a few hundred acres out this way."

"Ohhh, that rich buddy of Nadir's, right? You struck it lucky, dude. Rich friends *and* a fine woman." He whistled.

"I can't believe you looked her up on Facebook," Esteban muttered.

"Hey, it isn't my fault that the 'In a Relationship' status change blasted your business everywhere. If I had a honey that fine, I'd be glad to show her off to everyone. You need to bring her around."

I grinned mentally. That had been my idea. Last night while at the computer, a mischievous whim urged me to claim him. If I couldn't mark him with a bite, I had to settle for some other way.

Esteban cleared his throat and changed the subject. "I see a hog up ahead. Looks to be a decent-sized boar."

"Think you can get him?" Sergio asked.

"Not at this range and angle. Wouldn't be a clean kill."

They moved closer, and I respected that. With roughly a forty-yard distance between the hunters and their quarry, they had little chance of providing their prey a merciless kill. Once Esteban was in range, he nocked an arrow to his bow and aimed.

I held my breath. No guns. Not a single rifle in sight.

A trophy hunter with a gun had claimed my father's life. I didn't hate firearms, but I loathed men who slew their unarmed prey from afar using scopes and tools instead of skill. Esteban took his time aiming, waiting for the perfect shot before the arrow flew. He hit his mark with skill and precision, taking the pig down without more than a squeal.

A hunter. A real hunter. A man I could respect and track beside. I watched one of the guys clap him on the shoulder.

"Y'all can go ahead while I handle this. I'll dress my own pig."

"Make sure you cape him all the way back to his *cojones*, hermano. When Sergio did your last one for you, he fucked it all up," Angelo said.

Esteban chuckled. "Why do you think I'm doing it myself?"

"Don't take too long," Sergio grumbled.

"You know me. I'll have him quartered before you can spot a buck worth shooting."

Jesús laughed. He was one of the older men among the group, dark-haired with a thick handlebar mustache and a deep brown laborer's tan. His face reminded me of a bloodhound, all droopy and creased with wrinkles. "Right. We're moving up ahead, then."

"I'll catch up."

"If we don't catch up to *you* with another one," Sergio said, a challenge in his voice.

I followed Esteban back to their camp. The men had arrived in two double cab pickups loaded with gear for an overnight stay. They'd filled coolers with ice and had tents raised.

Within minutes, the scent of pig's blood filled the air. My mouth watered and the animal side of me wanted to advance. I crouched low, my tail swishing, and reigned in my baser instincts.

He cleaned and washed his hands with the tap from

their kegged water source on back of the pickup. Then he sat on the bed and took out his cell phone to make a call.

It rang and rang without an apparent answer.

Is he calling me? My clothes, phone, and vehicle waited for me at Russ's place. Licking my mouth, I watched him write a text then hesitate with his thumb over the send button. He sighed and put the phone away.

"She's probably busy at the hospital."

He *was* calling me!

While his pig bled, Esteban set up his supplies on level ground. I observed from the shadows as he skinned the boar with concise, confident slashes. Watching him nurtured a whole new respect for the man. His hands were skillful, strokes of the knife delicate, and he made the work of butchering seem like art.

I crept forward a little closer, hungry for more than the scent of fresh meat. Just one smell of the man I had claimed as mine would be enough to satisfy my craving for him.

I made a wrong step, distracted by the sexy Latino enough to lower my large paw on a branch. It broke beneath my weight.

His head snapped up, and he reached for his nearby compound bow in a single, quick movement. I froze. Our eyes met across the distance and his widened.

Shit. He spotted me. Following my desires over caution, I stepped out from cover and revealed myself. Esteban backed away with slow, unthreatening movements, smart enough not to run in the presence of a predator. As if he could outrun me if I wanted to give chase.

I wouldn't ever hurt you, I thought. His failure to nock

an arrow to the bow and aim at me proved the thought to be mutual.

My hesitation granted him time to retreat to the cab of the truck. The door drew shut. Then I prowled around to the driver's door and gazed up at the man behind the wheel. Without extending my claws, I rose to my hind legs and set my paws on the door. I rubbed my cheek against the glass, wishing for the first time in my life I could purr like a true kitten and prove I didn't mean him any harm.

Trust me. Please.

"Nice kitty... there's scraps in the pan for you." His muffled voice reached me through the window.

I don't want the damned scraps. I want you.

We watched one another for a while longer, his brown eyes trained to my face. When he didn't open the door, I hopped back and retreated.

Not now. I couldn't share our secret with him yet. Not now, but soon.

But for now, I guess I would settle for the damned scraps and pretend they were a gift from him to me.

∾

ESTEBAN

"I know what the hell I saw, man. It was a lion, a female lion, right over there watching me."

My younger cousin Xavier snickered. "Maybe you saw a cougar, homie. You know, a puma or something. From a distance, they can look like a female lion, right?"

"No. They don't look anything alike. This was a lion,

like safaris and gazelles in the bush. But she wasn't the right color, and she had blue eyes. I can't forget that. She came up to the truck and stared at me through the window."

With the most beautiful set of blue eyes I'd ever seen in a feline face. I wasn't a cat person, I preferred a dog any day, but something about the breathtaking creature had made an impact on me. I couldn't forget her.

"Yeah, sure. I know we're out in the boonies, but unless your friend is into exotic animals, I don't think you saw a lion on his property," Sergio said.

We argued until a phone call interrupted our talk.

Sasha Vogt, the glowing caller ID revealed. I answered it on the third ring and raised the phone to my ear. "Sup, Sasha?"

"Hi. Sorry, I missed your call. Is this a bad time now?"

"Not at all."

"So how did it go?"

"Good. I downed a boar, and my little brother, Sergio, took a stag a few moments ago. We'll have a freezer full of meat to last the winter at this rate."

"I make amazing venison chili, just to let you know."

"Dude, this isn't date time," Xavier complained. "Can't you do that shit later?" I made a threatening gesture with one fist, effectively shutting him up.

"I didn't mean to hold you up, Esteban. I can call you back another time."

"I'll call you when I get back in town tomorrow night, sound good?" The guys kept quiet, but it didn't stop them from making crude gestures. I flipped them off.

"That's great. You boys have fun."

"Night, Sasha."

Xavier spoke up the moment I disconnected the call. "You didn't tell your honey about your lion sighting."

"Yeah, because she'd think he was losing it, too," Sergio said.

"Why didn't you photo it through the window?" Alejandro asked.

"My phone was in the back. I set it down there after making a call. It wasn't exactly a priority when a safari predator was creeping toward me."

"Uh-huh. I think whatever they gassed y'all with over there during the Gulf War did something to your head, dawg. You're seeing things. There ain't no lions in these woods, and whatever you saw didn't leave any sign of it being here. Look." Alejandro nodded toward my boar. "If there was a lion, a real lion, she'd have taken that shit."

I grunted. He had a point. Could I have hallucinated the entire thing? There had been a brief period following my honorable discharge when I hadn't adjusted to civilian life right away, and self-medicating with the occasional joint had been a comfort. Unless those joints were laced with LSD, they shouldn't have affected my mind today.

"No. I know what I saw. Follow me over here."

I led them to the pan where I'd dropped the entrails. A few spots of blood glistened there, but the liver, heart, and kidneys were gone. She'd left only the intestines, and I couldn't blame her for that. No matter how Mamá cooked it, I'd never been a fan of the tripe she stewed for Thanksgiving.

Sergio stroked his chin. "Could have been anything, Esteban. Even a coon would run off with that."

"I know what I saw."

"Or a possum," Angelo said.

"Goddammit, I know what the fuck was outside of that car staring at me."

When my voice raised, the others quieted and stared at me. Claiming he'd give my story the benefit of the doubt, Angelo pulled up the news on his phone and searched for recent articles or breaking reports about an escaped lion from a zoo.

"Could have been an illegal exotic. You know how people are about setting shit free," Sergio finally relented.

"Yeah, maybe so. I'll let Nadir know so he can warn his friend."

Gut instinct said my lioness hadn't meant any harm. She could have mauled me at any point and might have been watching for several minutes before I even noticed her.

Looking back, I wished that I'd had the balls to stay outside the truck.

8

ESTEBAN

A week after my lion sighting, Sasha and I walked hand in hand through the Houston Zoo on a breezy Saturday afternoon. Wherever we went, appreciative eyes followed her. She looked amazing in her low-rise jeans and floral lace top, hair wild and free against her shoulders, a mane of silky curls and wispy white-gold spirals.

"Wanna check out the lions? They're up ahead." I pointed out the trail sign.

"Are they your favorite?"

"I guess you could say that. Plus, I thought…" My voice trailed off, and I rubbed my neck with my free hand.

"Thought what?" When I didn't reply, she nudged me with a hip and pressed. "C'mon, you can tell me."

"It sounds crazy, but when I was out hunting, I swear I saw a lioness."

"You mean, like, a mountain lion?"

I shook my head. "No, I mean an actual lioness. A pale

one, too, almost albino. No idea what she was doing loose in that forest, but she was there."

"So, I'm guessing you didn't…" Sasha's voice trailed off, and she looked up at me, curiosity brimming in her blue eyes.

"What? Shoot at her?" I snorted and gave another shake of my head. "Of course not. I mean, if she had charged me, I would have defended myself, but there was no harm in watching her for a while."

"That must have been scary for you."

I thought back to the encounter and the thrill of sighting a wild animal far from her native habitat. "Yes and no," I answered. "Would you think I was nuts if I told you it was sort of exciting? And beautiful to see her move?"

Sasha shook her head. "Where I come from, the slaughter of a lion isn't a big deal. They're dangerous, and they can kill a human within seconds."

"Isn't that pretty rare though? Like shark attacks here?"

Sasha's smile widened, transforming her thoughtful features into pure angelic radiance. Her warming expression glowed. "Yes, very much like that." Her arm curled around my bicep, introducing the soft curve of her breast to my arm. "Lions are my favorite creatures, and it hurts me sometimes to see them locked away at the zoo. Just the same, I always go to look at them to be reminded of home and other memories."

A casual stroll led us along a paved lane in the African Forest exhibit, weaving between sections of native flora until we eventually reached the lion habitat. For a better view of them, we descended a stairwell into a lower level. Two females looked over then approached us.

Both lionesses in the exhibit rubbed their faces against the glass, while their majestic male counterpart ambled over at a lazy pace behind them. The large feline nudged the smaller two away. At first, he sniffed the glass and fixed his golden gaze on my girl. I'd never seen the lions so interested in their daily visitors before. My little sister would have gotten a kick out of it.

As I reached for my iPhone to take a photo, the lion bared his fangs, growled, and lunged at me. His large paws struck the transparent barrier between us.

"Whoa!" I stumbled back, losing my balance until Sasha caught me around the arm.

"Uh, I think I pissed him off. Let's go check out the bears," she said. Her fingers slipped in mine before she dragged me up the steps and into the brightly lit walking path.

"*You* pissed him off? Baby, he roared at *me*."

"He probably took me as a threat to the females—oh look! Ice cream!" With our fingers laced, she dashed in her heels toward a kiosk and jumped in line. From lions to ice cream in seconds. I shook my head.

"The prices are robbery here."

"Put your wallet away. You already bought our tickets in. Let me treat you to something, Esteban. Which flavor do you want?"

I surrendered and shoved my wallet back into my pocket. "Cookies and cream."

We settled beneath a shaded table, an assortment of snacks between us. She fed me a spoonful of her strawberry then wound a tuft of blue cotton candy around her finger.

"I never had fun like this when I was a child. My mother struggled to give me everything, even to come here to America," she confided. "I guess because I didn't have much of a childhood, I like to go places like this as an adult. Does that make sense?"

"I can understand that. My parents grew up poor, too. When Pops started the family business, he and eight friends lived in a one-bedroom apartment. Then he met my mother while visiting Puerto Rico, they had me, and she left the island to move to Texas.

"So, you were born in Puerto Rico?"

I nodded. "My grandfather got his start in America as a laborer, but he was a real penny pincher. A good man, but cheap as fuck. Anyway, Abuelito knew a great investment when he saw it. He bought up a bunch of land in Texas, and when my dad started the company, he gave a large chunk of it to him and a loan to get the business off the ground. That's why most of my family lives in the area."

"I'm trying to decide if it's nice or torture to live down the block from your parents."

My grin widened. "A little bit of both. Your family not close by?"

"Not really. My folks live in California, and my brother is in Japan teaching English. We try to all get together once a year, but it usually ends up being almost every other year. Busy schedules and all that. Trying to figure out times and dates for so many people, well, you probably know all about that."

"I do, yeah. But I have six siblings and three times as many cousins. It's just the four of you then?"

"Sort of…"

"Oh? That sounds mysterious."

"So, okay, we need to have a talk about something important, but I don't know where to begin," Sasha said. She twisted a coil of hair around her index finger and fidgeted. "And I've met a lot of guys who aren't okay with this, surprisingly. Or if they are okay with it, they have their own ulterior motives and turn creepy."

"Baby, just tell me what's up. Your big secret is beginning to worry me."

She bit her lower lip and avoided eye contact, trepidation churning a minor rift between us. "It's… really personal," she whispered. "And I'm worried you'll judge me, or that this is going to be a deal breaker."

Was she really a man?

Why the hell was that the first thought to come to mind?

Because I'd never met a woman with the kinds of interests she had.

Did it matter if she wasn't born a woman? She was one now.

The thoughts raced through my head, evolving with each ridiculous query. I'd never considered dating a transgender woman before, nor did I know if I could. I wanted a big family full of kids like the home where my parents raised me.

I could adopt.

Was I willing to accept her, flaws and all? A woman I didn't know, who may have hidden a large secret from me? *Maybe she has kids. Maybe she's hiding kids from me and the reason we haven't met up often isn't because of work. Maybe she's got a litter of babies by some other man.* I imagined her leaving our date to return to an unsuspecting husband, some douche she escapes for fleeting moments of happiness.

Or a single mom. Maybe someone's watching her kids and she's waiting to find out if I'm some kind of fucking psycho eager to get my hands on a child.

"Nah. Whatever it is, I'm not going to judge you, chica. Now what is it?"

"My housemates aren't only housemates."

"Yeah?"

"We're together. The three of us are all lovers, and we've been this way for a while."

Lovers. The word ignited a hundred creative images in my head. All three girls naked under dimmed lights, twined over silk sheets, scissoring, grinding, fingering, and doing every other act red-blooded, heterosexual males enjoyed watching in porn videos. Once the fantasy died, anger and indignation remained.

"And what about this? Us? What the hell was the point of all this if you have girlfriends of your own already?"

"Esteban—"

"Did you get off on leading me on?"

"No, it's not like that all."

My stomach twisted. "Then what's it the fuck like? Am I an experiment or something? A dare?" I rose to my feet, the taste for ice cream and sweets gone.

"Esteban, please. I *really* like you, and I'd like to see where this goes between us, take that next step, but with full honesty."

"I'm not sure I understand, Sasha. You want to date me but keep your girlfriends, too?"

"No! Please, just give me a second to explain. Please sit down."

I should have walked away. My pounding heart and rising anger told me to walk before something regrettable left my mouth. The grief in her expression and tears shining in her eyes gave me a reason to pause despite the onlookers slowing their steps to stare. I ignored the passing couple and reclaimed my seat, drawn to listen to her a moment longer.

"It's not an experiment. We all want you."

I blinked. The drum beat inside my chest thundered like the hooves of a dozen racehorses galloping down the circuit. "Excuse me?"

"I know this sounds crazy, but I had this feeling you'd be open and willing to hear me out."

~

SASHA

I waited to watch the man of my dreams walk away. All my life, I held fond memories of Mom and Dad, rare fated mates who should have had their lifetime together. At the time, there'd been one other lioness in their pride.

She'd given her life to protect us when the new alpha tried to murder the cubs who didn't belong to him, guarding Mum's back as we escaped. We only knew Iminathi had died because my mother felt the death over the pride link.

Finding Esteban was a longshot, a once-in-a-lifetime miracle rarely given to any shifter. Swallowing the sour taste in my mouth, I waited for his judgment.

"What kind of game is this?" he asked, voice low and dangerous with restrained anger. I couldn't have picked a shittier place, but nerves had guided my actions. Esteban was a healthy, warm shade of sun-toasted brown, a tan attained during a Texas summer. Despite it, angry color had overwhelmed his cheeks. His silent fury unsettled me more than potential outspoken judgments.

He's one of those guys. The quieter he becomes, the angrier he is. My father had been one of those guys, and those fleeting memories I had of him, I remembered his silence was more damning than any verbal admonishments. I'd hated nothing more than upsetting my dad.

"No game, I swear. Nandi, Isisa, and I are a package deal. After you left the other night, they were so happy, Esteban. But they were also afraid you'd think we were…" My voice trailed.

"Freaks?" he suggested after an awkward pause. "It's not the strangest thing I've heard. You're all adults. But if you have each other, why do you need me? What was the point of involving me?"

"Because we want different things we can't give each other. Nandi wants a child someday."

Esteban shrugged. "Inseminate her."

"A child with a father."

"So, you want me to fuck your girlfriend and knock her up? Is that the plan? Con a guy into paying child support for eighteen years?"

The tears in my eyes threatened to fall. Through willpower, I held them at bay and shook my head. "No.

We're not after a sperm donor. We want a companion. Someone who loves us all as we are."

"I'm not a Latter-Day Saint. I don't know the first thing about polygamy, and if you didn't notice, the law frowns on that one-man-to-multiple-women thing."

"I know you aren't." I swallowed down the sour taste in my mouth. "Neither are we. What we are, is three women who find you very attractive mentally and physically. Three women who will give you back 100 percent of what you give to us."

"Sasha, I don't know…"

I wiped my face with the back of my hand and rose from my seat, finding my dignity. "If you think you can handle three of us, then we're yours. If you're man enough to handle us." Impulse spat the words out before I could control myself. And then I couldn't take them back. Insulting his manhood had been petty. An apology rested on the tip of my tongue.

Esteban stood. The muscles in his arms tensed, and his jaw clenched. I held my ground and met his gaze in silence. If we were over, then it was done. I couldn't take back the fun we had, the way he made me feel, or the joy experienced when my girls confessed to feeling identical connections.

If we didn't have an audience before for our tense conversation, we did now. His lips bruised mine, and he crushed me tight in an unforgiving embrace. Clutched to the hard outline of Esteban's body, I felt his every inch, every defined muscle, each angle, and the heat of him radiating through his clothes.

"Don't ever question if I'm man enough for something

again," he whispered against my lips. I practically melted against him.

"I won't."

We kissed again, gentler but no less intense. I curled my fingers around his nape and peered into his eyes when he drew back. "I'll give it a try, Sasha. No promises."

"That's all I'm asking. What *we're* asking."

"What what now then? You take me home and the three of you jump on me like a bunch of cats in heat?"

He had no idea how close to the truth his words were.

~

*W*e didn't go back to my place. Instead, we headed to his.

Esteban had a large home in a nice neighborhood that had plenty of space between neighbors. His particular lot was practically a forest, the house set back far enough away from the road that it was effectively hidden behind a line of thick maple and oak trees. In another month, the color would be gorgeous. Then he'd have a yard littered with an abundance of crimson leaves.

The idea of leaping into a colorful pile of fallen foliage in my feline shape sounded positively blissful, leading me to wonder if his backyard was private enough to attempt the endeavor. Russ and Ian both had the guaranteed privacy, but they didn't have maple trees.

The inside was as spacious as the exterior. After parking in the triple garage, he led the way into the house. The garage entry led into the kitchen and the cozy space put me at instant ease.

Pale yellow walls provided the perfect canvas for

cream cabinetry, accented in teal, with stainless steel appliances, marble countertops, and terracotta tiled floor.

Paned windows over the sink allowed in the light from the setting sun. Two prisms hung down in the light, casting rainbows across the room.

"My youngest sister put those up," Esteban said, catching me staring at them. He set our leftover dinner on the counter. Along the way home, we'd stopped at a Vietnamese dine-in for phở.

"They're pretty. I like it."

And then there were the dogs I'd heard about but never seen. An enormous crate had been pushed against the wall, one puppy brindle and brown eyed, the other white with big blue eyes. Their tails wagged wildly, mouths open and pink tongues lolling. A few squeaker toys covered one side of the crate along with a blanket.

"They're adorable, Esteban."

"Thanks. The white one is Rambo. The brindle is Ripley."

"You named them after action movie heroes?"

He grinned. "Why not? Your roomie named your dog after a Disney character."

I blinked a few times. "You remembered his name?"

Chuckling, he leaned down and released the latch on the cage. The dogs tumbled out, falling over themselves to have his attention. They kept distance from me and hid behind Esteban's legs until I crouched and offered a hand. Ripley ventured closer first, sniffed my fingers, and piddled on the tile.

Shit.

"Uh. Crap. I suppose I should have let them out first

before initiating an introduction. Sorry. Let me take them out into the yard."

Poor pups. I hadn't meant to scare them. Esteban let them out in a large, fenced-in yard and filled their water dish from the hose. After a few short rounds of fetch, he made his way back inside and closed the door behind him.

"There, they'll have fun out there for a while. Can I get you anything? Water? Beer? Something stronger?"

"Water's fine." After a whole day walking around, I needed it. Beer might have made the upcoming conversation easier to bear, but I wanted a clear head.

"All right. Go on in and make yourself comfortable. Pick out a movie if you want."

A wide archway led into the living area. I passed by a large dining table that looked too pretty to have gotten much use and down two steps into the living room. Colorful rugs spread out across the dark hardwood floors, and matching pillows added artful splashes of needed color against the charcoal gray sectional dominating the space. His flat-screen television hung on the wall over an entertainment cabinet packed with Blu-ray cases and a PS4.

"Whatcha in the mood for?" I called out.

"Anything's fine by me," he replied.

Anything, huh? I skimmed my finger across the various titles and pulled out a horror parody that I never tired of watching. By the time I popped it in, he had come out with our drinks and a little bowl filled with lemon and lime wedges.

"Great pick." He grinned and set the drinks on the coffee table.

Oh yeah, he's a keeper. As if there'd been any doubt.

We settled on the couch together to watch the movie, cradled by deep cushions covered in velvety microfiber. When I moved close enough to set my head on his shoulder, he curled his arm around my waist and drew me against him.

"Tell me about the other two. What do they like?"

"Well…" I circled my index finger over his pec, pleased with how firm his chest felt beneath the pressure, even through his shirt. His work had sculpted him into masculine perfection, every muscle cut like marble. "Isisa is always working, so she likes to kick back in her free time. She's pretty hopeless in the kitchen and has this infatuation with fine wines."

"And Nandi?"

"I've already told you this, I think, but she's our little homebody, always on her laptop writing her books and drinking overpriced tea. Or a small glass of Amaretto. She stresses out easy, and she's worried about her weight, so we don't pressure her into going outside."

"What's wrong with her weight?"

"Absolutely nothing, but try telling her that."

"I'll keep that in mind," he murmured, his gaze going distant a moment. When he snapped back to, he looked down at me and smiled. "So, the things we talk about won't necessarily interest them, because you're all different."

"Right," I confirmed.

"Good to know. Are you sure they're into me?"

"Trust me. After our first date out, you were all they talked about for the rest of the night until I fell asleep."

"They barely met me."

"Exactly. They interrogated me relentlessly."

He chuckled. "That bad, huh?"

"You made quite the impression." Enough to stagger all three of us, but I didn't think telling him that would help. More likely scare him off.

"So how long has it been since you three, uh, had a guy around for any long-term thing?"

"Nobody since we broke up with Taylor. That was almost eight years ago, give or take."

He let out a long whistle. "Wow. Mind if I ask what happened there?"

The question ripped the scab off a long-healed wound, bringing back painful memories. "It... We were too different and..."

Tell him, my wiser self urged.

But what if it scares him off?

Then he isn't worthy of us. Any of us.

"Hey, you don't have to tell me," he said in a gentle voice.

"No, it's okay. I had a miscarriage, and the relationship didn't survive it. We always found a way to blame each other for unrelated things after that. And... I was petty. Losing the baby made me into someone I didn't want to become, and our friendship meant more than romance, so we parted ways before things got ugly."

Esteban's arms tightened around me. He kissed the top of my head. "Sasha, I'm sorry for bringing it up."

"Don't be. It was a long time ago. Taylor was great through it all. He's married now, to a wonderful woman we all love very much. Jada is *great*. I mean, truly meant for him. It all worked out in the end."

"And you girls still have each other."

"We do, yeah." I tilted my head to gaze up at him. "I love them."

"You know, sometimes I wonder if I'm gonna wake up to find this is a dream. Or if I'm gonna walk into your place and discover I'm not some lucky bastard inheriting a harem because I'm on some candid camera show."

A harem? While snorting back laughter, I wiggled onto my knees to set him straight and tickled him. "Nah, no jokes, no dreams, and while you are lucky, we are *not* a harem. We're all equal."

"Even better." Esteban tugged me onto his lap and cupped a generous handful of my ass. His touch seared through the denim, and fantasies of having his fingers against bare skin flit through my overactive imagination. How long had it been since I'd have a man?

"I should warn you though, you're gonna have your hands full."

"I think I can handle the job."

I grinned. "Good."

9

ESTEBAN

*M*orning sun slanted across my face through the living room blinds. We'd fallen asleep with a quilt from the back of the couch thrown over us, the colorful orange, red, and blue blanket crocheted by my mother a few years back.

Sasha tucked her face beneath my chin and made a throaty rumble that didn't sound human, something I wouldn't describe as a purr or a growl, but something unusual and in between. At some point during the night, her camisole had fallen askew on her shoulder and revealed the plump upper curve of her right breast. She hadn't worn a bra beneath it. Didn't need one, the plump mound firm and perky. Enticing me to touch and caress her.

Fuck. My cock and my willpower remained iron hard. I set aside my lust to kiss her brow. "Sasha."

Nothing had happened the previous night aside from a little kissing and heavy petting despite my profound need to feel her writhing beneath me. We'd cracked open a few beers and both passed out fully dressed on the couch after talking late into the night.

Even so, waking up with her curled against me had felt good. Damned good.

"Sasha. Time to wake up, baby."

A quiet sigh whispered against my neck. She stirred, barely moving her face. "Morning."

"Buenos días. Did you sleep well?"

"Who couldn't when sleeping next to you?" She contorted her body into a kittenish stretch that seemed to defy the physics of a human body. My spine didn't move that way. What the fuck?

Before I could question her unusual flexibility, the remainder of her breast popped free. Cool air touched exposed skin. Puckered it. My gaze darted down to the tightened peak then flicked back to her face as she straightened.

She didn't blush. The gentleman in me warred against the pervert desperately wanting to sink balls deep inside her.

I adjusted her top, collected myself, and resisted despite the dire urge to take that perfect, creamy-brown tip into my mouth. "Hungry?"

"Starving."

While she freshened in the bathroom, I scrambled eggs, fried bacon, and poured tall glasses of juice. Cooking became the distraction I needed to cool the fuck down. We dined together and had casual conversation about her two lovers before embarking on a trip to Houston to meet them. Why wait? The longer we put it off, the more I'd wonder about them and our unconventional arrangement.

Wiping nervous sweat against my jeans, I followed Sasha off the private elevator and down the hall.

"Like I said, I'm willing to give it a shot, but I've never dated three girls at once."

"Just remember that we're all in it together and you don't have to worry about any jealousy." Her fingers slid over my arm. Then Sasha stepped close, her slim body pressed to my side. "We don't want to overwhelm you, so we get it if you need to spend time with each of us alone for a while first."

Overwhelmed is an understatement. "So, what you're saying is this isn't going to be the same as middle school days when girls flip their shit the moment you sit beside another girl?"

"Yes, exactly that." One touch of her lips against mine dialed my cock from relaxed to hard mode within seconds. Her intuitive fingers sought the aching bulge beneath my zipper and delivered a firm stroke. "I encourage you to. I don't need you all to myself every day. Part of this is wanting happiness for everyone. When Isisa and Nandi are happy, I'm happy."

Fuck, she turned me on, but there wasn't a thing I could do about it in the hallway. My fingers squeezed a handful of her round bottom as the door swung open and framed Isisa. She wore tiny, cotton jersey shorts and a matching heather gray tank top. Her dark hair had been arranged into a hundred thin braids resting against her shoulders.

"Are you going to bring him inside or not?"

Sasha rolled her eyes and stepped back. "Geez, give me a moment, brat."

"You've had a moment. You're molesting him in the hallway now."

"A kiss is hardly molesting."

The playful banter alleviated the lingering concern of being torn between three envious women. Isisa tugged me inside by the arm. "Naughty Sasha, keeping you out here in the hallway. Can I get you some coffee, Esteban?"

Behind Isisa's back, Sasha shook her head and mimed choking.

"Ah, no, I wouldn't want to put you through any trouble."

"No trouble. I've already made a pot." An enormous smile spread across her flawless face before she strode toward the kitchen... and the smell of burnt beans. Sasha smothered a giggle and took me to the couch.

"Where's Nandi?" I asked.

"Sleeping in. She was up until three or so pounding away at her latest novel. If you ask her, she'll tell you all about it. Sugar?" Isisa called over.

"Yes, please."

She returned with a hefty mug that may as well have been a beer stein. "Thanks. So, um…"

Isisa dropped into the love seat across from me. "She told you, huh?"

My eyes lowered to her bare legs. Lingered. Tearing my attention away from a mile of smooth skin took maximum effort. "About the three of you? Yeah."

"It's okay, right?"

"I'm willing to give it a try as long as no one gets hurt."

"Oh good." She relaxed against the cushions. "How's the coffee?"

Eager to impress, I raised my mug and sipped. No

amount of sugar could save this and cover the charred, oversteeped bitterness. I forced myself to swallow it down and smiled through the misery. "Good, thanks."

She shot Sasha a smug look then turned back to me. Her forward lean awarded an eye-catching glimpse of cleavage cupped in lace beneath her tank top. "The fact that you came back is nice. I look forward to getting to know you."

"Same. Sasha's told me a little. You're a lawyer, right?"

"Uh-huh."

"She usually wins all her cases, too," Sasha boasted.

"I don't take losing cases, and I encourage clients to settle when they are."

"Do you deal with criminal trials?"

"No. I did at first, but it was a dead end with too little pay for the headache and stress involved. There's no big money involved unless you're O.J. Simpson's dream team or you pull in a wealthy client with a complicated case."

"Plus, she'd come home in a rage sometimes. Or tears because the guys she had to represent were guilty and she knew it."

Isisa nodded. "I wasn't a nice person then. Or fair to Sasha and Nandi."

Sasha abandoned her spot beside me and joined Isisa, curling up beside her with an arm around the other woman's shoulders. "We still loved you."

"I know." Isisa kissed the fingers resting over her shoulder. "Anyway, when I left my last firm, Sasha encouraged me to study medical malpractice laws and associated cases. It was like finding my calling at last and knowing what I wanted to do."

"That's great. Do you work at the same hospital or is that a conflict of interests?"

"I've given counsel before, but mostly I represent patients with negligent doctors—"

"Which, of course, I am *never*."

"—and the occasional personal injury case." Isisa elbowed Sasha, but it was a tender gesture without force behind it. "Which you are never. Sasha is a wonderful doctor, and we're proud of her for achieving her dream."

"I gotta tell ya, we never had such a pretty doc out in the field with my unit. Not on the ships either. They were always old guys with gray hair growing out of their nose and ears."

Sasha shuddered. "Ugh, ugh, ugh, don't remind me. I did my required sea tours early on, but after that it was all shore duty. Or working with Ian's joint-ops group."

"Wait, you were a Marine?" Isisa asked.

"Once a Marine, always a Marine." I smiled. "I did an initial enlistment for six years since they lured me in with an enormous sign-on bonus. More money than I'd ever had in my hands at once. After that, I reenlisted once and went home. My father had a lot of medical problems back then interfering with his ability to manage the family business, you know? Mom never liked me being in the military to begin with, so that was the end of my career. I went home and took over for him."

"That's how he knows Nadir," Sasha explained.

A furry, golden shape streaked across the room and into my peripheral vision. Before I had the chance to blink and turn, it pounced on my lap, and I splashed coffee all over my shirt. I bit back a swear and soldiered through it, thankful it had cooled enough not to inflict a serious burn.

Isisa jumped up, panicked. "Are you okay?"

"It's not that hot anymore. I'm fine."

"Simba, get off him." Laughter filled Sasha's voice. She came to my rescue and reined in the excited dog, lifting him from my lap and cradling him in her arms despite his delighted wiggles. He resembled a teddy bear more than anything, tight yellow curls covering his body from head to toe.

"Sorry! He rushed out when I opened the door." Still dressed for bed in an oversized tee and fleece pants, Nandi descended the steps from the upper level. An uneven abundance of hair framed her round face, flat from a night of sleep on one side and fluffy on the other. When her gaze fixed on me, she stared until her eyes darted to her reflection in the decorative mirror on the wall near us.

"Good morning, Nandi."

"Your shirt. I'm sorry about your shirt." The words blurted out of her in a rush.

"Nothing a few paper towels won't fix."

"Take it off, and I'll toss it in the wash before it stains," Isisa said.

While it wasn't an expensive shirt, it was one of my favorites *and* a gift from my mother. After unfastening the charcoal gray Henley, I pulled it off and passed the shirt over. Simba laid down at Sasha's feet and wagged his tail, the picture of innocence.

While Nandi primped her wild mane of russet coils, Sasha pretended to be absorbed with her phone, but her blue eyes drifted from the screen to me. Sitting topless with three attractive—no, *sexy*—women hadn't exactly been my plan. Especially when those three women were a package deal and I was the one figuring out if I could handle it.

I cleared my throat. "So, Nandi, what sort of books do you write?"

"Romance." When she hesitated between the couch and love seat, I patted the empty cushion beside me. After another indecisive glance toward Sasha, she accepted my offer and sat down. "I write romantic suspense and, um, paranormal."

"Like ghosts?"

A tiny smile curved her full lips. "No. Well, I've had ghosts show up, but I mean like vampires, shapeshifters, and fairies."

"Ah. Shapeshifters, like werewolves and the like then?"

"Yes." Interest danced in her honey-colored eyes, and Nandi's personality finally came alive, emerging from behind the shy wall she'd erected since stepping from her room. "And I sometimes write about magicians and witches, but usually it's shapeshifters."

"That's cool. I watched the hell out of *Trueblood* while it aired on HBO. I've seen all of the *Underworld* movies too, but I gotta say, I usually rooted for the werewolves."

"Me too," Isisa said as she returned. "I thought the werewolves had the better half of the plot. You'd probably enjoy Nandi's writing now that she's broken away from romance a little."

"I don't mind a little romance."

Sasha cupped her chin against her palm and fixed her blue eyes on both of us. "Nandi actually has a signing in a couple weeks and neither of us can make it. I had already promised to help cover the ER for another doctor who is leaving on a cruise."

"And I have a string of court cases throughout October and November," Isisa said.

"Yeah? Where is it?"

Nandi twirled a spiral of her hair around her index finger and glanced out the window. "Chicago. I may just back out. I don't wanna drive up by myself."

"You can't do that," Isisa said. "It's your first ever appearance at a signing and people want to meet you. You have at least a hundred pre-orders, remember?"

"I can mail them out," she mumbled. "I'll eat the cost in shipping and deduct it on the taxes."

"I agree with Isisa. It would be a shame to miss your first appearance. When's the event? I'm due a bit of time off at the job. What if I go with you?" Three sets of owlish, wide eyes stared, and I wondered if I'd said something wrong. "If you're comfortable traveling across the country with a stranger, that is."

Sasha leaned forward. "You'd do that?"

"If Nandi agrees, why not?"

"Yes!" Nandi blurted out. "I mean, if you really don't mind. It will probably be boring for you."

"Oh, I dunno. I've never been to a book signing before, but I've been to Chicago. I could show you around the city while we're up there."

"Thank you."

Of the three, common interests with Nandi and Sasha hadn't been difficult to find. That left Isisa, the athlete among them. She'd fallen silent, resting both hands over the top of her lean thighs. I admired her without shame and took in the whole picture.

"Isisa, you should show Esteban the rest of the penthouse," Nandi suggested. "I'm going to get cleaned up."

Had she intervened to rescue me from the awful coffee, or because she sensed I was floundering and needing a lifeline? Isisa rose and led the way into unexplored territory while Simba followed on my heels.

"Cute dog. I really didn't mind him hopping on me."

"He's a rescue," Isisa said. "I drove all the way to Kentucky to pick him up. Cops had seized a dog fighting ring, and they found all sorts of neglected dogs being overbred on the property as well. Simba's mom died, and they were trying to save the litter.

"Poor little guy. Did the rest of the litter make it?"

Isisa shook her head. "No. I bottle fed him for weeks, but I heard some of the others didn't make it even with round the clock care."

When I reached down and offered my hand to the pooch, his moist nose skimmed my fingers and he shoved his head of sunny curls against them.

"I really am sorry about your shirt. He doesn't usually jump on people like that. He must like you." She grinned and opened a door to the right. "This is Nandi's office. She'll give you the grand tour, I'm sure, but just so you know, this is like no-man's-land. Even I don't bother her in here while she's working. Sometimes she's in the zone, so we just set dinner aside for her on a dish in the microwave."

The open door revealed multiple columns of floor-to-ceiling book shelves and watercolor landscapes on the other walls. A pair of ivory French doors with frosted glass led to a balcony.

"This next door leads to Nandi's bedroom. The one on the left is mine, and Sasha sleeps in the room at the end of the hall." She led the way past Nandi's room and opened the door to hers.

Red drapes trimmed in gold framed windows overlooking the Houston streets, a fraction of the vibrant colors inside Isisa's room and contradicting my first impression of her. A pile of unfolded laundry covered the bed. "Excuse the mess."

Stacks of books towered beside papers scattered across the floor in one corner of the room. Aside from that, nothing appeared out of place.

"No desk?"

"I actually like to sit on the floor when I'm researching." She tucked a braid behind her ear. "Weird, I know, but I have more room to spread out."

"I guess you do most of your work from another office?"

"Yeah."

"Are those awards over there all yours?" Two shelves supported over a dozen trophies and twice as many medals. "Wow."

"I used to compete in college. I still do one marathon a year if work isn't crazy. Do you do any sports?"

"I played soccer in high school. I haven't done a marathon in a couple years. Last one was with a crew from work for a charity fundraiser."

Her eyes lit up. "Yeah? I'm planning on participating in a zombie run in November."

"A what?"

She laughed and tugged on a braid. "It's a 5K run with mud, obstacles, and zombies chasing after you. You have to get through without losing all your flags. Sasha was going to go, but then she had to take over for that doc at work. Nadir is going though, and my friend Juni."

"Nadir? In mud? How'd you pull that one off?" My brows both lifted, and Isisa burst into another peal of giggles.

"Maybe you should join us. It'll be lots of fun, and we have an extra spot on our team open. Interested?"

"Heck, why not?"

She squealed in delight and threw her arms around me. Although she was the slimmest and least busty of the trio, she still had soft curves in all the right places. "Thank you, thank you, thank you. It's a week before the book thing, and it means so much to me that you'll join us."

I hugged her, relieved to have found common ground. "Thanks for asking me. Besides, I'd hate to miss a chance to see Mr. Perfection all muddied up. Think we can sling some mud at him?"

Isisa kissed the corner of my mouth. Her lips lingered, skin scented like cocoa butter. A spark zipped all the way to my toes as I resisted the urge to bury my face against her slim throat. "I'm sure we could arrange that."

"Is Nandi coming, too? You didn't say."

"No. She has a work call with her narrators that day, and since they both live across the world, setting up a time to get both of them online together was a bitch. She said she'd drive out to watch if timing allowed."

"Well, in that case, I promise to do my best to protect you from the brain-eating hordes."

"Or maybe I'll protect you." She grinned and slipped her arm through mine as we headed back downstairs. "There are a couple more places to show you."

After showing me to the guest bathroom on the lower level, she opened a door beside the stairs to reveal a sparse bedroom furnished with only a king-sized bed, dresser, nightstand, and a standing wardrobe near the closet. A couple floor lamps occupied the corners.

"Whose room is this?"

A gentle smile touched her face. "When we purchased our penthouse a few years ago, we wanted one with a bedroom for each of us and... our future husband."

I blinked at her. At my reaction, a throaty chuckle spilled from her like a feline purr. "We like our privacy, sometimes from each other. As much as I love Sasha, we've been together for twenty-six years now. I have my own things. My own belongings. I prefer dark colors on my bed. She likes pastels."

"So basically, you keep separate rooms to maintain your individuality, not because you fight."

She raised her chin, a devious smile widening her full lips. "Oh no, we do fight, but when we need each other, we aren't far."

I stepped into the room and let myself outside onto the small veranda. It didn't look like it would hold more than a table for two overlooking the park.

Isisa stepped up to my side at the iron rail and slid one arm around my waist, her cheek against my shoulder. She inhaled a low, calm breath, like she was breathing me in, followed by a satisfied rumble in her throat, like I'd heard from Sasha before. Before I could question it, she tilted her face up and met my gaze with her honey-colored eyes. "Would you like to see the sundeck? We have a pool."

"Sure."

French doors off the living room led to another

terrace framed by a stone ledge and a glass wall. I walked across the stone tiles toward a modest pool wide enough for two people to swim side by side, attached to a jacuzzi with a bench seat.

"Not much room to swim in there."

"It's more of a lap pool," Isisa explained. "You can activate a function to create resistance to swim against. Otherwise we just get in to cool off during the summer."

"Sasha's the strongest swimmer," Nandi spoke up from the open door.

"I've heard of those but never installed one." My gaze drifted from the pool to the Houston skyline. I whistled. Inhabiting the corner unit of the high-rise gave them an amazing view from both directions. "How do you like living in the city?"

"It's convenient for work, but sometimes I miss the privacy of having land, a backyard, and lots of acres. You know?"

"I'll have to have you all over to my place one weekend. I've got about twenty acres and a few ATVs for roaming if you're into that kind of thing."

Isisa and Nandi exchanged looks before the former answered, "As luck would have it, I *am* into that kind of thing."

"So am I," Nandi said. "I've always wanted to ride an ATV. And to try paintballing. I read that it's the most fun in the woods with cover and bushes."

I grinned. "It is. Tell me when you're down for it, and I'll arrange a campaign for you ladies. Even invite some friends if you'd like all-out war."

To ease into things, we chose to stay in with a movie and Chinese takeout for lunch. Just four friends hanging out. The awkwardness I'd expected never showed up. I sat between Nandi and Isisa on the couch, while Sasha sprawled out on the other end with her head in Nandi's lap. Simba flopped down on Isisa's feet and decided to use mine as a pillow. All things considered, I was pretty comfortable.

"So, since I'm new to this… any tips?"

"Be yourself," Isisa said. "You don't have to go to any great lengths to impress us."

"Yeah," Nandi added in agreement. "What would you do when dating one girl?"

"Ask her out on a proper date I suppose." I laughed and rubbed my nape. "I'm guessing y'all don't want me to take all three of you out at once."

"You can if you want," Sasha said. "Nothing says we can't go out and do things together. But no one will get pissy either if you want to take one of us out alone for something."

"Right, got it. Well, I'm pretty swamped during the week, but would you three like to hit up a movie some evening? Or, I dunno, bowling maybe? Pool?"

Isisa's eyes lit up, and Sasha cackled. "Trust me," Sasha said, "Isisa could cream you at pool."

"Oh really?" I asked, rising to the challenge. "What about you, Nandi?"

She wrinkled her nose. "I suck at pool. They always beat me."

"Yeah, but you're better at blackjack," Isisa said.

"Tell you what, Nandi. I'll give you pointers at pool if you share some of your card tricks with me. Deal?"

And just like that, I'd set up my very first date with my ladies. Lord help me.

10

SASHA

*E*steban was due to arrive at six for our date. Nandi had fretted in front of the mirror for the past hour, blending and reapplying her lipstick in different combinations until she found the perfect shade of cocoa and scarlet to suit her dark complexion.

When I'd tried on her red, it lasted less than five minutes on me before I removed it and chose a rose pink instead. Red on my mouth looked like I had one mission, and one mission only—to get dicked as hard and deep as possible before the night ended.

Isisa approached the couch and frowned at us. She wore snug, low-rise jeans—a rarity for a woman normally clothed in athletic wear or chic pant suits—and an off-the-shoulder ruffled blouse in pale pink. "What happened to the 'Come-Fuck-Me-Red' you were wearing ten minutes ago?"

"Removed for that precise reason," I replied. "We're not trying to send him silent cues to bend us over on the first date."

Isisa's frown deepened. "One, it is *your* third or fourth date with him, isn't it? Two, it was beautiful on both of you."

I toyed with one of my curls, deciding to wear my hair in its natural state of wild coils instead of ironed straight. "Thanks. Still, I like this better. I'll save the red for a fancier outing."

"If that's what you want." She stuck her tongue out at me. "I thought it was sexy though."

Nandi's silent agreement shimmered down the pride link, a warm buzz that touched my soul with love and laughter. Then she fiddled with the neckline of her blouse until I slapped her hand. Playfully.

"Stop that. No amount of readjusting is going to hide those unless you want to wear a turtleneck."

She moved to the edge of the couch cushion, poised to rise. "I could go put one on."

I grabbed her wrist. "Don't you dare. Sweetie, you look beautiful. And I'll wear the red tonight for you both."

The more I fretted, the more ridiculous I felt, my mind foggy with anxiety mirrored by two other women. Sometimes it struck me as more of a drawback than a bonus, a critical flaw to our shifter makeup that provided absolutely no emotional privacy.

Like on those nights when I needed to wake before dawn for a shift in the ER, but trembles of sexual pleasure vibrated through our link from Isisa or Nandi's bedroom.

Isisa shook her head. "Look at us. You'd think we had never dated a man together before."

Our shared laughter broke the tension and helped soothe our anxious nerves. I shook off the concerns and basked in the confidence of knowing Esteban could handle anything we threw at him.

"You're right," Nandi said. "We're worrying about nothing. Tonight is about getting to know him."

My phone chirped with an incoming message. I glanced down to see green bubble from Esteban. "Okay. He parked, and he's heading to the elevator now."

Isisa eyed me. "Good, but first we need to discuss something important before he arrives."

I sighed. "You said you would be the designated driver."

"Not *that*. What will we do if he expects something... physical from us tonight?"

Nandi pursed her lips. Despite her shy nature, she had the highest sex drive, a nuclear libido that kept her in bed with one of us or visiting Isisa's toy chest if we were otherwise occupied.

"I won't mind if it comes to sex, as long as you don't mind if I decline," Isisa said at last.

"Neither will I," Nandi said. "But... we don't have to. I'm okay either way."

"Then, we're agreed that we'll let things happen as comes naturally. If tonight ends in sex with one, two, or even all of us, we'll run with it without regrets."

"Deal."

I hurried to answer the bell when it rang, Nandi and Isisa on my heels.

Esteban waited outside of our door, too handsome in his collared shirt and jeans. His eyes took me in—devoured me like I was a snack laid before him on a platter—and a big grin spread over his face. "I feel underdressed. Is this how you ladies roll for movies and pool?"

I smoothed a hand down the sleeveless, blue shell top I'd plucked from Isisa's closet. It laced on the sides, accentuating my waist. The black leggings hugged my ass and revealed every curve. "Yes. Isisa has rules about how we're to be seen in public together," I said, accomplishing a straight face through sheer willpower.

"I do *not.*"

His gaze moved past me to Isisa and Nandi, still filled with appreciative male hunger. Relief finally released the long breath I'd held.

"Well, you ladies are stunning tonight. Ready to go?"

"Absolutely."

Whether or not he could hold his own against three of us was all that remained to be seen.

~

ESTEBAN

*T*he movie petrified Nandi. She sat motionless to my right throughout most of the film, alternating between gripping the armrest and clutching my arm while Sasha and Isisa laughed at inappropriate moments. They laughed at her, too.

"I'm normally the one she squeezes to death," Sasha whispered in my left ear. Our eyes were glued to the screen during the final act, Nandi frozen again, mouth parted in a silent scream during the inevitable jump scare. Someone a few rows ahead of us shrieked.

Isisa laughed harder. She reached around Nandi and

stole a few fries from my plate. "At least it wasn't Nandi this time."

"*This* time," I added.

Nandi elbowed me.

By the time the movie wound down to its final moments, we'd polished off our meals. My nephews loved when I took them to dine-in theaters, and since the ladies had never visited one, I'd prepurchased tickets ahead of time to the movie of their choice, upgrading our seats to the huge recliners in the middle row.

"I'm properly traumatized. Can we go drink now?" Nandi asked. She rose and stretched, arms above her head, pose accentuating the hourglass figure of her body and drawing my eyes right to her amazing tits.

Sasha reached around me to swat her. "You know they are going to scare you, but you always agree to one."

"The previews were deceptive. I was expecting torture porn and guts everywhere, not legitimate fright mixed in with jump scares and suspense."

I tossed payment and a tip onto the table then followed the three women outside to Nandi's sedan. "What sort of movies do you prefer? Romantic comedies?"

"Action, actually," Nandi replied.

"Yeah, she's dragged us out to every Star Wars, Marvel, and DC Comics flick that's come out." Isisa nudged Nandi in a light, playful manner. "I'm the rom-com junkie, but I love horror, too."

"Where to next, ladies?"

Isisa drove us to a pool hall in the Galleria. As our designated driver for the evening, she drank water while the rest of us enjoyed cocktails at a table near the back. We spent hours there, chatting about every subject that came to mind from dogs to video games, a woman on each side of me.

When Sasha excused herself to visit the restroom, Isisa took the chair to my direct left. "Sasha says you weren't born in the States. Tell me about Puerto Rico."

"Only if you'll tell me about Africa."

We closed the bar down after the girls displayed a drinking constitution that almost put mine to shame. At one point, Sasha and I were going neck to neck, slamming buttery nipples, kamikazes, and anything else Nandi claimed she needed to taste for book research. They kept up with me long after the buzz of alcohol spread warmth through my gut and turned my head fuzzy.

Nandi leaned against me from one side, Isisa on the other. Sasha trailed behind us to the car with her heels in one hand and this blissful smile on her face whenever her gaze drifted toward us. I'd ended the night hand in hand with Nandi.

One hell of an amazing date was over, and throughout it, it never felt like being out on a date with three different girls. Just… a date.

Coconut-scented ringlets brushed my shoulder when Nandi sank against me in the back seat. I held her every damned minute. Soft curves molded against me, her cheek burrowing against my throat. She cuddled the best out of the three, plush and warm with squeezable curves. Isisa hummed along to an R&B song playing over the radio, and Sasha snoozed until we reached the garage.

My Lexus sat in the adjacent parking spot. I'd had so much to drink, losing count toward the last two hours of the night, that I didn't even look at it in passing. Sasha slipped to my left side and Nandi on the right. I put an arm around their waists and squeezed them close during the elevator ride to the top.

"Did you have fun?" Sasha asked once we were inside.

"I had a great time."

Nandi tilted her head up. "With all of us?"

"I haven't been out drinking like this since I was in the military, but the company was never as great." Exhaustion had me in its grip, laying a blanket of fuzz over my vision. I was ready to dive into bed and sleep the inevitable hangover away.

Isisa giggled and bumped her hip into Sasha. "Next time Sasha gets to play chaperone while *I* drink and act ridiculous."

"Sounds like a date."

"Well, date's not over yet." Isisa skipped off to the kitchen and returned a moment later with four shot glasses balanced between her hands. "You still have to have a drink with me."

We all found spots on the couch and shared three more shots of vodka from Isisa's personal stash while we rehashed the movie. A few times, Nandi whipped out a notepad from the side table and jotted down notes.

"Another?"

I put my hand across my glass before Isisa could pour me anything else. "I'm good. More than good, really. In fact, I should probably get to bed if I'm not going to be worthless tomorrow."

Isisa crossed her arms over her chest, long nails tapping against her biceps. "Definitely not. You've had far too much to drink to drive anywhere."

"I wasn't planning on it," I muttered. "Figured I'd crash on your couch or something until morning."

"You will not."

"I can't?" Crap, my mind went a dozen directions at once, wondering if I'd overstepped my bounds somehow while also conjuring up an image of all of us tangled in a sweaty, drunken heap in one bed. Or on the floor.

Isisa cleared her throat, interrupting the fantasy materializing in my mind like a sexual phantom. "What I mean is that we wouldn't make you sleep on our couch when there's a perfectly good bed set aside for the purpose." She gestured to the door beneath the stairs leading to the bedroom intended for their future husband.

"It's your room. If you really are interested in pursuing this between all of us," Sasha said in a quieter voice. "We discussed it while you were in the restroom at the bar. We all enjoyed your company and don't need long weeks of dating to determine if *we* want to continue."

"I can't think of any reason why I wouldn't want to carry on. Y'all are amazing ladies, and the way I see it, it'd be my loss right now if I walked away. I haven't figured out how I'm going to mention any of this to my parents and my family, but that concern can wait until I'm sober. Besides, I know better than to argue about a comfortable bed, so I'm all for it."

"Good." Sasha's eyes brightened, and she leaned forward to kiss me—a quick, sweet touch of her lips on mine.

Isisa mirrored the affectionate gesture, then added, "You have your own bathroom, of course, and there are extra blankets in the closet on the shelf."

"I'm sure whatever's there is fine."

Nandi popped up to her feet. "I'll show you where everything is."

"Lead on, *corazon*."

I'd already seen the room, but I hadn't done more than chat on the terrace with Isisa for a minute. Thick carpet cushioned my feet as we crossed through past the bed and closet to another door. My gaze kept dropping to Nandi's rounded bottom, admiring the way her dress clung to the lush curves.

The bathroom was a work of art with an enormous shower beside a deep tub basin trimmed in marble. A large window over the tub, one I really hoped was one-way glass, revealed the Discovery Green below and the surrounding city.

"Am I going to be giving the city a peepshow?"

Nandi's quiet giggle brought a skip to my pulse. "No. All the windows don't let people see in."

"Does your bathroom have a view like this?"

She shook her head, curls bouncing around her face. "No. I have a smaller window higher up to let in light, that's all."

I leaned forward, hands on the marble ledge, for a better view. The twinkling lights of the park looked as amazing from above as they had on the ground.

"Believe it or not, Sasha has the better bathroom, but she paid to have some extra work done to it. Her shower is massive. All four of us could probably fit inside."

I tore my attention from the midnight skyline. "Tested that theory out yet?"

She bit her lower lip and shyly turned to the closet door behind her. "Maybe." She tugged out fresh towels and set them on the bathroom counter.

A combination of liquid courage and curiosity tore my attention from admiring the bathroom to checking out the woman in front of me. She bent to remove a wrapped bar of soap from the cabinet beneath the sink, raising her dress hem and flashing a hint of purple panties.

Now or never.

When she straightened, I stepped forward into the space behind Nandi until my hips pressed against her round ass. She blinked, and her eyes went wide in the mirror. But she didn't stiffen. I lingered behind her and wrapped an arm around her middle, my palm flat against her stomach. She melted against me.

"Thanks."

"For?" she asked.

"Choosing me." I kissed her ear and let her go.

"You didn't make it a difficult choice. You're..." She tucked a coil of dark hair behind her ear and moved to the door. "Goodnight, Esteban. I put some stuff for you in the dresser drawers."

"Goodnight."

After Nandi shut the door behind her, I crawled onto the bed without turning down the comforter and became dead to the world.

~

SASHA

*N*andi and I made breakfast while Isisa sulked nearby.

"We want to impress him," Nandi said.

"Not murder him with raw eggs and salmonella," I added.

Isisa sighed and gave us a half-hearted smile. "Is it technically murder if it's a well-intended accident?"

Nandi considered it, biting her lower lip while stirring the eggs. "Manslaughter then."

It was around noon when Esteban finally emerged from his bedroom, appearing rumpled and out of sorts, a pair of flannel pajama bottoms the only clothing on his fine body. They rested low on his hips, and his bare chest had never looked more delicious. Nandi had filled a couple of the drawers with fresh Hanes and pajamas after estimating his size.

She'd fretted over it before, afraid he'd think she was mothering him until Isisa reassured her there was nothing motherly about preparing for a guest, merely good manners. And reminded her of how frequently we bought each other panties and pajamas. Nandi knew all my favorite fandoms and never missed the opportunity to gift me with Harry Potter or superhero-themed apparel.

Esteban stretched his arms over his head, and I took a moment to admire his half-naked glory. He drew up short, aware of our appreciative glances. Then a cocky grin spread over his face.

"Well, good morning. Should I do a dance, too, or would that be too much?"

Isisa snickered from the counter and sipped her coffee. "Morning, Esteban, and please don't. Nandi will combust if you do, and then no writing will get done today."

I greeted him with a kiss to his cheek and pushed a mug into his hands. Black and sweet, the way I'd seen him take it before.

"Good morning," Nandi grumbled, removing a french toast bake from the oven.

While I plated eggs and bacon, Isisa flipped channels until she found the local Houston news. "Are you going to come outside with me for a jog, or close yourself away in the reading room as usual?" she asked Nandi.

"I'll jog with you this afternoon if the forecast is dry. It's kind of gray out there."

The news displayed the senior year book photo of a smiling young woman. "The family of Keshia Myers would appreciate any information leading to her safe return. Keshia is merely one among many young women of Houston to recently vanish without a trace. Tune in for the full story this afternoon."

Long after they cut to the meteorologist, I wondered about the missing women.

Ian didn't receive the Houston news in Quickdraw, so I'd mention it to him later, hoping it was another angle he could present to his cop buddies in the HPD. It couldn't be coincidence.

The phone rang as I collected dishes from the others. Esteban had settled on the floor in front of the couch with Isisa while Simba frantically rushed back and forth between them, unable to decide who had the better toy.

I plucked it from the cradle and peered at the caller ID window. Mum's cell number glowed back at me. Preparing for her to give me shit over failing to keep in frequent contact, I accepted the call.

"Hi, Mum. Is something wrong?"

"Must something be wrong to call my baby? We hadn't heard from you in such a long time we were worried. How are things?"

"Oh, they're pretty good," I said, aware of Esteban eyeing me. "How are things in California? Weather nice?"

"Sunny and balmy here, as always," my mother relayed. "You and the girls keeping warm?"

"It's Texas. It doesn't drop much below sixty this time of year."

"She cranks the heat up," Nandi called out.

"Does she really?" Esteban asked.

"Wait, is that a man I hear? Friend or...?"

I glanced over at Esteban and the other two playing with Simba on the floor. "More than a friend. For all of us."

"You have to tell me everything. Nikolai!" I winced away from the phone a little. "Sasha and the girls found someone!"

"Later, Mum, okay? I promise."

"You'd better. Oh, sweetie, I'm so happy for you all. Have you bonded?"

"What? No. Like I said, I'll tell you about it all later."

The phone clicked, and then Nikolai's deep, rumbling voice joined the line. "Your mother is an impatient woman, as you know. She will spend the rest of the day troubling me and speculating about this mystery man." His strong Russian accent was part of his charm.

I grinned. "Good thing she has you to teach her to relax and enjoy life."

My stepfather laughed while my mother grumbled. They were the perfect pair, even if he was a tiger.

"Well, we won't keep you since you have company. But you call me soon, baby, okay? I cannot wait to meet the man who has fascinated all three of you. Give Isisa and Nandi kisses for me."

"I will. Love you." I dropped the phone in the cradle again.

"Telling your mom about me?" Esteban grinned. Simba had claimed his lap after their tug-of-war game and seemed content to hold him hostage on the floor.

"As you heard, I didn't say a peep."

"Yet," Isisa said.

"Should I be worried? Are her parents gonna grill me then roast and eat me if I turn up wanting?"

He had no idea.

"Nah, my mum's a big softie. Nikolai, too."

"That's her stepdad," Nandi said. "He's nice."

"Sounds like a Russian name."

"He is," I replied. "They met, God, like ten years ago?"

Isisa nodded. "Yeah, it was that cruise, remember?"

"For her birthday, we all went in together and booked her a cruise to force her to take some time off work. Nikolai happened to be on board taking a vacation from his job, too. It took her days to work up the courage to approach him."

Nandi sighed gently and propped her chin against one hand. "Watching Nikolai and Phumzile was like viewing a real-life love story. Phumzile had a nice job, but she couldn't afford to fly to Russia to see him often."

"We helped where we could," Isisa said. "And Nikolai had troubles getting into the U.S. at first. They dated over the Internet for almost five years."

I nodded. "Finally, he managed to get a work Visa and surprised her when he came to the States. Isisa had made friends with an immigration attorney, and Ian nudged a few officials for me. Mum had no idea."

Esteban smiled. "It was really sweet of you ladies to help them."

My eyes burned a little, vision misty with

spontaneous, unshed tears. "Anything to bring her happiness. She's done so much for me, for all of us, that this was the least we could do."

"So you're all close to your family?"

"Not all of us," Isisa said. "I only see my mother anymore, and never often enough. If we're lucky, we can pull off a visit a couple times a year when we're not busy." And then she said nothing else on the matter.

Nandi cleared her throat and leapt in. "My family and I are... okay. I mean, I love them, and I see them, but they don't quite understand me. Or my personal preferences."

"That you're into other women?"

"Yeah. Phumzile and Isisa's mother came to America to escape... ahh... a war between their tribes, but my parents came here under different circumstances," she explained. "Dad has Mom and his second wife—"

"Wait, he has two?"

"Well, yeah. They get along—mostly—with some occasional drama since he couldn't legally marry both in America. Mom won because he had her first, and Lesedi is ultra passive-aggressive about it. She never misses a chance to bitch and moan about the other kids not being legitimate, and how it isn't fair for her to not have access to his bank accounts and stuff. I think she's a gold digger."

Esteban winced. "Yeah. I can see how that might be a problem."

"But it wouldn't be a problem between us," Nandi quickly said, words flying out of her in a breath. "Isisa doesn't care about marriage, and I don't either."

Isisa sighed. "Nandi."

"What? It's *true*. You called it a capitalist scam."

Isisa pinned Nandi under a murderous look, effectively silencing her.

At least she hadn't blurted the truth about our shifter natures. Esteban was silent, wearing the stony, neutral expression I'd seen him reveal on occasion. Leave it to Nandi to stumble onto a topic too hot and early for our relationship.

"So how would that all work exactly?" he finally asked when the heavy silence persisted. "Marriage, I mean."

I took his hand, placing it over my knee and stroking the back of his knuckles. "Legally, you could only marry one of us. But nothing stops us from living together. We don't have to rely on you for insurance and things like that."

"And what about children?"

"Your name would go on the birth certificates. We all know you don't have to be married to have a legal claim on children, so that wouldn't be an issue either."

"And you all... do you want kids?" he asked, sliding his hand off my knee and straightening. His posture changed, losing the laid-back and relaxed lean against the couch.

I fidgeted with the edge of my shirt. "Not all of us. Um, we don't have to have this conversation now. I mean, we've only been on a single date."

Esteban popped up both brows. "I think we do. You see, I know I want kids, and I've already wasted a long time with a dishonest ex-wife. Kids, marriage—all things we need to discuss early on before things get serious."

Isisa glanced away.

"Hey," he said in a softer voice. "If *you* don't want kids, that's fine. I just want to know up front if that's across the board—if I should expect to adopt."

Nandi reached over and took Isisa's hand. "I want kids. Sasha, too."

Isisa bit her lower lip and focused on Simba. The dog had crawled over on his belly, only to flop beside her and expose it for rubs. She leaned over him and gave all the scratches he needed.

Damn. And just like that, she'd already withdrawn and gone cold. After twenty-seven years, there were still days when I struggled with her. Only time would tell if Esteban would adapt to her quirks, too.

"I'm good with your personal decisions, and I didn't mean to make anyone upset."

"You didn't," Isisa mumbled. "Anyway, I should check my messages."

She kissed Nandi's cheek then mine and Esteban's before she headed upstairs. Simba trailed after her, ever doting and loyal.

Esteban exhaled a long breath and collapsed against the couch. "So how badly did I fuck that up?" He'd closed his eyes and tilted his head back against the cushions, throat exposed and vulnerable. I licked my lips, tempted to have a nibble. One claiming bite.

"You didn't," I whispered, voice low in case she lingered out of sight to listen. "Her father tried to marry her at a young age to an older man leading... another tribe. For children. It's why her mother brought her to the States. It was all their family cared about, and she was made to feel it was her only value to him."

Esteban frowned. "It isn't."

"We know that, you know that, but she doesn't know that. Her father, older brothers, and grandparents called her selfish," Nandi murmured.

"Selfish? She was a fucking child."

I nodded. "So there you have it. Nandi comes from a large family like yours, and I have my twin brother."

"So, uh"—Nandi rose and stretched, shirt rising high enough to show a sliver of her round tummy—"if you don't have any other plans today, I'm down for showing you the sights in Houston and then making dinner for everyone. I have a deadline, but the editor won't lose her mind if I'm a few hours late."

"If you haven't had enough of all three of us already," I added.

"What? Nah. If dinner is anything like breakfast, count me in. Just give me a few to get put together."

We both smiled. The moment the guest door closed behind him, Nandi spun to face me. "He's definitely the one."

I grinned. "Told ya."

And it was only a matter of time before Isisa let him through her defenses and saw it too.

11

ESTEBAN

Two weeks and three dates into our new arrangement, our relationship remained free of drama and irrational jealousy. Wednesday, Sasha pulled an overnight shift at the hospital, and I stayed at the penthouse watching movies on the sofa with Nandi and Isisa.

We fell asleep together, Nandi's head in my lap and Isisa leaning against my shoulder in front of the television, then stirred awake when Sasha tried to tiptoe past us around six.

After I showered in my bathroom and slipped on a fresh change of clothes, I emerged to find Sasha pouring coffee. Nandi and Isisa had vanished from the sofa.

"Morning, sexy," Sasha greeted me, rising on tiptoe and sealing her welcome with a kiss. Her damp hair hung in two braids against her shoulders, and she wore a thin, faded T-shirt over tiny pink shorts printed with white kittens.

Goddamn.

"Morning, *corazon*. Peaceful night at work?"

"The ER is never peaceful, but it could have been worse. You're here later than I expected."

"I'm here later than *I* expected." I grinned. "It's easy to oversleep when those two don't know how to end a night. Isisa wanted a *Halloween* marathon, and Nandi wouldn't agree to it unless I stayed to watch them all too."

Her bright eyes twinkled despite the hints of exhaustion shadowing them. "Aren't you glad you listened to me and brought extra clothes to leave here?"

I pinned her to the counter and kissed her again. "Very much."

An hour later, after coffee, eggs, and bacon with Sasha, I made my morning commute to the site. I drove through the gate to find the guys all standing beside our mobile administration office. Paint covered the side in a childish string of vulgar Spanish terms. *Mamón. Soplapollas.* I stared at the words I wouldn't repeat in front of my mother if someone offered me a million dollars.

Sergio stepped beside me. "Bad news, *hermano.*"

A section of chain-link fence had been cut open, allowing vandals inside to tag graffiti on a bunch of our equipment and the foundations we'd poured. I walked through the site, scowling at the images of swords and swears in Spanish.

"At least the security cameras will have caught our midnight artists, right?"

My brother cleared his throat. "Um, about that... It looks like the security system went offline."

"*What?*"

"About ten it dropped off. Looks like the power took a

hit and the backup generators never kicked on. I'll check the wiring on them."

"Great, thanks. I'll—"

"Hey, boss," Jesús called over. "I think you may wanna come take a look at this concrete load. It's lookin' *real* wet."

"Dammit, that'll be the third load this week I have to send back."

They say when it rains it pours, and today turned out to be a shitstorm of bad luck. While Sergio directed the crew, I dealt with the police and made a report.

The police thought a dangerous Texas gang was behind the graffiti. About twenty years ago, the Familia de Espadachines Latinos—the Family of Latin Swordsmen— were just a fast-growing group of Latino kids knocking over liquor stores and holding clerks at sword point because they couldn't always get guns. Occasionally, they even did some B&E. Today, they were smuggling drugs and frequently in the news for gang wars. About a few months ago, they'd killed the leader of a rival gang, decapitating him and leaving his head on the kitchen counter for his wife and kids to find. The sword they'd done it with was left in his body, penetrating the heart.

The officers suggested increased surveillance and promised to be in touch. Once the legalities were done, I grabbed one of our workers and began the tedious job of removing paint from concrete. By end of the day, we managed to pour the slabs for the next phase of the job, but it took all hands on deck, including mine.

Dirty and sore, I headed home to take a long, hot shower and pass out without dinner. My mother pulled in the driveway right behind me.

Having family within walking distance was often a blessing, but tonight it felt like a goddamned hassle. *Mierda.* If and when I got to sleep, it'd be hours from now, because I didn't have the heart to chase my affectionate and well-meaning mother away.

"Hey, Mamá. Did you need something?"

"You look like a mess," she said as she crossed over toward me. "You just getting home from work?"

"Yeah. Long day thanks to a few setbacks."

She pursed her lips and looked me over from head to toe. I knew I looked like hell, but hard labor did that, and she had seen my father in the same state on many occasions over the past years.

"Go get cleaned up, and I'll cook for you."

"You don't have to do that."

"I know I don't, *mijo*, but I want to. Besides, we need to discuss Thanksgiving plans."

"Right." Arguing never worked, so I did the smart thing and conceded. Besides that, my belly agreed with her plans despite my previous intentions to crash on an empty stomach. At this point, I'd settle for rice and beans.

Mom provided something much better. By the time I finished washing up and came out in clean clothes, she had all the fixings for tacos laid out on my counter. Somehow she'd managed to find that package of corn tortillas I'd been searching for all week.

"Thanks, Mamá. You're the best." I kissed her cheek and started putting together my plate.

We sat together at the breakfast bar and talked about the family. She shared pictures from her phone of Mariana on her extended honeymoon and chatted about

Selene's latest boyfriend drama. She'd dropped her asshole boyfriend like a sack of rotten potatoes.

"So that's one less mouth to feed at our big turkey feast," my mother concluded. "I'm still worried two birds won't be enough…"

I wiped my mouth and cleared my throat. "About Thanksgiving…" That got her full attention.

"Please tell me you are bringing someone with you."

"Maybe. We'll see."

She straightened and beamed at me. "Samuel said he saw you with a woman here. A beautiful one, too. Not a nice Latina girl, but that doesn't bother me."

"Wait, what? While it's nice to know *my* dating preferences don't bother you," I said with some sarcasm seeping into my voice, "but when did Samuel…?"

"Don't get smart with me. And it was a week or so ago." She waved her hand dismissively. "He came over to ask for one of your movies but said he saw you on the couch with a pretty girl, so he left."

I needed to learn to close my blinds earlier. "And you haven't said anything all this time?"

"I didn't want to push you."

"Who are you and what have you done with my mother?"

Mamá only chuckled and patted my arm. "You don't have any candy. Did you forget?"

The abrupt change of subject threw me off kilter. "Huh?"

"Candy, for the children. Only four more days, you know. The good stuff will be sold out."

"Oh, I'm not passing out candy at home anyway this year. I have a date to a party."

"Ah, all right then. I hope you have a good time." She rose from her seat, her satisfied expression the sweet smile of an old woman with diabolical plans on her mind. "Get some rest, Esteban. Let me know when you decide about the holiday so I can plan the meal. I need to know how many people to expect. Maybe I'll order that third turkey after all."

While I questioned my sanity, she returned to her car and drove away. Mamá *never* missed an opportunity to pry into my personal life.

And when she was ready to spring her plan, I probably wasn't going to like it.

~

SASHA

*D*ressing as my favorite *Game of Thrones* character for Halloween earned more attention than I anticipated when Esteban and I stopped to gas up along the way to Quickdraw. We'd been invited to participate in a costumed church function sponsored by my friend Julia and her husband Lyle for the town's kids.

I'd met Julia when we were both doctors serving at Navy Medical Center San Diego, and from there, our friendship blossomed into something greater. I'd been a part of Ian's group already, but after I introduced the two of them, she eventually became my stand-in.

But I'd never felt replaced by her. On the contrary, I'd felt confident and at ease with leaving the medical care of my best friends, my closest comrades, in her capable hands.

While steering my 'Vette down the narrow lane leading into Hawthorn Grove, subtle changes stood out since my last visit. A brand-new bronze sign on the left proclaimed the name of their sleepy little burg a couple minutes beyond Quickdraw city limits, and the roads had been newly paved. Prior to that, it had been dirt road and pea gravel, both of which I'd bitched about to him multiple times. The beginnings of a brick wall had been laid out to either side of the road, leading me to wonder if they planned to gate it off eventually.

Ian lived in a two-story brick home on the right-hand side, and a few yards down the road on the left, Taylor had purchased some property to build a house with his wife. At the very end of the lane, our other teammate, Russ, had built a cabin he shared with his wife and two children.

And then there was Jules in between them. She'd had taken a couple acres off Ian's hands. On it, she and her husband had built a gorgeous two-story home with an enormous, fenced-in yard and three-car garage. Her husband was a mechanic by trade and loved working on automobiles in his spare time as projects. When I pulled into the empty spot beside Lyle's massive tow truck, Esteban leaned forward and whistled at the classic Mustang parked beneath a carport beside the garage.

The tow truck shone black and glossy purple, the logo of Wildside Paint and Autobody visible on the side in stylish block letters hugged by the silhouette of a prowling wildcat.

Lyle worked for Taylor, a former drug dealer turned

good after a couple years in prison set him straight. Serving time had mellowed him. Changed him. Now he managed and ran operations at the Huntsville location opened last year. The two guys had become best friends.

I explained everything to Esteban along the way to Julia's house, not expecting him to retain everything I said, but wanting him prepared for the first meeting with all of my close friends. My *family*.

"See, I knew Nadir installed surveillance equipment, but I didn't realize there was more to it than that."

Ian's private security firm was one of the best in the country, and I'd been a member of it since the beginning. On top of government sanctioned missions, he hired out bodyguards and security personnel.

"Nadir is our communications guy, but sometimes Juni takes over for him. They're both good with tech and building stuff. Julia filled in for me as a medic sometimes when I wasn't available."

I expected it to overwhelm him, but he only grinned. "Does that mean you have an assortment of skills able to rival Liam Neeson?"

"Oh no. Not me. I just sew and plug things up," I fibbed, afraid of intimidating him with the absolute truth. "The one who lays down the calm threats before passing out judo assbeatings would be Ian. He's the big brains behind all of it. Anyway, now that they live in Quickdraw, the town is practically crime free. They took care of most of the criminal elements, and Lyle mentors the kids who enter the system. Speaking of which, there's something I have to warn you about before you meet him."

"Yeah?"

"Lyle lost his left arm in an accident a few years ago,

but he's not sensitive about it. Julia created his replacement, so feel free to stare at it and marvel over the design because it's her pride and joy."

"Okay. Stare and ogle away then."

"Right. But be sure to say it looks badass. Also, the triplets don't like to wear clothes. They're always whipping their diapers off and streaking the moment someone turns their back on them."

"Okay. I have a ton of cousins and little cousins. I can handle a few baby bottoms."

"And Elijah kind of stops to pee at random, so we try very, very hard to keep an eye on him for spontaneous diaper removal, and we leave all footwear outside or place them out of reach on the shelf inside because those are his favorite targets."

Esteban stared at me.

"Right. Let's go."

Dressed in an all-black, ankle-length gown with green highlights in her hair, Julia opened the door and met us on the stoop before I had a chance to knock. I left my slippers outside, and Esteban did the same.

The aroma of pumpkin spice and everything nice wrapped me in a hug before Julia's slender arms enfolded me, too. Her home smelled terrific, because she and Nandi shared a sincere love of everything scented from candles to wax melts and essential oil diffusers that released intoxicating aromas into the air. I didn't know who had addicted who first. And since Taylor's wife ran the spa in town, they were always trying out her latest aromatherapy discoveries.

Wishing I visited more often, I leaned back and gazed at Julia with a smile. "Where are my babies?"

"Harassing Lyle while I finish the goody bags. Are you going to introduce me first to your new man before you go spoil my kids?"

"Oh, right." Heat arose in my cheeks. I tucked my chin then stole a glance to the side at Esteban, gazing at him from beneath my lashes. "This is Esteban. Esteban, my best friend Julia."

When he held out a hand to shake with her, Julia tugged the dish from his hands, passed it to me, and stepped forward to hug him. "Welcome to our home. Now where are Nandi and Isisa?"

"One of Isisa's clients had some kind of emergency, and Nandi wanted to polish a draft before she sends it to her editor. They won't arrive for a couple hours but *did* send us ahead with this offering to appease you."

Julia leaned down and inhaled without removing the lid. "Apple dumplings. Call me successfully bribed."

"If you put them in the oven for a few minutes, they'll be warm and gooey all over again for the party. Nandi is a pro at making these things. And she managed to only save one for herself."

"We'll try and save her another then. You two head to the family room and grab a drink. I'll be in shortly."

Even if I hadn't known the way, the noise would have led us through the house. They'd built an extra room into their design exactly for times like this, big enough to hold all of us in comfort and still let the kids run around.

The triplets had all piled on their father, who lay on the floor playing dead. Thankfully, all three had their clothes on. For now.

"Kitty!" Charlotte abandoned Lyle and raced to me as

fast as her chubby legs could carry her, which was pretty fast. I caught her up in my arms and lifted her to my hips.

"Kitty?" Esteban asked.

"It's, uh, her nickname for me. Isn't that right, Charlotte?"

By then, both boys followed their sister's lead and jumped around my legs. Lyle groaned and picked himself up from the floor. He hadn't changed out of his oil-stained jeans and T-shirt yet.

"About time you came and rescued me," he said.

"But watching you suffer at such tiny hands is so much fun," I teased, trying to keep my balance while the boys attempted to crawl up my body. Esteban only laughed at my misfortune.

"Yeah, well, it's your turn now, and I get to enjoy the show."

I stuck my tongue out at Lyle, then nodded toward Esteban. "Esteban, meet Lyle. He's a jerk, but we let him stick around anyway because Jules is sweet on him. Lyle, this is my boyfriend, Esteban."

Esteban extended his right hand again. "Nice to meet you."

Lyle glanced Esteban up and down. My man had about four inches on the muscular dog shifter. They assessed each other in the way guys sometimes did, and then a smile broke out over Lyle's face. "None of that, dude. We're all family here." He swatted aside the offered hand and pulled Esteban against him for a one-armed bro hug. "Want a beer?"

"Man, yes."

Ten minutes later, they were both sipping beers on the couch while I sat on the floor with the chubby babies.

Only Charles and Elijah were identical. Recently, Lyle had begun to shift and lead them around the house and backyard in their animal forms, but they were still far too young to control their transformations on their own.

Charlotte patted my cheeks and gazed into my eyes. "Kitty."

Plucking her up and setting her on my left thigh, I distracted her from the request with a kiss to the cheek and tickles to her round tummy. Maybe next visit when Esteban wasn't with me, I'd strip down and transform to join them for a romp through the yard.

The door opened and shut, accompanied with a chime. "Anybody home?" Taylor's voice called out.

"We're all back here!"

Taylor wandered into the room, dressed to the nines in a pinstriped zoot suit, complete with a fedora and a replica tommy gun. A few steps behind him, Jada came into view, her luscious curves equally stunning in an Egyptian queen costume. There wasn't a hotter Cleopatra in all of Texas.

Lyle handled introductions this time around while I hung back and watched Esteban meet my ex. No posturing. No veiled hostility. He greeted Taylor with the same warmth and genuine kindness I'd come to know and love.

Russ, Dani, Ian, and Leigh arrived not long after, everyone dressed up in costume. Ian had been wearing the same Captain America costume for years now, and this year, we'd convinced our bear shifter pal he would make an amazing Colossus since no one could pull off a Russian accent better than him.

The guys fell into an easy conversation about hunting

out in the woods on Ian's property, which turned into a discussion about field dressings, camping, and an eager invitation from Russ and Taylor for Esteban to join them.

My heart swelled a little. Bless Taylor for being every bit the amazing man I knew he could be. They welcomed my guy with open arms, bringing him into our family without hesitation.

Julia poked her head into the living room. "Hey, Sasha, can you help me out for a few minutes?"

"Sure thing."

I passed Charlotte over to her father and followed Julia to her bedroom, only stopping to snag a mug of apple cider along the way. With the door shut, most of the noise from the party was muffled. Once we moved into her ginormous bathroom and shut that door as well, I could barely hear a peep.

"Think you can help me with my hair? I never manage to get the back to curl."

"Yeah, of course."

I traded my steaming drink for a curling iron. While I carefully formed curls, she worked on her makeup, applying green all over her face, smoky eyeshadow, and black lipstick.

"Witch?" I guessed.

She winked. "Wicked Witch. Nothing imaginative, I know, but—"

"Hey, sometimes sticking with the classics is the best. How boring would Halloween be if there were no witches with pointy hats and brooms around?"

She giggled and applied an opal gloss that turned her lipstick into a pretty blue-violet shimmer. "So Esteban seems nice."

There it was. I knew it was coming and chuckled. "He is, yeah."

"Looks like you two are doing good. Everything on track there?"

"I think so, but..."

"What?" Julia gazed at me through the mirror.

I remained quiet while finishing the last perfect curl. Julia didn't push, merely watching my reflection while I fussed with putting the curling iron away and arranging her cooling hair. "I need your advice."

"Okay."

While gathering my thoughts, I lifted my mug and sipped the delicious, fragrant brew for a few seconds, savoring the sweet taste melded with cinnamon. "Is it too early to tell him about shifters?"

Julia twisted around on her stool and studied my face. "How do you feel about him?"

"I feel... *we* feel like he's a dream come true. He doesn't seem real."

"So Nandi and Isisa share your feelings 100 percent?"

I nodded.

"He knows what he's getting into with the three of you and that you want this for the long term?"

I nodded again.

Julia crossed her legs and pursed her lips. "He fits in among the guys like he belongs here. Plus, he wore a *Game of Thrones* costume for you. I also overheard him telling Lyle that he doesn't even watch the show."

"He doesn't. Nandi requested for us to dress like this." I laughed. "It was some weird sexual fantasy she had and wanted to see fulfilled."

Julia's eyes twinkled with mirth. "A sexual fantasy means you need to be having sex. Are you having sex yet?"

"Not yet." I toyed with a lock of my blonde hair. "But I've been thinking about it."

"Better keep the costumes after tonight then. Besides, that man looks fine as hell as Jon Snow."

"He vetoed our original idea because it's too damned cold to be shirtless. He has the chest for it though. Trust me."

Julia sighed in echoing admiration. "Lyle wanted to be RoboCop since he has the bionic arm, but the kids picked out his costume. Cowardly Lion. The kiddos round out our *Wizard of Oz* crew with Dorothy, Tin Man, and Scarecrow."

"See? That's not boring and unimaginative at all."

"I suppose not, but we've veered away from the conversation. And since you're asking for my advice, I say go for it. Tell him before you all get involved any deeper. Especially if—" She paused, brows knitting together. "Have you, you know, recognized him? As a mate I mean."

"I think so. The first time I saw him at Nadir's place, I stopped dead in my tracks, like something had hit me with a sledgehammer."

"And the other two?"

"Same. Nandi was more flustered and shy than usual at first, and Isisa might have stuttered a few times. More than anything, though, I'm terrified telling him will be too much for him."

"On top of being in your unconventional relationship."

"Yeah." Relief flooded through me at her understanding. "He's still adjusting to dating all three of us at once, and no one but me has ever been off *alone*

alone with him yet. He and I are going camping tomorrow without the other two."

"Have you flipped a coin over who gets to bone him first?"

I shoved Julia in her shoulder. "Crude. You're picking up Lyle's dirty mouth."

"That's what you think. He'd have said fuck."

"Anyway, no, we did not flip a coin. We agreed that it would happen when it happened, with whoever he happened to be with."

"But you and he are going camping. Alone. Cuddled up close in a tent." She waggled her brows and made kissy noises.

"You're a brat."

"Admit it, you wanna claim him first, so you stacked the deck a little. No shame in that. *You* found him, and your lioness wants to have first dibs."

"Maybe," I mumbled

"Besides, I have no doubt whatsoever that Nandi would want you to go first. She's always been a little submissive to you."

"To me *and* Isisa."

Julia nodded. "To both of you, yes. And Isisa often waits for your leadership. You're practically the pride matriarch."

"Hardly. I just happen to be the oldest and most responsible. I'm not their leader."

"Sure, you aren't. That's why they look up to and seek your guidance. Anyway, clearly this means you should have him then report to them both about how amazing it is."

"So I should tell him, then. Tomorrow."

"I would, but the only thing you can do is follow your heart. Whatever you decide, I know you'll make the choice because it's what's best."

"Thanks, Jules."

"No problem. Always happy to help."

We divided the group between Russ and Lyle's trucks for the drive into Quickdraw and claimed a spot in the parking lot of the Methodist church. Isisa and Nandi arrived at the same time we did, and between the three vehicles, we set up a spectacular and spooky display for the Trunk-or-Treat event. Julia and Lyle abandoned us to pull the triplets around the parking lot in a wagon. Sophia dragged Ian and Leigh away to meet up with her friends from school and their parents to hit the neighborhood for treats.

Watching my friends with their children stirred a deep longing within me, and I saw that same desire on Nandi's face each time she happily passed each visiting kid a fistful of chocolate miniatures. My gaze drifted to Esteban, and I watched him playfully cross foam swords with a kid who looked to be around nine or ten.

He was the one, I knew it. Now I only needed to find the strength to tell him the whole truth about us, and hope that he accepted us for who we truly were.

12

ESTEBAN

A couple days passed before I saw Sasha again, since my dad's side of the family honored *Día de los Muertos.* For the Castillo family, it was two days of remembrance dedicated to our beloved relatives, especially Papá Sergio, my dad's father, and one of the biggest positive influences on my life as a kid. If not for him believing in Pops and giving him the initial loan to start his business, there'd be no Castillo Construction.

As much as I enjoyed meeting Sasha's friends, nothing excited me more than the promise of having her all to myself. When I picked her up from the penthouse Friday morning, Isisa kissed me goodbye on her way to work, and Nandi placed natural, bug-repelling wristbands on each of us before disappearing to her writing cave.

"This area is pretty." Sasha stretched her arms over her head and looked out over the clearing I'd driven us to.

"Yeah, it is. A family friend owns the property and lets us come out here to camp and hunt. Lots of wild hogs roaming the property usually. A few deer, too."

Frequent visits with the family had worn the area flat and made it an ideal area for placing the tent. I handled that while she inflated the thin air mattress she'd insisted on bringing. I'd laughed at the time, but then I remembered how cold the ground could be, even with blankets.

"You're going to spoil me," I muttered once we had everything tucked away inside. "How many blankets did you bring?"

"Nandi threw in at least two more and Isisa snuck one into my bag. We'll be toasty warm."

"That's what the fire is for."

"Yeah, but are you gonna leave the fire going all night while we're asleep inside? What would Smokey say?"

"Ha. Ha." A tug on the waistband of her jeans brought her close enough for a kiss. She met me halfway, one arm going around my neck. My dick hardened in a blink when the other hand snuck between us and stroked, like she was a cockwizard with a magical instant-erection touch.

Damn.

If she could do that with a kiss, what the hell would it be like when I finally got her into the bedroom? I let her go and shook it off, determined to keep my head in the game and dick under control. For now anyway.

While she found a patch of sunlight for the solar lantern, I brought out the portable shower kit and my heavy-duty campfire grill. "There's a deer stand, but I figured you weren't up for that lazy shit and would want to hunt from the ground."

Sasha flashed me a big grin. "You know it. Bows?"

I nodded.

We grabbed the rest of the gear from the rear cab and

armed ourselves. She removed a compound bow with few bells and whistles, its length green and brown camouflage instead of the hideous pink my little sister preferred.

We made our way through the forest without further words. Once or twice we paused to listen and watch, but eventually moved deeper into the property. Sasha proved herself a capable tracker, which surprised me a bit considering she was a doctor. I had to remind myself she worked in the field.

There wasn't much but rabbits and the occasional squirrel at first, both creatures Sasha turned her nose up at. She wanted the big prize and had her heart set on a hog or a buck. About two hours into our trek, we found signs of deer in the area.

Her hand went up and she stilled, a motionless predator who looked at home in the forest. She crouched and motioned me into cover. I ducked down and tucked my body behind a tree while Sasha leaned her back against another.

"Deer?" I mouthed at her.

She nodded then peered around the trunk behind her, signaling me to follow her line of sight. I leaned out of hiding enough to see her prey in the distance, barely visible between two enormous trees. I counted eight points on the buck's rack.

"Mine?" she asked silently, barely a whisper.

"Go for it."

Sasha was like silent death. I didn't hear the rustle of the plant life around her, and she didn't appear to even aim. The arrow flew, felled its target, and birds took flight from the golden-green canopy above us.

My jaw dropped. "Did you even aim?"

She shrugged. "I must have or I wouldn't have gotten him," she teased before jogging forward.

The buck was lying where she'd hit him, taken down by a shot so clean I'd have thought she used a scope or lined it up for several seconds instead of effortlessly letting that shit fly like the deer's heart had a magnetic draw. She crouched beside him and pursed her lips, studying the deceased animal before drawing her knife.

"Do you want me to give you a hand with—"

She slit him and poured his innards onto the forest floor without my help.

What the hell?

She'd propped the beast on an incline on his back and worked quickly, snipping and cutting, making efficient slices until the body cavity had been emptied. I stepped back and watched her work, mesmerized.

"Here, I'll take him back to—"

Sasha hoisted the deer over her shoulder and strode away like she'd picked up a sack of potatoes instead of an animal weighing as much as she did. I stared.

What the hell kind of wonder woman had I gotten my hands on? I knew she was fit for a chick, but I'd seen grown men struggle under a large buck's dead weight.

"Wait, stop, wait. Let me help you with that. Fuck. I know you can do it, as you've so aptly demonstrated, but it's going to sit on my conscience if I just follow behind you."

Sasha laughed and kissed my cheek, blue eyes twinkling with mirth. "My mother always taught me to handle my kills. It's a bit of an ingrained habit. An instinct, if you will." Her grin widened as she added, "Honest, I don't expect you to do anything for me."

"I know you don't expect it, and reasons like that are why I like dating you. Still, *my* mother raised me to help others, and I'd be down for taking this burden off your hands even if you were a dude."

About a mile from reaching our camp, Sasha relented and allowed me to take the buck. Together, we got the deer back to the edge of our camp and hung him nearby. We skinned him together then stretched the hide over the ground to scrape the flesh and skin out of it.

While her buck drained, we washed our hands then unpacked the picnic box Nandi had prepared for us. A pile of sandwiches and chilled apple cider had been packed inside.

These ladies were spoiling me.

"Want to go for a second now or wait until tomorrow?" she asked.

"Tomorrow's fine. To be honest with you, I have a request from Mamá for rabbit if we see any. We've got plenty of hog meat at home and a deer from our last campout. I'm mostly looking forward to the creek nearby though."

Her fair brows rose. "Creek?"

"Yeah. That's why I chose this place. There's a creek nearby full of mudbugs, and this is the best time of the year to go crawfishing. You ever been?"

"Once, a long time ago. They like meat, right?"

"Yup. I always come out here with Eduardo."

"Who?"

"My brother."

Her nose crinkled, and she counted on her fingers. "But I thought you only had six brothers and sisters."

"I do. Sergio, Mariana, Eduardo, Angelo, Selene, and Samuel."

"So who the hell is Lalo?"

I burst out laughing. "That's Eduardo."

She made a face at me, scrunching it up and scowling. "Why do you call him Lalo then?"

Chuckling, I took her by the hand and led the way to our crawfishing ground. "It's a nickname thing, *corazon*. My family sometimes calls me Stebi."

"That's… adorable." Her eyes sparkled. "Do *I* get to call you Stebi?"

"Please no."

Waist-high grass bordered a wide creek thick with algae and darkened by mud. I tested its depth with my pole then scooped water into a bucket. I'd also brought several coolers for storing the excess, figuring Nandi and Isisa would appreciate the gesture.

Sasha had brought leftover fried chicken as bait for our crawfishing in the creek, but I pulled out a Ziploc baggie holding a few pieces of ham. We both settled on the hard ground and readied our bait.

"That ham looks inedible." Sasha eyed the meat I held down in the water. "Like… I wouldn't eat it but *maybe* give it to the dog inedible."

Even my dogs hadn't wanted to eat it, but I wouldn't admit that to her. They were safe at home, babysat by Samuel until we returned. "That's why it's the best for crawfish."

"If you say so…"

"Fifty bucks says I catch more than you." As soon as the words left my mouth, I felt a slight tug on my lure and glanced down in time to sweep up my prize. The stubborn crawfish dangled from the meat without letting go, so him and his piece of ham went into the bucket. Sasha pouted.

"Fine, I'll take your bet."

Less than a minute after I sank my bait in the water, I dragged two more up. Sasha sulked at me. "It's luck."

"Uh-huh."

By the end of the first hour, I'd fetched over three dozen for our dinner, and Sasha had added half as many to our pile. I caught her staring at the dried out, forgotten ham leftover from my fridge.

"Ready to give in?"

"No."

Amused by her tenacious refusal to use my bait, I leaned in close enough to kiss her cheek. Defiant to the end, she caught another dozen with her remaining leg of chicken and sat pouting beside me afterward. I offered the ham again. She took a piece with a resigned sigh and a mock scowl. By the time we ran out of bait, we had more than enough for ourselves and our ladies back home.

"Guess I owe you fifty bucks."

"Yup," I agreed cheerfully.

We divided up our catch, cleaned our portions with fresh water, and readied the fire. Since I'd planned for a crawfish boil, I had packed the necessities. Onions, beer, red potatoes, corn cobs, and spices went into the pot while the water warmed.

Sasha cleaned up and packed away our deer in the meantime. Damn she butchered like a professional with my knife.

"Who taught you to cook?" Sasha asked while I checked on our boiling meal.

"My mom. She's a big cooker, always ready to serve up a meal on the fly. My dad cooks, too, but usually he handles the grilling. If he goes into the kitchen, he gets ordered around." I smiled at that last bit, thinking of my folks.

"They sound really nice."

"They are. I've never spent so much time away from my family before. It's only a matter of time before my mother questions what I'm doing and why I haven't brought you home." Considering the sensitive nature of dating three women in a non-traditional kind of relationship, I didn't look forward to explaining it to my old-fashioned Catholic mother, either.

"I'll come home to meet her if you'd like, but, um… just so you know, Nandi and Isisa don't mind if you don't mention them. The people closest to us accept what we have, but some people don't. We know that. It won't hurt their feelings."

"Seriously?"

She nodded. "You can talk to them about it if you want. We used to lie to a lot of our friends and pretend Nandi was only a roomie and a friend who lived with us. Then as time went by, we stopped caring."

"That seems…" Tension tightened my stomach. "It seems unfair to hide what you have."

"I guess so, but that's the world we live in. Most people don't understand, so we tend not to let those sort of close-minded people into our lives. There was a nurse I was friends with once, a few years back. The moment she found out I was in a same-sex relationship, she disappeared. Avoided me."

"Her loss."

"Isisa said the same thing. It still stung though."

"She still work there?"

"No. Last I heard she had gotten married and moved to Dallas." She shrugged and leaned forward to inspect the pot. "Are they done yet?"

"Looks like. You hungry or something?"

"I just don't want you to turn our food into rubber."

Cheeky. I guess that's what I liked about her. Sasha wasn't afraid to sass me. But she was also right. If I let them boil any longer, they would be ruined.

Once we had the pot off the fire and the crawfish spread out on newspaper, we both dug in without waiting for them to cool off.

Beer, butter, and spices flooded every inch of the meat. I slurped the juices trapped in the crawfish's head then tossed it aside to fetch another. Sasha slapped my hand.

"Leave some for me."

"You've eaten half of them."

"Have not." She stuck her tongue out.

"Have you even eaten any of the potatoes and corn?"

She wrinkled her nose at me. "No corn, but as you can see, my half of the potatoes are gone."

Damn, where did she put it all?

"You're the man. This is the moment when you accept that I'm hungrier and chivalry dictates you surrender the rest to me."

I grinned at her. "Consider me a feminist who believes in equal treatment."

"Damn. Foiled at my own game."

We divided the rest between us fairly and cracked open a couple cans of a delicious cider she'd brought. The sweetness of strawberry and sage offset the Cajun spices for a delicious, absolutely satisfying burn.

"This is some good stuff."

"I went out to Massachusetts earlier this year to participate in a conference covering some brand-new advances in medicine. Isisa came along with me since she'd never been, so once my business was over, we went sightseeing. Saw Salem and visited a neat local winery carrying these."

The sky was dark above us by now, no more sun to chase away the chill of the fall breeze snaking between the trees into our clearing. Leaving Sasha to sit by the campfire, I fetched our jackets and shrugged into mine. She didn't move, appearing transfixed by the flames.

"Sash?"

"Hm?"

"You okay?"

"Just thinking."

I offered her the jacket, but she shook her head. "About?"

"Something I want to tell you, but I'm not sure if it'll be a deal breaker after everything else."

"If I can handle everything else you've thrown at me, there's nothing at this point that can shake me, chica. So what's up? Is there a fourth woman somewhere?"

Her solemn expression didn't change, eyes quiet. Sad. "No."

My stomach sank. "A guy?"

Sasha blinked a few times. "A guy? No!"

The spike of adrenaline that kicked my heart rhythm eased. I relaxed, and the tension crawling into my shoulders and back diminished. A slow exhale deflated my chest. "Okay. That's about the only thing I don't think I could handle at this point."

"You're the only man any of us want, but it's a secret that isn't easily shared with anyone. I... I think you'll be okay with it, but it still worries me."

Sasha stood and unbuttoned her flannel shirt. She tossed it aside on the log, and nothing about her behavior stood out as unusual until she unfastened her jeans next and shoved them down her legs, revealing lean thighs I'd ached to have wrapped around me.

"Sash?"

"Just wait," she whispered.

The camisole was next, down to a shell pink bra with padded cups, not that they were needed. Once it came off, the fullness of her tits remained pert and high, capped with tight nipples. My cock tensed when her panties dropped next.

Beautiful. She'd waxed smooth, leaving a perfect strip of white-blonde, neatly trimmed curls between her thighs.

Tonight. After almost a month of dating, I couldn't think of a better night to take our relationship to the next level. The ache in my pants grew unbearable, my mouth longing for the taste of her skin.

She changed.

My Sasha wasn't there anymore.

Adrenaline rushed the blood through my veins, and a pounding pulse drowned out all other sounds beneath the night sky. In the glow of our campfire and the pale moon, a white lioness stood where Sasha belonged. Piercing blue eyes, identical to the eyes of the woman I'd come to adore, gazed at me from within a serene feline face.

Don't panic. Don't panic. Don't panic. Repeating it didn't help, and my fight-or-flight response won when she stepped forward. Jerking back, I stumbled over the root of a tree at the edge of our camp, lost my balance, and landed in the leaf-strewn dirt.

The lioness paused. She transformed again, back to a svelte and fair-skinned woman within seconds, crouched on the forest floor with her white-golden waves spilling over her bare shoulders. My hard-on didn't return, but I did manage to jump up to my feet again.

"You were a lion. What the fuck, Sasha? I mean, I saw that, didn't I?"

"Werelion would be the proper term, I suppose. Except I change when I want, not on the whim of the moon."

"Was… was there something in my drink?" I jumped to my feet and looked around.

"No, I didn't drug you with a sealed can of cider. What you saw is exactly what I am. What all of us are."

"You mean Nandi and Isisa are—"

"Lions too."

"Like one of her books."

Sasha nodded.

"And when she's writing about that shit, she's really writing about you guys."

"Not us specifically. There *are* more people like us. People who become tigers, bears, birds, and, um, other creatures. Nandi thinks it's funny to write about it all as fictional romance because… we all exist but don't have representation."

"Define other."

"Do you really want to know?"

"Yes. I'm guessing you showed me this," I waved my

hand toward her in a sweep that went from head to toe, "for a reason, so lay it on me."

Sasha stood and plucked her flannel shirt from the ground. She slipped into it, but the hem only reached a few inches below her hips after she fastened the buttons. "Sit down, and let me tell you this world's biggest secret."

For a brief second, I thought to argue and stay on my feet, but her serious expression made me reconsider and retake my place by the campfire. Instead of sitting, she paced on the other side.

"You said you liked that *Trueblood* show, right? Well, for people like me, it's real. Vampires, shifters, dragons, and magicians are something I've known exists my entire life, but we live the same way the rest of you do, hold down jobs, and start up families. Pay taxes."

"Back up. Did you say dragons?"

She rolled her eyes. "All of that, and dragons are the part that shocks you."

"Real dragons?"

"Yeah, real fire-breathing dragons. Well, some breathe acid or lightning. But there aren't many of them, and chances are you won't ever meet one. Doing okay so far?"

If I hadn't seen her shift with my own eyes, I'd have suggested a doctor, or a good shrink. "I think so."

Sasha's bare toes curled against the barren ground. Blue eyes gazed at me with hope and longing. "You haven't said how you feel about it yet. Is it *okay* with you?"

"Now that I'm not petrified you're going to eat me?"

"Yes."

"It's…" *She's still the same Sasha.* Still the same woman I'd hunted alongside throughout the day. Still the same incredible shot with amazing legs who drank me under the table when we'd gone out dancing together. "Kind of badass."

Mirth crinkled the corners of her eyes. "Kind of?"

Like hell if I was going to let her go now. I stood and crossed to her in a few steps. "Is 'fucking awesome' better? Come here. I can see you shivering."

Goosebumps speckled her skin despite the flannel shirt, not that it did her much good when it didn't even cover her ass. Chafing my hands up and down her forearms, I warmed her with my palms then dragged her in close enough to share body heat. The move prompted her to wrap both arms around me and thread her fingers through my hair, her mouth delivering sweet and drugging kisses to my cheeks and nose, occasionally finding my lips.

God. She rumbled again, this kind of sultry and feline sound that turned my knees weak.

"Every time I think you can't be any more perfect, you prove me wrong, Esteban."

Me, perfect? She was the one who turned into a damned lion. "Why? Because I'm not freaking out?"

"I've terrified a man or two with the news, but most of all, I didn't want you pissed because we kept a secret from you until the last minute."

"I'm actually madder that you scared the piss out of me at our campsite a couple weeks ago and made me look like a lunatic to everybody. No one believed me when I said I saw a white lioness."

"Yeah, well, I had to be sure what sort of man you were before I took you home to my girls.

"And what kind of man am I?"

Sasha's hips nudged forward, and firm pressure

restored the erection stolen by my terror moments ago. Cockwizard. For real. "The kind I trust with my mates. A good man who would make time in his plans to accompany a shy author to her first book signing. Compete with a shifter, even when he knows he can't win."

I slanted my mouth over hers and brushed my tongue between her lips. My cock twitched, cramped by too little room in my jeans. Desperate to free it, I dropped one hand between us and tugged my belt.

"No." Her fingers lowered to my hand and took over. "Let me."

I couldn't recall the last time a woman had undressed me. Sasha unbuckled my belt and snapped open my jeans. As much as I wanted to shove them down, I waited, letting her have what she wanted.

She didn't stop at only pushing down my jeans. No, instead she freed my cock from my boxer briefs and took me in her hand. I hissed out a breath between my teeth.

"In the tent," she whispered. "Now."

Like she had to tell me twice. Keeping me firmly in her grasp, Sasha nudged me backward until my hands hit against the tent. Once I unzipped it, we ducked inside, and then I was falling, pushed back onto the mattress and pile of blankets. The unusual number of them was certainly welcome *now*.

Sasha dropped down to her knees and finally tugged the rest of my clothes off, freeing my lower body to the cool air and her unobstructed view. It took my bedazzled mind a moment to remember she was completely naked underneath that shirt. She crawled forward, fingers skimming over my thighs up to my abs.

"Off with the shirt," she ordered.

I didn't think twice about coming back with some witty counterargument. In fact, I *liked* the way she went into boss mode. While I struggled to jerk my shirt off over my head, she removed her own and tossed it to the side. The campfire behind her cast flickering orange light against her porcelain skin. She hadn't bothered to zip the tent up.

"Baby, I don't have a—" The warmth of her mouth enveloped me, gliding down over my cock one inch at a time. She hummed, and I hissed a sharp, *"Fuck,"* between my teeth.

Aside from a few desperate one-night stands in the early years after my divorce and a scattered handful of dates, there'd been no one. I didn't keep condoms on hand, and hadn't considered picking any up from the store. Hindsight was twenty-twenty.

Sasha teased the round tip of my dick with her tongue, working over it until every contour glistened. "Don't have what?"

Groaning, I struggled to restrain myself. "I don't have condoms."

"I don't care."

We hadn't had the talk about sex or protection before, just kids and a mutual desire for them. With each passing second, the likelihood of having it now slipped farther from my mind and didn't matter, because if anything came out of this, I'd fucking love the kid for every second of his or her life. The way I was pretty sure I loved its mother.

Fuck. She'd gotten under my skin and clawed her feline way right into my heart. There was no going back now, no changing my mind. I couldn't lay down to rest at night without my thoughts drifting to three stunning women in Houston.

Her long, lean thighs straddled my hips. I jutted up between our bodies, the underside and my balls nestled against the neat strip of pale white curls.

Contrary to what Sergio thought, white-blonde was definitely her natural hair color. She ran her fingers up and down the length, caressing and teasing without removing our eye contact. I waited on the proverbial edge, half torn between watching her work and rolling her beneath me to end the torture.

"I want you exactly as you are with nothing between us, and when Isisa and Nandi have you, they'll want the same."

Damn. How did I argue with that?

Sasha released my cock and leaned over me, dragging the tawny tips of her breasts against my chest. I slipped both hands down to her rounded ass and squeezed double palmfuls of flesh, groaning when she nipped my lower lip. "Do you want to know why?"

"Why?"

"Because you are the one for us. Our special alpha. The *only* male we may ever want for the rest of our lives. Because finding one soul mate for one woman is difficult enough, but one to match three is as rare as aligning the stars. You're the one we've searched to find and always wanted. But as much as I want to do it right now, I won't claim you yet."

"Claim?" My heart stammered in my chest.

"Mark you as mine with my bite. Not yet. Not *tonight*. God, I want to, but I shouldn't. I should wait for them."

Whatever inhibitions she had against claiming me didn't prevent her from gripping the base of my cock and gliding the tip against her folds. The entry wasn't hard and fast like I craved, instead done second by tedious second of watching those inches disappear until I thought I could die from the wait.

Maybe I had.

Maybe this was heaven, and she was my angel.

I trembled beneath her and exhaled a swear. She was all liquid silk and sensual heat, riding me in slow and rhythmic movements, currents of pleasure cresting like the wild waves I once watched at sea. "What if I want you to do it now?"

"But—"

"Don't I get to decide?"

Sasha huffed a breath.

"Will it bother Nandi and Isisa?"

"No, but—"

"Then give me what I asked for."

Sasha leaned forward until her lips met my throat, a few golden curls tickling over my chest. Marveling over the goddess above me, I coaxed her to move faster with both hands on her hips, fingers curving over her round ass. Her kisses made a trail over the hot beat of my pulse, a featherlight caress.

Her teeth caught me between the neck and shoulder. Startled, I shouted her name and thrust my hips up, burying deep while she rocked against me. Ecstasy slammed into me like a sledgehammer, taking me by surprise when an orgasm tightened my balls and I spilled inside her. On the next thrust, I was spent, groaning beneath her until the tireless rhythm of her hips drained me of every drop. My head rolled back.

Maybe I blacked out.

When I did come to again and had some sense of my surroundings, remembered my name, and knew what the hell happened, she was lying against my chest with her eyes shut and a dreamy expression on her face.

Feeling like a teenager on prom night, I groaned and stirred at last.

"I don't... fuck. That's not normal for me. I swear."

She smiled lazily at me and kissed the corner of my mouth. "I know. I should have warned you that might happen."

"What kind of shifter magic shit was that?"

Her chuckle warmed my throat. "It's what happens when a soul accepts a bond." Lazily, she traced her index finger over my chest. "I should have told you more about it beforehand, but..." She sighed again, making a content, absolutely feline sound human mouths shouldn't have been able to make.

∼

SASHA

*R*esting my weight on my elbows, I leaned on his chest and peeked down at him. My hair skimmed his shoulders. "I don't know how to tell you how happy this makes me."

"What does? Sex?"

"No, silly. That you didn't... push me away."

"I'm not convinced this isn't a dream yet, so that may have had something to do with my decision," he retorted.

If anyone was dreaming, it was me. Esteban was the man we'd always wanted. Caring, compassionate, and hardworking. He loved his family, took care of his parents, and put the needs of others before his own desires.

My impulses drove me to kiss him again, savoring each second until I stretched out at his side and lowered my head to his pillow.

"I feel different somehow."

"That's part of the bond," I explained. "It's basically like... like I gave you a small piece of my soul. So you might find you're more attuned to me now."

"What, like a mind reader?"

I chuckled and turned my head to look at him. "No, but you might be able to sense my emotions. Know when I'm close by. It varies a little person to person."

"You know what I'm feeling right now?" he asked.

"No. What?"

He rolled and tucked me beneath him, sliding his cock back where it belonged in one smooth thrust. A gasp rushed past my lips.

"I'm feeling like you aren't done yet," he whispered against my ear. "And neither am I. This time, I want to watch your face when you come, and I want to hear you crying my name, chica."

13

ESTEBAN

*D*uring a rare moment of peace, I entered the break room and refilled my coffee thermos after chatting over the phone with our client. For once, we'd gotten ahead of schedule and weren't at risk of falling behind.

My little cousin Xavier stepped in, mopping sweat from his brow with his shirt.

"Sup, kid?"

He brightened and smiled. "Hey. Haven't seen you at all today."

"Lots of paperwork to complete and too many calls to make. I'm playing catchup on all the admin I missed when we were behind."

"It must feel good to not have to be out there every day with us now, huh?"

"Nah. It's okay. I don't mind helping you guys. It only sucks when I got other shit to do, you know?"

He filled a cup with water from the purifier. "So? How'd it go, man?"

I glanced at my younger cousin. "Hm?"

"How'd it go with your sexy blonde? Did she freak out over the blood?"

Knowing what I did about Sasha now, I snorted. "Nah. She's been hunting as long as you've been alive, kid. She could probably teach you some things."

"No way."

"It's true. She took down one of those deers I brought home without even aiming."

"Damn."

Damn was right.

"So, did you get lucky out there?"

"None of your business."

"So you did." He clapped me on the shoulder. "Lucky bastard. That girl is one fiiiine piece of ass."

A surge of irritation welled inside my chest. My left eye twitched and both hands flexed at my sides. Xavier was a real douche when it came to women, operating on a love 'em and leave 'em code of ethics that left a trail of brokenhearted girls in his wake.

"Bet she was a real wildcat in the sack, eh, Stebi? Bitch looked like her pussy'd be tight as a drum—Fuck!"

Xavier stumbled back three steps and pinwheeled his arms. He lost balance anyway and sprawled on his ass with blood dripping from his nose.

My eyes fell from his startled face to my bloody knuckles. I didn't even remember moving to hit him. It just happened. Reflex. One jab to the face like a cornered wild cat striking out.

"What the fuck?" His nose made a honking sound when he spoke.

"Keep your damn thoughts about Sasha to yourself, all

right? Aunt Laura taught you better than to talk about women like that. Let me hear you call another woman a bitch again, especially mine. She's my girlfriend. *Mine,* and the next time you disrespect her, I'll stomp your ass into the ground."

He backed away with both hands raised, palms out. "Christ, dude, okay. No disrespect meant."

When I turned around, three members of the crew were standing in the doorway, wide eyed and hesitant to enter. Sergio pushed his way between them and entered.

"Yo, what's going on in here?"

Xavier grimaced and tore a paper towel from a roll above the breakroom sink. "Nothing."

Sergio crossed his arms and stared me down. "That doesn't look like a bunch of nothing."

"We had a misunderstanding. I corrected him."

"Corrected him? You're twice his size, man. What the hell happened that you put your hands on family?"

"Good question," I muttered under my breath. As the heat faded and my sense returned to me, I shot a glance at Xavier. He leaned against the wall with his head tilted back and tissue cupped to his nose.

Angelo stepped inside and guided Xavier away. "Come on, cuz. Let's get you cleaned up."

While I washed my hands at the sink, Sergio leaned against the counter and watched me. "Wanna talk about it? You stressed? Something going on between you and your girl?"

"No. We're fine."

"Medrano family come to harass you again?"

"It has nothing to do with the Medrano family."

"You sure?"

"Yeah."

"Then what happened? This isn't like you."

I snatched a paper towel from the roll and dried my hands, a heavy lump in my throat now that Xavier was out of sight. Words. They'd only been words. Shamed by my behavior, I sagged into a chair and told Sergio what happened.

His mouth flattened. "I would have hit him, too, but not in the nose. Probably a good gut punch so Mamá and Aunt Laura couldn't see it. Even Uncle Lorenzo had a talk with that kid about the way he refers to women."

"Still, they were only words."

"I know how much you care about this project, but Mamá is right. You work yourself to the bone, hermano, and you need a break. You haven't taken any vacation time this year. You're a machine, always on the move arranging contracts, meeting with clients, working on the site to fill in for guys. You can't do it all."

"I know."

"Take some time off."

"Actually, I meant to have a word with you about that. A friend is heading to Chicago on a business trip in a couple weeks and could use my help on the road. You mind flying solo here for a few days?"

"Do I ever?"

I rose from the seat, a weight lifted from my shoulders. "Thanks."

"*De nada.*"

I found Xavier before the shift ended, his nose swollen and pink, both eyes smudged black. He shrank back from me, eyes darting to the side like a prey animal seeking an escape route.

"Look, if you came to finish the job, I'm sorry. I get it."

"No. I came to apologize. I should have handled it better. But you should know better than to speak about women like that. Aunt Laura didn't raise you to be a douche."

Xavier touched the tender tip of his nose and grimaced. "I know. I really didn't mean to disrespect your woman like that."

"Thanks."

A moment of silence passed between us with me on the end of his quiet scrutiny before he said, "You really must feel some kind of way about her. She's real pretty. Rich, too, huh?"

"Yeah, I do." I smiled, looking forward to another night at the penthouse. Another visit with my ladies. "Let me put it this way—her money is the *least* amazing thing about her."

14

ESTEBAN

*L*eaves crunched beneath our feet as Isisa and I crossed the grounds toward the registration tables. Dozens of people milled around, checking their Apple watches, stretching, and chatting on the phone. Excitement buzzed in the fall air, the wind scented of damp soil, dead leaves, and too many people.

A cloudless sky provided the perfect weather for our Zombie Dash, the air cool, crisp, and still.

"Isisa, Esteban, up here!"

Nadir waved us over to join him further ahead in the line. A dark-haired Asian woman in a matching T-shirt stood beside him, clothed in a pair of tiny turquoise running shorts exposing long legs with the impressive, sculpted thighs of an Olympic athlete. She greeted Isisa with a hug and passed us each a team shirt. The back read "Zombies can bite my dust" with bloody claw marks printed on the front.

"Glad you could join us," Nadir said. "Have you met Juni, yet?"

"I haven't had the pleasure, no." I extended my hand toward the diminutive woman. "Sasha's mentioned you, though."

"Only mentioned." Juni's brown gaze slid toward Isisa. "The betrayal cuts deep. She and Sasha talk about you *all* the time, and all I get is a mere mention."

"Juni," Isisa hissed. She swatted at her friend, but the other woman danced out of the way and grinned.

"You talk about me, huh?"

Isisa's embarrassment was adorable. She scuffed her sneaker across the grass and mumbled something incoherent before clearing her throat and punching Nadir in the arm since she couldn't reach the true source of her frustration. My buddy winced but wrapped an arm around her shoulder and squeezed.

"So talk me through this again."

"We each have three flags the zombies can snag off us. We have to make it through the run and obstacles with at least one flag left," Juni explained.

"What happens if they get all three?"

Isisa's brown eyes sparkled with mischief. "Then you've succumbed to your zombie infection and will be eaten. To cross the finish line into the safe zone, you'll need at least one flag as Juni said. Then the good 'Doctor' gives you a cure."

"Kinda morbid." I grinned. "I like it."

"You're not allowed to touch the zombies, and the only time they can touch you is when they're relieving you of a flag. The object of the game is to avoid contact with them altogether," Isisa said, gesturing to a shambling guy in zombie makeup. The volunteers on the zombie side must have sat in the makeup chair for hours.

I glanced at some of the other teams assembling near the starting line in team shirts of varying colors and designs. "How does the team part come into play?"

Nadir chuckled and gestured to the three flags pinned to his shirt. "Since we all have three flags, the team bit comes into play when it comes to saving a teammate. You can distract a zombie or sacrifice one of your flags for one or us, or vice versa. Maybe Isisa is on her last flag, but you have all three of yours and we're near the end."

"I'd take the bite for her."

"Right," he confirmed.

"He won't have to take a bite for me." Isisa's white teeth gleamed when she grinned. She was confidence personified, and nothing about her had ever seemed sexier.

We spent the five minutes leading up to the race stretching and preparing for the sprint. When the siren blared, we took off at a casual jog as planned, determined to pace ourselves until we saw the undead.

Without crossing a single zombie, we reached the first obstacle a quarter mile down the path. The runners in front of us dropped down to their bellies and crawled through a large pipe that led out into a mud pit.

Nadir and I had endured worse during basic training. I grinned despite cold mud soaking through my running shoes, a thick and cakey mess that squished beneath our fingers and clung to our hands. Juni hustled through ahead of us, the quickest and most agile, followed by Isisa and Nadir.

After that it was game on. The zombie horde exploded from the tree line to our left, at least three dozen of them to the two hundred or more participants in the race. With so many people ahead of us, we were able to weave through without taking any losses.

A new wave awaited us at each obstacle to whittle the competition down. We scaled a twenty-foot wall with a climbing rope and slid down to the other side, where we narrowly avoided zombies poised to attack. Isisa moved with incredible athleticism, a mesmerizing sight to behold despite the chaos taking place around us. The mere sight of her struck a blow to my situational awareness, and it cost me a flag before I had the chance to recuperate.

Worth it.

Zombies were closing in on us, spilling from the wooded growth bordering the path. The number of competitors had thinned, cut down by half, and the remaining participants were spread out in clustered groups.

We crawled through trenches teeming with submerged mannequins painted to resemble corpses, the howling screams of the hungry dead urging us to move faster. I ignored the slop soaking me down to my skin and burst onto stable ground with Isisa only a step before me.

Damn, that woman ran like a gazelle once she was on open terrain. Her long legs pumped effortlessly, and I had to push myself to match her stride. There were five zombies closing in on us. True to our team slogan, the four of us left them in our dust.

We climbed another wall and zip-lined to the bottom, coming in on our finish line after an hour of gritty obstacles and jump-scares from bushes. My muscles screamed, reminding me of how infrequently I worked out these days.

Construction work was no substitute for cardio.

My body told me to go lay in the dirt and accept my phony death. But Isisa's stride and the competitive light in her eyes forced me onward.

Juni and Isisa were neck and neck, entering a full-out sprint that left Nadir and me behind. He shook his head and continued his steady lope while I watched in awe of their performance. The zombie actors didn't even try to touch them when they breezed by.

"Dammit," Nadir muttered. "I told them not to show off."

My lungs protested speaking. I forced the words out anyway between measured gasps for breath. "Why not?"

"Draws unwanted attention. We were going to fall back and take second place, but..."

"Isisa really wants to win."

"Oh yeah. Can't blame her. Sucks to go your whole life surrendering first place."

The two women crossed the finish line ahead of us. Nadir and I made a last push and closed the gap, moving ahead with a final sprint to ensure our team's overall victory. A few steps past the finish line, I bent down with my hands on my knees and focused on trying to breathe.

"You gonna live or do I need to deliver CPR?"

Looking up brought Isisa into view. Her eyes crinkled at the corners, full of warmth and amusement.

"Fine." The wheeze in my voice made me cringe.

She moved closer and stroked a hand up and down my back. Eventually my muscles loosened up and it didn't hurt so much to breathe. I straightened after the discomfort faded.

"You did good. Fun, right?" she asked.

I grinned at my mud-covered girlfriend and thought she couldn't look any more beautiful than she did right now, her eyes bright and face glowing with happiness. Wanting to brand the memory of that look into my mine, I leaned down and claimed a lengthy kiss—the kind of demanding kiss that left onlookers flushed and envious, wishing they had the same kind of raw chemistry.

"Yeah, that was great," I whispered against her lips. "Thanks for inviting me."

Hose stations had been set up for the runners to use for cleanup. We sprayed each other down before adjourning to the large tents set up for the post-race buffet. I loaded my plate with two burgers fresh off the grill, creamed corn, brisket, and a couple cookies. Isisa's plate looked about the same. The four of us found a picnic bench near one of the space heaters and took a seat.

"So, Juni, what do you do?"

"I teach kickboxing at a couple different gyms."

"She's being modest," Nadir said. "She's also a personal trainer for a few high-profile clients."

Juni kicked him under the table.

"Ow, what was that for?"

"For being a big-mouthed blabber."

They picked on each other like siblings. I'd seen the same behavior time and time again in my own family.

"Never tried kickboxing, but my youngest sister is into that sort of stuff."

"It's fun," Juni said. "A good workout. I also have a self-defense class I run three times a year. Sasha helps me with that one sometimes if our schedules work out. Nadir, too."

"Putting that military training to work, eh?"

More racers trickled in over the next hour. A second wave went off, and the girls joked about running the race a second time, but Nadir and I bowed out. I had the feeling he did it for my sake and promised myself to buy him a beer later in thanks.

We stayed through the end of the event and accepted our awards as a team. Not only had we won our heat, but we'd had the best time out of all three waves, earning ourselves a second medal. After that, we posed for pictures with some of the zombies and shared another round of treats from the buffet because I'd never been so starved in all my life since leaving the Marines.

Once everything started to wind down, we headed out, going our separate ways in the grass field parking area. Isisa skipped to the truck, full of happy energy. The whole drive back, we recounted the event, laughing over near misses and the difficulty of some of the obstacles.

"I have to admit, the zip line gave me pause," Isisa said.

"Really? Didn't look like it from my end. You sorta just hopped on and went for it."

"Yeah, but my eyes were closed for half of it." She laughed and rubbed her face. "What was hardest for you?"

A grunt was my first response, followed by, "Climbing that damn wall. I'd forgotten how much I hated that in boot camp."

"Well, I think you did a great job. Some people had to skip the obstacle and take a time penalty. At least you made the effort and finished everything."

"All worth it, even though I'm sure I'll be sore for a week."

I scanned her garage pass then drove inside. In the weeks since they'd entrusted it to me, I'd learned to drop off and pick the ladies up inside, avoiding traffic and honking cars on the busy road.

Isisa turned in her seat to face me across the console. "Thanks for coming with me today."

"It was fun. I'd love to do it again next year."

Her eyes brightened above the most radiant, genuine smile I'd ever seen on her face. "Yeah? Good, I'm glad. It's more fun running with friends."

"It was."

"Anyway, I should get showered and dressed. I've got to work on a case. We'll have to go out again soon."

"I'd like that. Don't work too hard, Isisa. Get some rest."

One step at a time with her, I'd learned. She hesitated without opening the door, then leaned across the console and kissed me. Isisa never rushed. She liked her kisses long, slow, and deep. Sensual thoughts crept into my mind, imagining if she'd make love the same way, or if she would be as energetic and frisky as Sasha.

Isisa withdrew first. The kiss ended, seeming too brief, a damned tease compared to what I really wanted from her. "See you soon."

I watched her walk away to the elevators with a sway to her hips and bounce to each step, and I knew right then she'd be the last one I had. And every second until then would be worth it.

15

ESTEBAN

The couple of days between Isisa's zombie marathon and Nandi's book signing provided all the time I needed to get ahead of administrative work at the office before I turned the entire operation over to Sergio. I couldn't dump a shit load of work in his lap, even if he swore he was up to the task.

Brothers didn't do that to each other. Plus, he hated working the administrative stuff. Thankfully, Mariana had just returned from her honeymoon. I left Texas behind feeling confident about the job going smoothly in my absence.

After a long Wednesday on the road from Houston to Chicago, Nandi and I awakened Thursday morning to a free day before the hustle of her signing would take up the next two days. We'd fallen into bed sometime around two in the morning after checking into the hotel.

Her fluffy hair, fragrant with sweet almond and coconut oil, tickled my neck, and the plump curves of her nubile body invited me to linger in bed. Her soft breaths feathered against my skin, one of her legs twined between mine.

Nandi wore only a T-shirt and a pair of polka dot panties lacking enough fabric to cover her round cheeks. I squeezed one, tentatively at first, reluctant to manhandle the woman in her sleep. Her flesh was malleable and soft beneath my hand. Perfect.

She raised her head and smiled. "Mmm... Morning. Do I get to do the same?"

Prior to bed when we'd been too exhausted to do anything more, we'd stripped off our jeans and crawled under the covers of the king-sized bed.

"You're welcome to."

Nandi propped her weight up on one elbow and let her other hand wander over my chest, over a layer of cotton T-shirt I'd been too tired to remove the previous night. She edged it up, exposing my abs, and traced the chiseled lines until her gaze came to the morning wood I didn't have a hope of hiding. She blinked a few times.

"You're... so big," she whispered. Her fingers crept along the edge of my boxer briefs but didn't slip beneath the band or move any lower. As much as I craved one touch from her and kept imagining her delectable lips wrapped around my dick, I put the ball in her court and waited for her to make the first move. "Um. Muscles, I mean. Working construction gave you a lot of muscles."

I grinned. "And you're stunning even when you're just waking up." Smiling, I reached up and tucked a curl behind her ear. "What did you want to do today? Walk around downtown? Hit up the Navy Pier?"

"What's there?"

"Shops mostly. A few restaurants. The Ferris wheel."

"That sounds fun. I'll go get ready."

Was it wrong of me to feel a stab of disappointment as her hands fell away without exploring further? The question brought a well-deserved sense of shame.

Time, man. Give her time. Sasha said she was the shy one.

While Nandi showered, I brought her luggage up from the car and waited my turn. I made a call to Sergio.

"You're supposed to be taking a break," Sergio reprimanded instead of greeting me when he answered.

"I am. Just wanted to find out how everything's going."

"It's fine. No trouble and everything's on schedule. Now go have a deep-dish pizza for me or something."

"Brat."

"*Pendejo*. Have fun helping out your friend."

Unwilling to own up to having multiple girlfriends, I'd fibbed to my family and told everyone I was helping a friend with a business matter out of state. It wasn't far from the truth, but the lie put a sour taste in my mouth.

Two hours later, we hit the town. Chicago wasn't new to me. I'd served a stint as a recruiter in the area.

I grimaced and pushed those memories aside, focusing on making new ones with Nandi. It took some coaxing, but I convinced her to ride the Ferris wheel.

She clung to me, nails buried into my bicep, face against my neck the moment our car ascended in the air.

"It kind of defeats the purpose if you don't look," I teased.

"Lions aren't meant to be this far from the ground."

"Does that mean you don't fly?"

"On an airplane?" she squeaked. "No. No, no, no. Driving is what I do, and if I absolutely have to, I fly with the window shut." She peeked, raising her face enough to peer out the glass for a split second. Her iron grip tightened.

"Losing circulation here, kitten."

She hid her face again and lowered both hands to my thigh. "Sorry."

"No, it's fine. If I knew how much it scared you, I'd have never asked."

"You didn't make me get on. It's just…" She sucked in a breath and raised her cheek from my shoulder to look outside again. "I really *did* want to see the view, but it's terrifying. I can feel every tremble from the machinery. It's swaying and rocking and…"

"It's perfectly safe, believe me. It isn't like one of the county fairs out in the middle of nowhere. These rides undergo frequent maintenance. No one wants a lawsuit."

"Right." She nodded a few times and sucked in another breath. She went still beside me, staring out the window with large eyes, frozen by the view of Lake Michigan's crystal blue water stretching toward the horizon. There were boats out today in all shapes and sizes, dozens of them sailing at the harbor.

"I'm thinking of buying a boat sometime soon. My family has a timeshare up at Lake Conroe."

"A boat?"

"Yeah."

"Sasha likes boats."

"What about you?"

"I like water," she said, skirting the question. "I've never been on a boat."

"Well, if you'd like, maybe I can rent one for a weekend this spring and you can come out. It's quiet on the water. You could stretch out with your laptop and write or read."

"That sounds kind of nice."

"Good experience for your writing. I'll teach you how to sail."

The tension vanished from her shoulders, and a bright smile spread across her face that was more radiant than sunshine. "I'll look forward to it. We can try to surprise Sasha and Isisa, maybe. I'll give you dates free on their calendars. They tease me for writing all of the time, but no one works more than they do."

"Then this is long overdue, and Operation Lioness Vacation begins when we return to Texas. Deal?"

"Deal."

~

*A*t the end of a long day playing tour guide for Nandi, I slouched in a chair and passed the time with a puzzle game on my cell phone while she soaked in the tub.

We'd traveled over every inch of Navy Pier, saw the Field Museum, and visited the Adler Planetarium before meandering back toward our hotel on foot and discovering a local teahouse serving Russian cuisine.

I tossed my phone on the dresser and knocked on the bathroom door. "You alive in there?"

"I think so."

"Making sure you didn't drown. Or weren't needing mouth to mouth."

"I didn't drink that much vodka."

"You had two flights."

"You're the lightweight, remember?" she called back.

"You mean, I'm the human who lacks a supernatural tolerance for alcohol."

"Same difference."

Nandi emerged from the bathroom in a puff of steamy, coconut-scented air. We exchanged places, and when I exited in my shorts, it was to the sight of her sprawled in bed on her iPad.

"Have fun today?"

"Yeah. I'd love to bring Sasha and Isisa here one day and spend more time so we can all enjoy the sights."

"So I'm invited too?"

Nandi snuggled up to my side, swaddled in cobalt silk pajamas and the essence of vanilla and coconut. "Of course you are. All of us together for, like, a week. We can visit the museums and the aquarium, oh, and eat at that place again every day."

"Pretty sure you'd have to roll me outta bed and down the street if I had duck strudel, beef stroganoff, and everything else we ate every day."

She poked my stomach. "No worries there. Besides, they'd love the place I think. Sasha's the one who likes to eat adventurous, and she always makes us try new things."

"Speaking of, I was curious about something."

"Okay…"

"Isisa mentioned growing up alongside Sasha during their teens, but they didn't mention how you came into the equation."

"Oh, that. It's sort of embarrassing."

"You don't have to tell me."

"No, it's all right. Really. I met Isisa at the library. She was researching something for a case, and I dropped my pile of books when I saw her, like some idiot teenager facing their dream crush."

"She startled you?"

"Sorta. It's a shifter thing. When we meet our ideal mates, there's something about the way they look or the way they smell that our animal half senses. Our souls recognize each other, even if our minds don't realize what's happening."

"I see. What did you do about it?"

"Nothing." Nandi laughed. "I tried to run away, but I left one of my books, so Isisa chased me down outside of the library to return it to me. I was shaking so hard she guided me back inside. We had coffee at the cafe and talked all afternoon."

"When did you meet Sasha?"

"Not for almost six months. She was deployed at the time." She twisted a rust-red curl around her finger. "It was rough on Isisa."

"I imagine it was rough on you, too."

"Yeah. I didn't think Isisa felt anything in return," Nandi admitted. A fond smile curved her lips. She nestled closer and set her cheek against my throat. I ran my fingers down her back.

"So how did it develop into the relationship I know now?"

"Isisa and I became friends. I knew all about Sasha and was terrified to meet her, thinking I'd get ripped to shreds or something. But the moment she stepped through the security gate at the airport and came into view, I knew I could never want anyone else but them. I felt the same draw to her as Isisa. She came right up to me, pulled me into a hug while I stood there in shock, and told Isisa over my shoulder that I was welcome into their pride. If I wanted to be."

"And of course you said yes."

"I did, and I've never been happier."

"So… if it's okay to ask. Have you ever been with a man?"

"No, I only write about dicks." She waited a beat then nudged me in the arm and laughed. "Yes, I've been with a man. Taylor, remember?"

Somehow that both relieved me and made me jealous.

"Anyway, I should put my hair up for tomorrow if I want to avoid being a frumpy mess. I was so tired last night I didn't bother." Nandi slipped away and crossed the room to sit at the table where she'd laid out an assortment of jars and bottles alongside a wide tooth comb.

Fascinated by her routine, I sat at the foot of the bed and watched her for a while as she made precise parts and twisted her curls into long braids. "Do you need help?"

"Help with my hair?"

"Yeah. Let me rephrase that—do you *want* help?"

Nandi pursed her lips and studied me. "Have you ever messed with a black girl's hair?"

"No, but I can learn."

"If you want, sure."

Following her step-by-step instructions, I brushed sweet coconut oil into her dark hair and divided it into uneven sections. None of my clumsy braids resembled her examples, and we laughed together when a few unraveled.

I shook my head and rubbed my palms against both thighs. "I think you were better off without my help, chica."

"It doesn't have to be perfect when I'm only going to take it down in the morning. Besides, everyone has to start somewhere, and it gets easier with practice." She tilted her face up to me and smiled, features angelic in the glow of the nearby lamp. "Thank you."

"You're welcome."

Nandi fell asleep first once we were in bed. In the dark, with only a sliver of light from the Chicago nightlife penetrating the heavy curtains, I watched the peaceful rise and fall of her silk-covered chest. I tried to imagine the lioness within her and pictured golden-brown fur covering a cuddly soft body.

The image came easily. I'd seen Sasha at the camp, and maybe tomorrow, Nandi would have enough trust to show me the same in our private room.

~

*N*andi was up before the alarm, fussing around the room with her loaded cart and going back and forth on what to wear. Should she wear the skirt and sophisticated blouse or the dress? Would she be overdressed if she didn't wear jeans and a T-shirt? She changed three times then finally settled on a black pencil skirt paired with a pink, V-neck blouse that revealed enough of her tits to be sensual without showing off the entire package.

Outside of our room, it was a mess, especially when we reached the elevators. The entire hotel must have been trying to call them and they were probably stopping on every floor. By the time we were able to get on, Nandi had checked her watch a dozen times.

"Nandi Mokoena? Oh my gosh, so excited to meet you," the woman at the check-in table gushed. She passed over two tote bags and a table assignment map. "You can go ahead on in. Just be sure to wear your name badges, they're your lunch entry, and I hope you have fun."

"Thanks," Nandi murmured.

The woman beamed. "Don't hesitate to ask for help if you need it."

With the layout in hand, we wound our way through the busy room to Nandi's table.

"Where do you want the boxes? Under the table? Behind it?"

"Behind it against the wall. I'll help."

"Nah. I got it."

"But I can—"

"Look," I said, taking her by the shoulders. "I know you can lift these boxes just fine. I want to do this, because it's just the way I was raised, and it has nothing at all to do with you being a woman or me thinking you're weaker than me. Because I don't. Let me be nice to you."

Nandi bit her lower lip and nodded. "Okay."

I removed the boxes from the cart and set them behind the table while she fetched a tote bag of pens, stickers, and small objects of interest for her table.

"Each box has two titles in it. I need, um, let's say five of each out on the table for now. Please."

"Sure thing."

Clueless and out of my element, I followed Nandi's directions while the rest of the room exploded into chaos. Flyers, standing banners, and book covers featuring half-naked dudes dominated every corner of the convention hall. The tables followed the perimeter of the room, and then rows of them covered the floor.

Nandi's table appeared to be in a prime position, set in the center of the room against the back wall with a wide, open aisle directly in front of her that led to one of the three sets of doors leading into the room.

We'd been placed to the left of a young woman with pink and blue hair. Her model glanced at me and sized me up like a dog guarding his territory. I stared back at him until he looked away first. To our right was a table set up with gift baskets.

"Those are for various raffles," Nandi explained.

With all her books out, Nandi directed me where to set them up. We displayed paperbacks on plastic frame holders, and I unfurled her banner. The art displayed a man and a woman in a sensual embrace with a howling wolf in the background beneath a full moon.

I admired it for a moment.

"Did it come out okay?"

"It's eye-catching and sums up your books. It's great."

Nandi settled behind the table in one of the two chairs provided and folded her hands against her lap. She unfolded them again and fiddled with the stack of business cards on the table beside a candy dish overflowing with chocolate treats and cock-shaped lollipops on plastic rings.

I stared at those and mouthed, *what the fuck?* When had she put those out?

"Those were Isisa's contribution."

"I thought you were moving away from romance?"

"Most of my backlist is romance," she explained with a gesture to the assortment of covers baring male chests and muscular torsos accompanied by animals of some kind. Even the books featuring pale-skinned dudes with blood smearing their mouths were portrayed shirtless. "And this particular signing is the hottest romance convention in Chicago. I signed up and paid a year ago when I thought…" She shrugged.

"Thought what?"

"It'd be easier to talk to people in person. I'm a nervous wreck." She wrung her hands together and fidgeted in her seat.

"Why? Because of the line around the corner taking numbers to see you? You *did* notice that, right?"

Nandi dipped her chin. "Maybe. What if I'm not what they expected? Am I overdressed?"

"You look perfect."

"But—"

I kissed her. Driven by impulse and a spike of simmering desire, I cupped her face between both hands and brought her mouth up to mine. The older woman across the aisle gasped.

I ignored her.

It was supposed to be a brief kiss, reassurance and affection in one brush of my lips over hers. But it didn't end there. Couldn't. Once my tongue swept into her mouth, no one but Nandi mattered. Even when the kiss bordered indecent, I couldn't stop myself, because every taste of her was as intoxicating as the last, and something about her scent enveloped me, surrounded me, lured me in like a fucking siren's call. She made a startled little squeak, but then she softened and leaned into me. It wasn't how I'd planned our first kiss—not that I had been planning—but somehow it felt right.

"You look like a goddamned piece of art, and there isn't another author here as talented or beautiful," I told her in a rough whisper, startled by how little breath I had left in my lungs. My lips skimmed against her ear. When I leaned back, glazed brown eyes peered up at me. Her lipstick hadn't budged at all.

Nandi stopped fidgeting with her hands and skirt after that. Our neighboring author also faced forward, fanning herself with a flyer. She didn't introduce herself for another ten minutes.

We remained busy throughout the event with little downtime once the line of people queueing for specific authors were allowed inside the event hall. While Nandi ran credit card transactions, I took cash payments and arranged the purchased books in neat stacks for her to sign. By lunch, I'd assumed control of the phone and credit card reader too when a voracious horde of readers swarmed the table.

During a blessed lull, a tiny, gray-haired woman came by and paused by the table to lift a book from the holder. Her spectacled gaze drifted from the cover to me, and then she passed the novel to Nandi to be signed. "I'll take that one."

"Thank you. Who should I sign it to?"

"Bethie. It's for my daughter. Work wouldn't allow her to make it, so I'm visiting her favorite authors in her stead. She would have given anything to meet you, dear. Oh, and your model is so handsome."

Nandi's startled gaze flew up to the old woman's face.

"Oh, I'm not a model, ma'am. I tagged along to help out and give her some support."

"Really?" She smiled at Nandi. "Dear, you certainly

have a sweet boyfriend. You should put him on one of your covers. I'd snatch that right up."

"Oh, well…" Nandi turned her gaze on me. "I might try to convince him."

As much as I took pride in remaining in shape after the military, I didn't want to imagine thousands of ladies pressing their love buttons to my image. I kept my mouth shut anyway.

"Which book of hers is your favorite?" the lady asked.

"I actually enjoyed her newest release the most, but she didn't manage to get paperbacks in time. Out of the ones here, I'd say…" I scanned the covers, searching for the novel I'd completed a week ago on my phone, scanning the pages during lunch breaks at work. "This one."

While Nandi stared, I reached across the table and picked up a matte paperback featuring a bare-chested vampire on the cover. A large raven perched on his arm.

The old lady nudged the center of her spectacles and leaned closer. "What is it about?"

"An unlikely attraction between a vampire and a shapeshifter. Awesome premise. The love story is great and all, but my favorite part is the action. Nandi has a knack for writing out fight scenes. The hero has had his dream woman in front of him the whole time, but she has to sort of beat him around before he notices."

"Well then, I'll get this one for me. Could you make that out to Amanda, dear?"

"Of course," Nandi said. She signed in her looping script and passed it over with a smile. "And I'll see if I can sway Esteban here into a photoshoot."

Amanda beamed. "You do that."

The last few hours passed with the same hectic but fun

vibe. By the time the room closed for the day, Nandi and I both were ready to relax with our shoes off.

"Need any of this taken upstairs?"

"Just the money and iPad. They lock the room."

After I packed her valuables into her tote bag, we joined the line of authors and readers filing out of the convention hall. We didn't make it ten yards before a gang of writers approached to say hello and gush about Nandi's books.

From that moment forward, the next half hour passed in a blur of unfamiliar names and friendly faces eager to meet her. Eventually, the crowd thinned enough for the last of us to cram into an elevator with a panel of lit buttons destined to stop at every floor.

Fuck, socializing with so many women had exhausted me, and I wanted to kick my shoes off and lay down before the dinner party. By the time the last guest exited the elevator, my head throbbed.

The elevator doors closed behind the final passenger off and the box shuddered to a start upward. Then my back slammed against the mirrored elevator wall and Nandi's mouth slid over mine.

She stood on tiptoe with her fingers around my nape, body pressed flush to mine as her lips moved with sensual urgency. Her other palm flattened to my chest, and she stroked downward, petting my abs.

In one quick tug, I twisted her back against the wall instead and guided one of her thighs to my hip. The softness of her cradled me, plump, perfect, and real. A lush handful overflowed my palm when I squeezed her right breast and circled my thumb over the budding nipple. She made a small sound of pleasure, almost a purr, and pulled my shirt free from my slacks.

"You read my books," she whispered against my mouth.

"I wanted to surprise you."

Her scarlet lips turned up in a smile. "You did."

The elevator dinged, and the doors slid open. Nandi took me by the hand and pulled me into the quiet, blue-carpeted hallway. When we reached our room, the card reader rejected her first two attempts to unlock the door. She hissed a swear between her teeth and tried again, fumbling the door open on the third attempt.

One second, I was setting her tote bag aside, and in the next, the door had slammed and she was guiding me back against the bed, tugging my belt free, loosening the fly with agile and eager fingers. Clothes littered the floor in seconds, and then we were just bare skin against bare skin with her beneath me on the mattress.

The intoxicating scent of vanilla lotion wafted from her skin as I kissed my way down her neck then back up again to the hollow behind her ear. Every inch of her was satin smooth, cocoa silk beneath my hands. I molded a palm against one of her full breasts and laved my tongue over the tip.

"God, I love these."

"They're enormous. *Too* big."

"More for me then."

They weren't as round as smaller breasts, full and a little bottom heavy like plump teardrops with high, dark nipples. I suckled the tip of one between my lips. When she writhed and arched beneath me, I scooped both breasts together and tasted both at the same time.

"I love every inch of you. No part of you is too big, or too small. You're perfect."

To show her how much I meant those words, my lips found other interesting places to visit while both hands remained at her breasts, thumbing the nipples. With her sprawled before me, knees bent and feet planted against the sheets, I leaned back on my knees and surveyed all that was mine.

Thank God.

Nandi had the kind of sinful curves that could turn a heathen like me back into a praying man. Like she'd read my mind, her hands turned busy, stroking over my muscles and smoothing across my back. She kissed my shoulders, my neck, and traced her lips across my pecs before one of her small hands caressed my balls in passing but didn't linger. My cock jutted up straight, heavy and hard as steel, so stiff it hurt. Her and Sasha had a way of making me feel like a teenager again. I tried to mentally compel her to touch me, but it didn't work.

"I don't want to rush this, corazon, but I need to be inside you. *Now.*"

A coy smile came to her lips. "I know."

"Should I grab a—"

"No, I don't want anything between us." Her brown eyes studied my face, and after a quiet moment, she murmured, "Is that okay with you?"

"Not worried about me?"

"You're clean."

"And you know that how?"

"I trust you."

"That doesn't mean I'm clean."

"Even if you weren't, it wouldn't affect me." She snuck

her hand between our bodies and glided her index finger down my dick, stroking a straight line from root to tip. I jerked at the contact and sucked in a sharp breath.

Note to self: Nandi is also a dick magician.

I traced my hands down her ribs, hips, and thick thighs, molding my palms to every inch. When her legs parted, I took it as a hint and slid my middle finger inside her.

Her hips raised into the touch, and her expression turned euphoric.

"You're so wet, baby."

"I've been thinking about this since lunch."

I turned my face against her breast and chuckled. "That long, huh?"

"Let's just say that resisting the urge to straddle you on the table was a close call, and some readers almost received a free show."

"Ha! Maybe you should write that into one of your books."

She writhed against the sheets, fingers clutching against my shoulder while I stroked her. "I think I will. Now give me more to write about."

Determined to live up to her expectations—no, determined to outdo them—I kissed my way down her body until my lips and tongue replaced my fingers. That first taste of her nearly undid me. Nandi was the sweetest fucking thing I'd ever tasted, and her mewling cries stoked my ego.

She moved in subtle rocking motions, hands in my hair directing me where she liked it best. I teased her clit, toying with her by circling it one moment and avoiding it in the next, driving her up and up and up until her toes curled. My tongue plunged into her, and I licked, loving the sound of my name on her lips.

When I finally gave her the orgasm she deserved, I didn't stop until her quivering body went limp against the sheets.

"Don't think I'm done with you yet," I whispered against her skin, kissing my way back up to her breasts, then up again to her throat.

"Good."

I licked my fingers for a final taste of her. Her golden eyes locked on mine as her nimble fingers circled my dick. She slipped the tip of me against her entrance, and in one thrust, she was mine.

The way her body gripped me should have been criminal, her pussy just short of being a satin-lined vice grip for my cock. I groaned a low, guttural sound against her throat and lost myself with each thrust, aware of her fingers wandering my back, her nails scoring my shoulders, and the whispers of my name.

She thrust her hips up, meeting me stroke for stroke and never tiring.

Shifter stamina was infectious as fuck apparently, because my endurance carried on long after her first orgasm. Sweat beaded across my shoulders and brow, my entire body feverish from the efforts of pleasing a supernatural woman.

Nandi cried out the hardest when I pounded away at her, so I gave her that, our bodies slapping together at a furious tempo. Her ankles crossed above my ass, and her head fell back, expression filled with rapture and dark hair fanned over the pillow.

I came when she reached her third climax, the relief of

spilling inside her sweeter than all orgasms before it. I had no idea how I'd lasted so long, but she was insatiable and irresistible. Nandi rolled and curled up against me, eyes closed and breaths shallow.

"We have enough time for a nap before your dinner thing."

"I vote we stay here," she slurred in a drowsy mumble.

Grinning, I stroked my fingers down her spine. "But you paid for this, sweetheart, and after all that, I'm starving."

"Room service is an amazing thing."

"People wanna see you."

She cracked open her eyes. "I only wanna see you."

Nandi traced her fingers down my abs and took my soft cock in her hand. It tensed and then became rock hard again in her grip. Neither me or my dick could get enough of her. She grinned and straddled my hips, bracing both hands on my chest.

In the next moment, she slid onto me, and I thrust up, driving deeper than before, plunging into her anew with the boundless energy only a South African goddess could inspire.

"Fuck."

"Oh, I plan to." Her satisfied grin widened, and she rolled her hips, setting a demanding pace right from the start.

My hands found their way to her ass and gripped twin palmfuls of flesh. Nandi bent forward, lowering her hands to the sheets at either side of my head. Her breasts pressed into my chest, and she turned her face into my throat, teeth skating across my skin over my beating pulse.

"I know what you want. Do it." I threaded my fingers

into her hair and delivered a slight tug. "Don't resist, baby."

"But—"

"I want it."

A purr, or something very close to it, reverberated in her throat. The sharp sting of her teeth nipped my earlobe first, followed by a gentle suckle that made my toes curl and my hips thrust upward. She drew it out, taking her time, alternating teasing love bites with kittenish licks.

Her teeth caught me in the muscle above my left nipple, seizing me with a spark of pain and ecstasy. I didn't black out again this time, but her magical essence swarmed over me, a sizzling rush of sensation searing into my soul. I gasped.

She clenched around me. Any self-control I'd retained during our bonding crumbled into dust. I shuddered and collapsed against the bed, drained and vulnerable, trembling beneath her. My uncooperative limbs wouldn't even raise to wrap around her.

Her limp body covered me like a warm, velvet blanket. "Now you're mine, too," she whispered, and I wouldn't have it any other way.

16

SASHA

*S*ince Esteban and Nandi were away at a book signing, I had a little free time on my hands. I drove to Quickdraw Saturday morning, prepared for a day with my little ones.

Dressed in my favorite leggings and a thick, oversized sweater, I arrived to find Lyle raking leaves in the yard. He worked shirtless despite the weather, another example of physical perfection wrapped within one shifter body. His muscles gleamed beneath a thin layer of sweat, and he hadn't yet lost his summer tan.

"Sup, kitty? Come to take the pups off our hands?"

"And to spend a little time with your wife. Need a hand with that?"

He shook his head. "Nah. I got it. Jules is in the office."

I let myself in, crouched to pet Tux when the cat pranced out to meet me, and made my way to the back of the house to find Jules. Her office overlooked the fenced-in backyard with a pair of french doors, and a wide assortment of children's playground toys decorated the leaf-strewn grass.

"Sasha?" Julia called before I entered the room. She'd already twisted in the seat behind her desk.

"Kitty!" Charlotte threw down the pony figures she'd been playing with and ran over to me.

"Hey, doll, how are you?" I scooped her up, noticing Leigh standing near the window. Outside, the boys played with Sophia in the sandbox. "Hey, Leigh."

"Hey, Sasha."

"Kitty! Kitty!"

"Maybe later," I told the insistent toddler squirming in my arms. "Don't you wanna go play with your brothers and Sophia?"

Charlotte's little face scrunched up as she considered the idea. She looked at me, to the children beyond the window, then back to me. "Um…"

"It'll be fun," I told her. "And I promise a little later I'll be a kitty for you, okay?"

She grinned and pointed at the floor, so I set her down. The moment her feet touched the carpet, she took off to the door leading to the patio. Julia opened it for her and released a dramatically relieved sigh.

"I've been trying to convince her to go out there and play for an hour. How do you do it?"

"Auntie Sasha is awesome, that's how."

She chucked a pen at me, and we both laughed, but it was only the two of us. Concerned, I glanced over at our friend then back to Julia and mouthed, "Is she all right?"

Julia shrugged, a firm frown on her face.

I mouthed to her, "Did something happen?"

Julia shook her head then twisted around. "Leigh, are you okay?"

"Huh?" She blinked away from the window and flashed me a wan smile. "I'm fine."

"You've barely said a word."

"It's… it's nothing. Really."

Julia and I exchanged looks. Then we both descended on our friend and pulled her over to the couch, sitting her between us.

"Nothing doesn't make you look like you want to cry. We're your friends, Leigh. You can talk to us about anything. And if Ian's being a jerk, I'll bat his feathered ass out the air and show him what a pissed-off lioness looks like."

"No, no, it's nothing like that," she said in a rush. "Ian's wonderful. He's always wonderful."

"Then what's wrong, sweetie?" Julia asked.

"God, I'm so embarrassed to even say it, but..." She wrung her hands together and drooped her head forward, letting her blonde hair fall into her face. "We've been trying to have a baby, and I thought this time something finally happened. My period was almost *two* months late this time, and then today… it came today."

My heart lurched in my chest. "It takes time. Sometimes a year or more to become fertile once you're off the pill."

Leigh raked her fingers through her blonde hair. "It's been almost three years since I got off birth control, and nothing is happening. He's so depressed, guys, but he won't own up to it and just shoves it all away. Like, Ian always tells me that he doesn't care if we don't have any kids of our own because he loves Sophia like his own child, but…"

"She's not his biological child," I finished in a soft voice.

"I love him so much, and all that I want to do is give this to him. A baby who will share his eagle genes. Someone to fly with him. No matter how much he loves Sophia and me, we can't fly with him. We'll never be shifters."

Shaking her head and mopping her cheeks with her wrists, Leigh managed to blubber out a tremulous, "I'm sorry. I didn't mean to ruin our afternoon."

"There's nothing to apologize for," Julia said.

"Exactly." I squeezed Leigh's shoulders. "You haven't ruined anything. Trust me. Have you two been to the doctor yet?"

"Not yet, but I want to."

"Set up an appointment," Julia said.

"But Ian would—"

"Ian will support you if that's what you want to do," I said. "Hell, call and make the appointment yourself."

"I did call to get some information," she said. "But they said it could take a couple months to get in with anyone."

"What? Ugh, no, I'll ask around at work then and see if I can call in any favors. There has to be a fertility doctor in my social circle."

"Oh, Sasha, you don't—"

"I know I don't *have* to, but I want to. You and Ian are like family. Besides, what's the point of being an amazing doctor if I can't help people cut through the red tape now and again?" I grinned, relieved to see a smile returning to Leigh's face.

"Thanks."

"That's what friends are for."

～

The aroma of savory garlic and chicken greeted me the moment I stepped into the penthouse. I followed my nose to the kitchen where Isisa was carefully removing a foil-covered pan from the oven.

Thin, white candles glowed on countertops and on our dining room table. It had been set for two with salads on our fine china ordered from a local deli around the corner. I grinned. She'd placed cheesecake slices on small dessert dishes and set out two long-stem wine flutes. A corner of the dessert box protruded from the kitchen trashcan.

"What's all this?"

"Most of it was ordered, but I wanted to cook dinner for you. Nandi left this recipe out for me."

Bless Nandi for leaving a foolproof, anyone-can-make-this, recipe choice. Isisa tried her best in the kitchen, she really did, but usually her meals ended up in the trash while she sulked and we ordered Chinese. I'd been eating her kitchen nightmares for over twenty-four years, ever since we'd first moved out on our own together.

"Well, it smells delicious. Need me to do anything?"

"Nope. Well, unless you want to pick a wine maybe?"

"Sure thing."

She said for me to pick the wine, but what she really meant was for me to select one of the three bottles in front of the wine locker where she stored her ever-increasing collection of expensive vintages. I grabbed the closest one and carried it back to the table. Nandi and Isisa were the wine snobs, but I just drank whatever they put in my glass and sometimes wondered if their cultured taste buds were better than mine. Last year, I watched them fawn over a bottle of red from California. When I had a sip, it tasted like wet earth and chalk.

While she nuked a frozen veggie pack in the microwave, I twisted the corkscrew in and replaced the cork with her favorite stopper, a baby elephant that poured the wine through its trunk.

I sat and watched her putter around the kitchen, grinning. "Thank you for this. You didn't have to go through the effort."

"I know, but with Nandi gone and you and I so busy lately, I thought it'd be nice to have a good dinner before you take a sixteen-hour shift tomorrow."

"Ugh, don't remind me."

Isisa leaned over the back of my chair and kissed me. "Then I won't."

Despite past kitchen disasters worthy of a television sitcom, this meal turned out perfect, if a touch salty. A loaf of french bread—its wrapper from the grocery store also in the trash—helped with that, as did the vegetable mix of kale and butternut squash.

Afterward, once the dishes were loaded into the washer, we sat together on the couch with one of our favorite sitcoms on the television.

"Hey, Sash?"

"What's up, hon?"

"I'm sorry for the way I froze up that day Esteban asked about kids. I guess I worried he'd think less of me."

"That's been bugging you all this time?"

"Yeah."

"Oh, sweetie." I twisted around until I faced her and tucked my feet onto the couch beneath me. "You know we'd never hold it against you, and I hope you know by now Esteban wouldn't."

"I do. Still, I know I can be…"

"Moody? Bitchy? Broody?"

She flattened her mouth and tossed a pillow at my face. "Bitchy? Really?"

"Okay, fine, but the broody bit was spot-on, you have to admit."

Her sour expression melted into a sheepish grin. "You're right, and I'm sorry."

"You never have to apologize to me for being yourself. Have you talked about any of this to Esteban, though?"

"Not yet. I want to, but I wanted to tell you first."

I set the pillow down between us and leaned forward to kiss her cheek. "Apology accepted, but unnecessary. Now tell Esteban how you feel. He'll understand."

"I will, I promise. I've, uh, been thinking about it a lot lately, and I hoped that maybe I could tell him about what it was like after your miscarriage."

I stiffened. "You're free to talk about whatever you want with Esteban. I'm not going to put a ban on anything."

"I'm not asking if I'm banned. I'm asking if you'd like me to talk to him about it." In a softer voice, Isisa added, "So you won't have to. I know you did the same for me and explained about Dad. Nandi said so."

"We talked about it a little," I admitted. "And he does know I had a miscarriage. That's it."

Isisa eased an arm around my waist and drew me in close. "All right. I didn't mean to stir up sad feelings."

Soft kisses against my shoulder and collarbone eased the ache away. She meant well, I knew that, and I loved her all the more for caring so deeply about my feelings that she'd bear the burden of bad memories. My muscles relaxed, and I leaned into her embrace.

"You're the best."

Her dark eyes gleamed above a widening smile. "I know I am."

"Jerk."

"Brat."

My eager fingers slipped a few times on the pearl buttons fastening her blouse. I loosened them on the third attempt, and ivory silk slid back from her shoulders, leaving only pale pink lace against her dark skin.

Then her mouth was seeking mine, lips soft and pliant, tongue flavored with wine and a delicious hint of caramel-drizzled cheesecake. Between kisses, I managed to murmur, "I think I'm bored with this TV show. I'd rather enjoy some quality time with you upstairs."

"I like your thinking. You're a little overdressed though."

"Bet I beat you upstairs and out of my clothes first."

"Ha. I'm already half undressed."

And then the mad scramble began, both of us dashing for the stairs and shedding clothes along the way.

≈

*T*he cell phone dragged me away from pleasant dreams of Esteban and Isisa indulging in a round of double penetration with me trapped in the middle. I could still feel his touch on my skin, his lips whispering over my tits while Isisa teased me from behind with her favorite strap on.

It had felt so real. In the dream, we had been acting out a ménage à trois for Nandi at her behest, performing as she directed us to bring one of her book scenes to life while she wrote.

Wanting to murder whoever was on the other end, I raised my cheek from Isisa's chest and swatted at the phone, nearly knocking it off the nightstand. Through my blurry vision, I saw Ian's name pop up from his home office line. I accepted the call and placed it on one ear. "Hello?"

"Bad time?"

I squinted at the digital clock. One-fifteen? Ian was never up this late. "I was asleep. That thing most sensible people do at one in the morning. This had better be important or your feathered goose is cooked the next time I see you. Why aren't *you* asleep, too?"

"Working. Figured you'd be eager to receive an update about the missing young ladies in Houston. I took that information you gave me and passed it on to the people in charge of the case. If it's a bad time—"

"What do you know?"

"So," Ian said conversationally, a chuckle in his voice. "Does this mean you're up for a job?"

17

ESTEBAN

he office door banged against the wall. I jerked awake from my nap, leaping up from the chair and reaching for the concealed pistol under my jacket.

Sergio grinned at me across the desk, unaware of how close he'd come to receiving a new hole in his body to accompany his big mouth.

"You almost got yourself shot."

"You worried the Espadachines are gonna bust in? Dude, we're in the good side of Houston. There's no FEL here."

"Tell that to the assholes who tagged our shit before."

Sergio snorted. "Wannabes probably. Why come here and tag us? The real Familia de Espadachines Latinos got real shit to do. They're running drugs and murdering other gangbangers in the Second Ward, not painting swords on uninhabited buildings in the suburbs."

"So who did this?"

"Medrano probably paid some thugs. You said he's in our business."

"That's what bothers me. Medrano has enough money to buy off the FEL if he wanted. Probably runs them." I wouldn't be surprised.

"Now you're tired all the time *and* paranoid. Maybe this is just me, but I thought going away for a vacation meant you'd come back refreshed. You know, rested."

"We had a lot of shit to do in Chicago," I muttered instead of telling him the responsibilities of the job and dating three women were killing me.

"Yeah, I can see that. Mamá called to whine about you not visiting her when you made it back in yesterday afternoon."

"Christ. I've only been back to the state for less than a day."

"You know how she is. Give her a call and get her off your back until you find the time to visit."

"Yeah. I'll do that."

"Anyway, you look like you should have taken today off, too. If you're that tired, why'd you come in?"

"Paperwork. We're on schedule for once, and I want to keep it that way. Plus, I was sniffing around some other contracts last week and wanted to see if they were still available."

"We got the hands for another contract?"

I rubbed my chin. I'd hired more guys than necessary when we fell behind schedule, and now they were biting into our capital. "A small one. I was going to lay off Ted, Paolo, Jim, and Kyle, but they're good workers. We're still a month ahead of schedule, and Dupont doesn't want us to deviate from the draw schedule he penned out. Fact is, we got more dudes than we need now, and it's either lay them off or keep them for another job."

"Or put them to work on another project and make that paper."

"Exactly. Dupont should be paying us for the next phase in his project soon, so the important thing is to avoid falling behind again." My phone rang, caller ID window listing our client's name. I grimaced. "Speak of the devil."

"I'll let you handle that."

I put some warmth and professionalism into my voice before answering the call. "Hello, Mr. Dupont. Good afternoon for you, I hope."

"It's a *great* afternoon."

"I suppose it is. How may I help you today, sir? Did you need to come back or have me send another report?"

"Nothing like that, no. I'm proud of how far you boys have come since our little setback a few weeks ago, so I've decided to release additional funds—no, no, Susan, I'd prefer the peach syrup in my sweet tea." He fussed at his assistant for a moment then returned to our conversation, his exasperated breath whistling through the line. "Anyway, while I know this isn't part of our original contract, I'd like to amend a few lines to include top-of-the-line security and a guard station of some sort. Perhaps two. Our incident has given me food for thought."

"How top of the line are we talking?"

"Solar power with a secondary source."

"We can do it. I've got a pair of guys on crew with the experience to pull it off."

"Good. Shall we meet for dinner tomorrow to discuss the fine details?"

Dupont always insisted on discussing business at his favorite Italian restaurant. "The Venetian at seven?"

"Splendid. I'll talk to you tomorrow."

The line disconnected. I set the phone down and shook my head. "He wants to discuss security measures now."

"Weird dude," Sergio said.

We'd learned at the start of our business relationship that Dupont was a creature of habit. He didn't want us to fall behind schedule but also resisted us finishing the project early. He only visited the site twice a month to perform a walkthrough, always on a Monday, always at night, and always too chipper for a guy who was prowling around at the ass crack of dawn.

But we tolerated his quirks because the obscene amount of money poured into the project would leave Castillo Construction in a very comfortable position

"All right. I'm taking off. Any problems, give me a call as usual."

"There won't be a problem. Believe it or not, this place continues to move even when you're not here."

A Vietnamese restaurant provided dinner for me on the way home, and Sasha called minutes after I emerged from the shower. I placed her on speaker phone and settled on the couch with a groan, clothed in only boxers while holding a warm cup of bánh phở from a local place a few miles away.

"Is this a bad time?"

"It's never a bad time for talking to you. What's up?"

"I thought I'd check in to see if we should expect to see you tonight."

I'd gotten into the habit of popping in unannounced after spending a day at the site, given freedom to visit the ladies whenever I wanted. One of them was always home.

"Not tonight, chica. I think burning the candle from both ends is taking its toll on me now between the site, staying up with our night owl, and taking off on spontaneous vacations to hang with book nerds."

She chuckled. "You were kind of dead on your feet yesterday. I'll let the others know."

I dropped a few jalapenos and pieces of sage into my soup while listening to her. "Were they expecting me?"

"I think Nandi wanted to finish this movie series with you, but she can wait."

It was always Nandi who called or Nandi who couldn't wait to see me again. Sasha was a close second, visibly exerting will not to keep me all to herself.

"And Isisa?"

I raised the cup for a sip and enjoyed a few mouthfuls of savory beef broth.

"Oh, you know her."

"Actually, I don't."

I hadn't spent time with Isisa again since the race. Not alone anyway. She'd joined Nandi and me for a couple movies since then but only because the other lioness had dragged her onto the couch to join us, and even then, she'd sat on the other end of the love seat, warming up only towards the end and sometimes resting her head on my shoulder.

Those were the best fucking moments, better than the occasional kisses and the hugs.

"Are you sure Isisa feels the same way about me?"

A long silence hung between us. "She does."

"What am I doing wrong? I've spent more time with you and Nandi, hell, twice the time with Nandi, than I have with Isisa."

"Isisa isn't as physical as us. It comes and goes. One day, she might want to cuddle and have kisses, the next, she's quiet and standoffish when it comes to any sort of physical contact."

The tension knot in my chest eased. "So, it isn't me?"

"No."

"All right. God, I love you girls, but I don't have the slightest idea of what the hell I'm doing when it comes to her. I don't want to push her away. Or smother her. I feel like I put my foot in my mouth that day and she hasn't forgiven me."

Sasha hesitated again. "Isisa is... different. Do you remember what I told you about the prides our mothers escaped?"

"Yeah. An abusive asshole stepped in after your dad died."

"Yes, Mum left as quick as she could after that."

"And Isisa's father is an abusive asshole."

"Isisa's childhood wasn't the same as mine—it was cruel, and brutal, and many things happened she doesn't discuss with even me. For a long time when we were growing up, I thought she was a lesbian. So did she. Nandi was the one who introduced us to good sex with men, and for the right one, she's very happy."

"Yeah?"

"Yeah. It took her *months* to warm up to Taylor. Hell, there are days she doesn't want anything to do with Nandi or me. She's always been that way, and content to rely on her toys." She paused. "Disappointed?"

"Nah. Honestly, I didn't expect, and wouldn't want, the three of you to be boning me day and night," I said into the phone, chuckling at the giggle I received from Sasha in return. "Don't ever tell my brother—hell, don't tell *anyone* I said that."

"I won't. Now that we've settled the matter of Isisa's happiness, are you happy?"

"Honestly, I'm happy. I guess Isisa's welfare was my primary concern in all of this. It means` more to me than my dick, and juggling the well-being of three women is a little more work than I expected."

A quiet lull in the conversation lapsed between us before Sasha replied. "That's why I chose you. Why *we* chose you. I wasn't lying when I said I trust you with my girls, Esteban. I know you won't hurt her or Nandi. But if we're giving you too much too fast—"

"No. I can handle it. Trust me."

Her quiet exhale whispered against the line. "Good."

Eager to smooth away the tension, I grasped at straws, searching internally for something humorous to say. "Anyway, I'm due for a seven o'clock business dinner tomorrow night at the Venetian. It isn't far from you guys."

"I have some plans with Ian then, but I'm positive Nandi will be more than happy to be your dessert," Sasha said, beating me to the punchline of my joke before I had the chance.

"Tell her to expect me by nine to finish those movies."

~

*A*fter enduring Houston's evening traffic, I passed the car keys to a valet and strode inside the Venetian at a quarter to seven, earlier than necessary after factoring rush hour into my travel time.

A hostess escorted me to the rear of the restaurant where Dupont awaited me at a small table. As was typical for him, he wore a three-piece suit, his blonde hair perfectly smooth and in place.

"Mr. Dupont, good evening."

"Ah, Mr. Castillo." He smiled and rose, offering out his hand. "I do so respect a prompt guest."

"I figured I'd end up waiting on you," I admitted. "Traffic wasn't as bad as I expected."

"I always arrive an hour before any meeting," Dupont replied. "I enjoy the relaxing atmosphere and the wine. Shall I pour you a glass?"

"Thank you."

I'd learned early on that talking business never came until after we'd ordered. Dupont was a man who liked to do things on his own timeline. Once our meals arrived, he opened the discussion.

"There are other projects I'd like your company to consider undertaking once this one is complete," Dupont said. "I have purchased a considerable amount of land near San Antonio and have planned a third residential community in the Dallas Fort Worth area."

I nearly choked on my steak and made a valiant effort to chew and swallow. "I'd be happy to take your projects. It might take a little convincing for some of the crew, but I imagine most won't mind being away from home for a time."

Dupont waved a hand. "Of course I understand it will mean some extra dispensations. Travel and accommodations will certainly be factored into payments, as well as some extra time."

"That's quite generous of you."

"I'm a firm believer in family, Mr. Castillo. That's why I'm building these communities."

"For a family?"

His grin never failed to unnerve me, though it was nothing but genial. There was something almost predatory about it, his canines just a touch sharper than the norm. Sort of like Sasha and the girls.

Keep it together, man. Sasha said shifters were rare.

"In a way. This development will go to a private group who are as close to family as it can get without being actual relations. People who want to live close while maintaining their own space."

"Well, whatever it is, it sounds good and I hope it works out well."

"I'm sure it will—"

A shadow fell across the table. "Are you?" a deep voice cut in.

My appetite for bacon-wrapped steak dwindled in the presence of my biggest competitor. The elder Rafael Medrano towered over our table, a tall man with broad shoulders and rough hands, the kind of hands Selene would want to dip into a bucket of lotion. He'd wrapped his stocky body in an expensive, tailored suit, but the tie accentuated how little of a neck he had.

"Mr. Medrano." Dupont offered a polite smile. "If you don't mind, we're discussing business."

"My favorite subject."

He pulled out an empty chair and took a seat, as if he'd been invited. Dupont maintained a poker face worthy of the pros, his polite veneer never faltering in the least. If he could be civil, then so could I.

"How'd you know I would be here?" Dupont asked.

"You're a creature of habit, and I have a vested interest in this particular establishment. I've been trying to buy the owner out for the past year."

The polite facade cracked for the first time since Medrano's appearance, a flicker of irritation and a twitch of Dupont's left eye. "Well, for my sake, I hope he continues to hold out on accepting whatever snake oil offer you make. I happen to enjoy this restaurant as it is."

"If you enjoy your meat raw and bloody, I suppose it suits very well." Medrano smiled again and flicked his gaze toward me.

My brows rose. Dupont's hand was white knuckled, his expression frozen. An unspoken message passed between the two men, a stare down that could have ignited the table cloth.

I cleared my throat and leaned forward for the bottle. "Nothing wrong with that. I want the steak like it came from the cow directly to my plate when I can have it that way. No one likes a slab of ruined shoe leather, unless they've never had better."

"Lucky you aren't the cow yet. So, tell me, do you feel you're up to the task of handling Dupont's special little project? I hear you've had vandals and a host of other setbacks derailing the schedule. Quite unfortunate."

My smile remained. "Business must be slow for you lately, Medrano. Don't you have projects of your own to discuss?"

"You mean the high-rise in First Ward? Why yes, we've been contracted to build a second tower."

Inwardly, I fumed. That contract had been mine until he swept in and made some backroom deals, stealing it out from underneath me.

And then Dupont had come along and saved our asses with his dream project, throwing millions of dollars into our company while Medrano chased him doggedly. When that had failed, he'd sent his brother Luis and oldest son, little Rafael, to intimidate me, only little Rafael wasn't so little and they'd made veiled insinuations about the task being unsafe for us to accept.

Less than a month after we broke ground, one of my best guys was run off I-45 on the way to work. He was still bedbound, and the prognosis wasn't good.

Since then, there'd been a dozen smaller incidents, minor accidents and scrape ups, but nothing to prove Medrano was behind it.

"We were discussing further projects," Dupont said. His hand had unfisted and the tension in his face eased back into a calm mask. "Projects I fully plan to hire Castillo Construction to complete."

"If it's anything like the current job, Castillo may find his charming little company overwhelmed by the magnitude of it." Medrano helped himself to the bottle of wine on the table. A waitress appeared with an additional wine glass, assuming our uninvited guest was welcome. "Lots of special… considerations."

"Nothing my crew can't handle."

"Yes, I have full faith in Mr. Castillo," Dupont agreed.

"The wrong move, even a single mistake could cost many *lives*."

Dupont's expression didn't change. "Indeed it could, but as Mr. Castillo has already proven, my project is safe in his hands."

I clenched one fist against my thigh under the table. "Wait a minute. Are you *threatening* me?"

The elder Medrano had a smile like a shark. "Please, I have no need for threats, I'm merely reminding you of the possible repercussions of faulty work. Imagine the damage caused by an improperly installed window, Dupont."

Damaged caused by a fucking window? I'd seen the result of shit work on stairwells, floors, and rooftops, but I'd never seen a window cost anyone their life. I straightened in the seat, one second from jumping out of it altogether. Dupont laid a hand on my arm.

"Again, I have the utmost trust in Mr. Castillo's work. That's why I hired him. Should I ever require assistance from your company, you can be sure I will call." He paused a beat. "Which I'm quite certain won't be anytime soon."

Medrano grunted. Upon recuperating, he turned to me. "Do you like cats, Esteban? I may call you Esteban, right?"

"Excuse me?"

"Cats. You seem like a cat person to me. Good pets, I guess."

My eyes narrowed. "Not that it's any of your business, but I have two dogs."

"Ah. My mistake." He quaffed the remainder of his glass and set it aside as he rose from his chair. "We'll meet again soon, I'm sure."

He strolled away from our table with a casual stride. I clenched both fists against my lap, body tensed like a coiled spring.

Dupont coughed discreetly, effectively drawing my attention back to him. "You two are acquainted?"

Determined to recover the previous mood of the

evening, I shook off the fury and had a sip of expensive wine. Isisa would have loved it. "Nah. I can't say I've ever met Señor Medrano until now. I've only dealt with his son a few times and had the occasional run-in with their hirelings trying to intimidate us."

His fair brows drew together. "Intimidate you by what means and for what reason?"

"When you first approached my company and accepted our bid, they wanted us to refuse your contract. When I didn't do that, they wanted us to hire on some of their people and subcontract to them."

Dupont's features darkened, mouth pressed into a grim line. The pleasant facade faded and something else rose beneath the surface that I couldn't place. Something that made my skin crawl and a cool touch travel down my spine. "He's a foul little man, and I have no use for him."

"Then why is he so desperate for your business?"

"You could say we run in similar circles."

My brows shot up, betraying my desire to remain neutral and stone-faced.

"I know what you are thinking. No, I do not involve myself in his criminal mischief and enterprises, but we are acquainted by other means."

"I see." I didn't, but the more I tried to wrap my mind around it all, the more my head hurt.

"Now, enough of that cretin. What do you say to building a security center for the development?"

"It can be done. There's plenty of room by the area we planned to construct your gated boundary wall. You won't be cramped for space."

"And the other projects? Have I gained your interest?"

"You've certainly gained the interest of my wallet. I

like money as much as I appreciate a good challenge." Expanding the business to San Antonio and Dallas meant I'd have to hire and vet more workers, take on more apprentices, and ultimately needed to promote a few more of our best workers to oversee distant operations. I'd be traveling personally to each site frequently.

Dupont had handed me the means to expand Castillo Construction beyond a local family business into something more.

"Money is often the best motivating force." He smiled and refilled my glass, giving me the last of the cabernet sauvignon.

When he set it down, I turned the bottle around to look at the label. "How much is this? I'm not normally a wine drinker, but I think this won me over enough to take one for the road. My woman is one of those collectors who only drinks the fine stuff."

"Seven hundred and fifty a bottle."

I grimaced and discarded all plans of purchasing one for Isisa. What she didn't know, wouldn't hurt her. "A bit too rich for me."

Dupont raised both fair brows and twisted in his seat when the waitress passed by with empty plates from another table. "Excuse me, madame. When you are finished with that, bring three bottles of the Chateau le Sang and send the check, please," Dupont said.

"Of course, sir."

After she left, I leaned forward and lowered my voice. "Three bottles?"

"For you and your lady friend, of course. A true collector must have at least one to drink and two to cellar."

I blinked a few times while it sank in that the man was offering to send me out of the restaurant with two thousand dollars in wine. "I couldn't, man. That's too much."

"You will. I know I am not always the easiest client to work with, but you have done all within your power to satisfy my unusual requirements. Think of this as a tip. A token of appreciation from one businessman to another for the fine job you have performed."

It took a moment for me to form the words I wanted to say. "Thank you."

"It's my honor."

He paid by card and tossed a wad of money on the table, an enormous tip for the waitress that seemed to factor in the cost of the bottles as well. This was one of those moments that ended up on Facebook, spreading like viral wildfire.

"Mr. Dupont, I—"

"Please. Call me Julien."

After a pause to collect my thoughts, I said, "Thank you, Julien, for offering our company this opportunity. I give my word to you that we won't let you down. I'll get to the bottom of whatever it is that's happening out there and causing our setbacks."

"I believe we already know what is behind these setbacks," Julien said in a measured tone, absolutely calm. "And he just walked away ten minutes ago."

SASHA

When Ian asked for a favor, I couldn't help myself—I agreed. Juni and I were on our way to Club Hysteria. She hated skirts, so we'd compromised on artfully torn jeans and midriff tops instead of ultratight dresses.

Nadir had styled our hair prior to embarking on our mission and applied makeup with the talent of a Hollywood artist, achieving effects I couldn't do with my own hands even if I spent an hour in front of the mirror. I hated him.

Not really.

When Nadir had finished with Juni, she barely appeared legal despite being well into her thirties. Her face reminded me of a high school girl playing with her mother's makeup once his skilled hands completed the job.

If there was a pervert in the club hunting for Asian school girls, she'd fit the bill.

"I can't believe Ian has us doing this," Taylor muttered from the driver's seat. He'd come along for the mission and given us a ride, wearing his best hip-hop club attire, pressed jeans, brand new shoes sporting some basketball player's name, a white sweater, and two strands of bling around his neck.

"At least you don't have to spend the night letting drunken dudes come on to you," Juni fired back from the rear seat.

I grinned.

"If we should envy anyone, it should be Nadir. He

won't be doing a damned thing but sitting on his ass," I pointed out.

Nadir's voice came in crystal clear despite the distance between us. "Ha, ha, ha." He traveled on our rear in the communications vehicle. We'd already been outfitted with the best technology government money could buy, allowing us to keep in contact with him while in the club.

I hadn't entertained the thought of returning to Club Hysteria since beating a ridiculous amount of date rapist ass, but Ian had a feeling that I'd only disturbed one cog in the human-trafficking machine.

I shivered. Some of the girls in the tapes were currently missing person's cases. This mess was now officially related to the abduction of dozens of young women across Houston.

Juni tugged at her sequined top. "I feel ridiculous."

I slapped her hand. "You look amazing, and it's for a good cause."

"I know, but you have it easier. You don't look like you're still going through puberty."

We emerged from the car a block from the club, deciding not to be seen anywhere in Taylor's vicinity. Juni's stride on stilettos reminded me of a baby calf fresh from its mother's uterus, all awkward but adorable. Despite that, the bouncer at the door let us pass into a world of pounding music and flashing lights in multiple colors. Perfume, cologne, sweat, and alcohol hung heavy in the air like a choking miasma of human funk. Juni and I both took a moment to get a grip before the smell overwhelmed us.

"Where to first?" she asked.

"Let's scope out the bar, see if anyone is getting hassled or if we catch a whiff of drugs."

"Right."

Getting close to the bar was no easy feat in a crowd this large. We wriggled our way through until we slipped into a space at the counter. Juni ordered a cherry vodka sour, and I asked for a rum and coke. A couple guys glanced over at us, but no one approached.

Nadir's voice reached me through the small communication device tucked just inside my ear canal, nonexistent to human perception, but loud enough for shifter hearing. "I'm going to need you two to separate for a bit. No one is going to take the bait when you're hanging all over each other. Think like the predators you are."

"Not a predator," Juni muttered under her breath.

But I was, and I knew what he meant. I set my drink aside and rose. "I'm going to hit the restroom."

While wasting time pretending to touch up my makeup and hair in the harsh fluorescent lighting, I received compliments on everything from my dye job to my heels. None of the girls seemed in any danger, however. No one was puking, yet, and no one seemed to be in any distress.

Through the comm device, I picked up on everything going on around Juni, who had remained at the bar. She giggled, a quiet, girlish sound, and accepted a drink offer. While she flirted, I abandoned the restroom and hit the dance floor. Taylor caught my eye near the deejay booth. A gaggle of women surrounded him, a bachelorette party from the looks of it. Since he had his hands full, I made my way through the crowd toward the bar along the back wall.

Then I spotted him.

The guy wore the same tight-fitted college shirt as the one who'd nabbed me back in September. The girl he had his hands on looked like she was two steps away from passing out, her steps wobbly and her posture sagging. He kept a tight hand on her elbow and guided her away from the high-top table.

To be safe, I darted over and sniffed the glasses they'd left behind, but kept my eye on the pair as they made their way through the crowd toward the exit. The subtle odor of drugs wafted off the remaining liquid.

"Got one," I said in a low voice. "Tall blond in the red cougars shirt leaving with the drunken brunette. I'm following them out."

"Right behind you," Juni said.

"I'll watch for a tail," Taylor added.

Good. I trusted my team to have my back while I followed the pair out the club doors and onto the sidewalk. He led her to the left, to the parking garage at the end of the block. The nighttime crowd had thinned. Once we made it to the garage, no one else was in sight.

"Yeah, baby, c'mon, I'll get you to bed," the guy said. "I'll treat you real good."

She stumbled, but the guy gripped her around the waist and hefted her limp body against his side.

"There you are!" Feigning recognition, I rushed forward and grabbed the girl by her free arm. "I totally lost you in the crowd in there. God, you're a mess."

"You mind?" the guy asked. "We're just headed to my car."

"Um, yeah. This is my roommate, and she's coming home with me."

"She already said she came alone tonight."

Dammit. "Well, yeah, but we planned to meet up. So I'll get her home, okay? Thanks though, really."

"She asked me to get her home, so back the fuck off. This ain't got shit to do wit' you."

Juni appeared behind him and tapped his left shoulder. He twisted around to glance back at her. "What is this? Some kind of—"

Her fist crashed into his face. He staggered back and released his would-be victim. Without the guy holding her up, she became dead weight in my arms.

"You fucking bitch!" He lunged at Juni and swung at her, but she danced back in her heels, blocked his fist, and stomped down on the top of his foot.

One palm heel strike to the nose thrust her aggressor away. She was out of the shoes, kicking them off in the next second, barefoot in the lot when she twisted a roundhouse. Juni's thigh muscles were like steel cables, and I'd admired them before, even envied them.

Her attacker's head snapped to the side, bloody spittle and maybe a tooth flying from his mouth. He didn't fall yet, because she leapt forward, bringing her knee into his stomach. Men frequently underestimated her when it came to a fight, fooled by her demure appearance and meek stature until she juggled their faces with her feet.

The fight was over before it even began. She folded him like a sheet of paper, leaving him crumpled on the ground by the time Taylor arrived. He shook his head.

"Remind me why I'm here with y'all when you have everything covered?"

I passed the girl into his arms. "She needs medical attention right now."

"The call has already been made," Nadir said over the comm. "Police are en route with an ETA of about five minutes."

Juni crouched beside her human punching bag and searched his pockets, coming up with a wallet. "Martin Rodriguez, age twenty-one."

Nadir whistled. "Check him out for gang tags. Look at the arms, back, and chest. Throat as well. The Houstones are a bit of a problem in this area, and some contacts in the HPD gang division mentioned sex trafficking is their new big thing. They take girls across the border to Mexico, and they're never seen again. Hell, boys sometimes, too. Flesh is money, doesn't matter the gender."

I crouched beside him and raised his shirt. He had an enormous tattoo of crossed swords over his chest. Cavalry blades and a banner with something in Spanish.

"Live and die by the sword," Nadir said. "Looks like he's FEL."

Another guy came from around the corner, a huge Latino man who looked like he subsisted on a diet of eggs and cornbread. He had a shaved head and a snake tattoos crawling up his neck. "What the fuck is going on here?"

"Just a group of concerned citizens," Taylor said in an even voice, laying the girl across a car hood on her side. "Nothing for you to be concerned about."

"That's my boy on the ground right there. You did that to him, tough guy?"

Fury flashed in Juni's brown eyes. She whirled on her

bare feet. "No. I did, and I'll lay you out, too. Your pal tried to take advantage of a girl."

"Drugged a girl," I added. "So unless you want to be caught up in his illegal shit, I suggest you turn around and walk the other way."

The guy cracked his knuckles and planted his feet. "You have two ways to leave. On your feet, or in a bag. Your choice."

"Don't say we didn't warn ya," Taylor said. His fist swung out in a blur, knuckles colliding with Bald Guy's chiseled jaw. He didn't even flinch.

"Oh shit," I muttered.

Taylor's head suddenly rocked back, a lightning quick punch to his chin taking him off his feet and skidding him back on his ass. Before Juni or I could react, he hefted Taylor off the ground, his muscular body poised to perform a body slam against concrete. The cougar shifter twisted free and landed on his feet in a crouch instead. Spinning while low to the ground, Taylor swept the other guy's feet out from beneath him and toppled the mountain of muscle.

Juni came in with a kick to the ribs before he hit the ground. They were like a tag-team duo. It was how we'd been trained to fight when Ian first brought us all on, complementing each other with our strengths.

The guy didn't topple motionless to the ground. He didn't writhe in pain. He bounced onto his feet again like he was on a spring. Both of his meaty fists swung up, and he spun a ferocious clothesline that took Taylor off his feet.

I dragged a pair of brass knuckles out of my back pocket and kicked off my heels. Juni had ducked beneath his attack and come up again in an impressive tornado kick. She knocked the spit from his mouth, providing the distraction I needed to duck in and slam my fist into his kidneys. He howled in pain. Then the back of his hand cracked me in the face. I stumbled back as stars sparked across my vision, lip split and blood dripping down my chin.

Our punches and kicks rolled off him, and the way he twisted his body to avoid exposing his tender kidneys to me again put the contortionists of Cirque du Soleil to shame.

His sledgehammer-like fist buried in my stomach. All the wind left me at once, pushing me up on my toes. I collapsed to my hands and knees, wanting to puke and sob. He caught Juni by the ankle before her next kick landed, and then he spun like an Olympic athlete hurling a discus.

Our hundred-pound teammate struck a windshield with a loud crack and went still. Taylor's furious yell echoed through the garage. He wasn't fast enough, our opponent sidestepping, blocking, moving with the kind of footwork any boxer would envy. As I staggered to my feet, the big guy chopped the edge of his hand against Taylor's throat. My friend dropped to the pavement coughing.

"Sasha, down!"

I ducked the moment Nadir's voice in my ear told me to. The sharp report of a handgun preceded the guy stumbling back with a spreading red stain on his shoulder.

He swore a few words in Spanish I only knew from hanging around Esteban so often, and then he hauled ass down the ramp into the lower level of the parking garage.

Nadir stood at the end of the aisle with a few dozen automobiles between us and sweat on his brow. He must have run to make it. "He didn't look like he'd go down without help."

"Get him," Taylor wheezed. "Don't let him get away."

Nadir nodded. "I'll take care of them. Go!"

I sprinted down the ramp into the lower level of the parking garage. The guy was ahead of me, moving at a speed that belied the bulk of his body.

Had to be a shifter too. Or on PCP. I'd have bet money on drugs if the scent of his animal wasn't in the air and in his sweat, a musky smell like musty earth and sand. Something familiar teased across my senses.

He disappeared around a corner. The lot was like a maze, reminding me of a silly horror movie I'd watched with Isisa a couple years ago about parking garages and a woman trapped in one with a murderer. Chest heaving, heart thundering a relentless drumbeat between my ears, I charged straight out of my clothes and pursued on four feet, leaving my favorite jeans in tatters.

A thousand new smells hit my nose at once. As a shifter in my human form, my senses surpassed any normal person and became unmatched once I made the change. The scent of motor oil stained the ground, but my prey wasn't so far, his unique smell on the wind with the scent of cologne, perfume, and booze. I blocked out a hundred smells associated with city living and zipped around a corner. My claws clicked against hard ground.

Found him. Just ahead, I watched him turn a corner and vanish from my sight a second time. In the seconds it took to clear the distance between us, he'd disappeared again.

A rumpled pile of clothes lay on the ground beside a drain cover, the yawning hole it had once covered leading into darkness filled with moisture and dank smells. Whoever he was, whatever he had been, he was far beyond my reach.

~

*W*ith a cold ice pack to my cheek, I groaned and waited for Ian to dispense a few pain pills. That guy's fist had been like a pile of bricks wrapped in a flesh glove.

Two hours later, we were tired and bruised, recuperating from the event in our new Huntsville safehouse. Ian's plan was to establish several across Texas in the event of an emergency situation.

And it also kept our work away from home. It was one part office, one part armory, all of our gear sealed behind multiple locks.

"Man, was I glad you showed up with the cops when you did. Totally did not expect a shifter," Nadir said as he sank into the chair in front of the computer console. The enormous screen and numerous devices resembled the setup in some villainous mastermind's secret lair.

Or the Batcave.

Ian had arrived with the police minutes after our mysterious bad guy escaped, which helped smooth things over. An EMT tended to the victim while Nadir, Taylor, and Juni gave reports. I'd hidden in our van.

"I'm telling you, he was a reptile or something."

"Snake." Taylor cleared his throat and took another

swig of water. His hoarse voice made me wince. "Pretty sure, at least. Met one once, years back."

Once he made the connection, the memory clicked. "I knew it was familiar, but all I could think of was that scumbag Lyle used to work for, and the drain was way too small for a croc."

"Yeah. Reptile shifters have a peculiar kind of odor about them," Ian agreed.

Nadir spun his desk chair around to face the console again. "Now we need to ID this asshole. You mind looking at some photos for me, Sash?"

"Sure."

"Since that dickhead was FEL, I figure we should start with the database of known gang members." Nadir loved his job, and he went on to describe some sort of cooperative work between local police forces and the Texas Department of Justice. "If he's ever had a run-in with the law before, his photograph will be here."

"Does it let you narrow it down by height?" I asked.

"Yeah. About how big do you figure?"

"Fucking huge," Taylor rasped. "About six-foot-five and stocky as hell. Like Sasha's guy but twice as wide."

"Six-foot-seven, maybe," Juni said. She groaned as she eased into a chair with one arm around her ribs. "Sasha was wearing five-inch stilettos, and he was still way over her. Had a neck like a linebacker."

Nadir tapped a button. The number of results dropped down to a fraction. "How you feeling, Junebug?"

"Like I was hit by a sledgehammer. I'll live."

We tabbed through photo after photo, scrolling through the most recent to enter the system to the oldest until at last, I saw the guy. He was younger in the photograph by a few years, but built the same.

I tapped the photo on the screen. "There! Luis Medrano. Oh God no. The Medranos are the family harassing Esteban."

"No surprise. Luis Medrano is the kid brother of Papá Medrano. Construction is just one of their legitimate businesses, but they dabble in a bit of everything else apparently. This guy did a ten-year stretch at Ferguson Unit for assault and battery. He's been Medrano's muscle since he came out into the free world again."

Ian hadn't moved much throughout our chat, arms folded against his chest while he absorbed it all. Finally, he nodded. "All right. From what I hear among my buddies, these guys are a real problem lately. Constant blood in the streets. I'm going to make a few calls and see what kind of jurisdiction we can get over this. Right now though, you guys get some rest."

He didn't have to tell me twice. Crawling in bed sounded like a great way to end the night until I remembered Esteban was at the penthouse along with two easily worried wives who would fret and finish Luis's job for him once they saw my face. Shit.

≈

*W*hen I opened the door to the penthouse, Nandi was sprawled on the couch with a book while an action flick played on the television. She glanced at me. "You're back earl—Oh my gosh, Sasha, what happened?" She rushed over and fawned over me, touching my face.

"I'm fine. Really." Unlike the others, I'd gotten off lucky.

"You're a mess!"

"Shhh. Keep your voice down. Did Esteban go home?"

"No, I left him in bed, and don't you dare change the subject. What happened to you?"

"There was a little fight."

Nandi put her hands on her hips. "You have a swollen lip."

Did I? I raised a hand to my mouth. "Really, I'm fine, baby. Where's Isisa?"

"Taking a bath. So are you going to tell me what happened or do I need to go drag her out so she can beat it out of you?"

"You're super cute when you threaten me."

She scowled, scrunching up her nose, but amusement lit up her golden eyes. "Fine. I'll go grab you some ice."

"Preferably with some vodka over it. I could use a drink, and I'll tell you what I was up to if you add in some chocolate."

"All right."

A few minutes later, all three of us were curled on the couch with drinks and little discs of Mexican chocolate Esteban had given us. Isisa had showed up while Nandi was pouring, taken one look at me, and ordered me to sit.

Secrets didn't exist in our household, not unless we were forced to by work. We all understood confidentiality and classified information, but this wasn't either of those things. So I told them everything that had gone down that evening.

"Is the girl going to be okay?" Nandi asked.

"Yeah. The EMTs were taking great care of her. Ian's

going to ask her a few questions when she's medically cleared."

"What about the guy who ran off? A snake shifter? Really?" Isisa rubbed her neck and frowned. "I don't like snakes."

"Worse, he's a Medrano."

"You have to tell Esteban," Nandi said.

"No, he'll only worry."

"Sasha, he deserves to know."

"She's right," Nandi agreed.

My chest expanded with a deep, indrawn breath. I let it out slowly, eyes closed. "I know, but not right now. He has enough to worry about. I promise I'll tell him soon, okay? Please let me be the one to do it. Please."

Isisa pressed her lips together. "Fine."

"We promise. But, Sasha, don't wait too long. He's no different than us—no secrets between us. Not if we're going to be a pride."

They were right, even if it meant adding more weight to the considerable burden he already carried.

18

ESTEBAN

*R*ambo and Ripley loved the dog park at the Discovery Green. Despite the cool breeze of approaching winter, the sun shone bright above us. Isisa jogged to my right with Simba on a close leash, her dog a white-gold cotton ball of fluff no bigger than my two pits.

It had been love at first sight though. The dogs had been all over Simba when we met on the sidewalk in front of Hibiscus Gardens an hour prior. We jogged for half an hour then let the dogs loose in the park to play. The plan was to let them tire themselves out and let my rambunctious pair get some socialization.

Wins on both accounts.

Simba went straight to his kennel once we stepped inside. He sprawled across his padded bed and groaned. Rambo and Ripley sniffed around first then plopped down on the rug nearby.

I snickered. "I think we wore your little guy out."

"All three of them." She laughed and grabbed some

water from the fridge. "We'll have to get your guys some beds of their own if they're going to visit."

Smiling at the two dogs, I leaned close enough to scratch behind Rambo's ears. "They're not going to be with me too much longer. They'll probably have homes in the next month or two."

Her brows rose. "You didn't plan to keep them?"

"Nah. I never keep the dogs I foster. If I kept every pup that came into my house, I probably wouldn't be able to feed myself anymore." Rambo lurched to his feet, stretched, then came over to nudge his nose beneath my hand. I petted the top of his blocky, oversized head and grinned. "You'll have a real home soon, pal. Soon as we find someone who won't separate you two."

"Mm-hmm."

When I glanced up, Isisa had one of those big, secret smiles on her faces, like she knew something and wasn't letting me in on it. "What?"

"Anyway, I'm going to catch a shower because I'm a disgusting mess."

I fanned my shirt, trying to coax more air-conditioned current beneath it. "I'll do the same."

Isisa paused at the bottom of the steps and looked at me over her shoulder. "You could share mine."

"I wouldn't wanna impose."

"It isn't imposing if I invite you."

An invitation to join her in the shower didn't mean an invitation to sex, I just didn't think I had the kind of self-restraint and control required not to ogle every inch of her the moment she stripped. The way those leggings hugged her ass was almost obscene. And she'd worn only a peach sports bra beneath a bubblegum pink racerback tank. Isisa and Nandi loved the color pink.

"Don't have to ask me twice." I started after her then paused to look at the dogs. "Be good."

"They'll be fine."

As we headed upstairs, I tried to focus on anything besides her Lycra-clad bottom. Pictures hung on the wall, old snapshots of Sasha and Isisa as teens next to Nandi's graduation photos. Isisa in her cap and gown graduating law school was beside Sasha's Navy portrait and other photographs of the three of them together. No matter how many times I passed by, I never tired of looking, feeling like I caught some new detail with each observation. The distraction helped.

"Sasha said you were worried about me." She closed the bedroom door behind us.

I hesitated for a beat. "A little."

"I do like you. I like you a lot." While I was accustomed to Sasha's blushes against her fair skin, I had learned to study Isisa and Nandi for other signs. Nandi wrung her hands and toyed with her clothes. Isisa dropped her gaze to the floor and avoided eye contact.

I stepped close and took her face between both of my hands. "You don't need to explain it. I can wait."

"No, I do. I don't want you to feel like because I'm not jumping your dick every other night like Sasha that I don't care. Or that I'm disinterested in you because I don't want to sit in your lap all day like Nandi."

"Talking with Sasha helped me to understand why you haven't been physically affectionate all the time. It's fine. I'm not in this to pressure you into moving forward."

Her teeth skated over her bottom lip, full and plump.

I'd only tasted her a couple times, kissing her always the gentlest. She was the most controlled compared to the two insatiable wildcats beside her.

"I guess... I was worried you were too good to be true. I know Sasha and Nandi claimed and marked you," she said, stroking the imprint left by Sasha's teeth, "but I keep waiting for the other shoe to drop. For something to happen that proves you aren't perfect for us after all. Once I bond with you, it's sealed. It's forever. Permanent. I won't want to be without you, and it would take all of my willpower to separate if the need arose."

I nodded and stepped forward into her touch. "It is. And I'm willing to accept that risk if you're willing to have me."

She closed both hands around a handful of my damp T-shirt. "I know. Talking with her about your concerns made me realize we wouldn't find a better male."

"I want to be there for all of you, however you need me. That extends beyond sex, baby." I pulled her in closer by the hips. When I slipped my thumbs into the band of her leggings, she didn't draw away.

"What if I want it to be sex this time?"

"Then..." The mere thought and promise of sex sent a hot pulse of arousal straight to my dick. It tensed beneath my gym shorts, and a forward nudge pressed against her. She shimmied back in return, her lips eagerly seeking mine. The sweet taste of her invited me to sweep my tongue into her mouth. Her fingers danced over me, tracing the hard outline of my dick at first, and then delving inside to take it in her hand. Those slim and articulate fingers stroked up and down, exposing me to the cool air of her bedroom.

I nudged down her leggings and slid my fingers down the front of them, breaching the elastic band of pink panties. The soft warmth of her greeted my questing fingers, and she sighed my name.

"Tell me what's different about you from the other two." I'd already learned a few of Sasha's quirks. My lovely blonde and Nandi both loved snuggling after sex, but orgasms wired Nandi harder than a hit of coke. She'd remain awake chatting about anything that interested her afterward, or slip out of bed to write.

"I, uh… I like toys."

"I take it you don't mean the cutesy kind."

"Not unless you count fuzzy handcuffs."

The mental image conjured by her words made my breath catch in my chest.

"Do you want to see?"

"I'd be an idiot not to."

Isisa wiggled away from me and crossed the room to her bed. She bent at the foot of it, providing a delicious view of her exposed ass cheeks.

God bless the creator of the thong.

She pulled a trunk from beneath the bed and flipped open the lid, revealing an impressive collection of sex toys, jars of oil, and other novelty items I'd only ever seen in dirty magazines.

After rising to kiss me, she slid a small, bullet-sized vibrator into my hand. "It takes me a while to get… ready."

"I got all day."

Isisa led me into an enormous shower with an umbrella fixture angled toward us. We ended up beneath a gentle mist, soaping and washing each other between rounds of hungry kisses, her body pinned against the tile while hot water streamed over my shoulders. No matter how I teased, no matter the angle, she writhed in frustration and grasped, on the brink of orgasm but never there.

I took it as a personal challenge. After drying Isisa first, we moved to her bed. I lifted her with ease from the floor and set her on the edge of the tall sleigh-style bed with her long legs dangling over the edge. My cock throbbed between her soft folds.

Inch by inch, I slid forward.

She tensed, froze up beneath me with large eyes. She as so unbelievably tight the breath left me in ragged gasps, and when I started to withdraw, she curved a leg around me, drawing me back.

"Don't stop."

My head fell forward, and I groaned out a curse. Nothing had prepared me for the way she fit, making every second of preparing her worth the wait. Her body squeezed down around my cock and her back arched from the bed. The blankets bunched up in her fisted grip.

"Esteban?" My name became a soft whisper, a breathy moan.

"Hm?"

"I like the way *you* feel."

I turned my head and kissed the ankle balanced on my right shoulder. A tug on her hips brought her closer to the edge of the bed to meet my next slow thrust.

"Harder," she said. "I don't want gentle, baby."

"You sure?"

In answer, she thumbed on the bullet and lowered it between her legs, angling it against her clit and my taut flesh. The vibrations sent tingles racing up my spine. When I dragged out and thrust in anew, we made a slick, lewd noise together.

Isisa lifted her other leg and balanced it over my free shoulder. Hands on her hips, I gave her everything she asked for and more. Our position allowed for deep penetration and gave me the perfect view of her quaking breasts and mile-long legs. Each thrust pushed her across the sheets with only my grip dragging her back to meet the next stroke.

"Is this what you want?"

"Yes!

I didn't stop until she screamed. Her ecstatic cries bounced against the walls, and her legs dropped from my shoulders to circle around my waist instead. With another stroke, her body tightened around me. She drew me down by a hand to my nape and bit down on my shoulder.

Pleasure and pain combined into an explosive jolt that seared through every nerve and left me feeling like my blood was aflame. My eyes rolled back in my head, and I slumped down over her, struggling to maintain consciousness while her powerful claim rocked through me.

"Damn, girl."

"Now you're mine, too." A beautiful smile lit her face.

Once our bodies stilled and our breathing slowed, we crawled up over the blankets and stretched out. I gave Isisa her space, content to lie beside her and do nothing else.

"So, I'm just curious, what were you going to do if I had turned out to be some asshole since Sasha bonded with me weeks ago? What was the plan then, since I couldn't just walk away?"

"You would have disappeared, and I would have consoled them both as they mourned."

I studied her face, waiting for her to break out into a wide grin, waiting for the humor. It didn't come, and those solemn brown eyes told me she'd been prepared to leave my remains buried somewhere in the Texas wilderness, never to be seen again.

"Well," I said, running my fingers through my hair. The chill lingered a few seconds, warmed only by the weight of her breasts against my chest. She wiggled onto me, resting on her forearms. "If I ever have problems I can't solve through peaceful means, I know who to call."

Isisa leaned down and nuzzled my throat. A few of her loose braids tickled over my shoulders. "Being a lawyer gives me adequate insight into how to get away with murder."

"That is somehow both terrifying and sexy."

We both dozed until Nandi arrived sometime after sunset with dinner. We ate tender roast beef with her and celebrated the milestone in our relationship with one of Isisa's choice reds, putting her back to sleep again.

Nandi crawled into bed with us and snuggled against my opposite side, sandwiching me between her and Isisa. It was like dying and having a taste of heaven, two of my favorite women in one bed. The only thing missing was Sasha's blonde curls against my cheek. Nandi snuggled into my chest and burrowed her face against my throat.

At first I was content to lay there just like that, but my fingers seemed to have ideas of their own. I slid my palm across Nandi's back and sought out her bare skin. She didn't have a stitch on beneath her pajama shorts. I stole a stealthy look at Isisa but found her looking back at me.

Isisa flashed me a drowsy smile. "Go ahead. Just because I'm not always in the mood, doesn't mean I don't like to *watch*."

"Yeah?"

She reached over and stroked Nandi's curls back from her face in a loving gesture. "Well… maybe I'll help you out a little. I bet you and I can make little kitty here positively purr with satisfaction."

Lord help me, but I'd never been so turned on in my entire life. Or so eager to rise to a challenge.

～

*A*fter opening the floodgates to a sexual relationship with all three lionesses, I had to find time to rest. Between their different appetites, work, and spending time together, I spent less and less time at home and ended up bringing Rambo and Ripley along with me more days than not, because it seemed like they'd also bonded with Simba.

Apparently my absences had been noted. I'd barely been home half an hour before my mother texted to let me know she was coming over. Ten minutes later, she arrived at my door with a crockpot casserole in hand.

"I made you dinner," she announced. "Your food must all be bad."

"What makes you say that?"

"You haven't been here to eat it, that's why. Sergio says you head to Houston a lot."

My brother, the spy. I should have known.

While she fussed with the food, I pulled down two plates and glasses. Sure enough, the milk in my fridge was past its prime, but I had a brand-new bottle of sweetened iced tea I'd never gotten around to opening. Mom clucked her tongue but didn't say anything. In her house, tea was made from scratch.

"Sergio says you've had trouble at work."

Sergio said a lot of shit. Enough for me to decide to speak to him with my fists next time we crossed paths. "Nothing I can't handle. We had some vandalism, but I filed a police report and they have a patrol car drive by every night."

"Mr. Dupont is nice?"

"Yeah, I guess so. He's a decent guy for a man with too much money to spend. Fair. Doesn't mistreat us and keeps his word."

"Sergio called him strange."

"Strange is an understatement." The man lived like a recluse. Or maybe a playboy. His daytime hours were booked solid, and any of our meetings always happened past dusk, usually over dinner.

"Fine then, enough about your employer. Tell me about this woman you are bringing over, instead."

Her choice of conversation shift didn't seem any easier than talking about Mr. Dupont.

"Actually, I'm bringing three."

"Three? Oh, does she have friends in need of a place to enjoy the holiday? That's fine. The more the merrier I always say."

I hesitated. Did I own up to the fact that I was dating three women in a single, polyamorous relationship or did

I do as Sasha suggested and pass the other two off as friends?

Not only would I be dishonest to my mother, but I'd be misrepresenting a relationship with two amazing women. Nandi's shy smiles and Isisa's cheerful laughter deserved to be shared with the rest of the Castillo clan without a lie.

"No, I mean I am bringing three women over who are in a relationship with me."

Mamá stared at me, looking down her nose in a way I'd seen a million times over the years. "That is not funny, Esteban."

"I'm not making a joke."

"What do you mean you are seeing *three* women?"

"You asked me to go out and meet a woman. I did. Three of them, and they're all amazing. Sasha is a doctor, Isisa is a lawyer, and Nandi writes bestselling novels." Like ripping off a fucking bandage, I let it spill without holding back a single aspect of what we had, because somehow in the short time since I'd met them all, those three women had come to mean the world to me.

Because in the short time we'd been together, I'd come to realize they cared more about my happiness than Gabriela ever had. They were real and open, baring their relationship and trusting me to see them as people. The ladies, my ladies, had been open from the start about their expectations, save for Sasha's hesitation to reveal the entire truth at the beginning.

And hell, I understood that. Protecting Nandi and Isisa had taken precedence over providing full disclosure to me, a stranger they'd barely known at the time. They wanted the same things I wanted. The things Gabriela had once claimed to want, too.

And I trusted them to keep their promises.

"Ma?"

My mother clutched her rosary in a white-knuckled, bloodless grip. The color and warmth had drained from her face. "Tell me this is a joke, Esteban. A joke in poor taste."

"It's not," I said in a gentler voice. "I'm dating three of them. It's a little complicated, but I care about all of them. They're together too, but they want kids and—"

When she was truly upset with me, she always reverted to speaking Spanish. The language poured out of her all at once. "I didn't raise you to behave like this, going from woman to woman. What kind of girls could they be? Three of them? It isn't right. It isn't normal."

"Mamá—"

"No. I won't have this at my table. What kind of example are you setting for your brother, Esteban? What would Samuel think if he were to see this shameful behavior?"

When the rest of her Spanish tirade ended, I replied to her in English. "It *isn't* shameful. I care about them, and they care about me. I didn't set out looking for three women, okay? Now that we're together, I'm happy. I'm happier than I've been in the years since Gabriela left. And if you can't understand that, then I guess I won't be coming to Thanksgiving dinner."

Her expression hardened. Mamá straightened her spine and pushed her shoulders back to stare at me. "You would choose this over your family. Over your own mother?"

"If you won't give them a chance, then yeah, I guess I'm choosing them instead when it comes to Thanksgiving."

"This is not how I raised you to be." She peered down her nose at me.

"You raised me to be a good, honest, and charitable, hardworking man. I like to think you did right since I'm all of those things, but my feelings are what they are, and you aren't going to change that."

"It is against the law," she said, changing tactics.

"No, marrying all three of them would be against the law. There's nothing that says I can't be in a healthy physical relationship with multiple people."

"*Ay dios mio.*" She leaned against the wall and crossed herself like I'd admitted to fucking my way through a Satanic harem.

In her eyes, maybe I had.

Mamá turned on her heel and stalked to the door, skirts swishing and twirling around her ankles. "Wait until I tell your father."

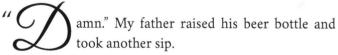

"*D*amn." My father raised his beer bottle and took another sip.

"That's all you have to say?"

"What the hell did you expect me to say? Pick one? Stop doing it? You're a grown-ass man and you can make your own decisions. Hell, I figure around Christmas when you're broke from buying them each gifts, you'll have second thoughts on your own."

"Says the man who bought a three-thousand-dollar meat grinder."

He grunted and took another drink. I didn't rush him, but he spoke up on his own when the bottle was empty. "So, how does that work?"

"How does what work?"

"Do you please them all at once?"

"Are you really asking me to go into detail about my sex life?"

"What? You're a Castillo. We pride ourselves on our stamina. When I was your age, I could have handled three just fine." He paused, considered his boast, then added in a mutter, "Don't tell your mother I said that."

"Your secret's safe with me."

In the hours since our argument, I'd already received calls from Sergio, Samuel, and Selene about our mother's irrational antics over my love life, and finally, she'd made good on her threat to send my father.

And as usual, Pops secretly had my side.

"Your mother will calm down."

"I somehow doubt that. She's all worked up."

He shrugged in the casual way of a man who knew his wife of four decades, and grinned. "True, but she'll get over it. Trust me. I'll talk to her. You know she wants you home with the family for the holidays."

"Then she needs to understand I won't put up with any disrespect against my ladies. If she can't be civil, I won't be there. End of story."

"Understood. And, for what it's worth, I agree with you, Stebi. You know, of all the kids, you've always made us the most proud—"

Stebi. No one but a few of my cousins and Ma usually

called me that. My father hadn't used it since I left for boot camp. "Pops, you—"

He held up a hand. "No. Let me finish. The rest of your siblings have done great things with their lives, but you've done so much more. You sacrificed years of your youth serving this country, years other men spend drinking with their boys or living at home. You took over this business and you turned it into something I could have never accomplished. Multi-million-dollar contracts and deals with billionaires. When this business started, it was only seven of us building homes in little rural towns, hoping to have enough money left over to put food on the table for our families. Papá Sergio believed in me when he handed me the money to start this business, believed we could do this on our own. Now look at us. More than we could have ever dreamed of having."

Tension squeezed my throat, tightening my jaw, and wrapped an iron fist around it. I tried to swallow it down. "You would have gotten there without me."

He shook his head and pointed to the driveway, where his shiny new Cadillac gleamed beneath the sun. It was lime green, a special paint job he'd had done to resemble a car he drove when he was young. "No. Under me, we made enough to get by. Enough to be comfortable and to meet our needs, but you've brought the kind of success that fulfills our wants. That new car out there, it's because of you that I drive it. The BMW your mamá always wanted, we have that now because of your help. Your sister has everything she needs at college. We go on family vacations. We tour the world. You sent us to Madrid last year for two weeks, you remember that? I enjoy these final years in retirement because of you."

Blinking didn't help. My eyes still burned. "Pops…"

"And now, your mother who loves you so much, is judging you for living your life in a way she doesn't like, despite all the good you've done."

In the past, Ma had forgiven me for a dozen ridiculous mistakes. I'd broken windows with baseballs, dinged her brand-new car against a tree when I was in high school, broken the dishwasher by using the wrong soap, and throughout it all, she always hugged me and forgave.

"She'll come around."

"I know she will, but it doesn't change that we have done you a terrible disservice. Your mother and I have kept something from you a long time, because we never thought it mattered. It never mattered to *me*, so we didn't bring it up."

"Bring what up?"

He shifted in his seat and took another long drink. The humorous mood of the evening had faded. My stomach felt heavy, chest tight. Why wouldn't my father make eye contact with me?

"Your mamá was pregnant with you when she and I met. Didn't bother me none, though she took some convincing to believe that. I just knew from the moment I saw her, she was the woman for me. I had to have her, and I figured that meant the whole package. You and her both. Eventually, she gave in to my charms and married me."

Everything I'd ever known about my life changed in the course of a few seconds. I wanted to be furious at him. Wanted to rage and sweep the phone from the cradle to make a call to their house.

Instead, I was numb. My dad wasn't dad. Mom had lied to me. Forty-two years of my life wrapped in fucking falsehoods because no one ever thought I deserved to know. "So you're saying you're not—"

"As far as I'm concerned, you *are* my son."

"Of course you are. Sorry, that's not what I meant." The conversation needed more than beer. I abandoned my seat long enough to grab two glasses and a bottle of tequila from the cabinet—one I'd been saving for a long time—then dropped back down beside him.

"You're angry with me. And you have a right to be."

"No," I said after a moment, furrowing my brow and focusing on the bottle in my hands. "I'm not mad. I'm confused. I feel kind of betrayed that nobody figured in all this time I should be told there's another man out there sharing half my DNA, but I'm not angry."

We drank for a while in silence, neither of us speaking while the truth rattled around in my brain and I gave it time to sink in. On the third glass, my tongue loosened enough to ask questions. "So, uh... what happened?"

He shrugged. "When she and I met, she was trying to figure out how to tell her family what she'd done, and didn't want to admit she'd gotten into trouble."

I hesitated, torn between wanting to know more and casting it all aside. I had a father right in front of me.

Did I need to know anything more? Did it matter who he had been?

Succumbing to curiosity, I sucked in a breath and asked a single question. "Do we know anything about him or who he is?"

"She knows his name, but he's nobody to me. Just someone she once knew in Puerto Rico, and nobody special. The bastard vanished on her. They'd only been together a few months before he did his disappearing act.

But it never mattered to me. His loss was my gain. He missed out on raising a great kid. And I'm proud of you, Stebi. Everything you've done with your life. It doesn't matter to me if you want three women as long as you do better for them than the *hijo de puta* I inherited you from."

I nodded. "I will."

Pops nodded, too. The drinking resumed in silence, both of us sitting with tears in our eyes. My blurry vision made the room shimmer around me and distorted my view of the only man in my fucking life who had ever mattered. "Treat them good. Always treat them good and make them feel loved."

That other guy, the dude who abandoned my mother, fuck him. This was Pops. I repeated that in my head a few times, making it an internal mantra. "I will."

And then I didn't need to repeat it anymore, because it was true. He *was* my dad, and no one else ever could hold a candle to him.

19

ESTEBAN

*W*ith a little help from Nandi—she'd tipped me off about Sasha's schedule—I was waiting for Sasha when her shift ended. They'd only needed her to work eight hours into the afternoon, a rare short day for her in the ER. I'd kidnapped her from the hospital with every intention of preparing a homemade dinner while digging for information on what to get Isisa and Nandi for the holidays. My plan was to get each of my ladies alone to get ideas for the others.

What did you get the women who had everything?

"I'm afraid my fridge is woefully empty, but we can run down to the store once we figure out what we're making."

"This is your show, remember? You pick, and I'll eat it," she said.

"Sure. You okay, though? You seem distracted."

"Huh?" Sasha turned her gaze away from the side mirror and blinked. "Sorry. I thought someone was following us, but they turned off a block or so back. Random black Escalade."

That news made my brows raise. I darted my gaze to the rearview mirror but saw nothing. "Do you always watch for a tail?"

Rosy heat suffused her cheeks. "Only when my boyfriend says creepy, swarmy jerks are threatening him."

"Trust me. I'm not worried about them."

"Esteban, the Medrano family has ties to the FEL. I've treated some of their victims at the hospital, so don't fucking tell me you aren't worried about them."

How the hell did she know that? "They'd be idiotic to actually do anything. Dupont isn't afraid of them, and he could cost them business in Texas entirely. Hell, the man probably could get them blacklisted across the whole damn country."

She stared at me.

"I'm being careful. Look, I know you work undercover and shit with Nadir for your pal, but you don't have to be on the job when you're with me. I can take care of myself, okay?"

"Okay. Um, we need to talk about something later. Not now. Just later, after dinner."

"All right." I parked in the driveway and killed the ignition. Before getting out, I leaned over and kissed Sasha, tipping her face up to meet mine. Her tension faded, and she melted against me. "How's enchiladas verde sound?"

"Mm. Sounds good to me. I'd eat anything you made."

When I slipped my key in the lock and twisted, it slid effortlessly to the side, silent. Had I left my door unlocked all day? My brows bunched together, and I locked it, testing the key. Unlocked it again, the lock mechanism clicked.

"What?"

Quietly, I withdrew the key and shoved the ring in my pocket. "Go back to the car."

"What? Why?"

"I think someone went inside my place."

"Doesn't your brother come over to walk the dogs?"

Intuition tingled down my spine. I shook my head. "No. Samuel knows better than to leave doors unlocked. And he texts me, 'cause he always borrows something." He always sent me a text message, letting me know if Rambo and Ripley had been good, because the kid took a lot of pleasure in helping me out with the two fosters. He'd been trying to convince our parents to let him adopt a dog from the shelter ever since I'd brought the two home.

"Then if someone is in your place, I think I should definitely be staying with you and not cowering in the car like a little girl." Her tone was even and calm, the voice of reason penetrating the machismo demanding to take charge.

I gritted my teeth. "Fine."

Keeping Sasha behind me, I touched the Smith & Wesson beneath my jacket. Cold metal met my fingers. Drawing it with one hand, I pushed the door open with the other and moved inside. To my left, the open living room appeared untouched, expensive equipment, television, and video game systems where I left it. Ripley and Rambo were standing with their bodies stiff inside their crates. Ripley growled.

The hairs on the nape of my neck rose. Sasha moved behind me, breath a whisper in my ear.

"Someone's here. A couple someones."

"Yeah." Intuition was a hell of a thing. The thing about being in the Marines is that, whether you had a job behind a computer or joined the special forces, the first and foremost thing we learned was how to kill and how to be damned comfortable doing it. No one enjoyed taking a life—at least, few people ever owned up to it—but we all had the balls to do what was necessary to protect ourselves and our squadmates.

Years of training flooded back to me. I moved forward past the living room after a glance at every corner and the blind spots. No one there. Dogs would have barked if someone was. Sasha moved with me, never in my way even when I swung to the left or right and swept the room.

There were at least five other rooms to hide in my house, including the upstairs bed and bath. Finally, I raised my voice. "If you're here, you better haul ass out of my place before I give you a reason to regret it."

Turning a corner into the kitchen brought me face to face with an armed intruder. We both leveled our handguns at each other, but after a moment of eye contact, the asshole shifted his a few inches to the left.

"Drop the gun, or your chick dies. I got her square in my sights, homie, and at this distance, I ain't missin'."

"Or maybe I'll shoot you first. Whatever you came to get, is it worth dying for, kid?"

A creak on the floorboard behind me alerted me seconds too late to what I knew was coming, but couldn't prevent. I knew every sound in my house, every loose board I'd intended to fix, every groan and moan of a loose rail.

The second spoke up. "You ready to die with him, old man?" His gun clicked.

Fuck. Two against one. Masculinity and years of training told me I could still take both of them with the element of surprise—but with an unarmed girlfriend in the room, I couldn't risk her life, too. Not with these odds. While I loathed to do it, I crouched down and set the gun on the floor.

"Good. Don't need you playing hero." The second thug kicked the gun aside and joined his cohort in the kitchen. From the corner of my eye, I saw the weapon strike one leg of the dining table. Sasha shifted her weight from one foot to the other, and her posture changed.

Assessing the lay of the kitchen and positions of the two gunmen, I curved an arm around her waist and guided her behind me, turning my body to place her between me and the sliding doors. The glass doors, maybe they'd shatter in a gunfight. Maybe she'd be able to escape.

Maybe it was foolish to keep a werelioness behind me, like she needed my protecting or saving, but something about leaving her exposed and out in the open rebelled against my sense of decency. Knowledge of the beast she could become warred against my perception of the very feminine and slender woman at my rear. One of her arms had encircled my waist, her palm against my chest. She curled her fingers into my T-shirt. A warning.

Sasha wasn't a fragile damsel in distress needing me to rescue her.

It didn't matter. Didn't matter if it was Sasha, Samuel, or one of the guys on my crew, I'd put myself between anyone and a bullet because it was just the way I was raised.

"Look, if it's money you want, we can do that. I have three hundred dollars in my wallet and an assload of cards, man. Take all of it."

One of them laughed. He looked young, eighteen or nineteen with a buzzed head and tattoos crawling up his neck. A sleeve on his right arm displayed a pair of crossed Mexican cavalry blades. Shit. Gangbangers.

"We're not here for money. We came for this blue-eyed bitch. Move out the way and we won't fuck you up, too, Castillo."

"What? You're here for *her*?" And they knew my name. The chilling realization turned my body to ice.

The thug tightened his grip on the gun. "Get over here, bitch. You gotta make amends for what you did to my homie, David, and his boys. Lost us a lot of cash."

I stared at them. "What the hell are you on about, man?"

"A bunch of sleazebag assholes who were drugging girls and videotaping their abuse," Sasha said in a low voice. "They picked the wrong target when they nabbed me."

Tension burned in my muscles and tingled beneath the skin, raising the hairs on my arms and the nape of my neck. Hell if I knew what kind of mess Sasha had gotten into, but I wasn't moving. Two tours in Iraq had introduced me to the faces of killers, and these two guys had the eyes of stone-cold murderers. It didn't matter that she was a woman.

It didn't matter that she'd burst out of her clothes and become a sleek killing machine the moment they touched her. Lions weren't impervious to gunshots. A coat of fur wouldn't make her bulletproof. It'd still punch a hole in her, and one lucky hit was all it would take.

A third voice spoke up behind us. "Yo. Hurry this up."

Sasha tapped her fingers twice over my heart. Two more men. The odds of us escaping the situation changed from slightly improbable to almost impossible.

"Not gonna ask again." The first man aimed his gun slightly to the left and fired. The round tore through my fridge, punching a hole in the stainless steel.

"The next one goes through your head, man. Or maybe I'll tag your bitch first in the leg. She doesn't need them for what we've got in mind."

"All this fucking playing around. Just grab her—"

One of the new arrivals barreled forward and shoved me aside. I resisted it, twisting my body with the momentum of his charge. His fingers closed around Sasha's wrist. My arm swung up and delivered a chop against his nape, all reflexes and muscle memory taking over.

The first shot hit me in the shoulder, a sharp in and out lance burning through me and splashing blood against the glass door.

"Esteban!"

A bone-deep ache began in the core of my arms and legs, and fire raced down my spine. It happened in the course of a few seconds, but it felt like hours, infinite agony dragging me into a white-hot abyss. The loose T-shirt I'd worn stretched taut across my torso and split at the same time my jeans burst at the seams. There were shreds of denim and cotton everywhere, my shoes obliterated, my senses overwhelmed. The light shone too bright, the air too thick with the smell of cheap cologne, marijuana, and the sour odor of fear permeating the air.

Because they were afraid. Because they were growing all the more terrified.

Instincts took the place of reason. When I charged forward to disarm the thug holding the gun on us, another poorly aimed shot whistled past my ear. Shattered the glass.

Anger. Fury. I had to protect Sasha. Mine.

The thug screamed, no match for the grip I took of his wrist. The next shot went wide. There was blood in my mouth, bone smashing, sinew tearing. Cloth ripped under my fingers. Fingers? Not fingers now. They were paws tipped with claws sharper than fish hooks, easily rending flesh and ripping through muscle. Blood welled up beneath them.

One was getting away. Prey. Fast prey on two legs dashing toward an open door. Seconds from fresh air and a shaded yard where I wanted to be. Sunlight and trimmed grass. Leaves. Birds. Neighborhood scents washed over me, the wind carrying the smoke of hickory from a winter cookout.

Sharp pain exploded in my foreleg. I ignored it, eager to catch prey. I overtook him in two bounds and pinned him to the cold floor. Tore his shoulder, severed a limb. Ripped him into shrieking, terrified pieces that couldn't cause more harm. Relief fell over me when the screaming ended. It had hurt my ears, their shrieks high-pitched and desperate. But that didn't matter, because I'd won and protected my woman. I'd shown her I was the strongest, the meanest, and the biggest. Shown her I was *worthy*.

Whirling, I turned to face my mate. A pair of big blue

eyes stared at me from the kitchen entrance, and all I could hope was that I'd made her proud.

~

SASHA

hy couldn't they have come for me when no one else was around, especially Esteban? I'd had a feeling my snooping around would anger someone, but I didn't expect them to send hired thugs with Esteban present.

How could I indicate to him it was okay? That I wanted this and needed to go with them to find out what the hell was going on? As a trained operative, half of my life had been dedicated to espionage and covert infiltration.

Four of them. The reflection in the sliding doors showed two men at the front door. The odds weren't great, even for me.

"All this fucking playing around. Just grab her—"

A big guy with a shaved head came up from behind and grabbed me by the wrist. His sweaty, meaty palms clamped a bruising grip, but before I even had the chance to pull away, Esteban turned and struck.

A shot fired, and the metallic tang of blood filled the air.

"Esteban!"

It happened too fast for me to do anything about it. One moment, Esteban had been standing in front of me playing the part of the unnecessary hero, and in the next, he was shifting and contorting into something else. One second, two at the max, and then there were pieces of clothing falling around us like confetti, and the biggest, angriest lion I'd ever seen lunged at our assailants. No. He didn't lunge; he became golden lightning, preternatural speed launching several hundred pounds of muscular male lion at a skinny gangbanger I could have snapped in half over *my* knee. This guy didn't have a chance.

"Esteban, no!"

Only it was too late and the young man was already dead. He twitched against the ground.

Of the remaining two, one bolted for the door and the other fired panicked shots at my lion. A round clipped his muscled foreleg and exited without striking the bone, but the other shots went wide. The side of my hand struck one thug's wrist and swept his arm to the side. The bullet meant for Esteban broke a lamp instead. Glass shattered.

I spun, twisting my body into roundhouse kick that snapped the man's head to the side. He staggered against the island counter, drooling blood on the pale marble surface. Springing forward, I brought an elbow down into the spot between his neck and shoulders. His chin bounced off the counter, and then he slumped to the ground.

Esteban caught the runner at the door and trampled him on the threshold beneath hundreds of pounds of muscle.

The last guy, the stocky bald one Esteban had dropped before his shift, groaned from the floor. He'd been injured but not knocked unconscious apparently. I stomped him in the balls with my medical clogs before crouching and cracking his head against the tiled floor.

Esteban's rumbling growls reverberated throughout

the house and echoed from the entrance hall. The first guy he'd mauled was in pieces nearby, not much more than shredded torso and a few dismembered limbs.

I turned the corner from the kitchen and stepped into the entrance to find him rising from his kill with blood on his paws and mouth, bits of flesh in his mane.

God, he was so handsome. At first, all I could do was marvel over the beauty of him and admire the thickness of his mane, all jet black and thick around his shoulders and neck. Eyes like burning amber studied me in return.

My senses returned, and fury flushed through me. I wanted to shove him. I wanted to walk away. Because in all this time we'd been dating, he had every opportunity, even after I'd shared *my* secret, to confess he was also a shifter. How the hell hadn't we noticed he was one of us? "Why didn't you tell me you were a shifter?"

He didn't reply.

"Esteban?"

He licked his mouth, silent. No comprehension shone in his eyes.

"Oh no. Oh no, no, no."

My boyfriend licked blood from his paws and stretched across the floor on his belly. He eyed the corpse in disdain, staring down his long nose at it for a while before he returned his attention to me.

"Esteban, please, return to your human body and answer me."

He yawned.

This isn't happening. This can't be happening.

Refusing to let down my guard just yet, I peeked outside and saw the same black Escalade I'd noticed earlier parked in the drive behind Esteban's Lexus.

Thankfully, the house was set far enough back no one would notice the extra car, but I wasn't so sure about the bloody body on his stoop. If his mom dropped by, we would be in deep shit.

Scratch that. His brother was more likely to pop by than his mother since they'd had their argument.

Only one number came to mind for an emergency like this. I whipped out my phone and hit the callback button. "Ian, we have a *big* problem."

"Yeah, what's that?"

"Um, you know that guy we're all dating?"

"Yeah? Esteban."

"Well…" Esteban nuzzled his enormous head against my chest and rumbled an intimidating, torso-vibrating noise.

"Sasha? What the hell was that?"

If I'd wanted to conceal the truth from him, I couldn't have even claimed it was Nandi or Isisa. This sound was deep and masculine, a throaty growl that ran shivers of delight down my spine. "It was Esteban. Ian, something is wrong. Four guys attacked us and tried to take me, and when they turned violent, Esteban transformed."

"Huh."

I tried to push Esteban away while I was on the phone, but a mournful look came to his face as if I'd wounded him to his soul.

"Yeah, that was pretty much my reaction. I think this was a first for him."

"How's he handling it?"

"That's where the problem is. He hasn't shifted back. I'm not sure he knows how, and I'm worried he might be lost to his animal side."

"Any injuries?"

"He took two gunshot wounds, but it's all soft tissue. Neither seems to be bothering him."

"Shifter regeneration will take care of that."

Esteban slumped beside me and threw his body across my lap. Between that massive black mane and his bulky frame, he covered everything from my upper thighs to my ankles.

After I gave him the address, Ian promised to arrive within the hour with backup. I just had to sit tight and keep my lion here.

I ended the call and wiggled the phone back into my pocket without standing, since Esteban had decided it was prime time for cuddling.

Despite the transition, he still smelled like Esteban, although the human scents I associated with the human man were an undertone beneath the musky scent of feline.

"You big, crazy lug. How did you manage to keep this secret, huh?"

He rumbled again and settled his head down, eyes closing. It figured he'd choose now for a nap, keeping me stuck beneath him. Instead of getting to clean up, I remained his unwitting prisoner.

An hour later, the familiar sound of Ian's Tahoe pulled into the drive. Esteban raised his sleepy head and peered toward the door. He snorted. I knew what he smelled, because I was also breathing in the scent of Juni and Nadir. Rabbit and golden jackal. Bald eagle, and the musky smell of feathers joined them as the cool breeze swept their individual aromas inside through the open living room window.

"It's open," I called out before anyone had the chance to knock.

"Safe to come in?"

"Yeah." My gaze dropped to Esteban, and I ruffled his mane. "Be nice, okay?"

For their sake, I exuded nothing but calm and reassurance, giving Esteban no reason to think the three were a threat.

Ian stepped inside first and blinked a few times. Neither Nadir nor Juni moved from the doorway, frozen in place as any wild animals would be in the presence of a massive predator like Esteban. Only Ian snapped out of it, and then he stepped forward with measured and slow steps, approaching a beast capable of crushing his human or animal counterpart into jelly.

"I'm not interested in your woman, big fella. And neither is Nadir. We came to give you a hand. You remember meeting me, don't you?"

"I wouldn't be so sure about that," I replied.

Ian nodded to the mauled gangbanger by the door. "And he did that?"

"And another in the kitchen. I killed one, and a fourth might still be alive. Not sure how hard I bounced his head against the kitchen floor, so no promises."

"Damn. You two don't do anything half-assed I see." He rubbed his face then pulled his government issued, encrypted phone from his pocket. After a glance at the screen, he shoved it away again. "There's some people on the way to handle this."

"His family lives nearby. I mean, like, *all* of them. We need to be discreet.

Ian's reassuring smile eased the worry churning in my

gut. "They'll be in and out. They're real professionals about this kind of thing, accustomed to cleaning up supernatural messes."

I nodded. "Okay."

It took Ian and me both to coax Esteban outside to the rear hatch of Ian's SUV. When I jumped into the back of the open hatch, Esteban hung back a step and eyed the dark interior. "Come on, big boy. Come on. You won't leave me to sit back here alone, will you?"

Encouraging Esteban to join me in the back of the SUV, I ran my fingers through his dark mane and beckoned him again. He tilted his head into the touch and closed his eyes while tickling his whiskers against my fingertips. After doing this a second time, Esteban caught the hint and leapt into the rear. Nadir shut the door behind us.

"Can one of you walk his dogs and feed them before we go? They've been caged for hours." I'd have Isisa and Nandi come to get the pups later.

Juni nodded and turned back toward the house. "No problem."

Nadir climbed into the rear, close enough to be supportive but still absolutely useless if Esteban decided to exert some muscle. My beastly beau eyed his friend, started to move, then the tension drained from him and he flopped bonelessly against me again. An ounce of recognition shone in his brown eyes.

Nadir had passed the test.

"That's right," I whispered, hugging him around the thick neck. "Nadir is a friend. You've known Nadir longer than me, and he won't hurt you or me. Isn't that right, Nadir?"

"Nothing could make me lift a hand against either of you."

Within twenty minutes, we were ready to go. A van marked with a local exterminator company pulled up by the garage. Ian spoke with them a few minutes before returning to his vehicle and climbing behind the steering wheel.

"They'll take the perps' vehicle back when they leave, and we'll give it a thorough search. I've already got someone tracking the plate numbers."

"I didn't get a chance to mention it on the phone but, uh, they were here about that whole fiasco I went through with those porno freaks."

Ian twisted around and stared at me. "Right. We'll talk about this when we get him somewhere out of sight. And safe."

Juni slid into the car again, carrying the scent of the dogs on her jeans. "All fed and cared for. Cute dogs. So, have you ever heard of anyone getting stuck in a shift?"

Nadir shook his head. "Never."

Ignoring the human blood in his fur, I kissed Esteban's nose. He stretched out his powerful limbs and relaxed again. "It's more than that. It's like... he doesn't realize he's human."

"I dunno, he seems to remember you at least."

"I'm not sure if it's me he remembers or he just smells that I'm a female of his kind."

Esteban tickled my lap again and rubbed his face against my breasts, eyes closed in euphoric feline bliss.

Ian grinned. "Maybe a mix of both. He knows he has it good right now. A woman's lap and some boob nuzzles? That's heaven."

I scowled at him but ultimately submitted to exactly that, my ferocious and fuzzy mate falling in love with my tits for the remainder of an hour-long drive to Quickdraw.

~

*I*an's place made the ideal safe haven for Esteban since we'd moved him from home. Sophia and Leigh were upstairs under strict orders not to come down for any reason while Esteban was on the loose, even though Sophia wanted desperately to see a male lion.

We promised she could have one look at him through the window as we led him from the SUV and into the backyard. Esteban seemed content to hang out there on the grass. Even with a slight chill in the air, the November sun shone with mild warmth. He flopped down on the patio and stretched.

Ian crossed his arms over his chest and studied the sprawling lion through the open sliding glass door. "Did you have any idea?"

"No. None." I peered back into the yard. "I mean, in hindsight, it makes a really weird sort of sense, but, no. No, I had no idea he was a shifter. And I don't think he did either. At all."

"It happens sometimes." Ian rubbed his nape. "It's rare, hell, I'd say you have a better chance of winning the Texas Powerball than a shifter does of having a child that can't shift. But it happens. Sometimes they repress it altogether and don't want any part in it. Or they're adopted. There was a term used among my grandfather's people. They were called Lost Souls. Shifter children who aren't acquainted with their shifter halves because they've been taken from their tribes too early to remember who they are. They're raised in non-shifter homes and eventually forget what they can do. They lose themselves and who they truly are. If Esteban had no one around to tell him what he was and teach him, the ability could easily remain dormant until the right stressor provoked the change."

"You've seen it before?"

"Once, a long time ago. It was a hazing gone wrong. I didn't arrive in time to stop it, but I saw how it ended. The kid was fresh outta boot camp, and as they were beating on him, he shifted into a falcon. He tore the lead aggressor a new one, and the guy needed about twenty stitches by the time it was over, most of them to the face and ears."

"Wow."

"Yeah, it was something to see. Then he flopped around on the ground, since he had no idea how to fly."

"What'd you do?"

"Only thing I could think of at the time during all the confusion." He chuckled. "I shifted, too, and gave him some flying lessons. Eventually his senses returned, and he was able to shift back. That was a long night of drinks and talk, let me tell you. Probably wasn't the smartest thing I've ever done, and after my CO finished tearing into me, I learned the proper protocol for handling spontaneous shifts in public."

Shifters almost always recognized shifters. Regardless of the inner beast inside us, we had a knack for picking our own kind out of a crowd, even if we couldn't identify the species. The military liked to sort us out early, often before we completed our physicals. Give us shifter commanding officers.

I imagined a much younger Ian—not a strand of white yet amidst his black hair—deferring to a pissed-off officer for his stunt. "What was that guy's story. Was he one of the lost ones?"

"Yeah. He was adopted, but he knew about it. I'm all for adoption when it's done responsibly, but when a shifter mother relinquishes her rights without notifying the proper people, lives are at stake. It's different when you're raised in the lifestyle and taught to shake off the animal instinct. We've had all our lives—entire childhoods —to grow accustomed to quelling the inner beast inside of us."

"What about Esteban? None of us recognized him."

"A true rarity. Have you met his family yet?" Ian asked.

"No, but I've never smelled anything but human on him."

"Then the best we can do is ask him when he comes to his senses." Ian sighed and ran a hand through his hair.

"Now what? What's going to happen with those four guys?"

"Taken care of. The great thing about working for the government is making problems like this disappear on a whim. His place will be good as new. As for the dead guys, we'll fabricate an accident and have the bodies turn up in a few days."

Ian could be so cool and collected when discussing these matters. And right now, I couldn't afford to do anything but mirror him while Esteban was counting on me.

"Sasha?" Nadir's voice echoed across the yard with a note of sharp concern.

"What?"

"I think you better get over here. Quick."

Esteban had been asleep a moment ago, peacefully sprawled in a patch of sunlight, but since our discussion began, the lion had awakened again and shambled to his feet. His body tensed with the posture of a predator stalking its prey, and when I followed his line of sight, I saw the creature in the distance. A rabbit.

Ian's privacy fence made a tight perimeter around the entire house, eight feet of solid wood boards with a lattice design adding another twelve inches to the top. Unaware of the beast lurking nearby, the rabbit nibbled on a plant in Leigh's vegetable garden.

"Oh no," I breathed.

Demonstrating the terrifying speed he'd displayed at his home, Esteban exploded forward. The rabbit dropped its lettuce leaf and bolted toward the fence line where it wiggled beneath it and disappeared.

"Shit, shit, shit," Ian said. "He can't jump that high, can he?"

Over the years of our service together in the group, we'd all seen each other naked so many times we didn't even keep count anymore. Modesty be damned, I yanked my shirt over my head and shoved my jeans down. "Doesn't need to!"

Ian took my cue and began undressing as well. Before he could shed his clothes, Esteban leapt onto the tree trunk beside the fence and scaled it in two powerful bursts. He jumped over the fence and the chase resumed beyond our eyesight.

I sprang forward and followed his path, bounding off the tree and over the fence in time to see Esteban's tawny ass disappearing into the bush. Damn, he was fast. A normal male lion wouldn't have a chance against a rabbit, but we weren't normal. Shifter genes made us the ideal example of our species, faster, stronger, and more resilient. A typical lion wasn't good for much but short sprints. Bursts of speed. They weren't built for prolonged chases.

But we weren't typical lions. If he had as much stamina now as he did in bed with me, this was going to be one hell of a chase.

I hadn't run like this in a long time, not since I'd last gone on a deer hunt with Nandi and Isisa out in these same woods. My paws kicked up fallen leaves and forest debris as we tore ass across the forest. Ian soared above us and kept pace.

God. How was he as good a hunter now in his lion form as he'd been as a man? Esteban rounded a corner, resembling a cheetah more than the enormous beast he was, and finally cornered his prey. One snap ended the rabbit's life, and then he laid on the ground to devour it, tearing off fur and swallowing meat.

Chest heaving, I slowed down and approached with cautious steps, respecting his boundaries as I would any male of my species in the wild. He was Esteban, but he wasn't at the same time, unaware of himself. Another step, a pause when he glanced up at me with big brown eyes set in the most handsome feline face.

I'm not going to take it from you, I thought, with all of my human awareness. Could he sense it and realize I'd never hurt him—never threaten him?

Esteban stood and grabbed the rabbit. He dropped it at my feet instead, appearing every bit the proud and mighty hunter, a reversal of the roles we'd have if we were wild lions roaming the savannahs of Africa.

He nuzzled my face and neck before dropping his haunches to watch me. He hadn't taken more than a bite of the tender creature. The rest was mine, a gift and token of favor as if some aspects of the human Esteban were seeping through his lion personality. I bumped my head beneath his throat and against the thick mass of ebony hair to show appreciation.

Unable to disappoint him by turning my nose up at fresh meat, I ripped away another layer of fur and tugged meat off its haunch. Esteban's instincts had taken over, gifting him with a knack for hunting that must have translated from his fondness for it as a human.

Maybe. Only time would tell if it was a fluke.

I shared the rest with him and then herded the big lion back to Ian's home. Nadir had waited for us in his human body to open the gate. We both strolled inside, though when Esteban tried to sprawl in the grass again, I nudged and guided until he rose to all fours.

Oh noooooo. We are going inside.

Like hell if I'd trust him again out in the grass.

20

SASHA

A couple hours later, Nandi and Isisa arrived with fresh clothes for both of us and lots of worries. Ian brought them to the garage where I'd settled down with Esteban on an old couch.

Nandi approached first with slow and measured steps, studying him with wide eyes. "Oh my gosh, look at him. He's *beautiful*."

"But how?" Isisa asked. She hung back in the doorway. "We are not like werewolves. It isn't contagious."

"Hell if I know."

Esteban raised his head from my lap and yawned. He licked his muzzle then met her gaze, gold on gold, his eyes as bright and vibrant as theirs. Nandi moved forward and held out her hand. He sniffed it then nudged his nose under her palm. She was won over in an instant, of course, enthralled by his powerful presence. Isisa, on the other hand, remained where she was.

"Hey," I said to her in a soft voice, crossing the garage to meet her. "It's still him. Nothing's changed."

Nandi had settled on the floor to hug him, resting her face against his mane and breathing him in. Esteban placed one paw against her back and bumped their cheeks together. "He's still ours."

I slipped an arm around Isisa. She leaned against my side while we watched Esteban and Nandi play on the floor. He was tender with her, soft paws and no claws, no touch of his teeth to her skin or aggressive growls. The male posturing and dominant behavior never arose. He rolled onto his back and let her pin him on the concrete.

Nandi pressed a hand against his paw and brushed her thumb over one of the individual pads. "He's gentle. Not like what I expected."

"He is," I agreed, "and right now, he's going through something we've never experienced. He's going to need us once he comes out of this and returns to his normal body. Need our support and our love until he can work his way through why this happened."

Isisa nodded. She swallowed and hung back a step, staring across the short distance between the door and Esteban. At last, she moved forward and pulled off her sweatshirt. "Then we should join him, yes?"

Nandi's eyes brightened. "Good idea. Let's take him outside for a hunt."

Between the three of us, Esteban didn't have a chance of getting away again.

~

*L*ater, after we'd had our fill of venison and rabbit, Leigh stretched three blankets over the garage floor and provided us with extra pillows. If Ian knew she'd been in there with us—with Esteban while his human awareness remained unconfirmed—he would have lost it.

"It'll be fine. I'm not worried about him. He's just a big kitty, aren't you, Esteban?"

Bless her loving, maternal heart.

Despite our worries, Esteban didn't move from the couch. We slept together in a big heap on the floor, cuddled together with blankets and all the comforts Leigh had provided.

When I awakened, Nandi and Isisa had already left and the aroma of bacon permeated the garage since it was located just off the kitchen. I spent a while with my head against his powerful chest, listening to the rhythm of his heart and easy breathing until my stomach rumbled.

I crawled away first and began to dress while he gazed at me with half-lidded eyes. "What? You know, if you would become human again, there'd be a delicious breakfast for you too. A breakfast with *cooked* food. You love bacon." I tugged on a shirt and knelt beside my sleepy lion again to cuddle him for a few last moments. The warmth of him soaked through my clothes. Perfect.

The door cracked open and Nadir stepped inside.

"Ah, good. You're awake."

"Yeah. I was just on my way out to join you guys."

"Uh-huh."

Lazily, I stroked a hand through Esteban's mane. "Did you need something or are you just here to interrupt my snuggles?"

"I came to ask if you'd tried to appeal to his human side again yet. You know, talk with him and see if you can stir some memories of being himself. I was going to give it a shot."

I gestured toward Esteban and stepped aside. "Be my guest."

Nadir took a slow approach before sitting on the ground at Esteban's level, leaning forward with his arms on his knees. "Hey, buddy, I really need you to snap outta this. Being lazy isn't you. You gotta shake this off and get back to work. Your brother's all worried, but we made some good excuses for why no one can contact you."

Esteban's ears pricked, but his head didn't lift from his massive paws.

"Do you remember the first time you saw Sasha at my parents' place? You couldn't stop looking at her out of the window. I told you to talk to her, but you were like, 'nah, man. I'm probably not her type. She looks expensive.'"

I snapped my attention toward Nadir. "He said that?"

"Oh yeah." He grinned. "Then after I introduced you as a doctor, I caught him in the attic and asked what he thought of you. He said 'totally beyond my pay grade' and nothing I said could convince him you'd be open to a date."

Laughing, I slipped down to join Nadir on the ground and placed both of my arms around Esteban. "I was never above your pay grade. But right now, I want to feel your arms around me again. I want you to hug me, and I want you to tell me how much you love me, so I can tell you the same."

I kissed the tip of his nose and closed my eyes, basking in the warmth of the mane tickling my throat. He made another one of his body vibrating rumbles, a sound that was pure heaven every time I heard it.

"He does love you. This happening to him, it's proof of that. We just need you to become you again, man."

The return to his human body happened faster than the transition from two legs to four. One moment I had a hold on his thick pelt, the next, it was a bare back. Long after Esteban's tawny fur became warm skin, his chin didn't move from my shoulder. Strong arms enfolded me within a tight embrace, squeezing the air from me, drawing me close, his body shuddering from the experience of returning from a shift for the first time.

Running my fingers up and down his back, I traced hard muscles and coaxed the tension from him until his grip eventually loosened. He didn't speak. A floorboard creaked, and a door gently shut. Nadir had left.

"Are you okay?"

He squeezed me again and shook his head.

"Take your time. I'm not going anywhere." I couldn't remember what my first shift had been like. I'd been a child, and many of us predators learned to shift at young ages, often taking our first tumble onto four legs around the time we learned to walk in our human bodies. It was a learned behavior, a talent we mimicked from our parents if we witnessed them changing often enough.

My father had been the one to teach my brother and me. If I searched deep into my memories, a vague recollection of his mane and the scent of savannah grass returned to me. And his blue eyes. The blue eyes my brother and I had inherited. But I couldn't remember that first time with the clarity I wanted.

Shifting for the first time rarely ever happened without a parent's guidance, which made Esteban, Ian's old Air Force friend, and the others like them anomalies in our community. Had he learned as a child, his shifter parent, or even both of them would have taught him to transition from beast to child, and child to beast, with the fluidity of rising or sitting in a chair.

I'd have to do it instead. We had time. All the time in the world. I kissed his throat, finding that little thump of his pulse, the scent of his lion still clinging to his warm skin.

Our embrace finally ended as Esteban sat back on his heels. He glanced down at his newly healed shoulder and the dried blood under his nails. There was another gunshot scar across his forearm. Both wounds were probably still tender under the surface, but eventually they would fade until only vague hints of discoloration remained. "I remember... I remember being shot by one of those guys. It's not a dream, is it?"

"No. You transformed, baby."

"I was... What the hell happened to me? *How* did that happen?"

Before I could answer, he twisted to the side and retched. He dry-heaved, but anything he'd ingested didn't come back up, too many hours passed since the mauling.

"Take it easy. Just breathe, baby." His knotted back muscles trembled beneath my palm.

"Where am I?"

"Ian's place. You met him at the Halloween party, remember?"

"Yeah and once before that, too, I think. You and Nadir worked with him before... I came and hunted on his property with my family and friends once."

"Yes."

"He didn't freak out?"

"Not exactly. You see, our whole team is made up of shifters. That's why I called them when this happened to you."

With my help, he sat up again and dragged his hands through his hair, eyes closed. "I don't even remember what happened really. We were heading inside and—" His eyes flew open. "That robber grabbed you. Two guys had busted in."

"Four, actually, but we handled them."

"You mean I…"

"The stress and emotions of the attack triggered your shift."

His eyes closed again, and he shuddered. "Shift."

Sympathy for his plight moved me to scoot closer and wrap my arms around him. "Ian said it's not unheard of to grow up unaware. Without other shifters around to teach them or anything to trigger the change, a person goes through life completely unaware of their animal side."

"What did I… what did I do? What *am* I?"

I pulled back, his face cupped between my palms, and held his gaze. "A lion. The most amazingly gorgeous lion I've ever laid my eyes on."

"What did I do?" he asked again, his voice barely a whisper.

"You protected me."

"Sasha, please don't try and sugarcoat this. What did I do?"

"You mauled two of them. I dropped the other two. Ian helped with the fallout from that. He's also making sure your house is cleaned up."

"I don't care about that. Are you okay?" Worry for

himself and his home were set aside, and he searched my body for signs of harm. "Did they hurt you?"

"I'm fine. They had no idea what they were dealing with. Plus, they underestimated you."

"Who were they?" He stopped his fruitless searching but kept his hands on my hips. "They knew us. They mentioned something..." His brow furrowed as he tried to remember.

"Thugs. I don't know exactly who, yet. Ian should be getting that info today from his contacts. You feeling up to seeing the others?"

"Yeah, I guess. Who all's here?"

A thought occurred to me. "Take a deep breath in through your nose and tell me what you smell."

"What?"

"You're a shifter. Even in our human form we have heightened senses. So, what do you smell out there? Who do you smell?"

"I smell motor oil because we're in a goddamned garage."

I rolled my eyes at him this time. "Beyond that. What else do you smell?"

Resigned to put up with me, he closed his eyes and drew in a few slow, deep breaths through his nose. "I smell... your shampoo. And that musky perfume you girls always wear."

I blinked. Had he always been able to smell it on us? "That's not perfume. That's just the way we smell."

He cracked open one eye. "In that case, why couldn't you tell I was a, um, shifter?"

"Because you've never been out of your human shape, so you don't have anything of your animal clinging to you. Now what else? Try to sniff out the others."

"I dunno. Fish, maybe? There's sort of a salty, fishy undertone to the place. Like a clean freshwater lake though."

"That would be Ian. He's an eagle shifter and loves flying over to Lake Livingston to catch a fish or two. With a little practice, you'll learn to differentiate scents and identify people, but for now, that's enough." I leaned over and kissed his cheek.

"Now what?"

"Now I get you some clothes and you get a shower. Go ahead and wrap up in the blanket so we can go inside."

I knocked on the door between the kitchen and garage then peered inside to see if it was clear of toddlers and children. Ian must have rounded everyone up, because the house was silent, but gleeful shrieking drifted in through the kitchen window from outside. With the all clear given, Esteban shuffled in with the blanket wrapped around his waist, and I guided him to the guest bedroom nearby.

We had a lot of ground to cover, and the sooner I had clothes on him, the better.

~

ESTEBAN

A shower and fresh clothes made a world of difference in how I felt. Isisa and Nandi had brought them from my bedroom in the penthouse.

I'd felt like Prince Akeem from *Coming to America*, two women in the shower with soapy breasts against my back and chest. More cuddling and hugging than washing went down. If there had been room for another person to squeeze into Ian's guest shower, Sasha probably would have joined us.

"Coffee?" Nadir offered out a steaming mug as I stepped barefoot into the kitchen.

"Yeah, thanks."

My ladies sat around a large breakfast table with an open seat between Sasha and Nandi. Isisa was between Nandi and Ian, and they had all gotten a head start on breakfast without me.

Leigh's warm and inviting smile welcomed me to the table, and then she placed an enormous stack of banana and chocolate chip pancakes in front of me, bathed in maple syrup and covered in a pile of bacon.

"Whoa. Uh, thanks."

Ian's wife had the soul of a 1950's homemaker and a smile twice as bright as the sun. She beamed at me. "No problem. It's about time you came out of there to eat. You must be starved for something that isn't so fresh it was running five minutes before you bit into it. How do you like your eggs?"

I raised a forkful of pancake. It was like tasting a buttery slice of sweet heaven. "However you want to make them is fine with me."

Sasha sipped her tea and gave me a sidelong look. "Don't be shy around Leigh. Cooking for others must be one of her kinks because the more you order her around in the kitchen, the happier it makes her."

"Honest truth," Ian confirmed. "How are you doing, by the way? Feeling good?"

"Scrambled then," I murmured. Leigh swatted her

husband with a dishrag then returned to the stove while the others studied me like a bug under a scope. "I guess. Feeling human again, yeah."

No one spoke while I ate, a kind of awkward silence falling over the kitchen nook. It persisted even after Leigh returned to set a small dish of scrambled eggs beside my pancakes.

After a couple more bites, I dropped my fork on the half-empty plate and leaned back in the seat, still starved but frustrated by the silence and lack of knowledge. "Are we not going to talk about what the hell happened yesterday?"

Ian offered a repentant smile. "My apologies. I was letting you get some grub in your stomach first. From what my acquaintances and I were able to determine, the thugs who broke into your home are tied to the same losers who picked Sasha up at Club Hysteria."

Someone had picked Sasha up at Club Hysteria? "Excuse me? When the hell was this?"

Ian's gaze cut toward Sasha. He stared at her. "You didn't tell him?"

"I wanted to wait until a good time…"

Nandi groaned into her palm.

I slapped my palms on the table. "Okay, is anyone going to fill me in? What the hell is going on?"

"Leigh and I are going to check on Sophia. She's a little too quiet for my liking." Ian abandoned the room in a tactical retreat and pulled his wife with him.

Nandi and Isisa stayed in their seats, but they both looked at Sasha with accusing, know-it-all eyes. Smug eyes. They knew something. Nadir, friend that he was, remained in his place leaning against the counter and occasionally raised his mug for a nonchalant sip of coffee.

Sasha's gaze dropped to her plate, but only for a moment. Then she looked up, straight into my eyes. "There's something I haven't told you about. I've been wanting to, but the timing hasn't ever been right."

"Tell me what? What have you been keeping from me, Sash?"

Nandi reached under the table and squeezed my knee in support. Isisa rubbed her foot against my calf.

"Before we met, I'd been at the bar. Someone roofied my drink and took me home. Tried to videotape me."

"Christ."

"I was fine. I knew what I was getting myself into, and I beat their asses. What we recently learned—what I *planned* to tell you after dinner yesterday—was that we discovered the Medrano family is behind it."

"Wait, what? Why—why wouldn't you tell me about this earlier? Dammit, don't you know how dangerous they are?"

"Apparently not *that* dangerous since you were gloating about how well you could handle them!" she shot back at me.

"That's different!" Furious heat swept into my face. I jumped up from the seat, fuming.

"Look, I had no idea until recently the Medranos were involved."

"You should have told me." Fear and anger pulsed through my veins, stirring the beginnings of an insidious tension headache.

"You're absolutely right. I should have," Sasha said, her

voice quiet. "I'm sorry. I... I didn't want you to worry, and I was wrong, okay?"

As much as I wanted to stay angry, it was next to impossible when she looked so miserable about her omission. The restless energy that had been building, that same tingling I'd experienced back at home, abated.

"I'll go tell Ian it's safe to come back," Nadir said. He stepped out, leaving us all alone.

I sighed. "Look, I get it. You were trying to protect me, but I'm not someone you need to protect. I'm your equal here, and I want you to trust me."

"I do trust you."

"Then don't treat me like a tender fucking plaything to defend." The words rushed out before I could bite them back, with more ferocity than intended.

Sasha flinched as if struck. "I've never seen you that way."

For the first time, Nandi and Isisa didn't speak up, quieting and averting their gazes.

I took a deep breath, letting it fill my lungs before I spoke again. "What am I to you?"

She blinked at me across the table. "Our mate. You know that."

"Treat me like one. From the start, I've had this occasional vibe from you ladies, all three of you—yes, even you Nandi—like I'm a pet to cuddle and fawn over."

"Esteban—"

"Let me finish."

Sasha's shoulders dropped, and she tucked her chin. I hadn't expected that to work. Isisa's back had stiffened, and Nandi had her lower lip between her teeth with her gaze lowered to the floor.

"All the time, I watch you three do nice things for each other, but when I try to help or do for you, too, you resist. I know you three have been on your own for years, and you can handle yourselves, but we're supposed to be in this together. That's fifty-fifty. That's not you protecting me, or me saving you. That's together. And I'd feel this way even if... whatever the hell is happening to me, didn't happen, and I was still a normal human joe."

"I'm sorry," Sasha murmured first.

"No need to be sorry. Just let me share the load."

Sasha nodded. "I promise."

"*We* promise," Isisa said.

"Nandi?" I reached over and tilted her chin up, hating the glistening tears in her amber eyes—but I had to be firm, had to make them understand.

"You've never been a plaything. I promise," she whispered.

Of the three women, Nandi was the least guilty of treating me like a fragile human. I hadn't felt like a two-legged Simba, or anything like that, but there'd been a noticeable difference from the way they behaved with each other.

Maybe shifting would help with that.

Maybe it was meant to be.

After kissing Nandi's pouting lips, I leaned close enough to squeeze Isisa's thigh. "Thank you." She relaxed at once, the tension bled from her body, and her eyes brightened.

"Safe to come in?" Nadir peeked around the corner.

With the weight off my chest, Leigh's delicious breakfast regained its appeal, and I was fucking ravenous again, unable to wait another second before digging into the enormous pile of bacon. "Yeah, we're good," I muttered around a mouthful.

He and Ian stepped in the room and retook their seats at the table.

"Let's pick this up where we left off. Why did they break into my house instead of getting her somewhere else?"

"Your neighborhood is a remote place with few witnesses, is my guess," Nadir said. "Why abduct her from a busy Houston street when they can drive an hour north and pluck her off your stoop?"

"That doesn't make any sense. I'm always at the penthouse with the girls. We don't go to my house much since I have nosy family nearby."

Ian ran his fingers through his silver-white hair. "Then it's possible they were following her from the moment you picked her up from the hospital. I should have had that video destroyed on the same night, but I think the footage of your involvement leaked, and they decided to get you."

"Get her for what?" Nandi asked, eyes wide in her face.

Sasha's grim expression didn't change. "To make me disappear."

"Is it too late to get rid of it?" Isisa asked.

That startled me. Law-abiding Isisa wanted to wipe evidence? Then again, she had been prepared to murder me and hide my corpse if I turned out to be an asshole to her mates.

"I'd say so." Ian glanced at Sasha. "Everything vanished from the evidence locker before it could be committed to the database. All of it's gone like nothing ever happened."

The moment I edged my chair from the table, Leigh

approached and refilled my coffee. The woman had to be a mind reader. I blinked up at her, but she only flashed me a smile and topped off Ian's cup too.

I sipped from the mug, mulling over the facts as we knew them so far. "Sounds like an inside job."

"Yeah, I said the same." Ian frowned. "Obviously, Internal Affairs is going to be all over this shit, but I don't trust them to handle it. Cops lost the evidence, and it'll take more than cops to shut them down. With that in mind, I petitioned the governor for his help and authorization to handle it my way."

When Sasha leaned forward, the sun glinted across her eyes, making them appear lit from behind like twin blue flames. "I want in on it, Ian. It's personal now. They tried to attack me and hurt Esteban."

"No," Nandi and Isisa spoke at once.

Sasha blinked at them. "No?"

Nandi tucked her chin and studied her lap, but Isisa spoke up for both of them. "You said you were done with the special operative gig. You promised you wouldn't have anything else to do unless Ian *needed* you."

"Isisa—"

"No. You said you were finished and that you'd no longer be putting your life in danger anymore. That we could settle and have a family and move on from all of that."

Shit. As hell threatened to break out between the trio of women, Ian shifted in his seat, trading glances with Nadir like they were going to tear out through the door again. I wanted to run with him.

"This isn't me going into a warzone. This is me

helping shutdown the creeps who have hurt dozens of women."

Nandi spoke up without lifting her gaze from her lap. "It's going to involve guns and gangs. That makes it a warzone. An urban one instead."

I licked my lips and considered the options. Letting Sasha go alone was out of the question, even if I knew she could handle herself. Had handled herself long before I came into her life. "What if I go with her?"

Isisa blinked. "Go with her?"

"I'm a Marine. I may not be in the service anymore, but I served for ten years. Plus, we know I'm not an ordinary human now." Dragging in a deep breath, I let the smell of them fill my nose and wrap around my mind until I could differentiate Nandi from Isisa, recognizing the hint of coconut and vanilla always clinging to the former. After that, I searched beyond those familiar scents of spice and lioness until the lingering hint of bird feathers reached my senses.

"You don't know how to control it," Sasha said, her voice gentle. "It took almost an entire day to get you to shift back."

"I'll learn." Before she could open her mouth again, I slanted a glance at her. "*You'll* teach me."

"So will I," Nandi said. "I'd feel better then."

Sasha turned a betrayed look upon her wife. "Nandi—"

"He's a Marine, and he's tough," Nandi continued in my defense. "I think you're being unfair. You want to go back on your word to us, then you need to take Esteban with you to do whatever it is you special agent people do."

"That isn't fair."

"Neither are you," Isisa said. "Those are the conditions

we're setting. If you want to return to duty, then you need an additional hand."

After releasing an exasperated exhale, Sasha turned to Ian. "Give me a hand with this."

"Their request isn't unfair, Sasha."

Her eyes flashed with indignation. Betrayal. "He's years out of training and doesn't know how to shift on his own."

"Right. I understand. But none of us learned over night, and this issue won't be solved tomorrow. We have time to whip him into fighting shape, and to be honest, Russ has no desire to return to duty. Now that he and Daniela are having their third—"

Some fury faded. Confusion clouded the anger stirred by Ian's apparent treachery. She blinked. "A third?"

Ian groaned into one hand. "Shit. I wasn't supposed to say that. *I'm* not even supposed to know. They want to do a whole party and everything this time around to announce it. Anyway, with a third coming along, Dani's not comfortable with him taking jobs. We could use someone else."

"There's Lyle. Julia gave him her blessing."

"She did, and I'm thankful. He's become a great member of the team with training, but we've both seen Esteban's power. He's fast. Not only that, but he's stronger than the rest of us. Maybe strong enough to make up for losing Russ. They're about the same size." Ian gave me another glance and whistled. "Esteban may be bigger. If he were any larger, we would have needed the van to bring him here."

I leaned over to take Sasha's hand in mine. My thumb swept over her knuckles, then I raised her fingers to my lips and kissed the tip of each. "We just had a five-minute conversation about this, Sasha. You can't protect me, but you can let me work alongside you. Give me a chance to learn."

"He has plenty of time. This mess with the Medrano family won't end any time soon. There's about a hundred of the slimy bastards," Ian said. "It'll take a while to gather the evidence we need and to put together an operation. Weeks. Maybe even months."

With the three of them—the four of us—against her, Sasha slouched in the seat and closed her eyes. Her head tilted back. "Fine," she finally breathed out. "Fine."

And with her blessing, I now had a limited amount of time to learn how to become a lion.

Something told me this was going to make thirteen weeks of basic training in the Marines feel like a piece of cake.

$\mathcal{T}$he unforgiving and frosty wind of a late fall afternoon wasn't kind to my bare ass. I shivered out in the cold on a blustery November day, Nandi's unfortunate student.

"No. You need to feel it," Nandi corrected me again. "You need to know what you are and feel it deep inside you."

"Feel it. Right." The only thing I felt was that I was an idiot because I was standing in the middle of Ian's yard without a fucking stitch of clothing on.

Between the three of them, Isisa's job kept her the busiest, Sasha a close second since the hospital actually needed her expertise for saving lives. That left Nandi, the homebody as they called her—my workaholic author—in control of my training. She'd taken the last few days off from writing to help me with shifting practice and concentration exercises to make it happen.

I glanced up and down the yard, taking in the height of the immense privacy fence. It stretched about eight feet up from the ground. "You sure nobody can see all this?"

"Private property for miles around and only shifters nearby. Anyone else would have to have a ladder or X-ray vision. Not shy, are you?"

"I'm not shy."

A big grin spread across her face. "I hope not. Didn't you have to shower with other guys in the military? You should be used to hanging free in front of other people."

I scowled at her.

"Anyway, you totally changed the subject. Come on, Esteban. If you can't get your shifting down, you won't be able to help her, whether that's today, next month, or next year."

"I know."

I tried to get my head in the game and think of it like any other skill that had taken time to master. Hadn't it taken time to learn how to roof a house and install a floor?

Standing with my arms at my sides and spine straight, I closed my eyes and let the cool autumn breeze whisper through my hair. It caressed my skin, and the grass stirred against the tops of my bare feet. Three days had passed since my accidental shift, and nothing had occurred since then. Not a damned thing.

Being thrust from one form into the next, I landed on all fours amidst the grass and arched my spine. A thousand scents and smells assaulted me. Fat and sassy squirrels in the trees. Rich vanilla body lotion wafting off Nandi's skin. Fuck, she was intoxicating, and everything about her smelled a thousand times better in this body.

"There's my big, handsome lion."

Nandi remained in her human shape and crossed over to me. Both of her hands caressed my face, and slim, articulate fingers slid through my mane.

"Now I need you to shift back."

Shift back? Why would I do that? Everything smelled amazing, her especially, and the sun warmed my fur. The teasing scent of prey drifted on the wind, something small and delicious like rabbit. I turned my nose into the wind, imagining the delicious morsel in my mouth.

Nandi turned my head and forced me to look at her.

"Take control of it before it controls you, Esteban. Remember who you are inside here." She placed her hand over my chest and touched above my heart.

I focused on turning paws into fingers and making forelegs into arms, but all I wanted was to rake my claws through the hard winter soil.

"You can do this," she continued. "Think about Sasha and Isisa. About me. Think about your family and remember what you have to come back to. Ignore everything else. Which would you rather have? Raw rabbit or a grilled steak with a beer?"

Fuck, I wanted the steak.

Groaning, I tried to step forward onto two legs, shedding the shifter skin and leaving the lion shape behind. I lost my balance and face-planted. Nandi made it seem effortless and fluid, and I was a clumsy baby in the dirt with a mouthful of grass. She didn't even try to catch me.

"See? You can do it. Shall we try again?"

"Already?"

Her cheek dimpled, and she leaned in, giving my cheek

a light peck. "Easiest way is just to do it over and over a few times. It'll get easier each time, I promise."

It did. I barely wobbled by the fifth time, although I was exhausted, and my body resisted the idea of trying again.

Leigh brought us hot cider, oblivious to my nudity.

"I read your new book, by the way. Brilliant."

Nandi brightened. "Really? I thought everyone would hate me for the ending."

"What? No. That was a beautiful sacrifice. I'm sure there will be a negative Nelly or two somewhere in your reviews, but I honestly think that was the most lovely ending out of all of your recent novels. Will there be another?"

Nandi turned euphoric, forgetting I was beside her with my hands cupped around a mug of cider. An animated book discussion took place less than three feet away while I stood beside Nandi with my dick exposed, praying Ian didn't wander out to greet us, too.

I shook my head and muttered, "Should I put on some pants again? I'm never going to get used to this."

Leigh laughed, radiating the kind of maternal warmth I always felt from my mother. A hint of pink touched her cheeks. "It took a while, but I'm used to it. Being married to a shifter means it's cocks and boobs all the time around here. Don't work him too hard, Nandi, and come in if you both get cold."

"We will. Thanks, Leigh."

My muscles and my bones ached, a dull throb ebbing through every joint. After we sipped more cider, we returned to the grass and to the next level of her training.

"Now, I need you to shift while running, making a

transition from two legs to four. The opposite is more difficult, but I won't tax you like that since it takes more practice. *Yet.*"

"How the hell?"

For someone so shy and quiet, Nandi became some kind of wicked cross between a cruel taskmaster and a dominatrix once she decided to implement a reward-based system for completing her objectives. I received a kiss for each success, and a tease for the failures, but I couldn't act on it or do anything in the backyard—once I mastered the objectives to her satisfaction, we could return to my place for the real prize.

Damn. An hour later, progress was minimal, and I was still shivering.

"I can't come out of a shift while running, Nan. I'll just end up eating grass again."

"Then I guess you won't be picking a special toy from Isisa's chest tonight to use on me."

"Goddammit, that isn't even fair."

"It's totally fair. It gives you something to look forward to. I *guess* we can stop for today though since you have to do the work thing tomorrow."

"Fine. Once more, then."

I didn't manage the shift gracefully, but I didn't face-plant either. More like belly flopped in exhaustion. Nandi took pity on me at long last and massaged my aching back.

"Sorry," she apologized. "I guess you'll want a raincheck on that toy box prize?"

"Please. I don't think I'd give you the deserved attention."

"All right. Let's get you home then."

Ian met us on the way out. He pulled his truck into the drive as Nandi and I were saying our goodbyes at the door.

"You look a little worse for wear," he said.

"Nandi put me through the wringer."

"It's always the quiet ones," Ian teased, winking at Nandi. She dipped her chin and smiled. "Anyway, thought you should know the house is all put together again and no one's the wiser about what we were really doing there."

"Yeah, they all just think I have a bug problem."

"Texas ants are notoriously stubborn beasties. But on the bright side, since we actually did lay down spikes and whatnot to appease your curious mother each time she wandered past, you should never actually have an ant problem."

"That sounds like my mom. Thanks again, Ian, really."

"It's the least I could do. I'm sorry you were caught up in the fallout from our op."

"Just keep me in the loop now, yeah? Whatever is going on with Sasha and these assholes, I don't want to be stonewalled."

Ian nodded. "Of course. And if you need more practice or the desire to hunt overwhelms you, you're always welcome here. Any time."

"I have to admit, this is all pretty damn crazy."

"Well, Nadir has nothing but praise for you. If I'd identified you as a shifter earlier, I'd have pulled you onto the team years ago when you were still in. So if anyone can handle this new part of life, it's you."

"Thanks, man."

Ian clapped me on the shoulder. "You're welcome. Now go get some rest. You deserve it."

Nandi drove while I dozed. Everything ached, and a satisfying post-workout burn settled in my muscles. It seemed like I'd barely closed my eyes when we pulled up to the house.

"Thanks, Nandi, for all of it.

She grinned. "No need to thank me. Watching you strut around naked is its own sweet reward."

"You gonna strip down next time and join me? Maybe that would have been a motivational tool."

"Maybe."

"Did you want to come in with me? Stay the night? I can't promise I'll be good for much, but I have a comfy couch and a huge movie collection we could explore."

"I'd really like that."

Every indication of a gunfight taking place had been removed, save for the loss of a couple lamps I'd purchased out of town. I marveled over the spotless carpet, the pristine kitchen tile, and the immaculate fridge. The bullet holes were gone.

Ian's people had even replaced the shattered patio doors.

"I'll be damned. They actually did it."

Nandi slipped behind me, arms around my middle, cheek to the back of my shoulder. "Ian always keeps his word. Anyway, why don't you go get in the shower, and I'll make you dinner. Okay?"

"Sounds like a plan."

If I could remain awake long enough to enjoy it.

22

ESTEBAN

To celebrate a rare day of November sunshine, a group of us sat outdoors at the table with our lunches. I'd been away from the site too long, missing the noise of construction and overseeing general operations for the business.

I had Nandi's leftover fried chicken from the previous night, while the guys beside me opened boxes of pepperoni pizza. Steam rose from the surface of a meat lover's with jalapeños and onion, Sergio's favorite. I grimaced at him.

"You'll be crying later over your heart burn."

He belched in my face. "I'll be fine."

I rolled my eyes and returned to my dinner. On top of chicken, she'd whipped together a pot of creamy mashed potatoes with the sparse ingredients in my fridge, using the last of some heavy cream I'd bought for Sasha to sip during movies.

"You'll be in the john later begging for Pepto."

"Whatever. Anyway, you coming to Thanksgiving dinner or not?"

"Seriously man?" I stared at him until he squirmed and looked away.

"What?" Sergio cleared his throat. "Ma asked me to check."

"When she's able to call and tell me she accepts my choices, I'll come to dinner."

He reached over and stole a fried chicken wing. I let him. "Man, you can't skip Thanksgiving. She'll be heartbroken."

"I can, and I will. Thanksgiving is a time for family, and that means my *whole* family. Girls included. If Mamá doesn't accept that, then it's her loss."

He remained silent for a time, expression gradually transforming from horror to silent rapture with each bite. "If Juanita fried chicken like this, I'd probably do the same. So which one made you dinner?"

"How you know I didn't make it?"

He glanced at me, scoffed, and took another chicken leg. When Nandi cooked, she made enough for several days, and I'd overpacked my lunch with the expectation of feeding my brother, too. "I know that bland shit you make."

"*Bland?* Eat your damn pizza and stay out of my stuff."

"For real though, good on you for standing up to Mamá. I think sometimes she forgets she can't run our lives the way she runs Pops."

"Yeah…"

We ate in silence for a while before the subject changed to our plans for the bonuses Dupont had promised for the holiday. Sergio wanted to take his wife and kids to Disney World.

I wanted to buy three identical engagement rings, but I lied through my teeth and gave him some bullshit about finishing the fence.

After lunch, we parted and went our own ways. I had phone calls to make, and he was overseeing work on the second wave of houses.

Around closing time, Jesús popped into the office. "Hey, where's Sergio? He's supposed to be giving us a ride. If he's going to be staying late, he should have said. I got places to go, man."

"Man, don't you have a vehicle of your own?"

"The Range Rover uses a lot of gas, amigo. It just isn't realistic to ride in it every day to the site when we live so far away. You seen Sergio or not?"

I glanced out the office window. My brother's ancient car hadn't moved. "He didn't say anything about staying late."

I called him twice. No answer.

A knot formed in my stomach. A nervous tingle in the tips of my fingers told me I hadn't done enough yet.

Jesús checked his phone too. "Not a single damn message. Man, this isn't like your brother to disappear. What do you want us to do?"

"We start searching for him. How many of you are left?"

"Almost everyone is gone for the day, boss. It's just me, Alan, and Paolo waiting on him. We carpooled."

"Find anyone else on site, split up and check the houses in wave two."

When I moved onto the unpaved roads and let the

smell of the site surround me, the wind brought the odor of motor oil, damp earth, drying cement, and a couple dozen men. There was dust and grit, the wide-open sky above us bringing in smells from miles away, and somewhere beneath it, I'd find my brother.

I tilted my head back and inhaled a long breath, letting it fill my human lungs. The subtle hint of Sergio's cologne came to me. Following it at a dead sprint brought me closer to the source, and the smell intensified, bringing another familiar odor.

Blood. I smelled blood. I dialed 911 along the way and gave the operator the address of the site.

"Sergio!" I called. "Man, are you here? Are you hurt?"

I couldn't remember the last time I'd prayed for anything or anyone. I prayed then, because I couldn't be the one to tell our Ma something took my little brother away from us under my watch.

I burst through the open door and found my brother sprawled across the uncarpeted floor with a big, wet gash across his bald head. He was surrounded by tools and the open box beside him wasn't far from his hard hat.

Wary of causing further harm by shaking him—fuck, what if he'd had a neck injury?—I crouched to one side and tapped his arm instead. "Sergio. Sergio. Say something."

After a few seconds, he stirred and groaned.

"Easy now, brother. Don't move."

I ducked over to the front door and threw it open, shouting loud enough for the bass to carry my voice to the remaining guys on our crew. "I found him!"

Sergio blinked his eyes in the dim light. "What the fuck happened?"

"I was hoping you could tell me."

When he tried to roll to his side, he gasped and abandoned the effort. Tears glistened in the corners of his eyes. "Shit."

"I told you not to move, *pendejo*. I think your arm is busted. Maybe your collarbone. You're lucky you didn't crack your fool head. Why weren't you wearing a hard hat?" I barked at him.

"Was scratching an itch and thought I heard something. Must have been a raccoon or something on the upper level. Something heavy enough to knock over that toolbox."

My gaze swept across the tools scattered around the rough floors. "Looks like. It shouldn't have even been up there."

I didn't smell raccoon either. Instead, a dusty smell filled my nose, like hot sand and moldy bones.

Flashing red lights filtered in through the plastic-covered windows and voices came into focus.

"Ah man, don't tell me you called an ambulance. Don't you know those are expensive? Juanita is going to kill me."

"So is our mother. Get used to it."

≈

*B*y the time I parked and made it inside the emergency room lobby, the paramedics had already wheeled Sergio in on a gurney and vanished into the back. Half my family had crowded inside the small room, and I imagined the rest would show up within the next hour once word got around about the accident.

My father paced the waiting room floor while my

mother spoke with a frazzled looking nurse. She abandoned the poor woman the moment she spotted me.

"Oh, Esteban!" She threw her arms around me and squeezed hard enough to force the air from my lungs. "You saved him."

"Ma, you're squishing me," I wheezed.

"Sorry." She released me and stepped back to mop her tear-streaked face with a linen handkerchief from her purse. Then the rosary came out in its place. "What happened? How could such a thing happen to my baby?"

Across the room I heard Samuel mutter, "Now *he's* her baby. I've been ousted."

Mariana shushed him.

"It was an accident, that's all. The paramedics said he was stable, and I'm sure a doctor will be out soon to speak with us." At least I hoped it would be soon. Patience, especially when it came to her children being hurt, wasn't exactly one of my mother's virtues.

My father joined us. His shirt was misbuttoned, a sign of how much he'd rushed once they received our call. "What happened? Sergio is always so careful when on the job. I always taught you boys to be cautious at all times."

"Yeah, you did. He messed up this time, and he knows it." I explained what happened with the toolbox, and that I suspected Sergio was in the wrong place at the wrong time.

Pops frowned, bushy brows drawing closer together. "That would be a strong raccoon to move something so heavy. But possible, I suppose. Damn. That boy is lucky. There must have been an angel or something watching over him. If all those tools hadn't come tumbling out of the toolbox, it could have crushed his—" He cut himself off, gaze darting to my mother.

Too late. Her eyes grew large and she clutched her rosary tighter, fingers white knuckled around it. "My baby could have *died?*"

"Ma—"

"You! What if it had been you instead."

I'd have probably shrugged it off already. I wanted to tell her I'd been shot twice this month already and bounced back, but now didn't seem like the appropriate time to have a heart-to-heart discussion about shapeshifting and my weird lineage. "But it wasn't. I'm fine—"

She hugged me again, tighter than the last time. "What if it had been you? Then the last conversation between us would have been that awful fight."

"Ma—"

"No more. I will not have our family torn in two. I want you home, *mijo*. I want you with us for Christmas, the way you should be. Bring your friends if that's what it takes."

Friends. I sighed, and the ounce of hope warming in my chest frosted over again. "They're more than friends, Ma. I told you that. They mean a lot to me—more than Gabriela did."

She gazed at me in silence for the span of a few heartbeats, eyes misty and shimmering with unshed tears. "Bring them home to meet us," she insisted.

"We'd love to have you home, Stebi," my father agreed. "You and your ladies."

While I was relieved to have her grudging acceptance, I wished the cost hadn't come at so high a price.

"Thanks, Ma. I missed you, too, and I'd love to be there for the holidays."

She swiped at her eyes and dipped her chin. "Good, good."

"Castillo?"

All heads swiveled toward the sound of the voice calling our name. A woman in snowman themed scrubs stood in the doorway leading back into the ER. She wore the same tired expression I'd seen on Sasha a hundred times after one of her busier shifts, but still managed to smile.

"I'm Mr. Castillo." My father stepped forward, and the woman met him halfway across the room.

"Hi, I'm Doctor Ringstead. I thought you might like an update on your... son?"

"Yes."

My mother hurried up to her husband's side. "Is he all right? Can we see him?"

"Your son broke his left arm. Good news, it's the only fracture he suffered and the break is a clean one. He'll have some major bruising around his shoulders but better that than a broken collarbone."

"Thank God for small mercies," I muttered. My mother sagged against my father and wrung her hands together.

"Can we see him?" Pops asked.

"Soon. He's been to X-ray and in for a scan already. He took a nasty bump to the head from one of those tools and has a definite concussion. We're also going to set his arm and get him in a cast. Right now he's been given something for the pain."

Ma fretted and fumbled through her purse for her cell

phone. "I should call Juanita. His wife is driving up from Houston."

"I'll do it, Mamá," Mariana said. She already had her iPhone in her hand anyway, the device a perpetual part of her palm.

"I promise to keep you up to date and let you know the moment you can see him. Though," the doctor glanced to the many worried faces, "we'll have to limit it to two at a time."

"Of course," Pops agreed. "Thank you so much."

Doctor Ringstead smiled and made her way back through the double doors.

"She's young to be a doctor. Too young."

At least she'd waited for the doctor to leave before she started fretting out loud. I reached over and settled my hands over my mother's twitching fingers. "I'm certain she's very capable, Mamá. Sasha's a doctor and looks about the same age."

She muttered something under her breath and let the subject drop, which I took as another small favor from above. Now that everything was relatively settled, exhaustion struck, replacing the adrenaline that had been fueling me since discovering Sergio missing.

Juanita arrived and my mother's attentions turned to her, granting me a few moments peace and quiet. Pops patted my hand and sat beside me in silence. As I sat there waiting for news, I closed my eyes and thought back to the site. Something about it still nagged me as wrong, and Pops had been spot on when he said the toolbox was too heavy for a racoon.

More was at play than a simple site accident, and I was determined to get to the bottom of it.

∿

SASHA

*M*oments after I shut my eyes after the shift from hell, Esteban's special ringtone jarred me awake again.

As my bleary vision cleared, my eyes focused on the digital clock on Nandi's nightstand. Esteban *never* called after midnight, my first clue something was wrong. When I wiggled away from Nandi to reach for the phone, she muttered into her pillow and scooted into my back again.

"Esteban?" I whispered, afraid of waking her. "What's wrong?"

"I... I really hate to wake you in the middle of the night, but I need a favor from you or one of your teammates." His voice sounded low and raw, an emotional tremble giving way to something dangerous.

"What happened?"

After Esteban caught me up on what happened at the site, I disentangled myself from Nandi and slid into a pair of jeans laying on the floor. "I'll be there in thirty."

"No, you don't have to do—"

"I'll be there in thirty."

"Sash?" The pillows muffled Nandi's drowsy mumble.

"Yeah, baby?"

"Where ya goin'?"

"Esteban needs help. We think snakeboy was at his site messing with shit, so I'm going to go with him and smell around. I caught a whiff of him in the parking garage that day, a good whiff of both his human *and* animal form."

"I'll come with you."

319

I tugged a shirt over my head and flipped my hair out from under the neckline. "To do what?"

"Help."

"If there's danger, I'd rather you be here where it's safe."

"If there's danger, three of us will take a bite out of it."

I paused, considering the odds of anything surviving a mauling from three adult lions. Esteban had already proven himself to be deadly even if it was feral instinct. "All right."

Leaving a note for Isisa if she awakened in the middle of the night to look for either of us, we made the trip to north of Houston and pulled up to the gate of his work site. Esteban was waiting for us in his truck, the glow of a phone on his face, and the engine cool.

He got out and slipped the phone into his pocket. "Hey. You both didn't have to come out like this."

Nandi stepped forward and hugged him. "Is your brother okay?"

I squeezed against the other side of him, one arm behind his back. "We wanted to."

"Yeah. They said he's got a concussion from one of the tools striking him in the head. He threw his arm up when he heard the commotion above him, and that's probably the only reason he's alive. The toolbox fractured his arm instead of crushing his skull. He'll be in a cast *and* a sling for a while. Something about how he was struck."

"Oh no," Nandi breathed. "Then he's out of work on top of it? It's almost Christmas."

"Yeah, tell me about it. He bitched and moaned about needing to afford their holiday plans."

"His health matters more," Nandi murmured, "but it must be difficult for him."

"Doctor said no physical work at the site for the next two months, but I'll figure out something for him to do." He glanced over his shoulder, nervous, then back to us. "C'mon, let's get inside. This house over here is finished. I can drag in a heat lamp if you need it."

"We're fine," I assured him. "But yeah, better to get out of the open. If someone is lurking, they'll see our cars, but they won't know where we are at least."

"Sergio claims it must have been a raccoon or something. Stray cat maybe."

"Does that happen?" Nandi asked.

"Yeah, it can in unfinished houses that are still open to the elements, but I don't think it was. I didn't smell anything like that. I smelled… I dunno what it was really, but it sure as hell wasn't a cat or racoon."

"Which is why you think it wasn't an accident." My lips pursed. "Is it safe for us to look around without setting off alarms?"

"Security system is off right now. I went into admin and disabled it for now."

Nandi unzipped her hoodie. "All right. Strip then."

A weak smile raised the corners of Esteban's mouth. "It's kind of hot when you get all bossy."

We dropped our clothes and shifted first. It took Esteban a few minutes longer, working himself up to it, even pacing like a caged lion when frustration stalled out his transformation, but he did it.

I bumped my head beneath his chin, proud of him. Nandi moved to his other side, and we followed him outside and down the dirt roads.

The stench I'd encountered outside Club Hysteria lingered in the air. With my nose to the ground, I followed the scent through the project zone. There had been three different uninvited snakes throughout the site at some point during the day, their scent trails fresh. Had they sabotaged some other area of the site?

Esteban claimed the lead. He caught a trail and started to run, loping through the development toward the far northern end. The buildings here hadn't been finished yet. As we drew closer to one house, I caught the faint whiff of blood.

He bumped open the door with his head and led the way inside. Nandi growled at the door and didn't follow. Instead, she twitched her tail and turned to circle around the large house.

Upstairs was almost as cold as the rest of the house, but they were in the process of closing it up and concealing its guts. I shifted back again inside and grimaced. Goose bumps arose on my arms. Esteban lingered for a few seconds, staring at me in silent admiration.

"You can do it, too. I know you can. Think of what you want most, use it as your motivation."

My lion stepped forward from four legs onto two and dragged me against him. His hands chafed up and down my back, warming me. "Did you smell it?"

"Yeah." My teeth weren't chattering yet, but I was cold. "And you're right. There was no raccoon in here. You had a snake. See these scuff marks over here? The toolbox wasn't anywhere near the ledge. Our Medrano buddy pushed it over."

"But of course there's no fucking way to prove it." He ran both hands through his hair and swore in Spanish.

"There may be." I glanced at the shadowed corners of the unfinished house and considered the blind spots perfect for a hidden camera. "Nadir is our surveillance specialist, and I'm positive he'd have something special to help with this."

"Special? You mean like concealed cameras?"

"Yes."

"Can I install hidden cameras though? Or is that crap inadmissible in court?"

"Honestly, Isisa might be the better one to ask about that, but my gut instinct would be why not? It's your site. Your security. I imagine your client would be the final word, and if you added extras without tipping off the crew for security reasons I don't see the issue. But maybe we can do one better than camera footage that people could claim was faked."

"What's that?"

"Set them up and catch them red-handed."

~

ESTEBAN

*A*fter the illuminating events of the previous night, I'd gone home and crashed a couple hours. With Sergio gone, Jesús had stepped up as a capable replacement until my brother was on his feet again.

Nandi had followed the snake's odor to the fence where it continued beneath a small gap and disappeared at the road about fifteen yards later. Someone had probably taken Medrano away by vehicle there.

"Hey, boss, is it true we're clearing out early today?"

I looked up from my laptop and forced a smile. Jesús, Xavier, and two other guys with families stood in the office doorway with hopeful expressions.

"Yeah, man. Since Thanksgiving is tomorrow, consider this my gift to you all. I'll still pay you for a full day."

"Still need me to come in this weekend to accept supplies?" Jesús asked.

"No, I'll handle it. It's just a matter of signing for them and ensuring they get laid down safely in one of the locked buildings. No need for you all to break away from your families."

"What's coming anyway?"

"The Italian marble for the countertops in phase one. Over three hundred bucks per square foot, man, and we have about two thousand feet of it coming."

Xavier whistled. "That's the good shit, ain't it, cuz?"

"Yeah."

Nadir had a theory about someone on my crew working as a double agent for Medrano. Man, I wanted him to be wrong. Step one in our plan involved making sure people knew the shipment was coming and what was in it. These loudmouths would get the word around.

Xavier lingered in the office after the others left. "You really not coming to dinner tomorrow?"

"I'm really not coming. I love you guys, but I have an invitation elsewhere."

"That's cool. Hope we see you at Christmas."

"I'll be there, just like I promised Mamá."

Julia and Lyle had invited the four of us to join them

for Thanksgiving in Quickdraw, so I'd jumped on the chance. Apparently, Lyle and Isisa spent the day playing video games while the women cooked the actual meal last year.

The crew cleared out early, the guys accustomed to riding with Sergio had arranged alternative ways home. After they left, I hung around to complete my work day, and Nadir arrived two hours later to help me set up cameras—after we confirmed the area was clear of any snakes hiding nearby.

Nadir shook his head in disgust. "Hard to believe anyone could be this desperate. This project should be small change for them."

"It should be, but it isn't. Dupont offered us another out in San Antonio for twice as much. Medrano missed out on a gold mine."

"Huh. Still, it's not like they're hurting for cash. I've been doing some digging around, and that family has their fingers in everything. Construction, real estate, entertainment, dining—"

"Yeah, shoot me a list of places to avoid from now on. I don't wanna funnel them any of my cash."

Nadir chuckled. "Sure thing. All right, this is the last of the cameras. The team and I will take shifts monitoring the site from a safe distance. No one will come in though unless we have to. Don't wanna tip them off."

"Then I arrive Saturday to accept the phony supplies."

"Yup. Make a show of leaving. Then we'll get you back in place with us."

"What's to stop them from smelling us?"

"Artificial pheromones and chemicals. Snakes have an excellent sense of smell, so they'll be difficult to fool, but not impossible. I plan to have a guy come in and fog the place beforehand, and we'll also have them in the shipment itself. By the time they get the packages open and realize they've been conned, we'll have the evidence we need," Nadir answered.

"What do you want me to do now?"

"Now? Nothing. Go home and have a nap. Go bang one of the girls and chill. Do lion shit."

"Lion shit," I repeated. "Why the hell not? I guess it's good to be the king."

23

ESTEBAN

*N*ervous tension twisted my stomach into knots while we waited. Maybe nothing would happen. God, I hoped nothing would happen.

Sasha and I sat in my truck a mile down the road from the site in a grocery store parking lot while Ian and his team held positions onsite. Damn, I wanted to be up there with them, but we had a plan and I intended to follow it through.

"It'll be okay," Sasha said. She set her phone aside in the cupholder, and I glimpsed a text conversation with Isisa and Nandi. All I could imagine was the two of them pacing their penthouse while they waited.

"Yeah, I know. Just makes me sick to think it's one of my guys."

"We could be wrong about that, you know. It could just be an eavesdropping snake—"

"Got movement on the eastern perimeter." Juni's soft voice spoke up over the comm line. She'd wanted to be involved, but Ian asked her to be our woman in the chair

—the boss overseeing the mission from behind a desk and computer monitor—since she was still healing from a serious injury. Broken bones, even for shifters, took time.

"What do you have?" Ian asked.

"A green Range Rover pulled off into the brush. Someone's climbing the fence now. No ID yet, sorry."

Except I didn't need her to name our mystery visitor, and my heart sunk. Only one man on my crew had that vehicle. "It's Jesús. My subforeman."

Nadir spoke up after a brief pause. "Do I get to remark on the irony of a dude named Jesús being your Judas?"

I laughed weakly, because if I didn't, I'd be crying. Jesús had eaten dinner at my goddamned table alongside me and my family before. He'd been a loyal member of the crew back when I discharged from the Marines. Fuck. My *dad* had hired him in the early days.

"Won't the security cameras film him coming in?"

My fists clenched around the steering wheel. "You said the eastern fence line, right? That was our blind spot. He knows that because I have him and Sergio patrol it a few times each day."

"Good thing he doesn't know about our extra additions," Sasha muttered. She reached over and squeezed my hand.

"What's he doing, Juni?" Taylor asked. "Wait, shit, lights outside just went dark."

"He's cut the power and disabled the generator," Juni relayed. "Got him moving toward the office trailer now. Looks like he's making a call."

I waited on the edge of my seat until Juni reported the arrival of two trucks a half hour later. Jesús opened the gates wide for them, and soon the sound of tires crunching over dirt and gravel reached my ears through the comm line.

"Wait for it," Ian cautioned. "We need to catch them in the act if we're going to have any chance of putting these guys away."

Waiting while men loaded up the first crates of "marble" tested the limitations of my endurance and sanity.

"I got two men, armed, outside the storage house. Medrano is there giving orders. Three more loading the goods. You sure you wanna confront them first, Esteban?"

"Yeah. Yeah, I do. This guy likes to talk and run his mouth a lot. He won't shoot me straight away."

"All right, you're green to go. We'll start moving into position in case things turn ugly."

I turned over the engine and looked at Sasha. She held a sleek, personalized Beretta in her lap and had a second matching handgun tucked into a holster beneath her left arm, a hint of the pearl grip visible, my own elegant and classy GI Jane. "Ready?"

"I won't be far behind you," Sasha whispered. "Be careful."

She vanished into the shadows and left me to make the walk up the drive alone. I didn't think my truck parked in the gate would do much to deter anyone from leaving, but I hoped it wouldn't come to that.

Their trucks came into view around the next bend. Ian's soft voice assured me he had me in his sights, and the others all reported the same. Even though I couldn't see them, I trusted that they had my back.

One truck faced the building they were emptying with the headlights on for illumination. The other had the bed facing the door for ease of loading. From here it looked like they'd loaded maybe a quarter of the shipment.

"Jesús?"

Everyone turned to face me at once. Two of them had guns, and having them pointed at my chest raised the hairs on my nape. The last time someone had pointed guns at me, I'd eaten them for lunch. Literally.

Control it. Don't shift. Don't shift.

"What the fuck is going on here?" I demanded.

Jesús stepped forward, both hands empty and down at his sides. He looked back at the truck loaded up with the stolen supplies then back to me. "You shouldn't have come, boss. I didn't want it to go down like this."

"Like what?" My left temple throbbed, and the familiar tingle of wanting to shift began in my fingertips. "How much did it take to make you betray us, huh? This job wasn't enough for you?"

"You give all of the good jobs to your brother. I worked here from the start alongside your dad, and all he did was hand it over to you. I was loyal to all of you—treated you like my own sons, and what good has it done me?"

I stared at him, cold fury pounding through my veins. "You call that loyalty, Jesús? You turned on us the moment you saw a better deal come along. We had two more jobs after this. Dupont and I signed the contracts last week, and I was going to surprise all of you before Christmas with first dibs to work the out-of-city crews. You would have led your own fucking site. You were first on my list to run the entire operation in San Antonio."

His eyes widened.

"They paying you enough for your dignity too? You

say you treated us like sons, but you were family, man. You ate at our table with us."

"Enough talking." Luis Medrano stepped forward into the light. I'd only ever seen the man once before, but he'd made an impression. Built like a bull, he tended to shadow his older brother like some sort of hulking bodyguard. Still, it didn't surprise me not to see the elder Medrano here. He didn't seem like the sort to get his hands dirty.

"You won't get away with this," I said.

"Why not? We have your marble, no one knows we are here, and you and your little cat won't be around to tell anyone after we're gone."

"Look, no one said anything about killing." Jesús stepped forward but stopped short when Luis turned the gun on him.

"You want to join them? No? Then shut up and do what we paid you to do. Finish loading the goods."

"What about him?" one of the thugs asked.

"Kill Castillo and toss him inside. We'll leave him as a message to everyone else not to fuck with us. Dupont will learn we are not to be ignored. Our money belongs with our own kind."

Our own kind? Was Dupont a shifter after all?

Before I could question him, before they could even think about following his orders, a red beam appeared on the center of Medrano's chest. He glanced down, bewildered.

"What the hell is this?"

"That, my friend, is a dot belonging to my friend Nadir's .357 magnum. He doesn't need the sight but…"

Nadir's voice reached us from the second-floor bedroom of the house behind me. At under fifty yards, he had Medrano dead if he pulled the trigger. "I like it, and it brings me a little joy when I see the kind of startled expression you're making right now."

A shotgun cocked. An unnecessary noise that carried a lot of intimidation with it. So did the guy holding it. Taylor stepped forward with his Mossberg. He'd been lurking nearby, outfitted in a black tactical vest and unseen by their gang members in the pitch-black night. None of Espadachines were trained for this kind of thing, accustomed to dealing with kids on the street and the helpless, not armed military operatives who knew how to fight back. "Easiest infiltration job I've ever worked."

"I've got you covered, too," Ian said cheerfully. He was on the rooftop of the house they'd robbed, wearing a black cap over his white hair. "Trust me, if I pull the trigger, even at this distance, Medrano, your people will be working with a closed casket funeral."

"You hired security?"

"The best security in Texas," I replied.

Jesús began to shake. In the glare of the headlights, he'd turned an ashy shade of gray. "I didn't think it would go down like this, Esteban. You gotta believe me. They made it sound like they were going to hurt my family if I didn't help them."

I ignored him. Jesús had an ex-wife and two kids, both of his sons living out of state in college.

"Place your firearms on the ground," Taylor said.

"There are two remaining threats inside the house. They're moving for the door," Juni announced over the comm.

"Guns down now," Taylor ordered again, prodding one in the back with his shotgun.

As one guy lowered his gun, another charged onto the porch, firing blindly into the group of us. The entire scene dissolved into chaos, from a neat and orderly arrest to a clusterfuck within seconds.

Nadir's red beam swung from Medrano to the initial shooters and plugged one neatly in the face, a split second too late to save me from taking a round to the chest. Taylor's shotgun roared.

Kevlar might stop a bullet, but the impact still hurt like hell. I stumbled back and hit the ground. In the same moment, Sasha appeared around the truck and drove her fist into a thug's face. He joined me on the dirt.

"Are you all right, Esteban?"

"Yeah. Go, I'm good."

"Medrano is running for it," Juni reported. "Eastbound!"

"He must be going for Jesús's ride. I got him." Sheer determination got me up off the ground and running after Luis.

Despite the considerable gap he'd gotten during his head start, I pushed my body and forced my lungs to cooperate. Sasha had promised awakening my shifter half would make me faster and stronger. It did. I flew over the ground and closed in on him.

Luis glanced over his shoulder. The full moon above us lit his panicked features, and raw fear rolled over me, the stench tangled with his smell.

He shifted. A pile of clothes fell, and his serpentine body darted forward toward the fence to go beneath it.

"Oh no you don't."

One thought, that was all it took to make me explode from my clothes. Cotton and denim burst at the seams, unable to contain my growing body. I may not have been as graceful as my girls, but I landed running on four paws and pounced with everything I had in me. Luis's serpentine body flattened beneath my paws. He struggled, twisting his thick length, but I'd caught him right behind the head.

This was the man who had hurt my friends. Who had threatened my mate.

A deep growl reverberated in my chest, and I pressed down with my claws. The viper went still. Dead? No, I hadn't killed it yet. I wanted to. One bite would sever his head from the rest of his body. One swipe of my claw would rend the olive scales to pieces.

"Hey now, big guy. I know what you're thinking, and trust me, I'd do the same, but we have to be better than them." Sasha stroked my ears. Then her voice hardened. "Shift back, Medrano, or I might decide to let him eat you anyway."

Medrano shifted back. His terror stank, and the adrenaline pumping through his body would have ruined the taste anyway. My paw remained on his chest, claw tips against bare flesh while Ian jogged up with his restraints.

"Look at you." Sasha tugged on the Kevlar vest still caught around my neck along with bits of cotton from my shirt. "You were amazing, but it's time to get you dressed, yeah? Don't think we wanna explain a lion or a naked site manager."

~

SASHA

*W*e secured the surviving FEL members, and I provided medical attention to Jesús while we awaited the authorities. Juni had already phoned in a report regarding the burglary attempt and assault, specifying that several members of their security team were armed, and that there had been two casualties among the attackers.

Esteban jumped to his feet and stared toward the open trailer door. "Mr. Dupont, I didn't expect to see you here."

"I wanted to see for myself how everything went."

No fucking way. The scent of iron and old blood wafted to me on the air, a metallic odor that we associated with all vampires. I stiffened and turned, slowly, resisting the urge to reach for the gun on the nearby desk. Bloodsuckers weren't exactly an every-day occurrence though I knew about a coven that lived close to San Antonio.

"Sasha, this is Mr. Dupont."

The vampire was all rosy and pink, fresh-faced like he'd had a few good sips of blood prior to visiting us. He smiled, unnatural gray eyes twinkling in the fluorescent lights. "I told you, call me Julien. We have worked long enough together to be on a first-name basis by now, I would think."

"Right, of course." Esteban's tired smile crinkled his eyes. "I think we won't have any more problems with the site."

"Yes, I saw Mr. Medrano in the back of a cruiser. Excellent work."

"Pleasure to meet you," I finally said. Our gazes met, and the man tipped his head in silent recognition. Did Esteban know? I doubted it.

"I hope this won't change your mind about working with me in the future, Julien."

"On the contrary, it's refreshing to know you're associated with such dependable people and that you'd go through this much effort to see my assets secured. In fact, I plan to speak with Mr. MacArthur about providing security in the future for all projects."

Julien took a step further inside. Natural instinct boiled up, and reflexes put me between Esteban and a possible threat. The vampire paused, and my mate shot me a confused look.

"You okay, Sasha?"

"Yeah, sorry." I moved back and ducked my head, mentally kicking myself. Esteban didn't need my protection, and not every vampire was a bloodthirsty fiend. He'd been around Dupont for months before I ever met him.

"Forgive me," Julien said. His composure never faltered. "Your lovely mate is reacting as would be her natural inclinations when danger is present."

"Danger? What danger?"

"It's nothing," I mumbled. "Really. I'm sorry."

"No, it's quite all right. Had I been aware that Esteban knew of our world, I would have revealed myself sooner."

"Is that what Medrano meant about keeping money in 'our world'?" Esteban asked. "Are you a shifter, Julien?"

"No." He folded his hands before him. "I'm a vampire."

Esteban blinked a few times, eyes drifting from me to Julien and back again. His mouth opened and shut until he regained composure and cleared his throat. "That explains a lot of things I'd wondered about but didn't question. UV shielded windows."

"And our dinner meetings."

Pride surged through me. No matter what life threw at him, Esteban handled every situation with tact and dignity. Only three months ago, he'd been a working man ignorant to the world of the paranormal, now he was a shifter bound to his own pride, working for a billionaire vampire. There was no better man in the world as far as I was concerned.

"Now what?" Esteban asked. "About Medrano, I mean."

"He goes to jail. I doubt he'll flip on his family, but between him, the gang, and Jesús, we should have enough to incriminate the family and call for an investigation," I said.

"Until then, I'll do what I can to ensure no further retaliation is taken against the project, beginning with speaking to your friend outside. If you'll both excuse me."

Dupont left us alone once again, taking his unpleasant scent with him.

"Wow. Vampire. I don't even know what to think right now." Esteban sank into his chair and rubbed his face.

"He seems nice though."

"Yeah, he is. Good man to work for. Uh... he's not gonna want blood or anything, right?"

"Doubtful. His kind have lots of rules and shit they follow, but we can talk about that later. How are you holding up?"

"I dunno, Sash, I really don't. Jesús's betrayal hurt bad. I don't know how I'm gonna tell my guys about this. Or my father. They were close friends."

"Just tell them the truth."

"Yeah." He closed his eyes and released a deep sigh. "At least now we should be able to finish the job on schedule. Everyone needs a break after this."

"Easy sailing from here?" I asked.

"Hope so, but we have one more adventure ahead of us."

"Oh yeah, what's that?"

Esteban opened his eyes, sat up, and smiled. "Christmas with my family next month. My *entire* family."

24

SASHA

*P*ulling a double at the hospital on Christmas Eve meant I'd be free to pursue an awkward Christmas Day at the Castillo residence with Esteban.

As a rule, few of us expected time away from the hospital over the holidays, but I'd pulled two days of double shifts and pleaded my case to another doctor, covering Christmas Eve *and* the day prior for him in exchange for having Christmas off.

I had crashed on a couch in the staff lounge for a few hours in the morning before the next rush of injured arrived by ambulance for everything from rooftop falls to head injuries on slick sidewalks.

With a stolen break that afternoon, I phoned Esteban to confirm our plans were still in motion.

"Yeah. Everyone starts to arrive for family brunch around ten. Show up at my place at nine and we'll drive over together."

"Paging Doctor Vogt. Paging Doctor Vogt to the ER."

"Damn. They're calling me again."

Esteban's chuckle weakened my knees. "Go be a hero, and I'll see you tomorrow morning after you've had some rest. Try not to freak out too much."

"Love you." Impulse pushed the two words out as I hurried into the elevator.

"Love you too, chica."

We spent hours stabilizing a young woman suffering multiple fractures and internal bleeding, the victim of a drunk holiday driver. Afterward, I sagged in the locker room and changed out of my scrubs. A colleague dropped me off in front of my condominium around six, saving me a walk and the cost of a taxi.

My beloved lionesses sat on the couch in front of a dark television in quiet conversation, matching expressions grim.

Isisa rubbed Nandi's shoulders and whispered in her ear, voice too low for even supernatural hearing to pick up. The talk abruptly ended when I walked up.

"Did something happen while I was gone?"

Nandi tucked her chin. Isisa sucked on her lower lip.

It wasn't like either of the girls to be quiet. "What's wrong?"

Isisa stood and moved to the kitchen. She fiddled with the tea maker, filling the kettle with water and spooning loose leaves into the automatic basket. "It's... it's Nandi's news to share."

Anxiety gnawed through my stomach, the solemn mood turning my worst fears into nausea-inducing, heart-pounding terror. "You're worrying me. What's wrong? What happened?"

Nandi toyed with the edge of her shirt and studied a frayed strand. "I'm pregnant. It must have happened when we were in Chicago, and I already took two tests and let Isisa take me to the doctor."

In all our time together, I'd never envied Nandi. Not once. But it struck me hard and fast, a merciless shock of cold jealousy seizing me in its grip. I didn't move. Couldn't breathe. It compressed the air from my lungs like a brutal, iron fist. "Are you sure?"

She nibbled her lower lip and nodded. "Are you upset?"

"What? No. I'm not mad."

"I didn't say mad. Upset. I didn't want to remind you of her."

Her. "Her name is Maleka." The baby I'd lost and rarely mentioned. I'd wanted her more than I'd ever wanted anything, and I'd had five months, five whole months to fall in love with her and the promise of motherhood.

Her conception had been an accident, one of those fluke 0.01 percent occurrences that sometimes happened on the pill, but she'd never been unwanted. Always loved.

"I know," Nandi said in a quiet whisper. We stood facing each other for a while. "I didn't want to remind you of Maleka. You're hurting now, and it's my fau—"

"No." I crossed the short distance and took Nandi's face between both palms. In one kiss, I tried to quell her worries, tenderly conveying thirteen years of love and affection. "I will love your baby like it's my own."

"Our baby."

The tears burned my eyes. I nodded and rested my brow to hers. "Our baby. I'm happy for you."

"You can still try."

A quiet laugh spilled from me with a hint of the warmth and genuine amusement I wanted to convey. "No, no. It wouldn't be fair to Esteban to bury him in children so early."

"He *wants* children. A lot of children."

"I know he does." Unable to help myself, one hand lowered toward her tummy, but I withdrew at the last moment. Nandi claimed my hand and pressed it flush against her instead. Although there was nothing to feel there yet, there would be in a few months once it swelled with life.

"You've never been afraid to touch me, Sasha. Please. Don't be afraid now. I'm still your Nandi. Nothing has changed between us, and I love you with all my heart. Tell Esteban how you feel."

"This is our time to celebrate your preg—"

"Do it or I will," Nandi threatened with an edge to her voice that sent a spark skipping down my spine. She'd always been our shy one. From the very first time I met her upon returning from deployment, I'd wanted her and known Isisa had chosen well. Known she would be *ours*. But she'd always been the tender and gentle submissive. The fleeting moments of dominance from her thrilled me. "Tell him how much you've wanted a little one, and I swear, Isisa and I will be your cheerleaders while you both fuck the nights away as long as it takes until it happens."

Warmth surged to my cheeks. I laughed in spite of myself and dipped my head. "You're right."

"Of course I'm right."

Isisa rejoined us, so I reached out and pulled her into

our joint embrace. "How the hell did I ever deserve you two?"

With the news out, the tension in the room popped like a bubble and the sheer joy and hope at what was to come took over. A crouch brought my face to her tummy, which I kissed.

"Okay, celebration time, but I want a shower first. I never feel clean enough when I use the hospital bathroom."

Nandi wiped one of her damp cheeks with her wrist and beamed. "Go ahead. Then I have presents for you."

The news perked me up. We had a tradition that Isisa and I had started during our youth, always opening one present before bedtime on Christmas Eve. Last year Isisa picked the presents we opened and this year it was Nandi's choice.

"I'll be quick."

Cleaning up took no time at all with the promise of gifts motivating me. Once I slipped into my favorite onesie—a purple dragon with a tail and tiny wings—I hurried downstairs and joined them on the floor by the tree. Isisa passed me a flute filled with sparkling apple cider and a few blackberries.

"To us," Nandi began. "May this be the start of the best Christmas ever."

"To us," Isisa and I echoed.

"Gift time!" Isisa said.

Smiling ear to ear, with big dimples in her cheeks, Nandi passed me a pink gift box tied with a black ribbon. Isisa received a mirroring black box with a pink ribbon.

Removing the lid of her gift revealed a peachy lace bra with molded cups and scalloped edges. The matching thong and suspenders had corset laces with ivory, matte ribbons and a tiny, decorative bow.

"This is beautiful," I murmured.

Her brown eyes danced with glee. "Do you really like it?"

"Have I ever disliked anything you've bought for me?"

She grinned. "No."

Our curvy girl couldn't fit into a single item in Agent Provocateur's catalog, but she had excellent taste in lingerie. They came short of fitting her impressive breasts by one cup size, but she lived vicariously through Isisa and me instead, clothing us like dolls in lace, silk, and anything she wanted her characters to don.

Isisa pulled out a gold lace corset with a matching thong. She squealed with unrestrained joy and held it up against her chest.

"This is perfect, Nandi. Thank you! I love it."

"I thought they'd be a nice gift for Esteban, too," Nandi said. She pulled over a gift bag for herself and showed off a plum-colored baby doll. "I managed to find this for me. I thought, maybe, we could go surprise him."

"Isn't he going to Mass with his family?" I asked.

Isisa nodded. "He is, but nothing says he can't get a surprise for after Mass…"

I looked over at the clock while I turned the idea over in my head. Esteban was part of our family now, which meant that he needed to open a gift too. Nandi's idea seemed a perfect way to introduce him to our special tradition.

"Well, if we're going to surprise him tonight, I need a power nap. Give me four hours and I'm fucking game."

~

*W*e reached Esteban's street at half past midnight. He'd already depowered his holiday ornaments, but the living room television set emitted a pale blue glow against the shades.

"He's watching *It's a Wonderful Life*," Nandi said, reading a text from her phone. Simba rested beside her on the rear seat. We hadn't wanted to leave him alone on Christmas. "And drinking eggnog. He said he needs to decompress after all that church pageantry and wishes we were here."

Isisa chuckled. "Won't he be surprised in a minute."

The moment I slid into the driveway, the porch light popped on and the front door cracked open to reveal Esteban in a pale pink button-down shirt and slacks. He squinted at us and shielded his eyes from the headlights. I killed the engine then took a few breaths.

"Ready?"

Nandi nodded.

We'd all worn winter coats over our naughty attire. The cold air whipped against my bare legs and stirred my hair as I climbed out. Isisa had brought the extra blankets, her and Nandi sharing the load and each carrying an oversized comforter. Esteban's bed wasn't large enough for all four of us without serious risk of someone tumbling onto the floor.

"Why didn't you say you were coming?" He held open the door and beckoned us inside. A fire burned in his fireplace, and as soon as the door shut behind us blissful warmth seeped into my cold limbs.

"Surprise," Nandi said, stretching her blanket in front of the tree while Isisa led Simba into the kitchen. "We decided you had to join us for our tradition."

"Oh yeah? And what's that?"

"Opening a Christmas Eve present, of course," I said. "And tonight, you get three."

On cue, we each unfastened our coats and shrugged them off. Esteban's gaze traveled over us, one by one, devouring our appearance with a hungry intensity that set my soul ablaze with desire. Fuck. How was it fair for one look to turn my entire body molten?

"All this for me?"

Isisa prowled closer to him and glided her fingers over his chest. She slid past his side, lithe and confident. "Part of our Christmas gift to you. Nandi picked our wardrobe. Do you like it?"

"Like is an understatement. I am absolutely 100 percent behind this tradition."

"There's more." I stepped forward and hooked my fingers in his belt. "Something for all of us."

Esteban's throat bobbed, and his pupils dilated. He settled his hands on my hips and stroked his thumb over the peach lace clinging to them. "What's that?"

I traced my lips from his ear to his pulse point, pausing to nibble his throat before I answered. "We've all marked you and claimed you as our own. Now we want you to do the same to us."

"How will I know what to do to make the bonding happen?"

"It's mostly instinct," Nandi said.

"It'll come to you," Isisa assured him.

The three of us had made love together a thousand times over the years, alone, with Taylor, and with other men. But Esteban was more than another man.

He was *our* man. *Our* fated mate. The lone lion we'd sought all our lives together. Despite my heart slamming against my ribs, I untucked Esteban's shirt and unfastened the buttons while Nandi unbuckled his belt. We undressed him together with the glow of the fireplace reflecting off our skin.

One at a time, we kissed him, light, teasing, and sensual. I thrust my tongue into his mouth when it was my turn while Nandi hugged him from behind with her full breasts against his back and cock in her small hand. The size of him was enormous in her fist. She slipped one of Isisa's favorite vibrating cock rings over the tip and nudged it down to the base, cradling his length in black silicone.

"Isisa first," Nandi whispered, "while Sasha and I watch."

Esteban turned his head and captured Isisa's mouth, groaning and pumping his hips to the rhythm of Nandi's deft hand movements. The low vibration hummed.

Watching Esteban make love to Isisa was every bit as beautiful as I'd hoped it would be. His talented mouth and fingers coaxed her to the edge, selfless and patient. Nandi and I drew her small breasts from the top of her corset and teased the tightly budded tips.

When it seemed Esteban couldn't take another second, he slid Isisa beneath him on her stomach, parted her thighs with one knee, and slipped into her from behind. The sound she made was pure satisfaction, a primal and low growl of pleasure. My core clenched.

Esteban gripped Isisa by the hips and dragged her onto her hands and knees. They made a beautiful sight, magnificent night and glorious day, his bronzed masculinity against the midnight canvas of her athletic frame. One of his large hands glided over her stomach, and two fingers delved between her thighs. She gasped and rolled her hips.

The slap of skin against skin persisted as Nandi and I entangled our limbs beside them. Her nimble fingers played me with agile precision, her lips a tease against my breasts. Esteban glanced left to look at us and stilled, lust smoldering in his eyes. Before I could ask if he liked what he saw, he murmured a low, "Get over here."

Nandi raised her head. "Both of us?"

"I can't watch you over there. I *need* to see you."

Eager to give him a show, I urged Nandi toward them until she lay spread eagle before Isisa and her waxed mound was bared to them both. Nandi always tasted the sweetest. Isisa and I took turns, sometimes licking and tasting her together, our tongues leaving slick trails over her dewy folds while she writhed against the comforter.

Nandi's cries filled the room first, followed swiftly by Isisa's triumphant shout and Esteban's groans. Then he bent forward, caught Isisa on her shoulder with his teeth, and bit down.

The shock of the branding seared through our shared line. It was pleasure and pain, a sweet and satisfying surrender to the man we all loved.

"Mine." Esteban kissed the teeth marks he'd left in her shoulder and chaffed his scruffy jaw against Isisa's bent spine. "My beautiful Isisa."

"Always," she whispered in return.

Released from direct participation for now, Isisa sprawled a few feet away on her back and didn't move again, too sapped to do anything more. I couldn't blame her. Sex with Esteban was always phenomenal.

He rolled onto his back for a while, perspiration glowing across his brow. I grinned and pulled off the cock ring to give him a break from it's buzzing.

"Think you can do that two more times?" I teased.

"Bring your mouth over here and find out."

I did, preparing him for the next round and savoring the taste of Isisa on his skin. It didn't take much, a trace of my tongue along the tender crown and a few playful nibbles. A few gentle laps of his glistening cock restored it to full mast.

"Fuck, I can't remember the last time I've gotten this hard again that fast."

I laughed despite having a mouthful of him. "Perks of being a shifter."

Then I grazed him with my teeth, each moan from his lips more delicious than the last. He fisted a handful of the comforter beneath him in one hand, my hair in the other, but I stopped and left him on the brink.

His chest was heaving by the time he claimed Nandi on her side, and I wondered if some sense of intuition took place. The position sandwiched her between me and Esteban, her plump breasts and nubile body quivering with pleasure. At the ideal position to skim my lips over the dark tip of one quivering breast, I tightened her left nipple with a teasing tongue flick then took it between my lips.

My little lioness moaned as I slipped my hand between

our bodies and teased her clit with my thumb, doubling her sensory pleasure. Esteban's muscles bunched and flexed with each smooth movement. He bit down on Nandi's ear and rumbled soft words too quiet for me to hear. She trembled and gasped. Of the three of us, she was the easiest to please, blessed with the responsive kind of body that practically came if we just blew on her pussy.

Her release came with a blissful expression and a keening cry that echoed across the large room. Esteban made his mark on her nape, and all three of us moaned in shared ecstasy.

"Perfect," he muttered. "God, the three of you are perfect."

"So are you," Nandi said in a breathy voice. "Perfect and ours."

He nuzzled her throat before withdrawing from her body, and then he turned his gaze on me. My heart skipped a little under the intensity of his stare. Nandi rolled aside and, for once, Isisa reached out for her and drew her close.

Esteban remained where he was, his cock only semi-limp, and held out his hand toward me. Once my hand was in his, he pulled me closer, yanking my body flush against his. He kissed me long and deep, until my lungs ached for air, and only then did I pull away. He leaned forward until I was forced to lay back.

"I feel like I saved you for last, Sasha." His thumbs rasped over my tightened nipples. The sensation zinged straight to my clit like a fine silver cord of energy had connected the three points. I sucked in a sharp breath, startled by my body's responsiveness to his touch.

How had his bonding with Nandi and Isisa changed everything so quickly when he'd yet to seal our pride link? I writhed beneath him, tortured by every flick, sensitive to the slightest movement of his cock. He hadn't even penetrated me, but my body remembered the perfect fit of him and yearned for it.

His eyes had lightened, brighter than I remembered— now the warm amber of molten caramel. They hadn't been that color before. Dazzled by the change, I looped both arms around his neck. "Why?"

"Were you jealous?" He nuzzled my neck and scraped my sensitized skin with his three-day scruff.

Quiet and sated, Nandi and Isisa lay beside us on the blankets with their long limbs entwined, the sheen of exertion glowing over their dark bodies like black velvet. As I'd watched him mate with my lovers one by one, they watched us while lazily stroking, touching, kissing.

There wasn't a woman luckier in this world than me.

"Never. I..." He sawed his length between my folds, gliding back and forth with the occasional notch of his cockhead against my clit. "I..."

"You what?"

"I wanted... wanted..." He slid down my body until he was between my thighs on his knees, hard and ready again within moments of sharing a climax with Nandi. Virile fell short of describing his incredible stamina, the word an understatement for the sheer masculinity of our chosen male. I watched the gentle bob and sway of his cock and dared to touch him, gliding my finger over the satin texture of its sinewy length.

A spark ignited and sizzled through my nerve endings

until the low throb in my core became an intolerable ache.

"Wanted what?"

"I wanted…" I moistened my lips with my tongue and arched my back. "Wanted to see them happy."

And they were certainly happy. Isisa made a content growl of approval from where she was actively burrowing beneath one of the blankets.

Nandi was the closest, the gorgeous length of her still exposed. "You always see to our happiness. Even before your own."

Not always, I thought, mind traveling back to the first night with Esteban in the tent, because I couldn't bear the thought of not being the one to initiate our physical intimacy. A flush of heat surged through me, but the brief flutter of shame abated the moment his fingers found the sensitive pearl between my legs.

And then Esteban nibbled my ear. "We have a confession to make."

"About?"

He never stopped torturing me, teasing and rolling, circling the bundle of nerves with a fingertip until he held me on the cusp. "I had a long conversation with Isisa and Nandi today while you were at the hospital."

"About?"

Nandi answered. "Your selflessness."

"I'm not that selfless."

"You are. You've always looked after both of us. After your team."

"After me," Esteban added. He kissed me again, demanding and urgent, mouth open and letting me brush my tongue against his. He ended it first by tracing his lips down to my throat. My head lolled back when his mouth found my pulse. "You see, this surprise wasn't for me. I knew you three were coming tonight. Tonight was for *you*, Sash. We made a decision."

Goose bumps arose over my skin as the building pressure between my legs increased. "What decision?"

"To make you the pride matriarch."

I jerked up and stared. "But—"

Esteban stroked between my legs again, this time with his cock. "It's decided."

"I didn't agree."

"We agreed for you," Nandi murmured. "We want this. We've always seen you as our unofficial leader. Always gone to you for guidance."

"I... I don't know what to say."

Esteban's low growl reverberated through me, a rumble against the taut peaks of my breasts. "Say yes." His teeth scraped over the edge of one and sent a tremble through me.

"*Yes.*"

He flipped me onto my front and ended my suffering with a thrust. One stroke sheathed him to the hilt, and then pleasure rippled through me like the wild tide surging from the ocean.

His teeth grazed the back of my neck, and a growl caressed his warm breath over my ear. From the moment he nipped me, the universe seemed to implode with limitless sensation spiraling down my nerve endings. I gasped from the shock of it, calling out his name and raising my hips to meet each thrust. The merciless slap of his body against mine became the only noise in the room, although I was aware of Isisa sleeping nearby and Nandi sprawled beside us, our silent and approving voyeur.

He gripped me by a handful of my curls and tugged my head back. I trembled, experiencing a new side of him. A delicious side. Something hidden within our tender and compassionate alpha.

I lost myself to his skill and the tireless rhythm of our lovemaking. The hand not buried in my hair cupped one breast, rolling the nipple and tugging until it beaded hard as a pebble. The same hand swept downward, smoothing over my tummy before teasing the slick cleft between my legs. I moaned in anticipation, on the edge before his fingers even stroked the hypersensitive bundle of nerves there.

Then he withdrew, leaving me empty. So empty it hurt. So empty I sobbed for relief and twisted onto my back, grasping at him desperately. "Don't stop."

"Baby, nothing could make me stop right now."

Esteban sprawled between my thighs and worshipped my breasts with his mouth. And in one thrust, he returned where he belonged, buried inside me. I jerked beneath him and grasped his shoulders. My nails scored flesh.

Although I wanted the moment to last forever, climax crashed over me. Head tilted back, my mouth opened in a silent scream. An orgasm unlike any I'd ever felt before trembled through my body, an explosion of limitless, unfathomable bliss. I gripped double handfuls of the blankets beneath me, unable to determine where one climax ended and the next began.

Thrusting wildly, Esteban found his release and spilled

into me, my name a guttural cry on his lips uttered over and over.

Fingers buried into the taut muscles of his back, I held onto him for a few moments more until climax robbed the remainder of my strength. Boneless and limp, my arms slipped to the blankets, and then Esteban sagged down atop me.

An aftershock rippled over his cock, dragging another shudder and low moan from him. At last, after some moments had passed and I'd milked all that he had, he rolled to the side and sprawled against the blankets, too spent to move again. I wiggled onto my side next to him and Nandi did the same. Isisa remained a foot or two away in her blanket burrito.

"I love the three of you so much. Fuck... I never thought... never thought anything could be like this."

"We love you, too," Nandi whispered. "*All* of us."

I murmured an agreeing echo of her sentiments and hugged my arm around his chest. Part of me wanted to sleep while the other wanted to stay up and bask in the euphoric sense of completion.

Isisa blinked open her eyes and smiled. "Feels good, yeah? Being marked, I mean."

He laughed and ran his fingers through his hair. "I don't even know how to describe it. I can *feel* you."

"It's the pride link. It's what happens when lion shifters are completely in tune with each other bond at once. It's..." I'd only known one pride with a link, and it had been severed the day my father's pride was broken.

"Very rare," Isisa finished for me.

"You girls have brought so much into my life. I feel... whole again, if that makes sense."

"It does." I kissed his cheek and stroked a hand down his chest. "I know I feel the same."

"Me too," Nandi and Isisa said in unison.

"Will it always be like this?"

"I think it can only get better," I said. "And we have all our lives to find out."

25

ESTEBAN

The sound of an incoming message woke me from what had to be the best sleep of my life. Of course, pleasing three healthy, voracious women would wear any man out, shifter or not. At some point before dawn, I'd made love to Nandi and Sasha again. Like her wild cousins, Isisa had growled at me the moment I disturbed her rest by touching her tits. We let her be.

Sasha mumbled in her sleep as I carefully extricated my arm from beneath her head and reached for the phone.

A green bubble displayed a recent text from Sergio.

Are you coming or not, dude? Mamá is pacing the kitchen.

I squinted at the time, blurry morning vision barely adapting to the bright screen. Promising to arrive early to unwrap gifts with the adults felt like a mistake now. *Overslept. We'll be there soon.*

Better hurry. You got one hour.

One hour and one bathroom split between three women. Fuck.

Forewarned about Isisa's tendency to bite first and ask questions later when awakening, I erred on the side of caution and nudged Sasha first. A kitten-like stretch elongated her slender limbs, her toes pointed and arms raised before she lazily slumped amidst the pile of blankets again. I nudged her a second time.

"Hey, lovelies, time to rise and shine."

One blue eye opened, fixed on me. "You better have bacon if you're waking me up this early," she replied.

"Um, it'll be better than bacon if you can get dressed and ready in an hour."

She squinted at me, skeptical. "Better than bacon?"

"Promise you'll love it. My mother should have brunch prepared by eleven."

"All right." She kissed the corner of my mouth and left, dragging a blanket around her before she disappeared around the hall. Nandi sat up before I had a chance to tickle her awake next.

"Hey, beautiful." I leaned forward and kissed the mark I'd left on her nape. "Wanna do me a favor and…" My gaze drifted toward Isisa.

"Let her be," Nandi replied. "Do you think you could grab our bags out of the car though. There's gifts for your family, Rambo, and Ripley in there too. And I wanna give the pups their toys before we leave."

"Yeah, not a problem. We only have an hour though, so…"

"Isisa is always the last one, but she's also the quickest," Nandi assured me. "She doesn't wear makeup, and she keeps her hair braided so it's always done. I'll just crawl into the shower with Sasha."

"All right. You scoot, and I'll get your things." And

hope there was hot water left over for me when they were all done.

~

SASHA

*E*steban had warned us that his family dressed nice for the holidays, jeans and T-shirts forbidden at the table. It was one of those old, unshakable traditions that had been going on since he was a child.

I donned a black pencil skirt with a pale lavender blouse and a high neckline, wary of causing offense with something too low cut and sexy. Isisa had on a gorgeous ivory and black jumpsuit with ruffled cap sleeves, a festive metallic red belt, and equally bold colored kitten heels. Nandi finally settled on a green blouse with lace, a loose black skirt, and gold ballet flats.

Isisa helped Nandi tame her curls while Nandi pulled my blonde locks back into a sideswept fishbone braid.

"You three look amazing."

As one, we all looked to the door where Esteban stood. It wasn't often we got to see him dressed up, but he didn't fail to impress in his charcoal slacks, black dress shirt, and Christmas red tie. He'd even trimmed his beard. The past couple of weeks had lent him an uncanny resemblance to his animal form.

"Same to you," I replied for all of us. "Are we dressed all right? If it's too much or not enough, we brought extra outfits."

"No, you all look great. Absolutely perfect."

"And you're sure about this?" Isisa asked. "Going to your family Christmas, I mean."

"My mother will love you."

Nandi raised her chin and studied him. "And if she doesn't?"

Esteban shrugged. "Then it's her loss. I won't abandon my family, but I won't allow them to disrespect us and our ways either. We're capable of making our decisions without their input."

His family. When I stole a look at Nandi, the corners of her mouth raised. We'd decided to tell him about her baby after Christmas dinner once we were curled up beneath the tree in his living room. Dividing our time between his home and our penthouse had been difficult but rewarding, providing a sample of his lifestyle and a taste of ours.

But I liked his place. I appreciated the silence and the peace of the country, making me wonder how difficult it would be to pack our lives into one house and leave our penthouse behind one day.

"Now?" she mouthed at me.

I blinked, startled by the change in plan. "If you're ready."

Esteban straightened his tie in the mirror, oblivious to our silent conversation. "If you're ready, we can drive over or walk down the road. It's only half a mile."

"I want to tell you something first before we meet them all," Nandi said. She picked at her nail polish and studied her hands before adding in a subdued voice, "We have something to tell you."

Given our cue to join her and stand alongside her, I took one of Nandi's hands. Isisa moved to her other side.

Esteban's smile dimmed. "What's wrong?"

Nandi's internal struggle filtered through the pride link, filling me with a sense of consternation and unease. "It's nothing wrong," I said for her.

"It's good news," Isisa said.

"What we hope you'll also see as good news." Praying he would see it as good news, I squeezed Nandi's hand and waited for her to take the lead.

"Well hit me with the news and don't keep me in suspense. If I can handle finding out I'm not human and that I've been working with a vampire this past year, I can handle anything at this point."

A hint of an uncertain smile touched the edges of Nandi's lips. "I hope so, because I'm pregnant. You're going to be a father."

Esteban stared. "You're serious."

"Absolutely."

"And positive?"

"The doctor says so."

He didn't say anything else, standing there with a shell-shocked sort of look on his face, eyes unfocused and distant. Nandi shifted from foot to foot in a familiar nervous gesture.

"Are… are you mad?" she asked in a whisper.

Esteban's attention snapped back to her with laser focus, and his lips parted in a silent "oh," as if realizing how it must appear to us. In three steps, he had moved over and pulled Nandi into his embrace.

"No, baby, no. This is the best news," Esteban assured her. "You have no idea how happy this makes me."

"Really?" she squeaked.

"Really. This is the cherry on top of what has already been the best, most perfect Christmas of my life."

When he raised his lips from Nandi's brow, Esteban fixed me with a quiet look, eyes smoldering with unspoken promises. "Sasha?"

"Yes?"

"You're next."

The husky tone of his voice sent my heart into rapid pulse. "You should probably know that lionesses have a tendency towards twins. Sometimes triplets."

"Did you think I was kidding when I said I want a lot of kids?" And then he paused with a thoughtful expression on his handsome face, brows notched. "Are we able to do that?"

"To do what?"

"Have as many as we want in this arrangement. Would it make you uncomfortable for me to father children with both of you? I know we mentioned kids, but we never went into specifics."

I exhaled a long breath, the tension draining from me at once. One of his arms remained around Nandi's waist, and the other hand reached for me, taking me by the hand. Our fingers intertwined, and he drew me in against them.

"I come from a seven-kid family, Sash. Three is nothing."

"Three at once isn't so easy."

He grinned. "There's four of us. We'll make it work. Won't we, Isisa."

She smiled back. "We will."

The last of my worries disintegrated like mist. Our perfect match had been out there all along.

We'd only needed the patience to find him.

$\sim$

ESTEBAN

"*Y*ou ready for this?" I asked when we stepped onto the porch. We each had a gift in hand, as it was tradition in my family for the adults to all blindly swap on Christmas Day with a fun game.

Nandi hung back a step and only came forward when Sasha guided her onto the stoop by the elbow. Despite a half dozen potted poinsettias, it was wide enough for all four of us to stand in front of the door, with a collection of chairs to our left next to my father's rocking chair where he liked to smoke the occasional cigar and have a beer.

If a day passed that he didn't have a beer in his hand, he was probably hospitalized, and we couldn't smuggle one to him.

Mamá's bench was to the right, wrought iron and wood with several plush pillows and a quilt. Those were all rumpled, a sign the kids had recently been on it. There were about a half dozen cars behind us parked end to end in the drive and three more parallel on the road. The entire Castillo clan was here, all of them aware of problems between me and Mamá.

"Ready or not, we're here for you," Isisa said.

I opened the door and gestured for the ladies to enter first. Sasha led, Nandi behind her, and Isisa to the rear. I stepped in last and shut the door behind me.

Christmas music and warmth greeted us, along with the aroma of Ponche Navideño simmering in the kitchen. I took a moment to breathe in the spiced apple and guava in the air. There wasn't a family with better holiday punch than mine.

A few steps brought us within view of the living room where most of the family had assembled, a wide arch revealing the long sofa and two love seats occupied by a host of cousins and some of my siblings.

"Whoa," my cousin Xavier said, only for his mother to shush him quickly.

Silence fell over the room and no one spoke. The four of us stood in front of my family, waiting for the worst to happen.

When no one moved or spoke, my father set aside his beer and rose from the chair in front of the television. "Ah, there you are. We wondered if you'd ever show up. And who are these fine ladies you have kept from us so long?"

"I'd like you all to meet Sasha, Isisa, and Nandi. Ladies, my huge family. That's my dad, Ernesto."

"It's a pleasure to meet you three when my son has had such fine things to say," my father said.

"He has nothing but great things to say about all of you, too," Isisa said, stepping up to play the outgoing one while Nandi hung back shyly.

Pops looked at me, grinned, then returned his attention to the ladies. He eased forward and put his arm around Sasha's shoulders, drawing her further inside. "Brunch will be served soon. In the meantime, make yourselves at home and take a seat. *Mi casa es su casa* is a phrase we Castillos mean with all of our hearts in this house."

Sasha blinked a few times, and a warm peach flush touched the apples of her fair cheeks. "Thank you, Mr. Cas—"

"I am only Mr. Castillo to the men who take orders from me. Ernesto is for family and friends. Or Pops if you will."

And that's where I'd inherited the charm, because Pops knew how to lay it on a woman when the situation required it. I grinned despite the trepidation churning in my chest.

Pops leaned close and dropped his voice to a whisper, "I warned everyone you'd be bringing three ladies, and I said if anyone had a problem, they can look for another Christmas dinner."

"Thanks, Pops."

"No need to thank me for doing what's right, Esteban. We love you, and it's time for you to be happy, even if some of our family doesn't understand."

"Where's Ma?"

"The kitchen, of course." Pops leaned around me and winked at the girls. "She runs that place like a general and won't leave until everything is done."

In my family, Christmas brunch became a creative opportunity for my mother to flex her culinary talents in the kitchen, blending breakfast entrees with Latino dishes. Breakfast tacos with chorizo and egg, spicy frittatas, and huevos rancheros. She'd always made the latter for me, pounding the corn tortillas herself because nothing was better than a hot and steaming tortilla fresh from the grease to hold the fried eggs, salsa, and beans.

"Is there anything we can do to help her?" Nandi asked.

"Trust me, you don't wanna venture into the kitchen. Think of it like your writing cave, baby. No Man's Land."

"Oh."

"It's nice to finally meet all of you." Sergio crossed over and welcomed me with a grin and a clap to my shoulder. His arm was still in a cast and covered in childish, holiday- themed doodles drawn in marker. "Leave it to my big brother to hoard you all."

"This is Sergio."

"How long until the cast comes off?" Isisa asked.

Sergio grimaced. "Another week or two hopefully."

Sasha's sympathetic smile made him blush. "Don't let him fool you into doing everything for him, though. He's been laying the pity card on thick."

Sergio put on a wounded expression. "I could have died."

"Wear your helmet next time," I shot back with good humor.

"You see the hard-ass I work for? Such a slave driver." He laughed and offered Nandi his good arm. "Come on, I'll introduce you to my wife and kids."

Despite my worries, the family welcomed all three ladies with warmth and kindness. We all found seats throughout the room, though it meant dragging in more chairs, and lost ourselves in conversation or the sports recaps playing on the television.

Eventually, Selene and Mariana brought out the brunch cart and served the family, but there was no sign of my mother. Once everyone was stuffed, we gathered around the tree and started sorting out things for our annual gift exchange.

When Mamá popped around the corner, the tight knot of tension in my stomach became an anxious tangle. She stood in the archway and fussed with her apron, brushing away specks no one but her could see.

"Merry Christmas, Mamá. Brunch was delicious, thank you."

"I am glad you enjoyed it, and I see we have additional guests. Hello, and welcome to our home." She put on a small, tight smile. "Please introduce them to me, Esteban."

"Of course. Mamá, this is Sasha, Isisa, and Nandi," I said, gesturing to each woman as I spoke. "Ladies, my mother, Rosalinda Castillo."

"It's a pleasure to finally meet you, Mrs. Castillo," Sasha said.

Isisa's tense shouldered loosened. "Thank you for inviting us to your home."

"Yes, thank you," Nandi said. "Your cooking is amazing, Mrs. Castillo. I never manage to make eggs so fluffy."

"Oh, well…" Their good manners and praise flustered my mom, who seemed caught between smiling and retreating back to the kitchen.

I took my mother by the hand and guided her to the couch. "Please sit down, Ma. You've been on your feet all morning, and we're ready to start."

The rules were simple. Once everyone drew a number, the first person picked a present. The next participant could either steal an opened present or pick a new one from the pile—but a gift could only be stolen three times before it was out of play.

My brother Angelo drew the first number and beelined to Nandi's package. He opened it to discover a set of luxury headphones. Samuel eyed him jealously.

"Freaking sweet. It has a mic! Thanks."

"Language!" Mamá scolded. "The Lord's day is no time for such words."

Nandi chuckled. "They're very comfortable."

"Too comfortable. She can sit in her office with those on all day and never hear a word any of us say to her," Isisa complained.

I nodded. "I can attest to that."

She only scowled at us all.

A couple of my cousins went next. One of them drew my gift and sighed at the utility belt and toolkit inside. My uncle stole it two rounds later, freeing her to unwrap another gift.

"Oh, this is lovely. The wrapping is so pretty." Mamá picked Isisa's gift and gingerly peeled the tape away from the paper. Inside, there was a wicker basket packed with two hand-painted wine glasses, two bottles, and a fancy new automatic corkscrew."

"Me next, and I'm stealing that wine basket," Mariana said.

"You cannot steal from your mother." Ma's expression was scandalized enough to make everyone laugh.

"Sure I can, and I just did. Pick again, Mamá."

"Esteban, you had better steal that back for me," she said as she had my father pass her another gift. This time she ended up with a brand-new e-reader, complete with leather case and a gift card.

"I have next pick," Nandi said. She promptly took Mariana's wine.

It took almost two hours to finish, and I'd never seen so much gift thievery in all my life. By the end, Mamá ended up with the wine since I stole her digital reader, allowing her to recover her preferred gift and freeze the basket Isisa had brought from further grabs. Sasha snuggled a blanket she'd unwrapped, Isisa geeked out over a video game, and Nandi delved into a movie-night themed popcorn tub filled with candy, bargain bin DVDs, and a gift card to a nearby cinema bistro.

Selene and Nandi bonded over novels while my brothers quizzed Sasha about being a doctor in the navy. I let it slip that she was on a special forces squad, and then no one would leave her alone.

"Like some Ghost Recon type shit?" Samuel asked. "Were there guns and infiltration?"

"*Samuel*," Ma chided him from across the room. "Language, *mijo*."

"Sorry."

The cashmere blanket draped around Sasha's shoulders and over her body looked softer than a cloud. She caressed her cheek against it, resembling a kitten in human form more than ever.

"Yes, a little like that. Only there were no save points and the graphics were too real." Her attention darted to my mother. Ma had been watching her the whole time my brothers questioned her about the life of an officer.

"This blanket is beautiful, Mrs. Castillo. Esteban tells me you made this one and a few at his house."

"Oh, well, thank you, Sasha. I understand if you'd like to trade—"

"Absolutely not. I love blankets for snuggling in at home."

"It's true, she does," Nandi chimed in.

Isisa chuckled. "She's always cold during the winter, so we buy her onesies."

"Then I am glad it found its way to someone who will appreciate it." She gave another one of her little smiles and stood. "Esteban, I would like to have a word with you in private."

She led the way into the kitchen, where she started bustling around with the dishes. Rather than press her, I kept my mouth shut and helped out. We washed the sink full of dishes and put leftovers away before she finally spoke.

Mamá gazed out the window instead of looking at me. "I like them. They are so lovely. And smart. And such nice manners, Esteban."

"They mean everything to me, Mamá."

My mother turned to face me at last, her brown eyes misty with unshed tears. "I can see that now. They make you happy. All this time I've wanted you to move on after Gabriela and to be happy. Then I was a hypocrite. I judged you, *mijo*. I judged the thing that made you happy. For so many weeks, I blamed these three women for corrupting you and dragging you down this dark path, but I drove this wedge between us."

"Mamá..." I couldn't remember a single time in over forty years when my proud mother admitted she was wrong.

"But there is no darkness here. Only joy. You're my first born, and not having you here made me sick. I wanted to go to you to apologize for my behavior, but... I thought... I thought you would hate me."

"What? No, never. I could never hate you. I didn't like how you behaved, but I could never hate you."

"You didn't come to family dinners anymore."

"My second family wasn't welcome."

"Is that how you see them now? Family?"

"Yes." I sucked in a breath between my teeth. "I'm going to ask Sasha to marry me. She doesn't know yet, but I don't need to wait years to know they're the women I want."

My mother wrung her hands together. "Oh no."

"Oh no?"

"But how can you marry one and leave out the others? That isn't fair, Esteban. Will they not get to have a wedding day alongside you?"

"You know I can't legally marry them. I'd hoped we could all exchange vows, even if only the one set would be recognized."

She considered the notion and nodded. "Then there is much planning to do. Do they have many relatives? A wedding for four people is four times the food and family. The cake will have to be immense." She spread her hands apart, indicating a cake large enough to hide a stripper.

"Ma, no, you don't have to do that. Besides, I haven't asked yet, and I'm sure they'd like to plan their own stuff. With your help, I mean."

"Fine, fine. But you will at least let me do this." She hustled over to the cabinet where she kept her prized vases, knickknacks, and tea service sets.

"We don't need tea right now."

"Shush. I know it's here somewhere. Ah! Yes, this is it." My mom pulled a small white box from inside a floral-painted teapot. As far as hiding places went, it was pretty damned good. All of us knew it was a death sentence to touch anything in that cabinet.

"Your grandmother had me save this for the day you married someone besides Gabriela."

"What?"

"You know how she felt about her."

Had everyone around me hated Gabriela and I was too blind to notice?

"We cannot divide your grandmother's ring by three, but we can remove the stones to have it reset. There are three stones, see? And when I saw these three stones a week ago, I realized it was like fate was telling me to let it go."

"You could have given this to Sergio. Why not save it for Eduardo, or even Samuel? Angelo was recently engaged, he could have used it."

She dismissively waved her hand. "Lalo is gay, Angelo always wants to do things his way, and Samuel—"

"Wait, he's what? Never mind, that doesn't matter right now. My point was that there are three other unmarried kids."

"And none of them would appreciate it. Your abuela asked me to do this, to give it to you, because she always saw you as the hardest working. You were the one who flew to Puerto Rico to fix her roof after the storm. You and your padre fixed her roof, Stebi, not the other children."

"About Pops... Ma, why didn't you ever tell me there was another guy?"

Her fingers went white-knuckled over the ring box. "He told you?"

"He did. I'm glad he did, and I'm not angry, but why lie to me all these years?"

"I guess… He was a good person, but his family was not always nice. One day he disappeared, and I thought it was a blessing in disguise when I met Ernesto. He never cared, and it was so easy to believe he truly was your father."

I nodded. "He is. I've never doubted that. He's always been here for me."

"As far as it mattered, he was your father. *Is* your father. And with nothing to tell you about the other but a name, I thought it best to let it be. I… I am sorry."

Worry and stress had weathered her features even more. She looked so distraught, I pulled her into my arms and squeezed her tight. "I love you, Mamá. There's nothing to forgive. Thank you for meeting my ladies and giving them a chance."

I took the ring box without another complaint.

It might cost more money to divide its stones into three identical settings, but the symbolism of having the blessing of the two women closest to my heart would be worth it.

EPILOGUE

SASHA

*S*ince I was a little girl I'd always known I wanted to get married wearing a dress like those I'd seen growing up in South Africa. Mum had worn beautiful ruffles in shades of gold, bronze, and cream, but her dress—along with most of our other belongings—had been damaged during our escape all those years ago. I thought it had been lost, but she surprised me when she sent me the remnants and told me to use them for my own dress.

After three months of fittings and creative consultation with a local designer, I had a dress that combined my heritage with my new modern life. We'd salvaged Mum's ruffled skirt and added new layers paired with a satin halter top trimmed by delicate beadwork. Isisa and Nandi wore different styles, but we'd all chosen pale gold over ivory and white. To accompany them, Nandi had found a South African store and ordered three matching bib collars with red, yellow, and blue beads, although Isisa looked the most elegant of all with her slim neck and swanlike poise surrounded by the layers of gold choker.

Someone knocked on the door to Leigh and Ian's guest bedroom, the one beside the kitchen borrowed as a makeshift dressing room and makeup studio.

"Safe to come in?" Sebastian called.

Isisa opened the door to let him inside. Despite being fraternal twins, my brother could have been my masculine clone. He was taller than me and broad in the shoulders with the same pale blue eyes and silky curls. He wore his hair natural and untamed like a white-gold cloud against his tuxedo clad shoulders, resembling his lion half more than ever.

He stopped at the sight of us and held his right hand to his chest. "I'm blown away. This much beauty in one room should be illegal."

"Sebastian."

He looked innocent. "What? Those people out there may never see a sight this breathtaking again. I should go warn them."

With too much distance between us for me to swat him, I mock-scowled instead. I was sitting at the chair while Julia fixed pearl-studded pins amidst my hair. We'd chosen not to straighten or curl it, instead twisting my hair into a fabulous updo. "Stop exaggerating."

"He's right. You look beautiful," Julia said after she finished. "All of you."

Isisa smiled and smoothed her fingers over the long dark brown feathers accenting her strapless bodice. Her corset and gathered, golden skirt gave the illusion of curves. Her matching hair wrap had hints of russet and cobalt as another nod to our African ancestry.

"I feel like a princess," I admitted.

"And today you are, my sister." My brother smiled, moisture gleaming in his eyes. "God, I wish Dad could be here to see this."

"Me too." I gazed up at him, blinking rapidly and at risk of losing the battle against inevitable tears. "But I see him here in *you*. I swear you're the spitting image of him today."

Julia dabbed her eyes with a small tissue. "God, I'm getting all weepy again. I didn't struggle as much to keep dry-eyed at *my* wedding. Lyle was the one who cried."

"Please don't cry," Nandi begged. "If you cry, I'm going to cry, and you worked so hard on our makeup."

That made us all laugh and kept the emotional breakdown at bay.

Sebastian kissed my cheek and hugged me. "I'll be cheering for you, sis."

Holding hands with Nandi and Isisa, we listened for the wedding march while our escorts waited to lead us to the man we loved. Occasionally, we stole a touch of Nandi's stomach, stroking her through the airy chiffon layers of her empire waisted dress—for luck, even though she'd told us a dozen times already that being pregnant hadn't made her a Buddha, no matter how much she showed prematurely.

"Are you ladies ready?" Nikolai asked.

Distrusting my voice, and also fearing tears would ruin my makeup, I nodded. My dashing stepfather stepped forward and offered his arm to me. He had sworn it was his solemn duty and his alone to give me away. Although Ian and even my own brother had volunteered to walk Isisa down the aisle, she'd ultimately decided to ask her mother to escort her to the altar instead. After all, her mother's strength and perseverance had saved her from a hopeless and dim future.

Initially, Nandi hadn't known if she wanted to invite her family or not, but on a whim, she'd sent them invitations in the mail. And they'd accepted, her father calling her a day later and asking if he could walk her down the aisle, much to her surprise and secret pleasure. Her family had never been close to us, so it meant the world that they'd set aside their disapproval to provide what she wanted and deserved.

"Yeah," Isisa answered. "Yeah, we are."

Someone must have queued the pianist because the music began a few heartbeats later. The wedding procession went out ahead of us. Leigh, Juni, Dani, and Jada paired up with Esteban's brothers and led the way down the aisle. Julia followed on her own, my matron of honor.

One of Esteban's little cousins held the honor of being the ring bearer. The red silk pillow had each of our rings tied to it with a golden cord. Sophia followed him with a flower-petal-filled basket, which she took great care in scattering across the long runner stretching across the yard.

Then it was our turn. I'd decided that the others should go ahead of me and put my foot down when they tried to argue about it. Nandi went out first, then Isisa, and finally me. All guests were standing and turned around to watch us travel down the aisle at a measured pace, but I barely noticed them. Esteban waited for us at the end, so handsome in his uniform he gave me tunnel vision, and everything else faded to gray.

We exchanged vows before our friends and family beneath the budding trees as hummingbirds danced around Leigh's feeders. Spring flowers provided pops of pink, blue, and yellow color against the green yard, and flourishing vines crawled pale purple blossoms over the fence.

I stood between Nandi and Isisa with Esteban across from us and fought back tears of joy as our shared love and happiness pulsed through our pride link. My fingers shook as I slid the platinum band we'd all picked out together onto his finger, with the promise to love and cherish him for all time.

"Since meeting you, my life has never been more complete," Esteban said in a quiet voice. He looked to each of us in turn. "And I cannot wait to watch our family grow. I love you all more than words can adequately describe, but you all know my heart, and it will forever belong to each of you."

Nadir passed over each ring one at a time, and Esteban slid them onto our fingers. Each one was beautiful and unique, with his grandmother's diamonds reset in the place of honor. A tear slipped down my cheek, and I darted my gaze toward his mother. She smiled at me and dabbed her cheeks.

"I now pronounce you all, husband and wife," the priest announced. "You may kiss your brides, Esteban."

"Gladly."

Applause and cheers filled the air as we all exchanged kisses, and then we turned to face them all as a united pride.

Only Esteban and I would be signing papers for now until legislation changed. Until shifters came out into the public and the world understood our bonds, one legal marriage would have to do. But in our hearts, the law didn't matter.

A piece of paper could never dictate the love in our hearts, the dedication of our bond, and the strength of our pride.

*A*uthor's Note: Sasha, Nandi, Isisa, and Esteban's story is not over and will continue in King of the Urban Jungle next year, but first, we'll be releasing another novel starring Ian and Leigh titled *A Man of Many Talons*.

Bet you didn't see Esteban's secret coming, now did you?! Due to the African slave trade, Latin America has a rich and varied ancestry. It's quite interesting to study. People with African blood can be found all throughout Cuba, Puerto Rico, the Dominican Republic, and many other countries in South America. Esteban's biological father happened to be one of those people with African heritage.

Now, I have a super, super big favor to ask of you. *Please* don't spoil the surprise for the other readers. I love, respect, and appreciate your reviews, but I'd consider it an amazing courtesy if when you review, you leave out spoilers of that nature.

OTHER BOOKS BY VIVIENNE

Fairy Tale Retellings

For the reader who likes their romance milder

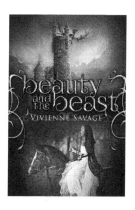

Beauty and the Beast

Red and the Wolf

Goldilocks and the Bear

Belle and the Pirate

Karina and the Djinn

Rapunzel and the Griffin Prince

Dragons

For the reader who likes their romance smutty

Loved by the Dragon

Smitten: Dawn of the Dragons #2

Crush on a Dragon: Dawn of the Dragons #3

God of Mischief: Dawn of the Dragons #4

Military Shifters

Hot and Wild military alphas

The Right to Bear Arms (Book #1)

Let Us Prey (Book #2)

The Purr-fect Soldier (Book #3)

Old Dog New Tricks (Book #4)

Texas Pride (Book #5)

Impractical Magic

Milder romance for the reader who loves action

Impractical Magic

Better Than Hex (Impractical Magic #2)

Blood Heiress

It's all about the plot and a slow burn relationship

<u>Blood Kissed</u>

Werewolves of San Antonio

<u>Training the Alpha</u>

Mythological Creatures

Making Waves

OTHER BOOKS BY PAYNE & TAYLOR

Epic Fantasy by Dominique Kristine

Shadows for a Princess

A princess who would rather die than wed. A warrior priest who would rather kill than see her harmed. A kingdom of shadows and treachery that threatens them both...

At the age of twenty-eight, Princess Ysolde Westbrook is a spinster duchess, the adopted daughter of Hindera's eccentric monarch. Commoners love their benevolent leader, but the kingdom's gentry take offense to the outsider among them.
Amid noble plots and demands for her to marry a local aristocrat, an assassination attempt places her life in peril--if she will not have one of them for a husband, they would sooner see her dead.

Finding allies in strangers with powerful gifts and even darker secrets, Ysolde must learn what it means to lead and find her own inner strengths. Whether or not she survives the tangled web of treason will determine the fate of her duchy, the royal family, and the kingdom she loves.

Blend the intrigue of Game of Thrones with a touch of Outlander's romance for an adventurous fantasy in a whole new realm of magic. Fans of Diana Gabaldon and George R.R. Martin will love the richly descriptive world of Terraina.

ABOUT THE AUTHOR

Vivienne Savage is the pen name of two best friends who write everything together. One works as a nurse in a rural healthcare home in Texas and the other is a U.S. Navy veteran. Both are mothers to two darling boys and two amazing girls.

All of their work varies in steam level, so pop by the VS website for details on which series is right for you!

For more information

www.viviennesavage.com
vivi@viviennesavage.com

84466111R00239

Made in the USA
San Bernardino, CA
08 August 2018